THE TURN

"Fans will clamor for this prequel and will enjoy the cameos from some series regulars, including demon Algaliarept. . . . it will leave longtime readers with an immediate desire to reread the main series."

—*Library Journal*

"Action packed with plenty of intrigue, mystery, a Machiavellian-like series of plotlines."

—*Smexy Books*

"My hat is off to Kim Harrison. She is a master."

—*Red Hot Books*

"Kim Harrison continues being one of my favorite urban fantasy authors."

—*Under the Covers Book Blog*

"*The Good Girls Revolt* meets urban fantasy, *The Turn* is an interesting glimpse of where the beloved characters of The Hollows all began. Seeing all the links between this closed world and Rachel Morgan's Cincinnati was fascinating."

—*All Things Urban Fantasy*

ALSO BY KIM HARRISON

Sideswiped

The Drafter

Waylaid

The Operator

KIM HARRISON

THE †URN

The Hollows Begins with Death

POCKET BOOKS

New York   London   Toronto   Sydney   New Delhi

Pocket Books
An Imprint of Simon & Schuster, Inc.
1230 Avenue of the Americas
New York, NY 10020

This book is a work of fiction. Any references to historical events, real people, or real places are used fictitiously. Other names, characters, places, and events are products of the author's imagination, and any resemblance to actual events or places or persons, living or dead, is entirely coincidental.

Copyright © 2017 by Kim Harrison

First Pocket Books paperback edition November 2017

POCKET and colophon are registered trademarks of Simon & Schuster, Inc.

For information about special discounts for bulk purchases, please contact Simon & Schuster Special Sales at 1-866-506-1949 or business@simonandschuster.com.

The Simon & Schuster Speakers Bureau can bring authors to your live event. For more information or to book an event, contact the Simon & Schuster Speakers Bureau at 1-866-248-3049 or visit our website at www.simonspeakers.com.

Interior design by Jaime Putorti

Manufactured in the United States of America

10   9

ISBN 978-1-5011-0876-1
ISBN 978-1-5011-0884-6 (ebook)

FOR TIM

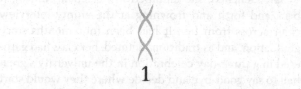

1

Trisk ran a hand down her Jackie Kennedy dress, not liking how it hampered her motions even if it showed off her curves. Grades and accomplishments were her primary weapons in the battle to attract an employer, but appearance came in a close second. Her long dark hair was pulled back into a clip, and an unusual whisper of makeup highlighted her angular cheekbones and narrow chin in the hopes of finding a businesslike mien. She was dressed better than most on the noisy presentation floor. *Not that it matters*, she thought sourly.

Anxiety pinched her eyes as she sat attentively at her booth, surrounded by the accomplishments of her past eight years. They suddenly seemed dull and vapid as she smiled at an older couple while they passed, their clipboards in hand as they shopped. "How are we for security?" one asked, and Trisk's face warmed when the other ran his eyes over her, making her feel like a horse up for auction.

"We could use someone, but how good could she be? She's in with the geneticists."

"That's because I am one," Trisk said loudly, shoulders hunching when they gave her a surprised look and continued on.

Jaw clenched, she slumped in her chair, shifting it back and forth and frowning at the empty interview chair across from her. It had been four months since graduation, and as tradition dictated, her class had gathered in a three-day celebration in the university's great hall to say good-bye and decide where they would start their careers. Much like a reverse job fair, past graduates came from all over the U.S. to meet them, assess their strengths, and find a place for them within their companies. Tonight her classmates would part ways, some going to Houston, others to Portland or Seattle, and the best to Florida and the Kennedy Genetic Center to work in the National Administration of Scientific Advancement.

Put bluntly, the gala was a meat market, but seeing as there were only a few hundred thousand of her people left on earth, hidden among the millions of humans, it was a necessity. Especially now. Their population was poised to drop drastically with this generation if they couldn't halt the ongoing genetic degradation caused by an ancient war.

The best of her people studied to become geneticists or the politicians who would ensure that government money kept flowing into the labs. A few who specialized in security aimed to do the same, though on a much darker, more dangerous level.

At least most of them did, Trisk thought, her gaze rising past the CLASS OF 1963 banner to the impressive chandelier hanging above her. The glowing light hummed with power, the crystal containing a room-wide charm policing all but the most innocent of magics. At the far end of the hall, a live jazz band played a snappy rendition of "When Your Lover Has Gone," though no one danced. Glancing down the long rows of tables, she scoffed at the hopeful smiles and cheerful platitudes of her classmates doggedly trying for a better offer as the final hour to register a contract ticked closer. But inside, she was dying.

Trisk and her father had entertained only three employers at her table, all of them more interested in her minor in security than her major in genetic research. Her doctorate in using viruses to introduce undamaged DNA into somatic cells had been marginalized. Kal, who used bacteria to do the same thing, was getting accolades and offers left and right.

Her attention shifted, seeing him sitting directly across from her. Her stellar grades had gotten her a place under the chandelier with the best of them, and Trisk sourly imagined that was a loophole the administration would plug next year. Her dark hair and eyes among their predominantly fair complexions were obvious and garnered unwanted attention. Olympian gods and goddesses, every single one of them—slim and fair, bright as the sun, and as cold as the moon. Though they didn't make her a second-class citizen, her dusky hair and brown eyes supposedly gave her a natural affinity for one thing in their class-stratified society: security. She was good at that, but she was better in the labs.

Kal, though, had been groomed for a high position since birth. Majoring in genetic studies and minoring in business, he had the skills to make him justifiably sought after. She hated his smugness. She hated having to work twice as hard for half the credit, and she thought it telling that he went by his last name, shortening it from Kalamack to Kal in order to sound more human. To her, it meant he relied on his family rather than his own self for his identity.

Depressed, she looked down at her dress and the

blah shoes the woman at the store had pushed on her. She'd wanted black to match her hair and eyes, a decision she was now regretting. It made her look like security, not business. A pillbox hat sat atop the coatrack her father had insisted on having in her booth, and she fought with the urge to throw it on the floor and stomp on it. *I'm tired of fighting this* . . .

"Penny for your thoughts," a pleasantly masculine voice said, and her sour mood vanished.

"Quen!" she exclaimed as she rose, thinking he looked exceptional in his interview suit, as black as her dress apart from a narrow, vibrant red tie. His eyes were a dark green, and his hair just as black as hers, though it curled about his ears where hers was remarkably straight. She warmed as his gaze traveled appreciably over her, and she wished his fingers would follow, but she knew they never would. They were both so damn focused on their careers, and if she got pregnant, hers would be over.

"Wow. I forgot how well you wash up," she said, her smile widening as she gave him a hug, lingering to breathe him in. His shoulders were comfortably wide, muscular from his daily regimen, and she missed him already. He smelled good, like oiled steel and burnt amber, the latter giving away that he'd been spelling lately, probably to show his skills to a prospective employer. "You shaved," she said, her fingers tracing bare skin. But then her eyes widened when she realized he was holding himself differently, an unusual pride hiding in the back of his gaze.

"You accepted a position," she said, grasping his hands. "Where?" He was going to leave in the morning and go to the rest of his life. But finding their place in the world was what the three-day gathering was for.

"I've never seen you look this amazing, Trisk," he said, evading her as he glanced at her contract basket and the three minor offers within, turned facedown in her disappointment. "Where's your dad?"

"Coffee run," she said, but he was really campaigning for her. "Who took you on?"

Quen shook his head. His thin hand, calloused from the security arts, felt rough as he tucked away a strand of her hair that had escaped the clip. They'd met in Physical Defense 101. He'd gone on to major in security studies as expected. She had not. Women, even those with hair and eyes as dark as hers, weren't allowed to serve in anything more than passive security, and after fulfilling her security minor with demon studies, she intentionally flunked out of business to get into the scientific arena. It rankled Trisk that her grades were as good as Kal's. She had the GPA to work for the National Administration of Scientific Advancement at the Kennedy Genetic Center, but she'd be lucky to get a job in Seattle, much less at NASA.

Kal's laugh sounded loud, and Quen shifted so she wouldn't have to watch the NASA representative and Kal's parents fawn over him. There was an opening on the team that had just recently solved the insulin puzzle, freeing not only elven children from diabetes forever, but also humanity, the species they'd tested it on. Kal's parents looked proud as they entertained the man. The Kalamack name was faltering, and they'd invested everything in their son to try to find a rebirth. Elitist little sod. *Maybe if your family weren't such snots, you could engender children.*

Trisk's lip twitched. "Did I ever tell you about the time Kal cheated off me?"

"Every time you drink too much." Quen tried to tug

her away, but she couldn't bring herself to leave, not daring to be absent if someone should seek her out.

"He has to win every time, no matter what. Even a spelling test. You know the worst part?" she said as she refused to move and his hand fell away. "He knew we'd get caught and I'd be the one called a cheater, because the Goddess knows Kal is too smart and clever to cheat."

"You think?" Quen grinned at her old anger. "I swear, Trisk, you should've majored in security. Maybe finished out that demon-study track. I bet you could find a demon name, and with that, they'd let you teach. Didn't your grandmother teach?"

She nodded as she dropped down into her chair, not caring that her knees weren't pressed together as they should be. Her grandmother had done a lot of things, not all of them in the light. So had her mother. *May they both rest in peace.* "Demon summoning is a dead art."

Quen sat on the edge of his interviewer chair, looking awkward and handsome at the same time. "Security isn't just guns, and knives, and stealth. It's technology, and demons, and sneaking around. You're good at that."

Her eyes flicked to his. *Not to mention security is the only place someone like me is allowed to excel.* "I want to help our entire species, not just one or two of us." She hesitated, astounded at the overdone display continuing across the aisle. "My God. His genetic code is so full of holes, I can smell the human spliced in from here."

Quen ducked his head, hiding a smile. "I'm going to work for the Kalamack family," he said, and shocked, Trisk felt her face go white.

"What? Why!"

"I have my reasons," he said, not looking up. "It wasn't the money, though I'll admit it's more than I thought I'd ever be able to make this soon."

She couldn't breathe, imagining the horror of working for the Kalamack family. "Quen, you can't. Kal is a prejudiced prick who learned at the knee of his prejudiced dick father. You'll never get the credit you deserve. They'll treat their horses better than you."

The sudden anger in his brow was surprising. "You think I don't know that?"

"Quen," she pleaded, taking his hand.

"I don't need recognition like you do," he said as he pulled away. "Besides, there are benefits to being forgotten and unseen among your betters." Finally he smiled. "The chance to sneak around and learn things is unparalleled. I'll be fine."

But I won't be, she thought, knowing her hope of finding a job near enough to him to stay in touch by any method other than letters was now utterly gone. The Kalamacks lived in Portland, and all the really good elven labs were in Florida or Texas.

She took a breath, hesitating when Quen rose, his attention fixed past her. She turned to see Kal, his smirk as he stood before them making it obvious he'd found out about Quen and wanted to rub her nose in it. "What do you want?" she said as she got to her feet, Quen's hand on her shoulder.

"Hi, Felecia," Kal mocked, and she bristled, hating her given name. It was why she went by her middle name, Eloytrisk, or Trisk for short.

"It's Trisk," she intoned, and Kal smirked.

"Felecia the flea. That's what we called you, yes?" he said, lifting the lowest contract in her basket.

She shoved him back before he could see the letterhead, her face cold. "Keep out of my space. You stink like human."

Kal's cheeks reddened, stark against his fair, almost white hair as he gracefully caught his balance. He'd been in and out of the hospital most of his early life, his parents spending a fortune tweaking his code to make him the picture of the perfect elf in the hopes that he would attract a successful house. He had the slim physique of a long-distance runner, a respectable height that did not stand out, and of course, green eyes. But no children meant no status, and the Kalamack name was ready to fall. Trent was the very last one in a very long line, but he *was* the last.

"Let it go, Trisk," Quen said in warning, and she shook off his restraining hand. She'd had enough of Kal, and after tonight, one way or the other, he'd be gone.

Kal drew himself up in the aisle, braver—or perhaps more foolish—with his parents gone, the two of them having escorted the NASA dignitary away for a drink. "I see Quen told you about his new job," he said as he idly looked at his perfect nails. "If I get my way, he'll be coming to NASA with me. I'll need someone to make me breakfast, pick up my dry cleaning. I would've asked my father to hire you, but everyone knows women can't drive."

"Get out of my space," she said again, hands fisted. Damn it, he'd gotten that NASA job. Everything was given to him. Everything. She stiffened when he moved closer, daring her to protest as he once more lifted the contracts to see who they were from.

"I got an offer from NASA. They want me to develop new strains of carrier bacteria that can repair a child's DNA as early as three days old with a simple inhalation. And you," he said, head tilted as he chuckled at the small-firm letterheads, "the closest you will ever get will be in some research facility's library, shelving books for old farts who can't work a Punnett square. Have fun, Flea."

Smiling that confident, hated smile, he turned to go.

Her anger boiled up, and she shook off Quen's restraining hand again. "You are a hack, Kalamack," she said loudly, and the nearby conversations went silent. "Your theory to use bacteria to fix DNA strands into a new host is seriously flawed. Good for a doctorate, but not application. You can't stop bacteria from evolving as you can viruses, and you will end up killing the people you are trying to save."

Kal looked her up and down. "Huh. A second-rate security grunt thinks she knows my job better than I do."

"Let it go, Trisk," Quen warned as she took two long steps into the aisle.

"Kal?" she said sweetly, and when he turned, she punched him right in the nose.

Kal cried out as he fell, catching himself against his own booth. His hands covered his face, blood leaking out from between them, a stark, shocking color. "You hit me!" he cried as a handful of flustered girls flocked to him, digging in their little jeweled handbags for frilly handkerchiefs.

"Damn right I hit you," she said, shaking the pain from her hand. Busting his nose had hurt, but casting a spell would have been worse. Besides, the chandelier would have stopped it.

"You little *canicula*," Kal exclaimed, shoving past the girls. Wiping the blood off, he stood stiffly before her, his fine-textured hair almost floating as he reached through the wards on the room and drew on a ley line.

People fell back. Someone called for security. Trisk's eyes widened, her attention rising to the huge chandelier as it shifted to a dark purple in response. A faint alarm began chiming.

"I can't believe you hit me!" Kal said, and as Trisk stared flat-jawed, he spread his clasped hands apart to show a glowing ball of unfocused energy. It was a lot for a lab rat, making Trisk wonder if he'd been tutored on the side.

"Kal, don't!" Quen shouted, and Kal sneered.

"*Dilatare*," Kal said, shoving the technically white, yet still dangerous spell at her.

Hands warming, Trisk yanked a wad of unfocused energy from the nearest ley line to block it.

Quen was faster, and Trisk started when his aura-tainted streak of power struck Kal's incoming bolt, sending both energies spinning wildly up and into the chandelier. They hit it with a shower of green sparks, and, with a ping that echoed through her hold on the ley line, the huge crystal-and-light chandelier shattered.

People cried out. Trisk cowered, arms over her head as broken crystal rained down on them in a weird chiming clatter of discord and sensation. With a harsh sound, the band quit.

Shouts rose, and the hall exploded into noise. Trisk straightened from her instinctive hunch, the power she'd pulled from the line still glowing between her hands, colored a golden green by her aura. Her lips parted and fear slid between her soul and reason. The eastern representative of the elven enclave stood before them, his hands on his hips and a scowl on his face. Broken crystal crunched under his dress shoes, and with a gulp, she pushed the energy down and away, letting go of the ley line.

"What happened?" he demanded, and the hall became silent. Faces ringed them: her classmates, their parents, prospective employers. It felt like the third grade all over again, and Trisk was silent. Kal stared malevolently at her, his face smeared with blood and someone's frilly handkerchief over his mouth. His nose was probably broken, and Trisk stifled a smile of perverse satisfaction that he'd have to get it fixed.

"You know there's no use of ley lines this close to the city," the bald man said, a tie pin the only show of his enclave status, but it somehow elevated his suit above the surrounding business attire and colorful cocktail dresses. "That's why we have the place charmed." His attention rose to the few crystals still holding. "Or at least we did."

"It was an accident, Sa'han," Kal said, using the elven honorific, as he clearly didn't know the man's name.

"Accident?" the man echoed. "You're both too old for this. What happened?"

Trisk said nothing. They'd never believe she hadn't broken the room-wide charm. She'd been the butt of too many jokes, taking the blame for all of them because to do otherwise would only increase the torment. She had a rep, even if none of it was true.

"Felecia?" the man said, and she started, wondering how he knew her name.

"I, ah, punched him, Sa'han," she admitted. "I didn't tap a ley line until he did."

"And yet the result is the same." The man regretfully turned to Kal. "Your temper is still getting the better of you, eh, Trenton?"

"She has no right to be here, Sa'han," Kal said haughtily. "There are only three offers on her table. The center is for the best, not slag."

Trisk's eyes narrowed, but he was only saying what they were all thinking. Behind her, she could feel Quen's slow anger building, but it was too late. His contract was binding.

But the man only handed Kal a spell with which to clean his face. "And your tongue still doesn't check in with your brain before wagging," he said as Kal used the very blood from his broken nose to invoke the charm, and, in a wash of aura-tainted magic, his face was clean. "You think she copied her way to her grade average?" the man said, and Kal's face flashed red. "You are drastically lacking in the art of stealth and misdirection. Your emotions and wants are as clear as a child's. Learn what you lack or forever be the shadow of potential that you are today."

Trisk felt herself pale as he turned to her. He could see right through her, all her grand hopes looking like a child's pretend. "And you need to find out who you are before you bring your house any more shame," he said, his rebuke hitting her hard.

Her chest hurt, and she dropped her head. In the near distance, the loud voices of Kal's parents became obvious as they tried to force their way through the circle of people.

The enclave member sighed, gathering himself. "Kal? Trisk? As neither of you has signed with anyone, you're allowed to remain on the floor, but you're confined to your tables. Quen, you have your placement. Go wait in your room."

Trisk snapped her head up, suddenly frightened. Quen would go through hell now, as Kal would blame him for everything she'd done. "Quen, I'm sorry," she blurted.

Quen's mood softened, and he managed a smile. "Me

too," he said. "Don't worry about it," he added as he gave her shoulder a squeeze, but what she wanted was for him to take her in his arms and tell her nothing would change between them. "I've dealt with worse. I'm proud of you, Trisk. You're going to do well. I know it."

He was slipping away from her, and she could do nothing. "Quen . . ."

He looked back once, and then he was gone, the colorful dresses hiding him as the band started up again. The enclave dignitary had vanished as well, and people began to disperse.

Trisk's eyes rose to find Kal standing with his parents. His father was trying to straighten Kal's swollen nose, and his mother was attempting to distract the NASA representative from the shattered remains of the hall's protection.

No one was venturing across the pile of crystal, and Trisk winced when her father's tall form stumbled to a halt at the fringes, hesitating briefly as he found her eyes and then turned to make his way around it. "The Goddess protect me," she whispered, nudging a stray crystal out of her way and collapsing in her interview chair. There was no way to make this look good.

"Trisk? Tell me this wasn't you," her father said as he worked his way into her booth.

A surge of self-pity rose, and she blinked fast, refusing to cry. "Quen signed with the Kalamacks," she said, voice cracking.

Her father's breath came in, but then he exhaled with a knowing, forgiving sound, the shattered chandelier and rising argument at the Kalamack booth suddenly making sense. "I'm sorry," he said, his hand warm on her shoulder. "I'm sure he knows what he's doing."

His quick understanding made her feel worse. "I wish he'd know what he's doing with me."

Her father dropped to a knee before her and took her into a hug. Her throat closed, and it was as if she were twelve again as he tried to show her all was not lost, that something good would come from it. "Have you made a choice?" he asked gently.

She knew he wanted her to take a position and move forward, but accepting anything other than what she'd worked for felt like failure. His arms still around her, she shook her head.

Slowly his grip fell away. He stood, silent, as a special crew began to sweep the crystal into shipping boxes for off-site decontamination. "I'll get us some coffee," he finally said. "You'll be okay for a moment?"

She nodded, knowing it wasn't coffee he was after, but the chance there might be someone who owed him a favor. Her breath rattled as she exhaled. There were no more favors to be had. He had spent them all getting her this far. She could probably be excused for the effrontery of trying to make it in a man's field if she looked like their ideal, her efforts excused by her probable goal of finding a better husband. But she didn't even have that.

He was gone when she looked up.

Numb, she sat in her chair as the conference took on its normal patter and flow, everyone seeing her but no one making eye contact. "You can't," a plaintive voice rang out, and she watched as the NASA rep walked away, Kal's mother following fast, her steps short and heels clicking. Kal met her gaze with a murderous intent, jumping when his father picked up one of his contracts and shoved it at him.

"Sign it," the older man demanded. "Before they all withdraw their offers."

"Father," Kal complained, clearly not liking that Trisk was seeing this.

"Now!" his father exclaimed. "Sa'han Ulbrine was right. You showed a disturbing lack of control and common sense over a woman you will never see after tonight. Sign."

Motions stiff, Kal took the pen and signed the paper. His father all but jerked it out from under him. "Go wait in your rooms," the tall man said coldly, then strode away to register the contract before midnight, when the gala would be over.

Trisk couldn't help herself, and she made a mocking face at Kal across the aisle.

Kal's eyes narrowed. "You cost me my dream job," he said, his melodious voice clear over the surrounding conversations.

"You went out of your way to hurt me," she said coldly.

He stood to leave, glancing over his booth as if only now seeing it as the vain display it was. Silent, he walked away. A cluster of young women flitted behind him, ignored.

Trisk slumped, tired. She watched him as long as she could, and then he was gone. The final hours passed, and in groups of three and four, smiling parents and happy graduates left the hall on their way to parties hosted by their new employers, and from there, to a new life. She slowly realized she was alone. The tables were empty, the family banners drooping unattended amid the stray cups of cold coffee and tea. Still she sat, her attention fixed on a glint of crystal missed by the cleaners.

The click of a shutting door roused her. Thinking it was her father, Trisk stirred, muscles stiff as she rose and went to pick up the forgotten crystal. It was cool in her hand, smooth but for one rough edge. There was no tingle of magic left—it was just dead crystal. The time to record her contract had come and gone. It didn't matter. She had no intention of accepting any of the offers. There wasn't much available for a twenty-six-year-old woman in 1963, but she'd find something. She couldn't ask her father to continue to support her.

A pang of guilt almost bent her double. He had tried so hard to give her what she wanted, and she'd failed him. The studying, the practice, the sacrifice—all for nothing.

A scuff brought her head up, and her fist closed tight on the shard. A suited official was moving slowly among the discarded chairs and scattered papers. It was the man from the enclave who had chastised her, and a feeling of defiant guilt rose high.

"What a mess," the man said as he drew close, and she stiffened.

"Good evening, Sa'han," she said, wanting to leave but unable to now that he'd addressed her.

"I think we're going to lose our cleaning deposit," he said as he wearily sat against Kal's table, left for others to break down and pack away. "But we usually do."

She said nothing, waiting for him to dismiss her, but he only leaned back, balancing precariously as he found a copy of Kal's transcripts, his bushy eyebrows rising as he looked it over. "I didn't know your GPA was higher than his," he said in surprise.

She shrugged, not having cared beyond acquiring a spot under the chandelier.

The man slowly bobbed his head, his thin finger tracing a line down Kal's last eight years. "My mother had dark eyes," he said softly. "When I complained to my father that she should get them fixed to be like everyone else's, he told me they helped her see past the crap most of us drape ourselves with. I was never more embarrassed of myself than that day."

He pushed off from the table, and Trisk backed up, confused.

"I saw what happened," he said, coming close. "You never used your magic, though you were ready to. I couldn't hear. What did he say before you punched him in the nose?"

Trisk warmed. "I made an error in judgment, Sa'han. You have my apologies."

The man smiled. "What did he say?"

She lifted her chin. "He called me a second-rate security grunt, Sa'han."

Nodding as if unsurprised, the man reached into his suit's inner pocket and handed her a card embossed with the enclave's symbol. "As you haven't accepted any of your *fine* offers, I'd suggest you put in your application at Global Genetics."

Trisk took the card, seeing it had his name and a phone number on it. *Sa'han Ulbrine*, she thought, confused. "In Sacramento?" she said. Global Genetics was a human-run lab, generations behind what any of her people were doing. The enclave was kicking her out, and her heart sank.

But Ulbrine put an arm over her shoulder and turned her to the door. His mood was one of opportunity, not exile, and she didn't understand. "Occasionally a lab we have no affiliation with makes a breakthrough, and we want to know about it before they publish it."

They weren't kicking her out then, but kicking her to the curb, reminding her of her place. "Sa'han . . ." she said, drawing to a stop.

He was smiling when she looked up, his amusement unexpected. "Your excellent grades and background give you a unique ability to infiltrate by taking a job as a genetic researcher. The enclave will pay you a small security stipend," he said, handing her a contract rolled up and tied with a purple ribbon. "And that is what your title will be on the rolls, but you will have your wage from Global Genetics to supplement your income to the point where you won't need a spouse to maintain yourself."

She stared at him, stunned. She'd be free, as few women were in the sixties.

"You will work in a lab," he said, drawing her into motion again. "It's where I think you ought to be, and I usually get what I want. You will maintain your job performance for your human employers, but your primary focus is to inform us of any unusual developments." He chuckled, rubbing his bald head ruefully. "Sometimes the humans get lucky, and we want to know of it."

"But you said I needed to learn where I belonged," she fumbled.

"I said you needed to learn who you are. You are a dark elf, Felecia Eloytrisk Cambri. And I'm giving you the chance to live up to your potential. Will you take it?"

Her heart pounded as she realized what he was offering her. On paper, being forced to work outside of an elven lab was a harsh punishment, but in reality, she'd be doing what she enjoyed, what she was good at, and working someplace where she could make a difference.

"Well?" Ulbrine hesitated at the door to the hall. She could see that the contract had been time-stamped an hour ago, legal and binding even if she signed it now.

Beyond him lay the world. She could be what she'd always wanted, had striven for. Quen was right. It didn't matter what anyone else thought.

Her hand trembled as she reached for a pen. "I'll take it."

2

Stifling a yawn, Trisk confidently made her way deeper into the underground labs of Global Genetics. It was nearing noon, and she could feel her body slowing down, forced to stay awake to hold to a human schedule. After three years, she no longer nodded off over lunch, but it was hard to fight the urge for a four-hour nap when the sun was at its highest. Elves were most alert at sunrise and sunset, but it had been ages since she'd allowed herself the luxury of her natural inclination to sleep at noon and midnight.

Her low-heeled baby-doll shoes were eerily silent on the polished floor, and the faint smell of antiseptic was a familiar balm, pricking the back of her nose. After noticing a few high eyebrows this morning, she'd closed her lab coat to hide her short, bright yellow skirt, but the matching hose still made a colorful statement. Her lab assistant, Angie, said the outfit was fine, but getting the new look past the stuffier old men she worked with was proving to be difficult.

"Hi, George," she said to the man at the glass double doors, and he rose from his desk to open them for her. There was no need to show her ID, and she didn't even bring it out from behind her lab coat.

"Good afternoon, Dr. Cambri. Save me a piece of cake?"

His smile was infectious, and her mood brightened. "One with a rose on it. You got it," she said as she crossed into the restricted zone. Immediately the drier air and tang of ozone from the massive computers under her feet made her long hair float, and she impatiently tried to corral the strands that had escaped her hair clip at the back of her neck. If she were at the elf-run NASA facility, the computer needed to comprehend the genetic code of just one organism would fit into a room. Here, with human-only equipment, it took an entire floor—at least until someone leaked the technology and humankind took another leap forward.

Trisk heard the building's head secretary before she saw her, the woman's trendy thigh-high vinyl boots clicking on the hard floor. "Hi, Trisk," the bubbly older woman said as she turned a corner and came into sight. "Are you getting him now?"

"Right this minute," Trisk said, and Barbara beamed, her eyes alight as she took Trisk's hands for a quick second.

"Outta sight! I'll make sure everyone is in the lunchroom," she said, the *click-clack* of her boots quickening as she ran in prissy, mincing steps to the security door and the elevators beyond. Her colorful dress rode high, and her hair was tall, but the day planner tucked under her arm had everyone's schedule in it, and the self-appointed mother of them all knew more than anyone about how to keep the small facility working, even if she did look and act like an aged stand-in on *American Bandstand*—which raised the question: If Barbara could get away with flaunting the new styles exploding into the shops this summer, why couldn't Trisk?

Because Barbara isn't helping design tactical biologi-cal weapons, Trisk thought as she passed her lab, still proud of her name on the door. Her outer office was dark, but she could see through the interior windows into the brightly lit testing bays, green and gold in the artificial sun. There had been a marked slowdown in her lab since the patent to the Angel tomato had been sold to Saladan Industries and Farms and the slow, year-long process of transferring data, seeds, and propagation techniques to Saladan Farms had begun. She'd have to find a new project by the first of the year, but for now, she still had a secondary, newly tweaked seed crop growing in the huge underground nursery—along with all the tomatoes she could give away.

Across the hall was Dr. Daniel Plank's lab, and Trisk hesitated at the window, waving to get the attention of the two people suited up in level-two containment suits. The suits were big and bulky compared to the ones she'd learned in, making her feel foolish the first time she'd climbed into one and not known how to zip the stupid thing up. Fortunately she didn't need one anymore in her day-to-day. Her product was two years in the field and doing well.

Both figures looked up, the taller immediately ges-turing for her to come into the outer office. She knew it was Daniel even if she couldn't see his blond hair and plastic-framed glasses through the thick helmet. He was the closest thing to an elf she'd seen since moving out here, and it bothered her that she'd been drawn to his slim build and light hair like a junkie.

Acknowledging him, she punched in the four-digit code to his door lock and entered his office. Only one window now separated them, and smiling, she went to the communication panel, as familiar with his office as her own. "Hi, Daniel," she said, making sure her cleavage wasn't showing as she leaned over the mic. "How long until you're done?"

Daniel turned from his setup, fingers clumsy in the one-size-fits-all glove. "Trisk? What can I do for you this morning?"

Stifling another yawn, she raised her wrist and tapped her watch. "It's noon. We have a plate of mac and cheese upstairs waiting for us. You promised."

"Noon?" Daniel turned to his assistant. "Larry, why didn't you tell me it was that late?"

"Sorry, Doctor." Larry's sour voice came faintly over the open channel. "I thought you were going to skip lunch. Again."

Trisk hid a smile at the faint accusation in the man's voice, but Daniel was known to forget to eat lunch. Go home at the end of the day. Have a life. She made a mental note to set aside a piece of cake for Larry as well.

"Oh, jeez . . ." Daniel turned back to Larry, clearly not wanting to leave him to work alone. "Trisk, can you give us another five minutes?"

"Just go," the assistant said in resignation. "I can finish this myself. Probably faster than with your help, even."

"Thanks, Larry. I appreciate that."

Trisk rocked back as Daniel gave Larry some last instructions, moving slowly and awkwardly to the decontamination room. Knowing it would take him some time to work through the SOP, Trisk settled herself at Daniel's terminal and punched in his password.

Fingers moving adroitly over the keyboard, she brought up the latest coding for the protein coat around the tactical virus he was working with. Again, she glanced at Daniel, his helmet off now as he closed his eyes against the glare of the decontamination light and scrubbed at his scalp as if he were in the shower. Returning to the screen, she compared the code to the one hand-printed on a scrap of paper she took from her pocket.

Perfect. Her last tweak to his work had taken. Now, even if his tactical virus should be deployed, it would have no effect whatsoever on her people. They were invisible to it. Ghosts.

Reaching out a sliver of her awareness, she touched her mind to the nearest ley line, squirming when the broken feel of it eased into her. The lines were fractured on the West Coast due to the constant mini-quakes. Both the movement and the slippery feel to the lines were big reasons why all the elven labs were east of the Mississippi, and though their vagrant feel still gave her the willies, she'd gotten better at using them the last couple of years.

Tightening her grip on the one running through Sacramento, she channeled the slip of energy through her, supplementing her body's natural energy. "*Flagro,*" she whispered to direct the influx of tingly power going into her hands.

The paper with its incriminating message of A's, G's, T's, and C's burst into flame, consumed so quickly it didn't even singe her fingers.

Sighing in relief, she waved the smoke to nothing. It was done. Sa'han Ulbrine had been correct in that human genetic studies needed to be watched, and she'd first brought Daniel's research to the enclave's attention almost eighteen months ago. Sa'han Ulbrine had advised her to completely sabotage the tactical virus, even after she'd explained that its intent was to sicken, not kill. She'd argued that in a world focused on biological weapons instead of space exploration, this was the first time anyone had tried to develop a tactical virus instead of a lethal one. Success here, she argued, might turn other human labs in a similar non-lethal direction.

To her surprise, the political body of elves had listened to her petition, accepting her plan to adapt the outer protein coat of Daniel's virus to make not just elves, but all paranormal species immune to it. That her research was being shared with every enclave-run lab in the states was heady. That the enclave had trusted her to complete the modifications before the virus went to live trials had worried her. Now that it was done, she was more than a little relieved.

Even to humans, the virus would do little harm, causing twenty-four hours of frightening skin eruptions, fatigue, and fever. Its effect was toxin-based, and with no host or natural carriers, it was short-lived and unable to reproduce outside of the lab. If the upcoming live tests went well, it would become the first of a proposed line of tactical biological weapons designed to down anything from a plane to an entire city held by a foreign force.

And now she and all her people were utterly immune.

She knew her face still held the pleasure of that when the door to the decontamination booth hissed open. "Sorry about that," Daniel said, still arranging his short blond hair as he padded on sock feet to where his shoes waited. "You should have knocked on my door earlier." He looked at his thick watch, brow rising. "I didn't realize it was that late."

Trisk pushed back from the desk, quashing a flash of guilt for her tweaks, some made with his knowledge, some without. "I know you get busy. Besides, they won't put anything away for another half hour."

"True, but I hate pulling the skin off the pudding." Sighing, he bent low over his knees, his sweater in warm shades of autumn matching his brown trousers. "I'm going to request a live trial next month," he said as his long fingers manipulated the thin shoelaces into behaving. "Maybe Cuba? It'd be nice not to have to worry about that anymore." He grinned as he looked up at her. "You shouldn't have the only project making money."

She smiled back, liking him this happy. "I think it's ready now," she said. "There haven't been any significant mutations in a hundred generations."

"Not since you helped me strip its redundant DNA out." Standing, he reached for his suit coat, and she rose, the scent of his aftershave strong as he shoved his arms into his sleeves. She liked the clean, woodsy aroma as she fixed his tie, not caring that his suit was stuck in the fifties.

"Trisk, I can't thank you enough for your help with the virus's coat," he said. "It never occurred to me to modify the protein skin so as to use the host's own immune response to create those additional, secondary side effects."

"Just making the value box bigger." She turned to the door, uncomfortable about everything she *hadn't* shared with him. Humans were so far behind, but perhaps that was because the elves and everyone else kept them that way. "It's what I did my doctoral thesis on," she said, not wanting to talk about it. "If I hadn't come up with it, someone else would have."

"Maybe, but you're the one who did," he insisted, and after a last look at Larry heading for the decontamination booth, he followed Trisk into the hall. "It's an entirely new way to think about viruses."

The silence stretched as they walked to the glass doors. The quiet was unusual for the chatty man, and his hard-soled shoes sounded loud and obvious. Grimacing, she forced her baby-doll slippers to make some noise, not wanting Daniel to notice she wasn't making a sound. Through the big glass doors, George read a magazine, oblivious to them approaching.

"How about dinner tonight?" Daniel said suddenly, surprising her. "Just you and me."

Trisk's step faltered, and she lengthened her stride to hide it. "Ah . . . ." she hedged.

"Aw, come on," he cajoled, pushing his glasses back up his nose as he got the door for her. "It's my birthday. Don't make me spend it alone."

"Dr. Plank, all you have to do is ask any of the ladies upstairs, and I'm sure they would be more than happy to keep you company," she blurted, and George chuckled, never looking up from his magazine.

"Is it my breath?" Daniel asked good-naturedly. "Did I forget to zip my pants again?"

She laughed nervously. "No!"

"Then what?" His expression became serious, and she sighed, wishing she'd done something different the last three years. Ignored him, maybe. But striking up a friendship had seemed harmless and made tweaking his virus easier. "Trisk, I've known you for three years," he said as they headed for the big silver elevators. "You don't have a boyfriend that I've ever heard of. You spend all your time here or at home. We have a great friendship, as far as I know. Did I do something wrong?" His eyes pinched. "Did I not do something I should have?"

She hit the elevator call button and turned to him. "Daniel, you're a great guy—"

"Oh no," he interrupted, and her eyes flicked up, reading real hurt behind the dramatic façade of being crushed.

"It's not you," she fumbled. "It's me."

Groaning, he dropped back a step.

"It is," she insisted as the elevator opened. She hesitated a moment, then taking a deep breath, she got in. Daniel was silent behind her. The doors shut, and she stared at the numbers counting up, wishing it would go faster. A relationship was fraught with more trouble than it was worth, not only endangering her career, but raising issues she wasn't ready to deal with yet.

"Trisk." She jumped when he took her hand, not moving as he searched for words. "I'm serious. Tell me what it is, and I'll change. You are a smart, intelligent woman. I like you, and I want to spend more time with you than ten minutes here, five minutes there in the hall or lunchroom. Just give me one night. One lousy candlelit dinner at Celeste's. If you don't have a good time, I'll walk away and not talk to you again."

"Daniel," she pleaded, never having imagined she'd be in this position. She'd never given him any indication of wanting anything other than a professional relationship. "That's not what I want."

"Then tell me what you do want," he said. "Is it because you've made it on your own? I'd never take that away from you, though kids would be nice . . . someday."

The elevator chimed and the silver doors opened. Relieved, Trisk strode out. She could feel Daniel's tension as he walked beside her, his frustration that she was putting him off. An unexpected pain took her at the mention of children. He wanted kids, lots of them, probably. So did she, eventually. But how could she tell him it would never work? That the biology wouldn't cooperate without intervention, and even then, her father would never accept him. Marrying Daniel meant the already slim chance that she'd have a healthy elven child would be completely gone, and with that, the possibility she could make something of herself, for when your species was on the brink of extinction, having healthy children equaled power, status. A voice.

She slowed as the doors to the cafeteria loomed close, and Daniel came to a stop before her. Trisk didn't know what she was going to say, but she couldn't walk into that room with this between them. Her breath shook as she inhaled. "Daniel . . ."

"There you are!" Barbara called as the door to the lunchroom opened and the woman bounded out, completely missing Daniel's dark look as she took control of his arm. "We need you in the cafeteria," she said loudly. "Right now!"

"We?" Daniel caught his balance as she jerked him to the door. "We who?"

Trisk didn't move as Barbara all but pushed him into the lunchroom. Miserable, Trisk crossed her arms over her chest when the entire building shouted "*Surprise!*" and began to sing "Happy Birthday." Her eyes closed, and depressed, she slumped back against the wall beside the doors. Her birthday was in the spring, but elves weren't known to celebrate them, as there were too many memories of babies who never grew up.

Unable to go into that room full of happy people and pretend, she opened her eyes and pushed herself up from the wall.

Starting, she jerked to a stop, almost running into the

man standing before her. She hadn't even heard him approach. "Oh!" she exclaimed, her gaze going first to his ID badge before dropping to run over his tall frame. He looked almost exotic in his slim-waisted suit inspired by the latest British fashion, his narrow, brilliantly red tie the only nod to old-school business Americana. Dark, gently waving hair almost dared to touch his broad shoulders, and her face warmed at the unusual pull she felt toward him. "Excuse me," she added, faltering at his intent gaze, his pupils widening ever so slightly to make his dark eyes even darker. They seemed to be looking right to her core, and she stifled a shudder, becoming very much awake despite it being noon.

"You must be Felecia," he said, his mellow voice sounding as if he should be announcing jazz on the radio, not standing in the hallway of a scientific center.

A faint hint of brimstone tickled the back of her throat, and in a cold wash, she realized she wasn't standing with a human. Suddenly his allure became . . . threatening. *Don't witches smell like brimstone?* "I'm sorry. Are you supposed to be here?"

Smiling with his lips closed, he extended his hand. "I'm Rick Rales. The new CEO."

"Oh." She cautiously tapped a line, letting a bare hint of it run through her as she took his hand. If he was a witch, he'd notice and give himself away. Only witches and elves could tap into and use ley lines. But the man's hand gripped hers with only a professional strength. "Everyone calls me Trisk or Dr. Cambri," she added, pulling away when she remembered: Witches didn't smell like brimstone. Vampires did.

He was a vampire. Not an undead one, as the sun was up, but a living vampire, born to parents who were the same before they died and became truly undead. He'd have some of the strength and charisma of his undead brethren, but none of the liabilities, and he probably only dabbled in blood whereas the true undead needed it to survive. Probably. *What is he doing here?*

"Ah, nice to meet you," she added as Rick touched the side of his nose and smiled, clearly recognizing that he'd been outed. She should have known right away. The undead bred their living kin like horses, designing entire family lines to be compliant, mentally flexible, and most definitely beautiful. And Rick was breathtakingly handsome. In his midthirties, he was clearly too old to be a plaything anymore. It would make him smart, ruthless, and very . . . subtle, to have survived this long under his undead master's attention.

Trisk hadn't dealt with the undead much. Indeed, apart from elected officials and very old vampires regulating human-Inderland affairs, there was a "you go your way and I go mine" mentality that kept the peace. Showing fear, though, would be a mistake. She knew that much.

"I, uh, wasn't aware we were getting a new boss," she added, glancing in at the festivities. "Is Dr. Hartsford okay?"

"He is." Rick's lips split to show normal-looking teeth. He was wearing caps over his slightly elongated canines, though nothing would hide the truly long versions he'd get once he died. "You might say you invited me," he said, head inclined in amusement.

"Really? How so?" Her pulse had quickened, and she didn't like that he probably knew.

Rick leaned in, and she froze as he whispered, "You need to keep your nose out of human progress."

Trisk pulled back, hating that she had flushed. "I created a drought-resistant tomato."

"Your *boyfriend's* virus?" he asked, thick eyebrows high.

"He's not my boyfriend," she said quickly, wanting to walk away, but turning her back on him wasn't an option and might invite him to follow.

Rick breathed deeply, and she wondered if he was tasting the emotions that lingered long after those responsible for them had left. "He wants to be," he said, voice as soft as black silk, and Trisk felt ill, wishing there were a vampire handbook she could consult. "Play with him. You have a hundred years to make more elves."

Lips pressed, Trisk took a long step back. *No sense of personal space.* She knew what he was, and he needed to stop trying to pull an aura on her, which was a polite way of saying trying to charm her into being his blood slave. "Why are you here?"

Immediately Rick lost his avarice, glancing into the lunchroom as if it helped him find a calmer state. "You tweaked his virus," he accused. "There are elven fingerprints all over it. We are in the government as much as you are, and we know it's been slated for military use. I'm here to make sure you're not creating something to further your species at our expense." His eyes found hers. "You elves are tricky little bastards."

By *our expense*, he meant the vampires', and she found her courage, hands on her hips as she leaned into his space, brave here among the humans as she couldn't be in a dark alley. He wouldn't dare bite her to try to bind her to him. Not here. "I may have given him some ideas," she said, smug as he blinked in surprise at her lack of fear. "Don't get your panties in a twist. If you'd bother to look at the code, you'll see that I made everyone immune to it. *All* of us," she emphasized. "Not just elves. It's human specific, right down to its mRNA."

"Mmmm." Rick dropped back a step, a hand over his mouth. "I can't read code."

Trisk's expression soured. He couldn't read code, and yet here he was, the new CEO of Global Genetics. "Only those who share a common ancestor with humans will be affected," she said. "It's safe."

"Vampires share a common ancestor," Rick said, his suspicions returning.

"I took that into account," she said. "I was the best in my class, Mr. Rales," she added, proud of her skills. "Even at artificially high levels, Daniel's virus will do nothing but make you and anyone else sick. Multiple safeguards keep it tactical. I wouldn't have even bothered to make us invisible to it, but I didn't want to take the chance that an immune-depressed elf baby coming out of gene therapy might get a pimple from being exposed. Look, you can talk to my boss if you want," she said, exasperated. "Sa'han Ulbrine, not Dr. Hartsford."

"I did," he said, lips parting to show teeth. "Ulbrine is why you and Dr. Plank are alive."

Threat, threat, threat, she thought, not impressed. The only thing more suspicious than a living vampire was a dead one. "You're not going to slow down the trials, are you? Rales, he's worked too hard for this. It's perfect. I made sure of it. It *cannot* harm us. I'd stake my life on it."

"Good. Because you have." Rick frowned, but his expression suddenly shifted, the hard mistrust falling from him to show a comfortable camaraderie. Shocked at the change, she floundered, at a loss for words as the cafeteria door opened. Clearly he'd felt whoever it was coming before his or her shadow had touched the glass, and it creeped Trisk out.

"Mr. Rales!" Barbara burst forth, clucking like a

mother hen. "I should have known you'd be out here hiding with Dr. Cambri. She's *such* a wallflower. Come in and meet everyone you missed yesterday. It's Daniel's birthday and we have cake!"

Mouthing a soft platitude, Rick let the woman lead him away, giving Trisk a threatening stare as he crossed the threshold and was taken in among the naive, fragile humans like a cat among mice. He was here to watch her, but he'd play if he thought he could get away with it.

Turning, Trisk walked briskly to her lab, her mind pinging from the threat of Rick's presence to Daniel. She needed to talk to Quen. He knew more about vampires than she did, and if he came out to spend a weekend, Daniel might misunderstand and stop trying to make a date with her.

Better than a hundred awkward conversations he wouldn't believe anyway, she thought glumly, feeling even more guilt-ridden than before.

3

The scent of salt and low tide was almost lost behind the reek of burnt cooking oil and over-done shrimp as Kal handed the keys of his Mustang convertible to the valet. "Keep it somewhere available and in the shade," he said as he gave the old man an extra twenty.

"Yes, sir!" the valet exclaimed, jogging to the front of the car and carefully getting in.

It was unusually hot for Daytona Beach in early October, making Kal more drowsy than he normally would be, even at high noon. He uncomfortably adjusted his tie as he waited for a second valet to get the door for him. Sa'han Ulbrine, too, would be sleepy this time of day, making Kal question why he wouldn't wait until the sun went down, but perhaps it had been easier to get a table at the exclusive restaurant now than at night, when the waterfront came alive and the Sandbar would be packed.

The inside was no cooler, loud and noisy with wealthy snowbirds. A few businessmen were bellied up to the bar as if it was their second home, drinking their lunch and comparing notes. Resigned to an uncomfortable hour spent justifying the slow pace of his research,

Kal approached the host. A couple ahead of him were trying to get a table on the patio, arguing that they'd had reservations.

Sighing, Kal rocked back on his heels to wait. The large placard beside the restrooms touted a live band playing everything from the Beach Boys to Buddy Holly, but it was probably the restaurant's location on the water that made it such a hot spot. Finally the couple were coaxed by free drinks to a less desirable table. "Kalamack," he said, impatient as the host made eye contact. "I'm meeting someone. Reservation under Ulbrine for two."

Immediately the man's bored expression shifted to one of excitement. "Yes, sir. Your party is here already. Would you like me to take your hat?"

Kal shook his head, reluctant to hand it over as it sported one of his orchids, cut from his tissue-grown plants. "No, I'll keep it. Thank you," he said as he pushed forward to follow the man into the restaurant proper.

His grip on his hat tightened. He could think of only one reason the enclave would want to talk to him away from his work, and it probably had everything to do with that brilliantly researched and written paper that Trisk had published last week in an elf-exclusive journal. It made his work look clunky and almost criminally timid, but even a pared-down virus was potentially dangerous in his view. Far safer to use bacteria to introduce new genetic code than a virus that couldn't be stamped out with antibiotics if it took on a life of its own. All he needed was a clean host bacterium, and he and his team would be poised to create an entire line of genetic fixes to keep his people alive for another generation. He had gambled his career on it.

Pace stilted, he wove through the crowded restaurant, not liking the loud chatter brought on by too much wine too early in the day. Trisk had a product on the shelf, but it was her theory to use a stripped-down virus to introduce new material to both somatic and germ cells that dogged him, not her drought-resistant, shippable tomato that was tart and firm even after weeks from the field. The human-based journal featuring her T4 Angel tomato claimed the desired traits had been introduced by careful splicing, but Kal was betting that a donor virus, not mechanical butchery, had introduced them.

And now the enclave wanted to talk to him. *Have I made an error?*

"Sir?" the host said, pausing at the open door to the patio.

Kal looked up, appreciating the cooling breeze coming off the ocean to shift his fine hair. He hesitated briefly at the empty tables, remembering the host saying the patio was closed, but then he saw Sa'han Ulbrine, looking like a tan, somewhat overweight tourist in bright clothes and flip-flops, his bald head shiny with sweat even under the shade of the palms.

He wasn't alone, and Kal's pace slowed as he took in the three men with him. The most striking was a small but tidy man in an army summer uniform, clean-shaven and trim, with a panel of ribbons on his chest. A businessman with a decidedly Asian cast sat opposite him, seemingly oblivious to the heat in a suit and tie, one leg propped up on the other knee as he smoked a thin cigarette. The third looked uncomfortable in his trendy, tight dress pants, his silky, wavy hair almost to his shoulders. His face was pale, and he was squinting despite being in the shade. A suit coat was carefully draped over an adjacent chair, but he still looked hot, even with his narrow tie loose about his neck and his top two shirt buttons undone to show a soft, old scar about his collarbone.

Ulbrine's voice rose in welcome upon seeing Kal, and everyone stood. With a shock, Kal realized the one with the long hair was a living vampire; the grace he moved with and the uncomfortable squint at the sun gave him away. *Not to mention he looks like a god*, Kal thought as he scuffed to a halt.

"Dr. Kalamack," Ulbrine said, beaming as he extended his hand. "Thank you for joining us on such short notice. I ordered iced tea for the table. Would you like something stronger?"

He did, but not with a vampire present, even if it was noon. Though living vampires could tolerate the light as their undead masters couldn't, meeting when the sun was high would help tamp down any urges for blood that afflicted even the living ones. Ulbrine had probably rented out the entire patio for privacy.

"Iced tea is fine," Kal said as he shook the elf's hand. His eyes went to the military stiff, realizing that for all his smooth face and collected mien, he was a Were, an alpha by the look of it. A NASA pin hung at the end of his bank of ribbons, and Kal's eyebrows rose. *Good news, maybe?*

"Colonel Jason Wolfe, with an *E*," the small man said to his left, his handshake firm as he pumped Kal's hand once and let go. "Right on time. I like that in a man."

"Timing is everything," Kal said, his flash of hope that this might be a job interview faltering as he realized the man with the cigarette was a witch. The scent of redwood coming off him was detectable even over the reek of tar and nicotine. *Shit*, Kal thought. He might be in trouble. Interspecies meetings to discuss territory rights, population control, and long-running plans weren't unheard of, but they usually didn't involve genetic engineers.

"Max Saladan," the businessman said, voice rough as he extended his hand, and Kal shook it, feeling the tingle of the ley lines as their internal balances tried to equalize. He was a ley line practitioner, and fairly competent, judging by the pressure imbalance between them.

There was a decided coolness about him, and Kal decided he was using a charm to block the heat. Not a drop of sweat marred his severely straight black hair or lightly lined face despite his wrinkled black suit. His eyes were hidden behind sunglasses, and he looked nearly asleep. A cup of coffee steamed beside him in opposition to the three other half-empty glasses of iced tea.

"Dr. Trenton Kalamack," Kal said, reclaiming his hand. "But Kal is fine."

"Kal," the vampire said, smiling a politically polite but warm smile. "I'm Rick Rales. CEO of Global Genetics."

Kal stifled a shudder as he shook his hand, not liking that the man probably enjoyed his sex with blood and wasn't picky about the container it came in. "That's where Trisk Cambri works, is it not?"

Rick nodded as he sat down beside him, his satisfaction obvious as his gaze strayed to the distant servers in more than mild interest. "It is indeed where *Doctor* Cambri works."

"Sit, sit," Ulbrine said as he took his own seat, clearly comfortable in his lighter clothes. "It's hotter than the demons' ever-after out here. Kal, I asked the colonel, Rick, and Max to join us. I have a proposition for you that involves them."

Uneasy, Kal handed his suit coat to the server who had darted forward to take it. He kept his hat, though, dropping it carefully on the table beside his chair before sitting down between the vampire and the Were. An ice-clinking drink dripping moisture was set before him, but he waited until the waiters vanished before sifting a spoonful of sugar into it with a casual slowness. *A witch, a vampire, a Were, and an elf go out for lunch*, he thought sourly, hoping he wasn't the punch line. That he was by far the youngest man at the table didn't bother him half as much as the fact that all four major Inderland species were represented.

"My research is far from a dead end," Kal said to try to head off the coming accusations. "Once we have a stable host, the possibilities are endless."

But Ulbrine held up a restraining hand. "You misunderstand. It's not your research we have a question about, but Trisk's—er, Dr. Cambri's."

Intrigued, Kal settled back under the shade of the shifting palms and took a sip of tea. "She's working on coding new information into germ cells by way of a virus, is she not?" he said, looking at Rick in expectation. "Creating a true-breeding tomato that will save the world."

Rick grinned to show perfectly normal teeth, capped, no doubt. He looked svelte and trendy enough to be an undead's favorite. Scion, maybe. "Or at least save Global Genetics' bottom line," he said, dabbing the sweat from himself with a handkerchief.

Expression idle, Max Saladan blew smoke to the ocean. "It's not your tomato anymore, Rick. It's mine. Bought and paid for."

"Like I said, Global Genetics' bottom line," the vampire said, laughing good-naturedly.

Ulbrine leaned over the table, his brow furrowed. "Have you seen Dr. Cambri's paper on incorporating code into somatic cells by way of a virus?"

"Of course he has." Colonel Wolfe chuckled, his short fingers carefully manipulating his spoon so it didn't ting against the glass as he stirred it. His NASA pin caught a glint of light, and Kal felt a jolt of envy. "Can you not smell his jealousy?" he added, dark eyes knowing as they found Kal's. "The boy reeks of it."

Kal's lip twitched. Setting his drink aside, he leaned back, his hands resting confidently on the arms of the wicker chair. He didn't like that he was unable to see Saladan's eyes, lost behind dark glasses. "Why am I here?"

Max snorted, and Ulbrine gave him a brief irate look before saying, "After your *stellar* display at presentation three years ago, I had no recourse but to put Trisk on the enclave's payroll as security somewhere. We have standards, after all, and I'll not have the university's one-hundred-percent placement record tarnished. I sent her to Global Genetics on the rumor they were working up another planet killer."

Kal's eyebrows rose. He'd thought her position had been a step down, but apparently not. "So . . . she's been working on something other than drought-resistant tomatoes?"

"I do not waste talent like hers on farm produce." Ulbrine slurped his tea, getting a face full of ice when it slid. "Humanity is hell-bent on developing a line of bio-based weapons," he said as he wiped the tea from his face. "So far, we've managed to sabotage the worst of the lot, but there are too many smaller labs without current governmental ties to keep track of."

"We can't allow another Cuban bioweapon crisis,"

Colonel Wolfe said, his expressive eyebrows high as he handed Ulbrine a cocktail napkin. "With Vietnam heating up, we can no longer afford to ignore the possibility that a small group not under our control is making great strides. We can't infiltrate every lab from pole to pole, so the easiest method to control them is to give them an outlet, a direction of study we *can* control."

Rick brought his eyes back from the servers moving like fish behind the plate glass that divided the haves from the have-nots. His tongue was a sexually charged hint as he slowly licked his lips. "If they had the ability, humans would wipe us all from the earth."

"No one is going to break the silence," Ulbrine said placatingly as he wadded up Wolfe's napkin. "But we can't risk them accidentally destroying us along with themselves. Focusing humanity on tactical weapons instead of mass destruction is key. Developing a base virus we're familiar with and can control seems more than desirable; it's prudent."

Kal felt a sinking sensation. "And Cambri has done this?" he asked.

"No, but her colleague has," Ulbrine said. "Dr. Cambri assures us that due to her tweaking, not only is this new virus incapable of causing mass death, but that all of Inderland will be to some degree immune. We'd like to allow it to go to live trials, but we've been requested by several Inderland factions to get a second opinion."

Relief spilled into him, and Kal nodded, the presence of the high-level witch, alpha Were, and vampire now making sense. "You want me to go over her work," he said, not sure whether that was a compliment or a slap in the face.

Rick beamed at him. "Who better than the man who would give anything to see her fail?"

"Of course," Kal said, suddenly relishing the idea. "Send the file and I'll—"

"Send the file?" Colonel Wolfe interrupted, chuckling. "You have no idea the shit that woman has to wade through to do her job on a human platform. It would take three semis to carry the electronic files, and then you'd be unable to read them. Global Genetics' computer system is large and unwieldy. Takes up an entire basement floor. You have to go there and read it on their system."

"To the West Coast?" Kal's enthusiasm faltered, and Rick beamed, nodding unapologetically as he downed the last of his drink. Exhaling in satisfaction, Rick set his empty glass aside, ice tinkling.

Max Saladan slumped, his hand shaking as he found his coffee. "We want the assurance that this new virus is safe as well. You will go in as my employee, assisting in the patent transfer of the T4 Angel tomato. And if you start chewing that ice, Rick, I swear I'll spell you into a bat."

"What about my work here?" Kal said as Rick sullenly pushed his glass of ice aside. Kal's work wasn't going well, but there had been progress.

"Ulbrine," Max said, his thin voice taking on a trace of an Asian accent, "I did not stuff myself in a tin can for six hours and fly out here for a maybe. *Make* him do this. I thought the enclave could *make* him do this."

Kal's eyes narrowed. Across from him, Colonel Wolfe leaned back, his hands laced across his middle in expectation. Ulbrine shifted as if uncomfortable. "Ah," the enclave member stammered. "Kal? We've gotten you a six-month guest pass at Global Genetics through Max. Saladan Industries and Farms acquired the patent to Dr. Cambri's Angel tomato, and as his field manager, you'll be assisting in the patent transfer. From there, Rick will get you access to Dr. Plank's records on the tactical virus. The colonel will be on-site occasionally as the government's contact facilitating the military acquisition. You will report your findings to both me and him."

Six months! I can't leave my research for six months, Kal thought as the small Were in his tidy uniform inclined his head, his expression still holding that wary expectation.

"There can be no question," Ulbrine was saying. "No mistakes. The balance between the four major Inderland species has been maintained for over eight hundred years, and if the effects of this new virus are more detrimental than Trisk promises, there will be problems."

Realization snapped through him, washing Kal with an icy breath despite the heat. The enclave could send anyone to double-check Trisk's work. They were sending him so they could quietly mothball his current research with bacteria. They'd given up on it in the face of Trisk's more promising, quickly evolving theory. Trisk's results were attractively fast, but that's where the danger lay. His theories were slower, yes, but safer. Why couldn't they see that?

A feeling of alarmed urgency broke over him, but Kal kept his breathing even. His theory that bacteria could safely insert genetic code into mature cells would have as much chance of being developed now as a man had of walking on the moon.

Rick cleared his throat, drawing his attention. The living vampire beamed at him, his hand rising in a gesture of *Well?* as Max lit another cigarette, clearly not caring. Colonel Wolfe's eyes narrowed in threat. And still, Kal couldn't move, the heat of the day making it hard to breathe. If he left for six months, they'd close his project. He'd never find another lab willing to pick it back up. Trisk's code-carrying virus would become a potential threat in their very children's cells until something went wrong, and something always went wrong.

"Dr. Kalamack, a word?" Ulbrine said as he rose, chair scraping the worn wood.

I should have worked harder. Kal sat for three heartbeats as his failure trickled through him. With very little grace, he stood, pushing his chair back with a loud noise to follow Ulbrine to the railing, where the crashing waves might cloud their words. The wind was fresher, tugging at his short hair as the dampness wound its way past his shirt and coated him in a sticky, salty film.

"Trisk's research is dangerous," Kal said bitterly, not caring if the three men at the table now discussing the agony of jet lag could hear. "You expect me to leave my lab to become a field manager? For a witch? To help *her?*"

Ulbrine's expression creased as he took Kal's shoulder and turned him to the ocean. "This isn't about Trisk, it's about Dr. Plank's tactical virus. We must be sure it will function as designed before other labs take it up as their template. Our numbers are too low to risk outside strife impacting us, and if it should go wrong, we won't survive another species-specific war."

They want to close my work down, he thought, seething. Trisk would laugh her ass off.

Ulbrine's expression darkened, clearly thinking jealousy, not the loss of his own work, was making Kal reluctant, and he felt his face burn. When NASA had withdrawn their offer, he'd been forced to accept his second choice. It was still in Florida, but he felt like damaged goods. And it was Trisk's fault. No wonder he hadn't made any progress. Even his colleagues doubted him.

"I'm giving you this opportunity as a favor to your father," Ulbrine said, and Kal's focus cleared.

"Don't do my father any favors," he said coldly, turning to take his leave. But he stopped short when Ulbrine grasped his elbow, the tingle of ley line energy warning him to stay.

"Then consider it a last-ditch effort to save your family name," Ulbrine said, his eyes inches from Kal's. "You're the very last one in a very long line, Trent. Your parents were lucky to bring you to full term, and they spent their entire fortune keeping you alive."

He let go, and Kal caught his balance. He remembered the bitter medicines, the painful experimental treatments. It had been akin to torture, and he had lost most of his childhood, but his parents had tried to make it up to him in other ways. Part of why he worked so hard was so that no other child would ever have to go through what he had.

Apparently satisfied Kal was listening, Ulbrine turned to the ocean to prevent anyone from reading his lips. "There are two ways elven lines maintain power," he lectured. "Through money, which your parents utterly spent to keep you alive, or by having many children. You haven't had much luck there, either. If you do nothing, your name will die with you."

"I haven't—" Kal started, feeling his masculinity threatened.

"Stop." Ulbrine turned from the two women walking the beach to look him up and down. "Our race is dying, but some families, once the most powerful, are dying faster than others. Yours is on a knife's edge. Tell me I'm wrong."

Kal thought about the women he had had relations with over the years. None of them had gotten pregnant. Not even for a month or two.

"Which brings me to the second reason I want you there," Ulbrine said softly. "If Trisk successfully used a donor virus to introduce new code into an established individual such that it breeds true, I want to know. People are not tomatoes, but technique is technique, and if it can be applied to repair our genome, she has to be moved into a real lab."

A job at NASA, perhaps? he thought bitterly. Trisk's ideas were dangerous, not only because they were inherently flawed, but also because they would suck the funding from his own research, research that wasn't based on hasty assumptions. Somehow he kept it from his face. Trying to explain it to Ulbrine would only reinforce the old man's idea that he was being jealously stubborn, not stubbornly pragmatic.

"She's done more in that wretched human lab than ten men with access to all our elven advances." Ulbrine hesitated. "This opportunity is a gift, Kal." Hunched with his elbows on the wooden railing, the older man eyed Kal, the dappled shade of the palm making his eyes look black. "If you find errors in the immunity of the tactical virus, it will be your task to fix them."

"You want me to fix her work?" Kal asked in disbelief, but in his very question he saw the beginnings of an idea.

"What I want is for you to give us control of something worth having," Ulbrine said. "It will take stealth and cleverness and test your ability to manipulate to the utmost. These are the traits that define the best of us, Kal, and your father was the epitome of the warrior poet steadfastly doing what needed to be done to keep our people alive. Even the most ugly of deeds." He hesitated, focus going back to the water. "Perhaps I made a mistake. Sometimes it skips a generation."

But Kal hardly heard, his mind racing forward, seeing this for the golden chance that Ulbrine never dreamed it was. He could do what the enclave wanted *and* bring it to their attention that Trisk's donor virus was not the savior to their species it looked to be, prove that other avenues of research shouldn't be shut down in the name of fast results. He could stomach Trisk thinking he was a field manager if it might bring the perils of her flawed research to light.

Pulse quickening, Kal gripped the worn railing. "I'll do this," he said. "But if I have to make repairs to her work, I want my name on it, not hers." If it bore his name, he could keep her techniques and utilize them on his own organism. And with that, NASA would again be in his reach, his family name restored.

"That sounds fair, Ulbrine," a light but resonant voice rumbled, and Kal spun, shocked to realize Colonel Wolfe had come up silently behind them both. Rick and Max remained at the table, the older man slumped in what Kal now recognized as jet lag.

"I knew he'd do it," Rick said, jostling Max's elbow. "Didn't I say he'd do it?"

Max waved a listless hand, the cigarette dropping ash into his coffee.

"I need a few days to wrap up my life here," Kal said softly. He had no emotional ties, and he'd accumulated only a few belongings in three years. It would be easier to leave everything behind. Except for his orchid collection, of course, carefully developed and tended like the obsessive-compulsive hobby it was.

"Wonderful." Standing, Rick took his coat from the

adjacent chair and put it on as if getting ready to depart. "I'll let you three finish up. There's a flight leaving in an hour, and I want to be on it. I don't like to be away from my family." He extended his hand. "Kalamack. Good to have you on board."

Max leaned forward to look at Kal over his glasses as Kal and Rick shook hands. His eyes were a dark brown, and bloodshot. A thin hand held back the metal charm hanging around his neck. It was probably the spell that was keeping him cool. "I'll have my secretary book you a flight for late next week and send you a listing of nearby apartments," Max said. "Consider it part of your salary."

"Thank you," Kal said softly. "I appreciate the offer for transportation, Mr. Saladan, but I'll make my own way out there if you don't mind. I'm not leaving my orchids, and I'll not risk them on a plane. The pressure shifts are damaging." Not to mention he wanted to bring his car.

Rick peered at him in disbelief as he settled his coat about his shoulders. "Are you sure?" he asked loudly. "Eight hours versus three days? A small ear pop, and it's as comfortable as your living room. Pretty women bring you drinks and food. Max, buy him two tickets so his plants can sit next to him."

"No, thank you," Kal said. "I'd appreciate the drive time to change my focus."

Colonel Wolfe leaned in, whispering, "I don't like my feet off the ground, either."

"Suit yourself," the vampire said, clearly not caring. "Ulbrine," he said, shaking the man's hand before giving Max Saladan and Colonel Wolfe a nod and walking away. Kal watched the waiter he passed shudder, the human clearly not knowing why.

Mood expansive, Ulbrine sat back down in the shade, his satisfaction obvious as he beamed at Max's listless expression. "Gentlemen, shall we order, now that the predator has left?"

"I could do with a mimosa," Max said as the waiter hustled forward. "And the breakfast special with the shrimp and scrambled eggs."

"Meat tray," Colonel Wolfe said as he found his place. "And no fish on it. I want meat." He hesitated. "And a bowl of chowder."

Kal slowly sat down. He was going west to work as a field manager to infiltrate a human-run lab headed by a vampire CEO. His loss of his own work would be temporary, and once he'd gained Trisk's techniques, it wouldn't matter. From there, he could fix the elves' failing genome so that no one, not his child or anyone else's, would have to go through the hell that he had endured.

"I'll have the roast duck," he said absently as the server hovered expectantly at his elbow. "With honey drizzle," he added as he took the pollen-laced flower from the centerpiece and replaced it with his own faded orchid bloom from his hat.

Ulbrine was wrong. The elven savagery to survive hadn't skipped a generation. He would do anything and everything to bring his name back to greatness and save what was important to him. Just the idea that Trisk's theories were better than his burned holes in him. They were faster, maybe, but not safe. He'd find fault with Trisk's work—even if he had to invent it.

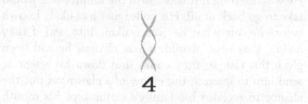

4

Kal's steps were silent as he walked up the stone-paved path to the large ranch home snuggled between rugged palms and dunes held down by long grasses. Cocoa Beach was a ten-minute drive, the Atlantic an easy five-minute walk. The house afforded him a large private yard that kept his neighbors at arm's length. It had been remodeled only a few years ago and had all the bells and whistles, not that he used the modern kitchen much. It was the walled garden that had attracted him. With mature fruit trees and a shallow koi pond, it had spoken to a part of him he hadn't known he possessed. Turned out he wasn't the only one it spoke to.

His parents thought he'd been crazy for wanting the solitary living space over the condo with a communal pool and private beach, even as they'd bought it for him as a graduation present, a consolation, he'd always thought, for having to work at a secondary lab in the hopes of someday transferring to the nearby NASA facility.

A tiny lizard skittered from his front door, and Kal juggled his keys with a doggie bag sporting the Sandbar's logo. He hadn't gone back to his office after lunch.

He was debating if it was worth the hit his pride would take to go back at all. His colleagues had likely known before he left what he was walking into, and if they hadn't, they soon would. It was obvious he had been given this task so they could shut down his research, send him to learn at the elbow of a classmate. But the chance to reclaim his family's status kept his mouth shut and his resolve firm.

Dr. Trisk Cambri. Enclave security and their own private genetic engineer, he thought, grimacing as the key smoothly turned and he entered, shoes scuffing on the stone entryway. Her dark complexion and ebony hair made it easier for her to move freely in the human world than the fair, almost white hair that most elves were born with. Some said dark elves were the originals, and that the light hair and green eyes their race now almost exclusively possessed was a result of generations of captive, selective breeding by the demons. That dark elves usually had a stronger genome supported the theory. Kal didn't care, but he couldn't help but wonder if Trisk's thick hair would be coarse or fine in his fingers.

He shut the door behind him, tossing his keys into the empty flowerpot on the table beside the door. "Orchid? You around?"

The clatter of dragonfly wings pulled his head up, and he smiled as a glimmer of light barely visible through the expansive, open floor plan flew from the distant living room and adjoining patio to him in the entryway.

"Hi. What's up? You're home early," a high-pitched feminine voice called as Orchid came to a silver-dusted halt before him. The pixy was a dangerous secret, his friend and confidante, an attentive ear at the end of a difficult day, a way to feel special when the darkest hours of the night insisted he wasn't. The entire species was on the brink of extinction, and he was honored that she trusted him. Most pixies lived in the deepest wilds, where predation kept their numbers low but their existence a continued secret. He'd risk everything for her, and he didn't know why. She was like a piece of him he hadn't known was missing.

"I brought you a flower," he said, but she'd already spotted it, her tiny angular face lighting up with avarice.

"For me?" she said, wings blurring to nothing as she darted to his hat, now in Kal's hand. A bright silver dust spilled from her, vanishing before it hit the polished floor. "Oh my *God*, look at the stamens on that thing. Thank you, Kal! I've not had hothouse lily pollen since Easter."

"Then I'll steal you another tomorrow." Pleased at her excitement, Kal strode into the gold-and-yellow kitchen, half a wall knocked out so as to look out over the sunken living room and the walled garden beyond. It was made for entertaining, but he'd never had more than one person over at a time. The greenery was red with the low sun, and he liked to pretend that the insects rising silver in the glancing light were pixies. He knew Orchid did as well, though neither of them would say it.

"Ooooh, perfect!" Orchid exclaimed, following the hat down as Kal set it on the stark white counter. "Lemon pollen is tasty, but I love the rich tones of a good lily." Her hands turned brown as she packed a handful into a ball and began nibbling at it. "Where did you get it?"

Kal smiled at the tiny woman, her dress of gossamer and spider silk and her little feet bare to the world. She was not his pet, being as independent and fierce as his people had once been: a garden warrior. "It was on the table at lunch. I brought you something else, too." A rare, mischievous mood on him, he opened the doggie bag. "If you want it."

Orchid dusted her hands together, the last of the pollen falling from her. "What?" she said, rising up on a clattering of wings. "Honey?" she guessed, breathing deep. "Good *God*! Do I smell honey? Did you find me honey?"

Kal beamed as she hovered at the opening of the bag, her dust an excited red. Her pride wouldn't allow him to buy her anything at the store, but he'd found that if he gathered it from fortuitous sources, as a courting pixy buck would do, she would accept the odd gift. "I did," he said as he reached in for the duck and threw it in the trash before going back in for the small container of honey drizzle it had come with. "For you," he said as he set it on the counter.

"Outta sight!" Orchid used the tiny but potentially deadly knife at her hip to break into the container. Experience told him she would've taken offense if he had opened it for her. "Thanks, Kal," she added as she used a pair of pixy-size chopsticks to eat it, her head thrown back to make her long blond hair cascade almost to the laminated countertop as she dribbled it in. The fair strands mixed with silver dust to make her almost glow.

"Orange blossom honey is the boss," she said as he got himself a bottled beer from the fridge. There wasn't much else in there. It would make moving easier. "The wild hive across the street. You know the one? I'm thinking I might smoke 'em out the next cold morning. Grab me some bee spit. I have enough to make it through the winter, such as it is down here, but some variety would be nice." She spooned more honey into herself, a tiny, appreciative moan rising. "I like not having to hibernate, but it is a drag stockpiling enough until the flowers bloom. It would almost be easier to sleep through it."

"Whoa, whoa, whoa!" Kal exclaimed as she almost toppled over backward, wings a blur as she giggled. "Take it easy. You know, you *can* save it. Honey never goes bad." Beer in hand, Kal went into the living room, long legs going everywhere as he collapsed in his favorite chair. It was set perfectly to see his new color TV and the garden equally well. He'd never used the fireplace. Orchid did, thinking it made a grand door. He'd been thinking about putting in wall-to-wall carpet this fall, maybe a shag. But that wasn't going to happen now.

Distracted, he leaned to flick on the record player, staring at nothing as the preloaded album dropped and silence filled the room until the arm swung across and settled into place. He chuckled ruefully as "Monday, Monday" spilled out of the speaker. The Mamas and the Papas always seemed appropriate to whatever mood he was in.

Orchid flew an erratic path from the kitchen, her dust intermittent as she skidded to a halt on the table beside him. Kal figured it was the honey inside her more than the honey she was carrying that ruined her flight. "What's got your panties in a twist?" she asked, beginning to slur as the honey took a grip on her. "Your aura is all mixed up, Kallie-Wallie. Did they fire you?" she said, laughing merrily as she fell backward on her butt, wings bent awkwardly behind her.

Six months, he thought, his grip tightening on the bottle. "As a matter of fact, they did."

Orchid stopped laughing. "They can't fire you," she

said indignantly, struggling to get up, but she was still sitting on her wing. "You have a five-year contract. You're a friggin' genetic engineer! In the top of your class. Dr. Trenton Kalamack."

The sight of a six-inch warrior in tie-dyed silk and gossamer defending him made him smile. He knew the slurring would vanish as quickly as it had come, leaving her with no headache. She wasn't drunk as much as in overload. Pixies had a high caloric need when active. Combine that with a need to remain out of sight and undetected, and it was a wonder any of them survived.

"I had lunch with a member of the enclave, an alpha Were in the military, the owner of Saladan Industries and Farms, and the CEO of Global Genetics," Kal said, and Orchid reluctantly looked at the remaining honey and tucked her chopsticks away. "The enclave is sending me to the West Coast to check on a colleague's work. They want me to make sure it won't kill humans and that elves are immune before it goes to live trials." He took a sip, lips curling at the bitter hops.

Orchid made a wobbly flight to his hand. The dust spilling from her created a warm spot against his beer-chilled fingers. But it was her fierce expression that touched him the most. "How is sending you to check a colleague's work firing you?"

Kal shrugged, his eyes on her garden. He might own the land, but she tended it, lived like a true homesteader in a broken flowerpot under the prickly pear that kept cats and big lizards away. He always felt like a guest when he went out to feed the koi. "Trisk's theories to embed DNA into somatic and germ cells is moving faster than mine. By the time I get back, my research will be six months further in arrears. It's a no-conflict way to pull the plug on my work as the enclave puts all their resources into her donor virus." He grimaced, feeling a sense of urgency rising. "It's flawed, Orchid. You can't control a virus as you can a bacterium. I don't care how clean you get it by stripping out the redundant DNA."

"They're killing your research? On purpose? That's so not cool," she said indignantly, and then her wings drooped. "Six months?"

He forced his face to remain still, not wanting to show how much he was going to miss her. Size aside, she was the closest thing to a friend he had amid his rival colleagues. "They think if I work with Dr. Cambri that I'll change my focus. Carry her work further," he said, vowing that he'd show them just how dangerous her theory really was. Her techniques, though . . . those might be useful.

Eyes wide, Orchid sat down, right there on his hand. "They want you to work *under* someone? That's not going to happen." She snorted, reaching up for a drop of condensation from the bottle with which to clean the pollen from her hands. "Not Dr. Trenton Kalamack."

"I have to do this," he said, and Orchid's wings hummed, making a cool breeze on his hand. "Showing them how dangerous her research is might be the only way to keep mine alive."

"So you're going out there to shut her down?" the small woman asked.

Kal smiled at her glum expression. "Officially?" he said, and she took to the air so he could sip his beer. "Officially, I'm going out there to find the holes in her patch job on a human-created tactical virus she's been monitoring. She tweaked it to supposedly have no effect on Inderlanders, and since it can't replicate out of a lab and has no host to carry it out of the intended range, it should be relatively harmless to humans apart from the initial reaction. If I fix the holes she left in it, the enclave agreed to put me in charge of it."

"The better engineer," Orchid said, saluting him with her drop of condensation. "She's going to freak out."

He shrugged and sipped his beer, turning introspective. Perhaps this was the enclave's way of keeping the world spinning the way they liked it. Trisk was talented, true, but she was a woman, and a dark elf to boot. "It's rare that the person who invents something is the one who's remembered," he said softly. "It's usually the person who makes it marketable or safe. That minor in business my father made me get has got to be good for something." Kal's focus blurred. It was easy to make money with the right product at the right time. Handover-fist easy. If nothing else, he could use the funds appropriated to her research to jump-start his own.

"You should just let the humans kill themselves," Orchid said as she flew to her stash of nectar behind the TV. "The world would be a better place without them. It would be cleaner, for sure."

Kal sat up, buoyed by his predictions but still feeling the sting of having to leave Orchid. "No. A world without humans, or even with too few of them, would be a disaster."

"For you, maybe." The small pixy flew back with a cup she'd made from the carapace of a large ant. "But not me. They need too much room, too many resources. We're pushed into smaller and smaller spaces to avoid them. There's nowhere left to be pushed. If there were no humans, we could come out of the closet," she said in satisfaction. "We all could. Witches would let us in their yards, I bet." She looked wistfully to her garden, thriving but limited because of the salt and heat. "They might even keep the birds out."

"Inderland needs humans," Kal said, his thoughts on what to bring and what to leave. Setting his beer aside, he stood.

"I don't," Orchid grumbled.

"Yes, you do," Kal said, voice loud as he went into his room. "We all do. That's why the enclave is treating this so seriously. Fewer humans means vamps would be tempted to prey on witches and Weres. They wouldn't tolerate that, and we'd have another underground war."

Kal stood in his room and frowned at the double bed. He'd been sleeping alone in it for the last few months, but it hadn't always been so. Orchid insisted she didn't mind the occasional visitor, but they all left with blisters caused by pixy dust. *I'm not sterile, am I?* Grimacing, he flung his closet open. If he could not engender children, even ones who never survived to term, his voice would never hold weight, especially if his family's millionaire status was in danger.

Orchid followed him, sitting on the lampshade to sift a blue dust that pooled on the table. "My people thrived in the Middle Ages," she said, oblivious to his dark thoughts. Their higher populations and rare sightings were probably how pixies and fairies had made their way into fairy tales. Fortunately, there hadn't been a way to preserve images back then.

"Mine didn't." Kal looked at his suits, taking only one to hang on the back of the door. It would be easier to buy new. The ties, though, he gathered down to the last and draped on the bed. "We need the resources that a large population brings: advancements in technology, medicine, a higher standard of living. You like your sprinkler system, don't you? The electric wire that helps keep the cats out?"

She nodded, and the light brightened as her dust hit the bulb. "I'd like a family more."

"I'd like that, too," he said softly as he cleaned out his sock and underwear drawer. "If I could, I'd give you an entire field surrounded by a forest." Orchid didn't need him, but only now, faced with leaving her, did he realize how much he needed her. Even his colleagues did little more than tolerate him. Some of that was probably his fault. Hell, it was probably all his fault. He held too tightly to his pride, but it was all he had left. He'd known his parents had been strapped lately despite the show of wealth, but until today, he hadn't known why.

The light dimmed as Orchid grew depressed. "Six months is a long time to be gone," she said softly, and Kal pulled his golf bag from the back, silently weighing the trouble of bringing it with the hassle of buying new clubs. Finally he took out his three favorite clubs and a putter, setting them on the bed before putting the bag back.

"Can I come with you?" Orchid said suddenly, and Kal jerked, shocked. Emotion washed through him, honor, perhaps, that she valued his friendship as well.

"Are you serious?" he asked, and she flushed. "You'd leave your garden?"

She beamed, the light under her going almost painfully bright from her dust. "For the winter?" she said, giggling. "Why not?" Her mood dulled. "For everything I've done to it, my garden won't come alive."

Kal's smile faded as he glanced out the patio window, thinking the yard was beautiful. Beautiful, but empty.

Wings clattering, she flew a blue-dusted path to him, hovering between him and the view. "If we go out there slow, stop at rest stops and stuff, maybe I could find a husband."

Kal nodded, a hint of melancholy brushing through

him at her need to search for another of her own kind. "That's a great idea," he said, though if she found a pixy buck to settle down with, she'd likely abandon him rather than return to the garden she'd made.

"Don't make such a face," Orchid said, clearly able to read his moods. "I don't think there are any bucks left to find."

He forced himself to smile. "Nonsense," he said as he turned back to his closet. "Human's haven't killed them all. They're in hiding. Not every pixy buck likes the challenge of living among humans as close as you do." He could leave most of his clothes, but shoes he liked were hard to find, and he put four pairs on the bed, then a fifth. "We'll go through the wild places if you like. Set out honey and leave a notice at every rest stop. I bet by the time we get to the Pacific, you'll have a bevy of bucks trailing you, wanting to make your acquaintance."

She slipped a pale pink dust, her mood brightening. "You think?"

"Absolutely." There wasn't much more he wanted other than his toiletries and the rack of genetically modified orchids currently taking sun on the screened patio. He wasn't going to scrap eight years of tissue grafts and DNA splices. Leaving his work to arrange permanent funding for it was one thing, abandoning his plants to die of drought another.

Suddenly it felt more like an adventure and less like an exile. "You finished stockpiling for winter, right? Bring it all, and you'll have enough until you're settled and growing more. Sacramento has a twelve-month growing season."

Hovering before him, Orchid looked to the garden, her face glowing. Her land was her life, but she'd been here for two years creating a place to raise a family and had yet to find even one prospective mate. Perhaps Florida had none. He'd found her in the back of a truck full of heat-dead plants someone had left on the interstate. Even now she was too embarrassed to tell him how she'd gotten there.

"Unless you want to stay," Kal said, wondering if she was having second thoughts. It was more than risky traveling with a pixy. It was damn stupid if they were seen. "I won't sublet it out. It is yours." But he knew she'd suffer if he left her. Pixies weren't naturally loners. Neither were elves.

"I want to go," she said again, her flash of worry vanishing behind a quick smile. "When do we leave?"

Anticipation filled him, unexpected and heady. He'd have to work at a human-run facility with a woman he could hardly stand, but with Orchid coming with him, he felt whole. He could do this with his head high, not down in shame for failure.

"Is morning too soon?" he asked, willing to give her all the time she needed. "I'd like to get some miles behind us right away. The sooner we leave, the slower we can go."

She took to the air, her dust a bright, happy silver. "Morning is fine. It won't take me but a few hours to move my winter stores. Can I stash them in one of your orchid pots? You're taking them, right?"

He nodded, sure he had a cardboard box in the carport. "Of course. I can move your entire flowerpot if you like."

She clapped her hands, spinning where she hovered to make her dress and hair fling out. "I'm going to find a husband!" she cried, then darted out and up the flue and into the garden.

Kal couldn't help his smile of prideful happiness that he could do this for her. He had long since seen his own people's faltering mirrored in hers, and knowing she was happy, even if she found a mate and left him, would be a calm spot in his fractured moods.

Unlike his species' decline, the pixies' was a direct result of human activity. There were simply not enough wild places left for a small Inderland species forced into hiding and unable to mimic humans. It was a shaky balance, but the more humans there were, the happier the vampires were and the easier it was for the population of witches and Weres to integrate seamlessly. They'd had enough practice, having walked hand in hand with humanity through the ages since before Jesus, and yes, rumor had it he'd been an Inderlander. Never before, though, had any species had the ability to end not just its own people, but all of them.

Kal reached under his bed for his largest suitcase. It was dusty, and he brushed it clean before filling it to find he had room to spare. Pleased, he put in two more pairs of shoes and zipped it shut. No one would thank him for letting the humans die out from a virus of their own making. He'd go to Sacramento and make sure Trisk's virus was everything she said it was. Fixing what she missed would put his name on her research. He'd make sure of it. Ulbrine had given him a chance to earn a career that would increase his opportunity to find a productive wife, or at the very least, the higher salary that would pay for fertility treatments or the gene therapies just now being developed.

What could go wrong?

5

Trisk rose from the fertilizer-stained cement walk, wiping the growth substrate from her fingers onto a rag tucked into her lab coat. A stiff, artificial wind blew dry air over the sturdy tomato plants as she stretched her back in satisfaction. The leafy, tart-smelling greenery spread nearly a quarter acre under artificial light, healthy and strong. It would be cheaper to have her largest testing field aboveground, but after the Cuban bioweapon crisis, legislation forced all true-breeding GMO research into facilities that could withstand a 747 hitting them.

This would be the last year her Angel tomato would reside in Global Genetics' largest quarantine field, and in actuality, what was here was the seed holding the final tweaks that Saladan had demanded. Her project was making money, and it felt more than good.

It did, though, beg the question of what would fill the perfect rows between the dirt and the raised irrigation system next year. Perhaps after she had proved herself with Daniel's virus, an elven lab would offer her a job.

Trisk bent over one of the ripening fruits, examining it for any hint of cracking to find only a perfect red skin. The tiny little hairs that helped retain moisture were a soft fuzz on her fingers. Her feelings were decidedly mixed. It would be wonderful to leave the clunky, labor-intensive techniques that a human-run facility was saddled with to work directly on developing her donor virus, but she wasn't sure she wanted to leave the comfort of where she was, fighting only the expectation that she should be cooking in a kitchen, not at a Bunsen burner. Her reputation was here, and to leave it, even to help her people, would be hard.

"Dr. Cambri?" Angie's voice came across the intercom, shouting to be heard over the massive fans. "Mr. Rales wants to talk to you."

Trisk turned to the observation window with a grimace. She'd skipped the man's first staff meeting this morning, and he probably wanted to nip that in the bud. "Sure!" she exclaimed, hoping the mic could pick her up from here. "Can you take a message? I'm busy."

"Uh, he's in your office?" Angie said apologetically, and Trisk winced.

"I guess I'd better get my ass in there, then, eh?" she said softly, and then louder, "Got it! Thanks!" Making her way back, Trisk plucked a tomato to take home for supper. It wouldn't hurt to remind Rick that her work paid some of the bills when he made whatever lame-ass request he had buzzing around in his vampire-infested brain.

Wanting to make him wait, she carefully knocked the growth substrate off her field boots before slipping into her office shoes. She took the time to wash the tomato in the decontamination sink. The minimal procedures were nothing compared to Daniel's elaborate precautions, but seeing as the Angel tomato was on the market, they were all she needed.

Rick's shadow loomed close to the observation window. He was smiling, but Trisk didn't like the way he was looking at Angie, and she hustled to the door.

"Dr. Cambri," the man said as the air lock hissed open. His disapproving glance at her slacks rankled, and she held up a hand to shut him up for a moment and maintain control of the situation.

"Angie, I want the field to go another three days without water. Could you adjust the irrigator for me?"

"Certainly, Dr. Cambri." The young woman gave Rick a lovelorn look. "Have a great weekend, Mr. Rales."

"You too," the living vampire said with a closed-lipped smile. "See you Monday."

Never taking her eyes off him, Angie stumbled out the door Trisk had come in through and into the field. Eyebrows high, Trisk shifted to stand between the closing door and Rick. She didn't like him watching her lab assistant. "What brings you down to the basement, Rick?"

Rick's attention went to her, Angie clearly forgotten. "You," he said, and Trisk blanched as his smile widened to show his capped teeth. "You weren't at my meeting this morning."

He looked better than good in the lab coat he'd begun to wear lately over his tailored slacks and crisp white shirts. He smelled good, too, sort of a dusty-book-and-wine scent. Knowing the man had made a game out of learning what turned on each of the female staff—not to mention that he'd pegged her correctly in two days flat—Trisk cocked her hip belligerently. "That's right," she said, offering no explanation. The monthly staff meeting had been a waste of time under Hartsford, and probably would be doubly so under Rick.

Making a small noise, Rick turned to a shelf of reference books stacked beside her terminal. "I'm sure you heard everything through the grapevine," he said, and she stiffened as he ran a finger sensuously over the spine of the most worn.

"No," she said, feeling her pulse quicken. Daniel had been in a sour mood—the little she'd seen of him. "What can I do for you?" she said, wanting him to stop touching her things.

"Me?" He turned, shoe squeaking. "Nothing. But I need you to clear out the office next to yours by Monday morning for an incoming researcher."

Trisk's lips parted. "That office connects directly to mine, Mr. Rales, and I'm using it." Damn it, why did new management always think there was a better way to do things?

"Your assistant is using it, not you," he said, going still.

The barest widening of his eyes was a clear warning at her argumentative attitude. It wasn't that he didn't like it, but that he did. The sun must be down. It would be harder for him to keep a lid on his instincts. "Yes," she said, eyes down to give him space to collect himself. "But it's connected to mine. My work is proprietary, and the security risk alone—"

"Your work has been on the shelves and in every third-world field for over a year," Rick interrupted. "There's no security risk. Perhaps next time you can make a product that doesn't self-seed."

She'd taken a lot of flack for that from Hartsford as well. "Species that don't reproduce on their own shouldn't be taking up resources in the field," she said, her face warming at the hypocrisy. Two-thirds of the elven population was alive due to genetic tampering.

Rick turned away, clearly struggling to maintain an

even temperament as she argued with him. "We can put in a lock between your offices if you like," he said, voice low, "but he needs a terminal linked to the main-frame, and your assistant's is the only one available."

"Mr. Rales," she protested, and he spun, shocking her to silence with how fast it had been. His shoulders were hunched and his lips parted. His eyes held the need to dominate. Trisk's mouth went dry. *Quen said to never argue with a vampire . . .*

"This isn't a request, Dr. Cambri," he said, inches away, his aftershave coating her like a heavy blanket to make her pulse quicken. "Dr. Kalamack needs access to the mainframe to verify that the modifications you made to Daniel's virus will hold through multiple gen-erations."

"Kalamack!" she exclaimed, her fear vanishing at the thought of the prideful snot in her office. Eyes darting, Trisk glanced past Rick to make sure the intercom was closed. "Does the enclave know about this?" she all but whispered, and Rick made an ugly face.

"Of course they do," he said, as if she was being stu-pid. "He's here to assist in the patent transfer of the T4 Angel tomato to Saladan Farms, but you will give him access to Dr. Plank's tactical virus. Everyone wants to be sure it is safe before it goes into live trials, and that means a second opinion. Get that office cleared out by Monday. Stay late or come in this weekend if you need to, but get it done. And be at the welcome meeting at nine A.M. Monday morning, or I'll bring the party down to your lab."

Trisk jerked as Rick strode to the hallway door, almost looking as if he was fleeing. She knew the tweaks she'd made to Daniel's virus were perfect. She'd checked the original code herself, taken steps to be sure the organism wouldn't easily mutate. It wasn't her universal donor virus, but it was clean. And Kal was coming to check it? *Bullshit.*

"Rales!" she shouted, but the door had already swung closed. Lips pressed, she yanked it open and strode out after him. He was halfway down the long hallway, moving fast. Quen had told her in his last letter to never follow a fleeing vampire, but he'd also told her the enclave was cutting off Kal's funding. He was coming to steal credit for Daniel's work. Either that, or hers. *Or both.* "Rales?" she called as she ran to catch up.

Rick spun, a savage, almost pained expression on his face, and Trisk slid to a frightened halt. "Are you following me, Dr. Cambri?" he all but rasped.

Breathless, she backed up. "Was it your idea or the enclave's that Kal check my work?"

"The enclave's," he said, hunched as he looked at his clenched hands, exhaling as they opened. They were shaking, and Trisk put more space between them. "His findings will be going to the witches' coven of moral and ethical standards through Saladan. The Weres have Colonel Wolfe as their representative, and the vampires have me. This is not a small matter, Dr. Cambri, and I'd advise you to cooperate with Dr. Kalamack and give him what he wants." His eyes narrowed as his hands crooked into claws again. "I'd also advise you to stop following me."

Damn. Every major Inderland species was involved, and she nodded her agreement, cursing herself for beginning to sweat. "Daniel's virus is perfect," she said, her thoughts going to her own secondary research on a universal donor virus. It was vulnerable and easy to steal if you knew where to look.

"Then there should be no problem."

His closed-lipped smile chilled her, but she had been counting on her hidden contributions to Daniel's virus to advance her reputation in the elven field. That would be gone if Kal claimed it as his own, and so she reached out, her hand falling before it touched him. "Wait," she said as Rick began to turn away once more. "I know what is going on. This is Daniel's virus. His research. I won't let Kal put his name on it."

Rick smirked. "I believe what the enclave said was 'We're not so foolish to allow a potentially deadly virus to reach the public without our best people vetting it.'"

"What?" she exclaimed, face warming. "Kalamack is a research-stealing hack who hasn't had a unique thought since the third grade. I know, because I was there! Bring in someone else."

Eyes pupil black, Rick leaned close. "I don't care, Dr. Cambri," he said, inches from her ear, his beautiful voice reaching deep into her and twisting until fear oozed out, thick and black into her veins. "My master and the rest of Inderland simply want a tactical virus that is what you say it is, and nothing more. Whose name is on it means zip." He pulled away from her, and she began to breathe again. Turning, he walked away, lab coat furling and his steps loud on the tiled floor. "Cooperate with him!" he exclaimed, back hunched as if in pain.

Suddenly Trisk realized she was pressed up against the wall. She didn't remember putting herself there. "Damn," she whispered as Rick stiff-armed the security door open, his voice pleasant as he told George to have a good night. And then the door shut, and she was alone.

But the thought of Kal near her research was even more frightening than a living vampire fighting a thousand years of instinct to not break her skin. If Kal was coming here, it wasn't to double-check her work, it was to steal it. And sure as spoiled boys grow up to be small men, the enclave would turn a blind eye. Everything she'd worked for would be gone. *How many times*, she wondered, *is this going to happen before they give credit where credit is due?*

Anger began to push out the lingering fear that Rick had instilled. She would *not* let Kalamack walk over her again. She'd finally gotten his footprints off her back from the last time. The enclave wouldn't help her. Her father . . . no, she couldn't ask him to fight her battles anymore. She was alone. But she had skills—skills she'd never dared use before.

Pace fast, she blew into her office, jerking to a stop when she almost ran into Angie. Her assistant was waiting for her, the clipboard in her hand clearly needing her signature. "Angie," Trisk fumbled, wondering if the woman had seen Rick pin her to the hallway wall.

"Is everything okay, Dr. Cambri?" the young woman asked, and Trisk took the clipboard.

"Saladan has a guest researcher coming in to facilitate the patent shift on the T4 Angel," Trisk said stiffly as she scrawled her name across the bottom. "He needs your office and the terminal to the mainframe. I'm sorry about this."

"That's okay," Angie said, the answer to the question of whether she'd seen Trisk and Rales arguing still ambiguous. "I've already got my desk emptied."

Trisk frowned at the box of belongings by the door. "You're taking this better than I am," she said to try to explain away her anger. "Go on home. I'll clear out the computer. There're some sensitive files in there, and if there's a problem, I don't want it to fall back on you."

Angie nodded, accepting that. "It's going to be okay, isn't it, Dr. Cambri?" she asked again, her expression pinched in worry, and Trisk managed a thin smile.

"Of course. He'll only be here for a few weeks." But she didn't believe it. Her fingers began to twitch, and she hid them in her lab coat pockets.

"Okay," Angie said, clearly not believing it, either. "I'm going to bug out then, unless there's something else you need. See you Monday."

"Monday," Trisk echoed, her hands now in fists as Angie gathered her things and left.

Trisk didn't move until she heard Angie's cheerful good night to George. Frowning, she locked the door to the hall, then strode to the adjoining office, yanking the door open and going into the spacious but nearly empty room. Immediately she pulled the blinds that looked out onto the hall, then locked the main door as well.

Wincing at the grinding squeak, she pushed the desk all the way to the wall to leave an open space half circled by built-in terminals that overlooked the tomato field. Kal might have been sent here to check her work, but he would try to steal it, change it enough that he would feel justified in relegating her to the footnotes. She'd be lucky to be listed as his assistant in the history books. But Trisk was a Cambri, damn it, and they never gave up.

In her flowed the blood of dark warriors who'd stood and killed demons when others fled. It was said that it had been a Cambri who learned how to travel the ley lines and escape the ever-after. Her kin had carried the survivors to safety, and because of that, she had one more card to play.

Nervous, she checked both doors again. It was after

sundown. Demons couldn't be summoned when the sun was up and the natural energy flow of the ley lines was contrary.

"Okay, let's see how useful that minor in demon studies is," she whispered as she took a key from her keychain and opened a locked cabinet. It was empty but for a cardboard box loosely closed by its interlocking flaps.

Her motions slowed as she took it out and set it on the displaced desk. With a methodical reverence, she pulled the flaps, stifling a sneeze at the dust. Peering inside, she exhaled in relief. Everything was still there. Gaining help from the same species who'd cursed the elves' genetic code into a slow, cascading decay would be a chancy game of truth and misdirection. She had the basics, but even her professor didn't have a demon name to summon one with. Demon summoning wasn't illegal, just foolish, which was probably why the university hadn't minded her minoring in the dead-end study.

Trisk's fingers shook as she draped the purple satin ribbon around her neck, the tails brushing the top of her lab coat's pocket. It was for show, but any form of protection was appreciated. Still inside was a jewelry box full of sea salt, a candle, a stick of magnetic chalk, and a small jar of cremation dust from her grandmother: all definitely not for show.

It was the cremation dust that was the most valuable, not so much for the cremains themselves, but for the small stone she'd found among the ashes when she'd accidentally broken the original container. Trisk was betting her grandmother had swallowed it before she'd died, a gift to whatever family member might find it. The river-worn stone was engraved with a long, complicated word Trisk hadn't found in any dictionary or encyclopedia. It had to be the name of the demon her grandmother was rumored to have been able to summon.

"This is so stupid," she whispered as the magnetic chalk rolled to the metal stapler sitting on the desktop and stuck. But her fear of what Kal would do was greater, and she pulled the chalk free and turned to the open floor.

Breath held, Trisk scribed a six-foot-diameter circle, practice making it absolutely perfect. Hesitating, she went over it again to make sure the holes were filled. Still not trusting it, she made a second, larger circle around the chalk line with the salt. Salt was cheap, her life was not, but if her grandmother was brave enough to summon a demon, she could be, too.

"Thank you, Grandma," she said as she carefully shook a tablespoon of ash into the center to attract the demon. Stretching, Trisk set the candle beside it before rising to wash any hint of ash from herself. The candle was there to direct the demon to the pile of ash and not any residue on her hands, but why take chances?

Stupid, stupid, stupid, she thought as she stood before her double circle and shook out her hands. Exhaling, she stretched out her awareness for the strongest ley line. It wasn't always the closest, and here on the coast, it was rarely the same one from day to day. Small quakes disturbed them, making the connection unreliable and chancy.

Settling on one outside Sacramento, she pulled the energy into her to fuel a hard-won, often-practiced series of mental gymnastics. Reaching out, she pinched the wick of the candle. "*In fidem recipere,*" she whispered as she released both the wick and the energy swirling through her. The candle flickered and steadied, the pure scent of wax rising unsullied by the hint of sulfur. It was set with her will, and would be stronger than one lit using a match or lighter.

It wasn't too late to walk away, but instead, she strengthened her hold on the ley line to set her containment circle. "*Septiens*," she whispered, using the power of the lines to shift a molecule-thin span of reality into the ever-after. A wavering barrier of alternate reality sprang up, rising until it began to fall back in on itself to create a half bubble of containment.

Another half sphere mirrored it under the floor, and she'd already taken pains to ensure that no pipes or electrical lines crossed it, possibly giving the demon a way out. The word to set her circle wasn't as important as the intent behind it. Any nonsense word would work. Latin was the language of choice because it wasn't used in regular conversation and the chance of accidentally setting a circle when, say, asking someone to pass the salt was nil.

Tension tightened her jaw, and she retreated to the desk, resolving not to move from it until this was over. She had her ash to draw him in, the candle to direct him where to materialize, and the circle itself to contain him. She'd done all of this before for her final, but the teacher had only a nonsense word to use in place of a demon's name, and there'd been no danger except of looking like an idiot if her circle hadn't formed. If she did it wrong now, she'd die. Or worse.

"*Facilis descensus Tartaros*, Algaliarept," she whispered, hoping she hadn't made a mistake and that the word engraved on the stone buried in her grandmother's ashes was actually a demon's name and would pull him from the ever-after.

Breath held, she waited. *Nothing.* Trisk's shoulders slumped. She shifted her weight to push from the desk, but with a wash of fear, she stopped, stifling a shudder at the blossoming scent of burnt amber, cloying and thick, slightly acidic and sweet in the half-light coming in from the underground field. "The Goddess help me, it worked," she whispered as she pressed back against the desk, and then louder, "I know you're here."

The candle flame hadn't flickered and the ash was untouched, but she could smell him. *Damn it, what if I had dropped my circle?*

"Who, little elf, are you?" a bored, masculine voice with a noble British accent said as if from nowhere. "And how, between here and the ever-after, did you get my name?"

Trisk stifled a shudder. He was here. It had worked! Excitement mixed with her fear, and she clasped her arms around herself. "Show yourself and I'll tell you," she said boldly, shaking inside. She had summoned a demon. She had *summoned* a demon!

"You offer me Felecia Ann Barren's ashes," her demon intoned, and she grimaced as a haze condensed over the ash. "Are you her daughter, by chance? I never did finish with Annie. I could finish with you."

"Show yourself," Trisk demanded, not liking the disembodied voice. Her hands were cold, and she unclenched her jaw. *The Goddess help me, I'm talking to a demon!*

"Gra-a-a-anddaughter," the demon said confidently, and Trisk's attention darted to the malevolent, goat-slitted red eyes that blinked owlishly at her from a haze of nothing. "Felecia Ann Barren would *never* allow her daughter to be so . . . *attractively* aggressive."

The demon chuckled, the sound tripping down her

spine to make her squirm. Mouth dry, she watched the haze condense into a man's shape. Contrary to popular belief, a summoned demon wasn't her slave. He could vanish at any time and couldn't stay after sunrise even if he wanted to, but he'd probably indulge an inquiry or two on the chance she'd make a mistake and he would have her body and soul.

"I've waited long for someone like you," Algaliarept said, and like a Cheshire cat, he blinked his red eyes at her from the darkness, hovering a few feet above the floor in the middle of her circle. A wide, blocky-toothed smile was next, and then a disembodied face, his cheekbones strong and his complexion ruddy. He grinned at her, his body a bare hint of a silhouette sitting crosslegged in her circle. "Now that I have found you, I curse the years you waited to call my name. Love."

Trisk forced her shoulders to relax. If her circle hadn't been strong enough to contain him, he'd be out by now, dragging her back to the ever-after. "I have a problem," she said as his shape became more substantial and the shadow of a crushed green velvet frock coat appeared.

"Don't we all. My God, are those . . . tomatoes? Why you growing tomatoes underground?" Algaliarept tugged a misty lace from his coat sleeves as he looked past her to the field, lit softly by security lights. More lace appeared at his throat, and with an unheard wave of energy, he became entirely solid, the buckles on his boots shining as he sat beside the ash and candle. He appeared for all the world like a Victorian dandy. Perhaps her grandmother had liked the look, but she thought it silly.

"Tell me your name. You promised, yes?" he said with a disparaging sniff, and round, blue-tinted glasses materialized on his nose. "Don't be cliché and start our association on lies."

She forced her arms from around herself. "Felecia Eloytrisk Cambri."

The demon started. "Annie let her daughter marry that Cambri bastard? No wonder she stopped calling on me." He sniffed again. "I'd be embarrassed, too."

Trisk's lip curled as he found fault with her father. "She didn't have much choice."

The demon's eyes flicked up, finding hers from over his blue-tinted glasses. She felt herself warm as he looked at her brown eyes and dark hair, his silence almost as hard to take as the racial slur he was probably thinking. "Indeed," he finally said with a pout, brushing at his frock. "Tell me, Felecia Eloytrisk Cambri with the dark hair and eyes, what ails your heart to risk calling me? *Ple-e-e-ease* tell me you want more than a vanity curse to shift your locks to the color of ripe corn and your eyes to the shade of a verdant valley."

Trisk glanced at the clock humming on the wall. "I need help keeping what's mine."

"Where am I?" The demon smoothly stood, her circle humming a warning when his softly curling black hair neared the top. "Fractured lines, faint quakes. I smell fires, mudslides, and an *asto-o-o-ounding* number of vain egos." His smile brightened to show thick, blocky teeth. "West Coast?"

Trisk pulled her lab coat tighter about her shoulders, uneasy with how good he was at guessing. But then her nose wrinkled as a wash of black haze seemed to raise itself from his skin, coating him for an instant in the scent of burnt amber before it soaked in again.

He'd changed. The Victorian dandy was gone. Rope-and-wood sandals now poked out from under a loosely made pair of brown trousers embroidered with thin ribbons. The trousers were held up by a wide black sash, tattered tassels on the ends. A bright red long-sleeved shirt and a baggy vest had replaced the crushed green velvet and lace. His soft curls were now long black waves held back with a metal clip. A thin, silver-streaked beard went down to his chest. His eyes, though, were the same, watching her from over his round, blue-tinted glasses. They glinted at her reaction as she relaxed at the less imposing image, his smile going even wider to show drug-stained teeth.

"Do you like my Jesus boots?" he said coyly, showing her his sandals. "I stole them. Right off his feet before they nailed him up."

Trisk frowned, her dislike growing. This vision was probably closer to his true self than the other. He looked harmless—just another hippie, until you realized that like the worst, the most dangerous beach guru, he lived solely for sensation, taking without thought as if it was his right, taking in order to feel, whether it be a mind-altering drug or a willing or unwilling woman to relieve his baser urges with. In his eyes, she saw that manipulation was his weapon only because brute strength had lost its flavor until whim and fancy drew him that way again. She was something to be experienced, and he would use and discard her on his way to his next fix, never finding enough to be satisfied.

"We're in a lab," Algaliarept said confidently, looking at his knobby hands as if he missed his gloves. "A *human* lab," he added disparagingly. "The science here may as well be in the Middle Ages. Daughter of Cambri, my love, have they trodden you so low?"

"I'm working two jobs."

"No doubt." He ran his hand across the inside of her

circle. A crackle of burning flesh hissed, and he rubbed his thumb against his index finger, rolling the blackened skin off. Under it was new. "You'd have to in order to maintain an elven lifestyle with a human's wages."

"I meant I'm working a human lab position so I can fulfill my real job for enclave security."

His eyes rose to hers, mocking. "Come with me. Right now. Drop your circle and let me take you. You'd be a slave, but you'd probably be working fewer hours."

Frustrated, she put her hands in her pockets and leaned against the desk until it scooted back a noisy, grinding inch.

"Ooooh, now I see what scares you!" he said brightly, and he vanished in a swirl of black-tinted smoke. His wide shoulders slimmed down to a pleasant span, and his waist shrank. With a shake of his head, the black waves vanished to a closer cut, the white strands almost not there. His ruddy complexion cleared to a light tan, and his face became angular with a narrow chin and small nose.

Trisk felt her expression go blank. He'd become the image of Kal, dressed in a business suit with a vibrant red tie that matched the demon's eyes. Only the glasses remained.

"I like the hippie better," she suggested, and he laughed, low and long, running a hand suggestively down his new lanky height.

"No, this is nice," he said. "Who is this, little bird, and why are you afraid of him?" The demon smiled at her with Kal's face. "Nasty dark elf shouldn't be afraid of the light. He's pretty, though." He posed, shifting his hips suggestively. "He'd fetch a fair price on the block. You'd probably bring more, despite your dark hair, having dared to summon me. Tell me now. Would you like me to make it fair for you? I'd only ask for one year of service. This pretty man would die for you. I promise."

Trisk grimaced, wishing he wouldn't prattle so. "His name is Kal," she said impatiently. "He's trying to steal my research. That's why I summoned you. And I'm not afraid of him."

Glancing at the humming power over his head, Algaliarept sat back down, his smaller guise of Kal looking odd on the floor in his suit and tie. "You are, or I wouldn't be here. He wants your research? Is it that good?"

A flash of affront quashed her nervousness. "I found a way to fix the damage you inflicted on us before we left the ever-after," she said, and the demon cocked his head, a mocking slant to his eyebrows. He looked so much like Kal—apart from the red eyes and blue-tinted glasses—that it scared her. "A donor virus. With it, I can insert healthy code into somatic cells to repair existing damage, or possibly the germ cells to improve the next generation even before they're born."

"Why would I help you with this, love?" the demon said, the image of Kal making talking-hand motions. "I would just as soon see you all dead. I am curious, though. Why did you let him *do* that to you? You are a dark elf. *You* are a warrior."

"I'm not letting him," she said, offended. "Did you not hear me say he was going to steal it? Did I not just summon you to be my sword and shield?"

He beamed at her show of anger. "I make a better mirror," he said slyly, then sighed. "You want me to help make you famous. I thought you were special, grand-daughter of Felecia Ann Barren, spawn of Cambri, but you want the same boring thing everyone who calls me does."

"I want to keep what I earned," she said, then louder when his shape became misty at the edges, "I have not dismissed you!"

His form solidified. "No, you haven't," he said calmly. "But you should."

Trisk pushed away from the desk, and Algaliarept's evil smile, looking odd on Kal's face, widened. "Will you do it?" she asked, pulse hammering.

"To ensure you get credit for your research? Mmmm. I could kill him," the demon suggested, eyes on his manicured fingernails.

"I don't want Kal dead. I want to stop him from claiming my research."

He looked up. "It would be easier to kill him. I'd enjoy it. You'd enjoy it. I'd let you watch. No?" Algaliarept sighed as if in regret. "Well, if I can't kill him, I need something in return for my services. Your soul, perhaps?"

Trisk shook her head. If he had her soul, he had her body.

"Why not? You're not using it," the demon coaxed. "Take a bare moment. You think you have nice computers? I've got the entire power of your basement mainframe in the palm of my hand. I'd let you play with it in your downtime."

"If you don't take me seriously, I'm going to send you back," she threatened, knowing he was bored out of his mind, and the demon predictably stiffened.

"Tell me his name. His full name," he asked.

Trisk's eyes widened. "You'd make sure my name is on my work for Kal's given name?" she asked, shocked, but the demon shook his head, eyeing her over his glasses.

"Names are power, Felecia Eloytrisk Cambri, and

you should swallow that stone you found my name on before someone else sees it. It won't leave you. I promise that. Curiosity prompts me to know the name of this man you hate with so much of your heart. Call it a retainer to continue to entertain your dismally small aspirations until you're ready to sacrifice your soul to retain your life's work." He smiled. "I give you a week."

A frown pinched her brow, and she clasped her arms around her middle. She hated Kal, but giving a demon his name went against her morals. Algaliarept gestured from the floor with a *Well?* motion, and she licked her lips. "Trent Kalamack," she said softly.

The demon's eyes widened. He looked down at himself, then back to her. With a whoosh and thump of moving air, he vanished to reappear as the Victorian dandy. "Kal-l-l-l-amak," he drawled, as if tasting the word. "Goes by Kal, you say?" the demon mused aloud, tugging his white gloves tighter onto his hands. "The little bastard is proud of his family name and insecure about his place among his kin. A man-child eager to make his mark." Eyes fixed on hers, he leaned in until her circle hummed a warning. "Full name," he demanded, and she blanched at the anger behind it.

"Trenton Kalamack," she said softly.

"The boy has a middle name, does he not?" Algaliarept inspected his pocket watch.

"I don't know—" she started, jumping when Algaliarept hit the wall of her circle with an angry fist. Stress lines rippled out, threatening to fray. "Trenton Lee Kalamack," she said loudly, pulse fast.

"There. Isn't that better," the demon purred. And then he looked to the door and laughed, white-gloved hands clapping. "I do so love working with the novice. You forgot to lock your door."

6

"I locked that!" Trisk exclaimed as the door to the hall was pushed open, spilling a bright light in and across the demon sitting cross-legged on the floor. "Daniel?" she gasped as he staggered over the threshold, a bottle in one hand, a master bypass key in the other.

"Oh, this is beyond brilliant," Algaliarept said merrily. "Hello, little man." He saucily winked one goat-slitted red eye. "What are *you* afraid of?"

"Trisk?" Daniel slurred, and she bolted to get between them. Daniel seeing a demon was a major breach of the silence, and right before Kal showed up. "What are you doing in my office?" Daniel said, trying to look past her. "That's not my lab. That's your lab. Trisk, why is Angie's office empty?" He blinked, looking over her shoulder at the leafy green field. "Who is that? Does he have clearance?"

"Daniel . . ." She rushed to say, and then spun, horrified, when Algaliarept stood and shoved his fist into her circle.

He was trying to get out.

Smoke billowed behind the barrier, curving up the sides until it slithered its way through the membrane and up to the ceiling. Algaliarept ground his teeth in pain as his skin peeled and fell away. Just the smallest gap, and he'd be through. Her soul was apparently worth the pain.

"*Finire!*" Trisk exclaimed, shoving both hands at Daniel. Whooping, Daniel backpedaled into the hallway as if pushed, his head slamming into the far wall. Groaning, he slid to the floor.

Trisk spun back to Algaliarept, her hand pulsing in pain. She'd hit Daniel with the full force of what was still coursing through her circle, and with a panic-born strength, she yanked more energy into her from the ley line. "You will stay!" she shouted, vertigo swamping her, pulling her down to a knee as she became a conduit for more energy than she'd ever dared channel before. Her hand, already burned from knocking Daniel out, flamed.

With a cry of frustration, Algaliarept pulled his fist back. His red eyes glared with a frustrated wrath, and the circle holding him crackled with energy. It dripped from the sides, hissing as it met the tile floor and magnetic chalk outline. Shaking, Trisk rose from her knee, her burned hand cradled to her middle. "You will . . . stay," she panted, panicked but steady.

"For now—little bird," Algaliarept snarled.

Only now did Trisk turn to see Daniel out cold and slumped against the hallway's wall. A ribbon of alcohol from the dropped bottle was running a slow path to her circle, and with a frightened quickness, Trisk took off her lab coat and dropped it on the rivulet, stopping its advance. From behind the barrier, Algaliarept made an angry noise of frustration.

Flustered, Trisk looked up and down the otherwise empty hall before grabbing Daniel's foot with her good hand and awkwardly pulling him into the room. Still hunched, she went back for the master bypass key.

"You will be mine, someday," the demon intoned. "And then you will pay for this, in ten times the agony you put me through."

Trisk eyed Daniel, hoping he was okay. "I didn't make you push your hand into a focused barrier," she said. "Leave."

"You just told me to stay," Algaliarept said, giving his tortured hand a shake. It wreathed itself in a gray mist, dissipating to show untouched skin and unblemished lace. "Now you tell me to go," he muttered, examining his ruddy hand for signs of damage. "I want to see you explain me to him. You looked adorable together in your matching lab coats." The demon's eyes widened, and his form went misty until he reappeared looking like Kal. "Well, well, little bird. Your passions are showing. We are alike, are we not? Trenton Lee Kalamack and your human?"

She shuddered as Kal's full name fell from the demon's lips. Maybe it had been a mistake to give it to him. Trisk looked up from Daniel to Algaliarept, the demon posing coyly within his circle of confinement. "Apart from the eyes, of course," the demon added, having apparently forgotten his attempt to escape. Trisk knew it would haunt her nightmares.

"You look nothing alike," she lied, testing the strength of her singed hand and wincing. Daniel would be fine, spelled into unconsciousness until she woke him. Flustered, she took her purple ribbon off and dropped it back into the dusty box before going to peek out into the silent hall, close the door, and lean back against it. Algaliarept stood, beaming at her.

"Demon, I banish you directly to the ever-after," she said, and Algaliarept pouted.

"No. I want to stay," he said petulantly. "I promise I'll

be good. Quiet as a mouse. Hell, I'd even *be* a mouse if you wanted." His gaze dropped to Daniel. "Did you intentionally find a boyfriend who looks like an elf, or was it purely subconscious?"

She said nothing, embarrassed, and Algaliarept's smile widened. "You *envy* Trenton Lee Kalamack?" he said, and her jaw clenched. "You hate him, but *envy* him as well. Of course you do!" His face lit up, scaring her. "I have an idea . . . growing in my brain," he said. "It will solve all your problems, but you won't like it."

Daniel doesn't look like an elf. Bothered at the thought, she edged closer, knowing he did, apart from the glasses. "Algaliarept," she said forcefully. "I banish you directly to the ever-after. Go now."

But Algaliarept pressed closer to the circle, his excitement obvious. "Why call me if you don't listen to my counsel?"

"Go!" she shouted, and his expression clouded.

"Good God. You don't have to be so bitchy," he said, and with an inward-rushing pop of air, he vanished.

The candle went out. Not trusting he was gone, Trisk leaned forward. But the ash had vanished, and knowing it meant he was no longer there, she let her circle drop. The energy flowing through her left with a scintillating feeling of ice sparkles against her burned hand, and she exhaled. At the ceiling, a faint residue of burned fat remained. She'd leave it for Kal to find. He'd know she'd been summoning demons, and the little dipstick might give her some respect lest she set the demon on him. Not that she ever would. Summoning demons wasn't illegal, but setting them to kill people was.

Edging past Daniel, she wiped the chalk lines to nothing and swept up the salt, her motions awkward with her burned hand. She grimaced at her whiskey-soaked lab coat, putting it and everything else into the dusty box to take home. Finished, she crouched beside Daniel. "*Ita prorsus*," she whispered to undo the charm she'd knocked him out with, and Daniel took a quick breath. Eyes still shut, he straightened his legs, grimacing.

"Something is burning," he slurred, then blinked his eyes open. "Trisk?"

She smiled thinly, wishing she could turn on the exhaust fan, but the stench might bring someone investigating. "You passed out," she said. "Why are you drinking whiskey?"

Struggling, he sat up against the desk. "That's not whiskey. It's regret, with an 'I'm screwed' chaser." He felt the back of his head, wincing. "Ow. You heard, right? The government is sending someone to look over my work before they buy it. You weren't at the meeting. How come you never go to meetings? Everyone else has to."

"It's in my contract," she said, glad he wasn't talking about demons and candles and circles. With some luck, the episode would be lost in his drunken stupor. *Thank God*. If he remembered, Daniel would be killed to keep the silence. "Are you okay?"

"No." Hand on the wall, he got to his unsteady feet. "Colonel Wolfe doesn't have a degree in anything scientific. Rales says it's a formality, but I've seen this before. Wolfe is going to slap 'top secret' on it and shut me out. Give my work to those bastards in Florida. NASA doesn't give anyone credit but their own staff. My name won't be on it anywhere. Worse, once they have it, they can do anything they want. I made this to save lives, not end them."

Trisk's jaw clenched, her hand on his elbow as she

helped him to a rolling chair. "I don't think they'll turn it into a planet killer. They want a tactical weapon, too."

"NASA never did anything for anyone," Daniel said, not listening as he collapsed into the chair, his eyes on the empty whiskey bottle. "Apart from curing diabetes. And childhood leukemia," he added. "And Legionnaires' disease. Malaria." He frowned, passing a hand over his brow. "Never mind," he said faintly. "Maybe they should check my work. Give the credit to someone else. What would I do with a Nobel Prize, anyway?" He looked up, blinking at her. "Why are you clearing out Angie's office?"

"Because I've got my own snot-nosed brat coming Monday to help with the patent transfer of the T4 Angel tomato to Saladan Industries and Farms. An old friend from my alma mater, if you can believe it. I probably won't get my name on my product, either."

"Oh yeah. I heard about that," he said, unknown thoughts passing through him. "We are so screwed," he whispered, then met her eyes, clearly embarrassed. "Excuse me. That was uncalled for."

She drew back, a rising feeling of disquiet in her. Wolfe didn't have any scientific credentials, but Kal did, and Rales had told her to give him access to everything. She wasn't the only one Kal was screwing over. Two for the price of one. "No, it's entirely appropriate," she said, sympathy rising high. "You want to have dinner at my house?" she asked suddenly, not wanting him to hurt himself trying to get home. It was a mistake, but she didn't care. Both their lives were being ripped apart by Kal.

"Yes. That would be really nice. Thank you," he blurted, falling back into the chair when he tried to stand. "Ah, I don't know if I can drive."

A smile curled her lips up as she slipped her shoulder under his and lifted. "I'll do it."

"That's . . . probably a good idea," he said, swaying as she tucked the dusty box under her other arm and they headed to the door. "You really went to school with him?"

Trisk held the door with her foot as she eased him into the hallway. The charm paraphernalia was under her arm, and she resolved to bury it in a corner of the barn, never to call Algaliarept again. She didn't like the demon's opinion of what scared her. "Unfortunately, I did," she said as she checked to see that the door locked behind them. "I'll tell you how he cheated off my third grade spelling test over dessert."

"Sounds great." Daniel hesitated. "You've known him since the third grade?"

But she didn't answer as all the ugliness returned: the hidden barbs, slights, indignities that were easier to swallow than do anything about. The question of what was going to happen was still out there, but one thing was clear. She'd spent the last three years being treated as an equal. She couldn't go back to living and working among her brethren, the better computers and working environments aside. She wouldn't.

7

"*I held my nose. I closed my eyes . . . I took a drink.*"

The peppy music wedged itself between Daniel's disjointed dream and his awareness, pulling him awake. His head hurt, but that was nothing to his gut, threatening to rebel when he shifted and the afghan over him slipped to the floor. "*Love potion number nine,*" the soulful man sang, and Daniel groaned as he sat up, his elbows on his knees and head in his hand. *Whiskey?* What had he been thinking?

With a click, the music cut off. It cracked through Daniel's head like a shot, and he sent his gaze about the room, trying to remember having seen it last night. Nothing seemed familiar apart from the few aboriginal knickknacks on the mantel over the huge fireplace, which still held smoldering coals. Behind him was an entire wall of books—the hardcovers mingling with the paperbacks in a joyous chaos that set his teeth on edge. Wide floor-to-ceiling windows looked out onto gently rolling hills, yellow with sunrise and a thin strip of fog glowing just over the earth.

He was on a square-cornered, stiff-fabric couch. Two equally uncomfortable-looking chairs sat at either end of the coffee table pressing into his shins. A lighted globe sat on the tidy desk, which was angled to take advantage of the view. It felt more like the lobby of a resort than a private residence, but he hadn't seen anyone, and most hotels frowned on their guests sleeping one off in the lobby. Still, he appreciated the earthy and subdued colors. Even the soft light coming in seemed dappled, though the only trees he saw past the huge windows were rows and rows of sapling sticks.

"Never again," he moaned softly, then turned his head, squinting at the square of brighter light coming in from a kitchen. It looked as if it had recently been remodeled, one wall brightly wallpapered with an orange-and-black pattern that somehow went with the original stone-slab floor and varnished-wood cabinets. *Where am I?* he thought as he pulled the knitted afghan off the floor and tried to fold it.

But he froze when Trisk's silhouette moved between him and the smaller kitchen window. *Oh God. Trisk,* he thought, the sight of her and the soft clinks as she arranged something on a tray overwhelmingly domestic and soothing. Wisps of the night came reluctantly back: her awkward help getting him to the parking lot, their almost one-sided conversation in her car, her distant, almost preoccupied admission that an old friend had taken a job with Saladan Industries and Farms. *To work with her?*

Adrenaline woke him up fast as Daniel searched for his shoes, not finding them. He ran a hand over his stubbled cheeks, then fumbled to straighten his tie only to realize it was missing, too. *And then she drove me to her house,* he thought when Trisk turned, tray in hand. Maybe she'd reconsidered and wanted to change their relationship.

"Good morning," she said cheerfully, her low voice

blessedly soft, and he stared as she came down the single step and into the sunken living room. The sun glowing through her hair was amazing, until she passed out of the beam and it was gone. "How are you doing?"

"Trisk," he said, wincing at how rough his voice was. *God help me, this is not how I wanted to do this.* "I haven't woken up on a strange couch in a house I didn't recognize since my undergrad." He hesitated, embarrassment making him squint. She was absolutely gorgeous in a casual halter top and wide-bottomed jeans, nothing like her usual self. Not that her usual self wasn't gorgeous, too. "Ah, sorry about last night. I must have been a real ass." *But I wouldn't know, seeing as I was stone-cold drunk.* Almost his entire night was gone. He would've sworn he hadn't had that much to drink.

Trisk set the tray down, the slight scrape it made going right through his head. "You were a complete gentleman. Fell asleep before the pasta was cooked."

Daniel looked up from the four muffins and coffee. "I fell asleep while you were making dinner? You offered to make me dinner, and I *fell asleep?*"

But she was beaming as she sat down kitty-corner to him, her feet almost lost in the thick-looped red rug. "Don't sweat it. It was canned sauce."

Between his head and his gut, he was reluctant to try eating anything, and he absently tugged at his rumpled shirt again. He vaguely remembered using the bathroom last night, but not where it was, and he was too embarrassed to ask.

"The coffee is black and the muffins are guaranteed to sit well," Trisk prompted, and he looked from the tray to her folded hands, feeling ill. "Promise. It's my grandmother's recipe. Apparently she was known for her parties that lasted until noon the next day."

If he didn't eat something, she'd think he was an ungrateful slob, not just a slob. Hand shaking, he reached for the coffee, surprised when the bitter brew slipped into him with hardly a twinge from his middle, relaxing him even as it brought him awake.

"Thank you. Is this your house?" he asked when Trisk took her own cup in hand, clearly pleased. "I mean, it's really nice," he added, hearing how that sounded. "They must pay you more than me," he muttered.

Trisk laughed, making him feel better. "It was an old farm that someone tried to turn into a bed and breakfast. They remodeled everything, added bathrooms and a kitchen to code. But it's too far out from the city. I got a great price for it because they redrew the floodplain and it's in it. I put in twenty-five acres of trees the first year I was here and turned it into a pecan ranch."

He followed her eyes to the rows of sticks beyond the windows, his mood softening as he saw in her a slow anticipation. It made her more beautiful yet, and he again wondered why he was sitting on her couch. She'd been gently adamant yesterday that she wanted to keep their relationship just as it had been for the last three years, but here he was.

"Low-maintenance, long-term investment," she added, seeming to give herself a shake as she brought herself back. "I originally bought it because of the stables. I might have horses someday."

"I like horses," he lied as he reached for a muffin. Bolstered by the coffee, he gingerly took a cautious bite, surprised to find that the dry texture mixing with the sharp bite of cherries went a long way in settling his stomach. "I like these muffins even more," he said appreciatively. "These are really good. Thank you, Grandma Cambri."

Trisk's smile widened, and a new sense of camaraderie swept him, dangerously hopeful. He took another bite, wiping his mouth with a napkin. "And thank you for not letting me wake up in my lab," he said softly. "That's so unprofessional."

"You're welcome," she said, sounding just as vulnerable, and he looked up, embarrassed that she was seeing him hungover and freaking out at the end of his project.

"I'm so sorry," he added, hoping she'd understand. "This isn't the way I wanted to spend our first evening together: you in the kitchen, and me passed out on the couch."

"Don't worry about it," Trisk said, but she was gazing out at her trees. "No one but George saw us leave. And even if they did, I don't think anyone would think twice about it." Now she brought her attention back to him, and he felt his heart clench. "You worked hard on this project, and no one blames you for wigging out when someone comes in at the eleventh hour to possibly try to claim the credit for your work."

It truly seemed as if she understood, and he wondered what had happened in her past that she wasn't telling him. She was one of the best researchers he'd ever had the privilege of working with, and even considering her relatively young age, it was strange that there were no papers, no journal articles with her name on them. He'd looked. Perhaps she'd had her work shanghaied by other colleagues before.

"Trisk—" he started, reaching for her hand.

But she yelped when their fingers touched, and he drew back, shocked until she sheepishly turned her hand palm up to show that it was a bright red.

"My God, are you okay?" he asked as he scooted to the edge of the couch to see.

"It's fine," she said, but he saw a second flash of pain as she hid it in a loose fist. "I got a steam burn draining the pasta. Stupid. So, uh, you don't remember anything from work?" she asked as she took a muffin, carefully wrapping it in a napkin to catch the crumbs.

"Bits and pieces," he said wryly as he resettled himself against the hard couch with his coffee. "Not much."

Her smile returned, confusing him. "You honestly don't remember bursting in on me while I was cleaning out Angie's office for the Saladan Farms researcher? I must've screamed loud enough to be heard upstairs."

The coffee was warm against his fingers, and he shook his head. "No. Maybe?"

Trisk's half smile made her absolutely charming. "You scared the ever-loving crap out of me. I thought the floor was empty. You fell back into the hall. Hit your head on the wall."

He reached back to touch it, feeling a sore spot. "I don't remember that at all."

Trisk's eyes dropped as she hunched forward over her knees. "I didn't think you should be alone after hitting your head, so . . ." Her attention flicked up and away as she shrugged.

That's why I'm here, he thought, suddenly angry with himself. She'd made it perfectly obvious earlier that she wasn't interested in going out with him, and when she took him in, concerned over his personal safety, he'd turned it into something it wasn't. Coffee between his knees, he slumped. *I am so stupid.*

"Maybe you should get your head examined," Trisk said, and he started, having been thinking the same thing.

"I'm fine," he said, resisting the urge to touch the back of his head again as he set his coffee down and took another bite of a muffin. He ate when he got upset, and they were really good. "Besides, if I have to take a sick day on Monday, Colonel Wolfe will make Larry salute him."

"I bet he does that anyway," Trisk said with a dry chuckle. "Daniel, I can't tell you how sorry I am about your project, but I just can't believe that they will turn it into something dangerous. There're easier ways to kill people than a virus with no host or way to reproduce."

"I suppose," he said, sneaking glances at her between bites of his muffin, not believing anyone could look that good in sandals and jeans. *No wonder her old friend from college came all the way from Florida to work with her.*

Oblivious to his thoughts, Trisk began bobbing her foot. "With some luck, both your soldier and my farm boy will be gone in a few weeks, and everything will return to normal."

"I don't know if I want it to anymore," Daniel said, and her foot stilled. Meeting her eyes, he lifted a shoulder and let it fall. "I don't know if I can keep working for Global Genetics if they're just going to sell my work like that. I mean, I don't mind it being sold because my heart is in research, and you have to let go to find the next thing, but to have your contribution utterly obliterated?" His focus went distant. "The government can put any name on it they want. And that's assuming that they don't turn it into a deadly weapon."

"They can't," Trisk soothed. "There is no way. You engineered it so it can't replicate outside of a lab. It has no host and mutations are lethal or nonexistent."

He stared at the fireplace, watching the thin trail of smoke rise from the defunct fire he didn't remember. "I hope you're right. I never imagined they would close me out completely. Maybe I don't want my name on it after all."

Trisk leaned across the space between them, startling him when she touched his knee. "I know I'm right."

He looked at her hand, eyes rising to hers. "Thanks for not saying it's going to be okay."

"It will be that, too," she said, and he frowned, confused at the mixed signals he was getting. Did she want to be more than friends, or just friends? *Damn it, I'm too old for this.*

"Maybe," he hedged as he pulled out from under her touch and took a sip of coffee. "You said you went to school with him?" Daniel asked, needing more information. "Your farm boy," he added when she stared at him in confusion.

Understanding, she slumped and rolled her eyes. "Kal?" She exhaled, hiding her face behind a sip of coffee. "Yes. He was in my class. Went to work in Florida when I came here."

"No kidding." Daniel was silent for a moment. "Kal, huh? Cute name."

"I can't believe he's working for Saladan Farms," Trisk said. "He's good enough to work for NASA, almost as good as me. And now he's coming here?"

All the better to rekindle a school romance, my dear, Daniel thought, and she laughed at his sour expression. "You want to see him?" she asked suddenly.

"You have a picture?"

Her mug hit the table, and Trisk rose to go to the bookcase behind him and take out a slim volume. Her pace was slow as she came back, thumbing through the yearbook. "That's him," she said, pointing down as she handed Daniel the book.

It was heavy, bound with real leather. He didn't recognize the school name, but if it was on the East Coast, he might not. Lips pressed, Daniel studied the black-

and-white class photo for a moment, freezing when Trisk leaned over him, her hair brushing his cheek.

I should go, he thought as he breathed in her scent mixing with the fading smoke from the fire. He liked seeing her this casual, so unlike the usual stiff professional face she had to show the rest of the world in order to be taken seriously. He liked it a lot.

"Where are you?" he asked, and she pointed. He was silent as he took in her image from the past, standing at the outskirts in her cap and gown while Kal was in the middle surrounded by a bevy of young women fawning over him. "Huh," Daniel said, still studying the photo. "He looks like me."

"I hadn't noticed," she said as she almost jerked the book out of his hands and shut it with a snap. She strode quickly back to the bookcase.

Frowning, he stood, the need to leave growing stronger. *No one walks away from a Florida lab to work for a farm, even one as large as Saladan Industries, unless they're trying to rekindle a past relationship*, he thought. But Trisk didn't seem happy as she shoved the book back in its place. A worried frown pinched her brow, changing into a questioning smile when she saw him standing at the couch.

"I should probably go," he said, patting his pockets for his keys. "Thank you for breakfast. And for making sure I didn't make an ass of myself last night," he added, then winced when he realized his car was probably still at Global Genetics.

"You're welcome." Her smile turned real at his sudden consternation. "I'll drive you. Let me grab my purse."

"Thanks," he muttered as he finally spotted his dress shoes by the door and made his unsteady way to them. "I feel like such a bother."

"No bother." She breezed to the double front doors, the entry all glass, stone, and beam. "Besides, I need to finish cleaning out the office before Monday. Unless by some miracle Farm Boy doesn't show."

Daniel leaned against the wall and scuffed on his shoes. His coat was draped over the chair by the front door, and he winced at his image in the ornate mirror next to it. He still didn't know where his tie was, but he was afraid to ask. "No chance of that," he said as he ran a dismal hand over his stubbled cheeks. There was no way to make anything look better. "Dr. Kalamack has been in Sacramento since last night. They've got a get-to-know-you luncheon planned to introduce him and Colonel Wolfe both on Monday. You should really go to the meetings once in a while."

She stopped, purse swinging as her hand fell from the door. "What?"

Daniel's eyebrows rose at her flat utterance. "Go to the meetings?" he said. "Barbara always has doughnuts."

"No," she said urgently, and his expression went empty at her sudden flush. "Kal has been in town since last night?" she asked. "Are you sure?"

Daniel slowly found his full height, a sour realization turning into a heavy lump in the pit of his soul. "Rales said he came in early to find a place and get settled so he could start work Monday morning." Depressed, he opened the door for her. The cool sounds of October spilled in, but he hardly heard the flocking birds. It had become obvious why Trisk wanted to keep everything the way it was. She clearly liked Kal, was excited at the thought of possibly rekindling their school romance—if it had ever truly vanished at all. Long-distance relationships were impossible, and now, with her wildly successful project ending, she had the freedom to work anywhere she wanted.

"Uh, did Rales happen to give out a phone number for where Kal can be reached?" Trisk asked as she locked her door and followed him down the wide stone steps.

Daniel slumped as he reached her little two-seater parked right at the bottom of the steps. His tie was on the floor of the passenger side, but he felt nothing. "I know what hotel he's in," he said glumly. "Will that do you?"

"Yes. That would be great, thanks," she said as she hustled around the front and got in, settling behind the wheel with a nervous haste. Daniel slid in beside her, taking his tie and smoothing it out between his fingers. Trisk started her car up with a *brum* of sound, jerking them both back with her sudden acceleration. Silent, he brought a casual fist to his mouth and stared out at nothing as they bounced down her drive and onto the smoother road back to Global Genetics.

He had moved too slowly, content for too long with the solid friendship they had, and now a friendship was all there would ever be.

8

K al pushed the rolling chair from terminal one to terminal two, glancing up at the smoky fat ring on the ceiling as he passed under it. He stifled a shudder, knowing it was atomized demon flesh. Apparently Trisk had found a summoning name and was practicing. That she could turn that demon on him was a real concern. Death by demon was illegal, but if it worked, he wouldn't be around to lodge a complaint.

Losing himself in the familiar task, he ran his finger down a string of text, recognizing the pattern as a protein coat that would prevent the organism from bonding to an Inderland cell. *Perfect*. Rick had called him when Trisk had left for the night, bundling her drunk coworker into her car and off-site. Kal had been in her office ten minutes later. It was past daybreak now, and he was tired, hungry, and in a bad mood. He'd expected to find something he could point to that would justify bringing her research to an end. Instead, he found perfection, not just once, but twice.

A clatter of wings pulled him straight, and he cracked his back against the familiar ache of long study.

"There's a woman in the building," Orchid said, landing atop the bulky monitor. "She's coming downstairs."

The flickering yellow text blurred, and he waved her dust away before it shorted out the old system. Rick had said no one worked on the weekend. "That doesn't sound like security."

"I'm guessing a secretary," the tiny woman said. "I doubt it's Trisk. She doesn't look like an elf, and she's wearing jeans and sandals. You want me to follow her?"

She was probably just what Orchid had guessed, and Kal shook his head, not wanting to risk the pixy being spotted. "No," he said, scrolling through page after page of code as he looked for anything that might attach to an Inderland cell. "How are you doing? Warm enough?"

"I'm good," Orchid said, but she'd parked herself right next to the terminal's vent, her wings moving slightly in the air being pushed through the clunky system. "How bad is it?"

Kal frowned, his darting eyes recognizing patterns and loops of code that would need a computer to forecast results. "It's beautiful," he muttered, mood worsening. "All the data points to a twenty-four-hour toxic response, and then it dies." He pushed the rolling chair back to stretch his legs out. "The perfect tactical weapon. It has no carrier, and according to this"—he shuffled through the printouts—"it can't replicate outside of the lab." He shook his head, wondering if he had made a mistake. "I don't know how they did it. With the tools they have to work with, it would be like trying to plow a field with a horse."

"You've only been farming without horses for forty years out of thousands." Clearly warm again, Orchid darted up, her hands on her hips as she inspected the atomized demon fat on the ceiling until she realized what it was and flew to the windowsill, clearly shaken. "The only good human is a dead human," she said as she landed next to the tomato sitting there. An entire field of them lay beyond the thick glass, out of her reach with the door closed.

"Everyone needs humans, Orchid. Besides, I don't want the enclave angry at me."

Orchid ran a hand over the tomato, then rubbed her hands, a frown on her face. "Why would they be mad at you? She's the one who tweaked it." She looked at her fingers as if they were dirty. "Dude. This tomato is fuzzy."

"If I can't prove that her tweaks to the tactical virus are faulty, I'll never be able to prove her theory to use donor viruses is dangerous," he said as he shoved his chair over to the shelf to look at the tomato. "And it is." He took it up, seeing that it was, indeed, fuzzy. It was irritating. That her fix was perfect, not that her tomato was fuzzy. His research to save their species would falter and die without funding, a surety if he couldn't bring Trisk down.

Orchid stood at his eye level, her wings drooping as he felt the fuzz between his fingers. It must be part of what made the tomato so drought resistant. "How can it be any good? It's fuzzy," she said, and he set it back down.

"It's put together even tighter than Daniel's virus," he muttered. Somehow, she'd taken a sterile tomato cultivar that had most of the required traits, bettered it, and then gotten it to breed true. He could almost hear his work slipping into obscurity, and his chest tightened. He couldn't save his species if he had no lab, no funds. *Her work can't be better than mine.*

Frustrated, he pushed himself away from the shelf, the chair rolling back under the demon smoke ring and to the other terminal. He'd been searching the mainframe all night, and he still hadn't found any hint of the universal donor virus she must have used to accomplish it. If he could find that, he could prove it was unsafe. *Maybe*.

"Mind if I give it the pixy test?" Orchid said, and Kal shook his head, his fingers a fast staccato on the keys as he went to the main menu to search again. "Smells good," the small woman said behind him. "Not so sure about the fuzz." Kal started, surprised, when he heard her punch it, and smiled at the obvious smacking of her lips. Unless Orchid had found something in the corridor, she hadn't eaten in several hours.

"Mmmm. Sweet *and* tart. It can be as fuzzy as it wants if it tastes like this."

"Great," he said sarcastically, then stiffened, startled at the beeping door panel. Spinning in the chair, he gestured Orchid into hiding.

"Maybe it's that cleaning lady," the pixy said as she flew across the office to hide among the reference books.

Kal stood to wave her dust to nothing, but his face flamed when Trisk walked in, finding him looking just like the thief he was. "Trisk!" he exclaimed, holding a sneeze against the dust.

"I knew it." Hip cocked, Trisk narrowed her eyes. "This is low, even for a Kalamack."

Kal pulled himself upright, his gaze running over her. She was just as slim, just as dark, just as angry as he remembered, looking markedly casual in bell-bottom jeans and a bright halter top that showed off her curves. "I have every right to be here," he said. "Rick—"

She came in, and he stumbled back, wanting to keep distance between them.

"Get out. It's not yours until Monday," she said, pointing to the open door.

"Rick knows I'm here," he said. "I have every right—"

"*Flagro!*" Trisk shouted, and Kal ducked, hardly even feeling her tap a line, much less marshal it into a spell.

"Hey!" Ducking, Kal deflected the spell into the glass window, where it hit with a wet splat to spread out into a flickering greenish-gold glow that mimicked her aura. With a final hiss, it dissipated to leave nothing. "Ulbrine sent me!" he exclaimed, strengthening his hold on the ley line. He'd forgotten how wickedly quick she was. "Will you relax?" Orchid was peering out from between the books, and he hoped to heaven that she stayed where she was.

"Relax?" Lips pressed, Trisk kicked the door closed behind her. "You ruined any chance of me landing a good job, and now that I've made something of myself, you think I'm going to step aside and let you take credit for it?"

"Stop throwing that shit at me," he said, dodging another ball of unfocused energy. It hit the floor and smoldered. *Not unfocused, then,* he thought, wondering if she was using black magic. That nasty glob bubbling against the tile looked ominous.

"Will you listen?" he said, then frantically brushed at a spell fragment that had scorched his pant leg. *Stay hidden, Orchid,* he thought, not wanting to know which was faster, the pixy or Trisk's spells.

"Daniel's project is perfect," Trisk said, her long ebony hair almost floating with the unharnessed energy flowing through her. "How *dare* you think you can come in here and find holes in his research."

"I couldn't agree more."

"*Leno cinis!*" she shouted, shoving a wad of green-tinted, aura-laced energy at him.

"Trisk!" Kal darted out of the way, then gasped when

the spell hit his printout and the ream of paper burst into flame. "Will you knock it off?" he said, shoving it to the floor and using his suit coat to put it out. A sliver of panic iced through him. He was outclassed. He couldn't beat her with magic. But elves' greatest threat had never been outright force, but guile, and he'd gotten better at that the last couple of years. Maybe enough to do more than survive her.

"I said I agree!" he said again, still beating the flames off the paper. "I agree! Daniel's research is top-notch. Stop trying to burn everything!"

Kal's expression eased in the sudden silence, and he cautiously stood. She was glaring at him, her feet spread wide and brow furrowed. "You agree?" she said caustically.

Kal edged away from the smoldering paper. "I agree," he said. "Dr. Plank's virus is perfect. I can see your handiwork in it, and it's an exquisite use of the materials and systems available to you. I'm impressed. I can't make it better. Or safer."

Trisk shifted her weight, clearly not trusting him. "All the more reason you shouldn't be putting your name on it."

He backed up, glancing at the monitor with its incriminating message of FILE NOT FOUND in line after line. "I looked at your T4 Angel files as well," he said, and she stiffened. "It's beautiful in its simplicity. I understand it's been in the field for over a year. Turning enough profit to entice a global farm to buy it. It's all they're planting in Africa and Australia. Rick says it's going to end their famine."

Trisk's attention flicked to the shelf of reference books and back again. Her eyes were narrowed in mistrust, but her hands had lost the rim of concentrated aura. "You honestly think that pap is going to work on me?"

"Maybe I grew up," he said, wishing she'd relax a little. "The last few years . . . It's hard going from a small pond to a large one where everyone thinks you're riding on your family's coattails."

Her expression went empty, and excitement zinged through him. Ulbrine was right. There was power in the soft word, the gentle compliment. "I'm not afraid to admit I'm wrong anymore," he said, twisting his lips into a rueful smile. "It gets easier when you're wrong a lot, and I was wrong. A lot. You belong in a lab, not in the hallway protecting it. What you did with the Angel was beautiful. Imagine what you could do in a real facility."

Her eye twitched, but she kept looking back to the shelf where Orchid was hiding. "I'm not showing you my universal donor virus studies," she said flatly.

Kal raised a hand in placation, head bowed. "I wish you'd reconsider. Especially if they're anything like what you did with the tactical virus." He smiled. "Does Dr. Plank know you modifed his virus?"

She shifted uncomfortably. "Of course. And why should I trust you? I'm not a human whose work can be stolen with impunity."

"I agree, but what good are your theories doing here?" he protested. "You can't publish them in a human journal. You're generations ahead, and if you do, you'll never be allowed to work in an elven lab again."

"Like I'm allowed now?" she said, gesturing at the outdated technology she was forced to use. "Get out. Before I throw you out."

"I'm just going to come back on Monday," he said, even as he edged to the door, wiggling his fingers at

Orchid to stay where she was. "The enclave sent me to look at your universal donor virus. They think it has an amazing potential."

Trisk put her arms over her chest, poised belligerently. "Out."

"Just . . . let me explain," he said as he paused by the door, and her eyes narrowed. "Yes, I came to check Daniel's research and make sure your modifications are foolproof, but after seeing how stable it is and what you've done with the tomatoes . . ." He hesitated, looking at the ceiling as if pleading to the gods to give him the words to convince her. "Trisk, show me your universal donor. If it's as good as I think it is, Sa'han Ulbrine will want you to come back—not just your research, you." Which was all true, even if none of it would happen if he got his way.

Trisk blinked, a shocked amazement on her face as she took her attention from the bookshelf. "What?" she managed, her voice sounding nothing like her, soft and low instead of hard in threat. He'd never heard her voice gentled like that, and he thought it was pleasant, tripping down his spine like warm sand. "They want me to develop my donor virus?"

"How about it, Trisk?" he asked, vowing he'd sabotage the dangerous idea into obscurity before it got anywhere close to being developed. "You could work in a real lab with real resources and people you don't have to hide yourself from."

Her lips were parted, and he followed her gaze to a grainy color photo of a lab get-together. She and Daniel were arm in arm, silly party hats on their heads. Rick had said he had a thing for her, and since the man looked like an elf, it was a good bet Trisk had a thing for him. It was hard to leave perfection.

"I know you miss us, Trisk. It won't be school all over again. I promise."

She was flushed, her gaze sharp as it fell on him. "I don't trust you."

"Fair enough. How about we go for coffee? You and me. We can talk about it."

Trisk's eyes narrowed. "I'm not telling you anything about my research."

The harsh tone was again in her voice. Bringing back the softness would be a challenge—one he wanted to accept. "Fine." Kal raised a hand for patience. "I'm not going to hurt you."

"Why would today be different from any other day?" she said, and then her expression shifted. "What is that smell?"

"I'm sorry for what I did," Kal said forcefully as Trisk strode over to the shelf where Orchid hid. "I was stupid and insensitive."

"You spelled my hair blond," she said, intent as she took first one book down, then another. "Do you have any concept of how embarrassing that was? I was ten, Kal."

His lips curled up at the memory. He'd done it on a dare. She'd looked awful, worse than he'd ever imagined. Dark elves were built differently, and seeing those fair wisps on her only accented her strong features. "I'm sorry," he said, wiping the smile from his face when she turned. "I was a dumb shit."

The dark look at the back of her eyes told him he was losing her, and he took a step forward. "Just one cup of coffee. I want to introduce you to someone."

Orchid's wings clattered a warning, and Trisk spun. "What did you bring into my lab?" she said, hands glowing again with loosed power.

"Orchid?" Kal called, seeing the dust at the ceiling. She'd flown to the light fixture, and he'd never even seen her move. "Trisk won't hurt you. If she does, I'll see her into the ground."

"Like an elf could catch me," Orchid said, and Trisk looked up, her face pale.

"What did you do?" Trisk whispered as she followed Kal's attention to the sifting dust, clearly not knowing what it was. Hardly anyone did anymore.

Kal couldn't help his smile when Orchid peered over the rim of the fixture, her wings folded prettily behind her head.

"Oh my God," Trisk whispered, walking backward so she could see better.

"Promise you won't throw a spell at me," Orchid said, and Trisk nodded, almost falling when Orchid took to the air to come to a dust-laden hover before her.

"Where . . ." Trisk whispered, and satisfaction filled Kal. "Where did you find a pixy? I thought they were extinct."

"Not yet," Orchid said, her dust changing to a melancholy blue. "But the humans are trying *very* hard."

Kal held out a hand, and Orchid flew to him, no doubt appreciating the warm perch and safety. "Orchid found me two years ago."

"Yeah, right," Orchid said with a snort. "That's how it happened. I found you."

"She's my friend," Kal said, always having felt that Orchid rescued him, not the other way around. "And if you tell anyone about her, even the enclave, I will hurt everyone you care about, Trisk."

Trisk pulled her eyes off Orchid long enough to give him a dry look, as if begging him to try. "Who would I tell?" She held out a hand, and Kal felt a stab of jeal-

ousy when Orchid flew to her, hesitating only briefly
before landing. "I'm honored to make your acquaintance, Orchid. You're the most beautiful person I think
I've ever met."

Orchid flushed, the dust spilling from her shifting
to a faint pink. "Thank you," she said coyly, and then
her wings drooped. "You haven't seen any bucks then,
huh?"

"Give the notes we left time to work," Kal said, and
Orchid grimaced impatiently. Kal breathed easier when
she came back to him and landed on his shoulder.

"Notes?" Trisk asked, and Orchid brightened.

"We left honey and notes at every rest stop between
here and Florida," the pixy woman said. "Kal promised
to help me find a pixy buck. You sure you haven't seen
any?"

Trisk shook her head, the softness returning. "I'm
sorry, no. Are you hungry? I've got a grove of young
pecan trees you can safely gather in."

"She's fine," Kal said. "Orchid brought her entire
winter stocks with her."

Orchid rose up, eyebrows high. "Something fresh is
always appreciated. All you have is a windowsill."

Kal stifled his pique. The two of them bonding was
not exactly what he had intended. "Then how about we
go to a coffee shop and you can snitch whatever you
want from the back?"

Spilling a bright dust, Orchid turned to Trisk, and
they both stared at her, waiting. "So," Kal said slowly.
"Coffee with scones and honey?"

"Sure." Trisk pointed to the door, and Kal almost sang
as he scooped up his singed coat, beating the ash off it
before taking his hat from a counter. Orchid immediately settled atop his head, and he carefully put his hat

over her before going out into the hall to wait. Trisk would likely want a moment to shut everything down. He wasn't so vain as to think he had brought that softness back. It had been Orchid. But trust in him would come. In time.

"Sorry about forcing you out of hiding," he said softly, and Orchid's tiny sniff reached his ears.

"She was going to find me, anyway" floated out from under his hat. "That woman has skills. And claws."

"Yeah?"

"Yeah," Orchid said, voice serious. "She'll rip your eyes out if you look at her wrong. I've never seen a dark elf. What did you ever do to that woman?"

The light flicked off in the lab, and he moved a few feet down the hallway. "I was mean to her, and made sure everyone else was, too." Maybe that had been a mistake.

Trisk came out, awkwardly resetting the lock with her left hand. Kal remembered her favoring her right hand when attacking him. She probably had a burn from whatever had tried to force his way out of her circle, leaving that rime of fat on the ceiling. "I know a few places in town that have palatable tea," she said. "It's taken me two years to educate them on how to make it."

I am going out for coffee with Eloytrisk Cambri, he thought in amazement as she came even with him and they headed down the hall together.

Orchid stomped on his head, the signal that they were being watched, and he caught sight of Daniel lurking in the hall far behind them. *Curious.*

"Is that a sensory burn?" Kal said, snagging Trisk's hand.

"Let go," she said, trying to tug free.

"No, let me fix it," he said, tightening his grip to make it look more natural. "I know a healing charm, but it works better if I'm touching you. I'll be careful," he said, sending a gentle warmth through his hand and into hers.

"That's nice," she said, her tone guarded, but she hadn't let go. Everyone at school had abused her, but she'd wanted to be one of them nevertheless. "How's Quen?" she asked, and excitement zinged through him. Knowing Daniel was watching, he walked confidently down the hall, his hand in hers.

"I don't know. He works for my father, not me. Do you want to go back to my hotel and order room service?" he asked loudly, then leaned in, whispering, "Orchid could join us, then."

Trisk turned to look at his hat, but Kal was sure all Daniel would see was her enraptured look up at him, their lips inches apart. "Okay," she whispered back.

"Okay," he echoed, letting go of her hand just long enough to get the door for her and gallantly gesture her through.

He had six months. He only needed two weeks, and everything she had would be his.

9

The late-October sun was warm, but Trisk was glad for her lab coat as she walked the long rows of sturdy tomato plants, fondly touching one here, another there. It was nearing the end of the season, and they'd grown tall in the strong summer light at Saladan Farms' seed field just outside of Sacramento.

The leafy green stalks were almost over her head; the main trunk lines had become woody when the same hairs that gave the plant its superior drought resistance had unexpectedly matted together in a rude, keratin-like substance able to support the heavier growth. Even the simulated outside conditions of the underground labs hadn't produced it, and she'd come out to take some final measurements before the field was razed next week. It never failed to surprise Trisk how an organism could respond unexpectedly to stimuli and do something completely wonderful.

Such as creating a summer-smelling canyon of shade, she thought as she took off her gloves and tucked them into her lab coat pocket along with her tape measure, pencil, and spiral notebook. The press conference to publicly release the patent to Saladan Industries and Farms was next week, and it felt as if she was saying good-bye.

Content, she scuffed through the ruts back to the farm's office building. It was little more than a shack with running water and a single phone line connecting it to the outside world. She'd make her final report at Global Genetics this week and move on to a new project.

A smile crossed her face at the sound of kids in the field, and she laughed, shouting after the handful of exuberance that thumped past her in bare feet and exotic accents as they played tag in the setting sun. There was a farm-run school right on Saladan's property, but it was patently obvious that it was only there to give the kids somewhere to go until they were old enough to work the field without the government crawling up Saladan's back.

Trisk slowed as she saw her farm truck parked beside the rusted flatbed Fords and the decommissioned school bus waiting to take the migrant workers back to Saladan's shantytown when the sun went down. She didn't like bringing her little two-seater out to the fields on her rare inspections, but today, it would have been right at home beside Saladan's black Jag and the red convertible Mustang that Kal had driven out from Florida, both now parked in the shade of the single tree hanging over the office shack. They hadn't been here when she'd arrived, and she wasn't eager to talk to either of them, as nice as Kal had been the last few days.

She'd first met Mr. Saladan last year when he'd bought the patent, suffering his large ego and patronizing slights as she fulfilled Global Genetics' obligations during the patent transfer. She hadn't liked the witch then, and she didn't like him now.

Her faltering mood utterly soured when the door to the farm office banged open and Kal and Saladan came out, their pace and direction making it obvious they wanted to talk to her. Saladan was in slacks and a white dress shirt, his inappropriate shoes coated with dust and his hem discolored with it. His black tie was loosened, and as she watched, he took a pair of dark sunglasses out of a front pocket and put them on. Even with his eyes hidden, she could see the scowl making his few wrinkles fold into each other.

The older witch didn't look hot, though, and was probably using a charm to keep himself cool. She'd heard the workers call him the Ice Man, and she thought he had better be careful lest the magic he used become obvious and break the silence. Seeing both men stomping toward her, she couldn't help but wonder how many missing people were really unfortunate deaths needed to preserve the silence when some witch or vampire made a mistake.

Squinting, she brushed her hair back and tried to look professional in her slacks and white dress shirt. Kal, at least, was dressed appropriately for the field, his jeans worn and casual, and his lightweight shirt open at the neck. There was a bandanna in his pocket to mop up his sweat, and it was obvious that he'd been inspecting Saladan's fields for most of the day; the dust was thick on his boots and had turned his fair, almost translucently white hair to brown. His quirky smile made her wonder if Kal might be responsible for Saladan's bad mood.

Why not? Kal sure irritates me, she thought as she stepped from the field to the parking lot and wisps of her hair rose in the radiating heat. But even as she thought it, she flexed her hand, remembering how he had eased the sting of her sensory burn last Friday. She hadn't expected that. It didn't make up for anything he'd done to her as a kid. Neither had the coffee and dessert in his hotel room.

"Dr. Cambri!" Saladan called even before they closed the gap between them. "Did you get my memo concerning the modifications I want to next year's crop? Those hairs must be removed. They're getting into the workings of the washing machinery and causing trouble."

She pulled herself straighter, halting where she was to force him to keep going. He was trying to weasel out of the final payment owed to Global Genetics. Again. "That's why I recommended the wider screens, Mr. Saladan."

His long face tight, Saladan halted before her, a breath of coolness continuing its momentum and washing briefly over her. She held her breath, not liking the reek of cigarette smoke that came with it, barely hiding the scent of redwood. "I wouldn't need to retool my machines if you would retool your tomato. I don't like the hairs in everything."

Kal ducked his head, that same mischievous glint in his eye that she remembered from school when he looked up. That it wasn't at her expense was an odd feeling. "I've been trying to explain," Kal said dryly. "Removing the hairs would damage the drought resistance that's making it so successful in Africa."

Saladan smiled insincerely, clearly not liking their united front. "I spent a fortune on this product, and by God, it's going to be exactly what I want. I don't like tiny hair filaments in my ketchup, and neither do my buyers."

Trisk exhaled, not caring that Saladan heard her exasperation. "Mr. Saladan," she started patiently, "I have tweaked the organism per the original agreement to your specifications. No more modifications are allowed under the current contract. You have an entire year of profits already in the bank that say you're satisfied with the product as is," she continued, voice rising to drown out Saladan's coming protest. "If you like, I can arrange a meeting with Rick. I'm sure he'd be more than happy to draw up a new contract for additional modifications not covered by the original agreement."

"Bullshit," Saladan swore, but the crass, unbusinesslike word didn't faze her as he clearly intended it to. "I asked for a sterile cultivar, and I didn't get that. If you can't give me what I want, you've failed to provide the promised modifications and the contract is nullified."

The Goddess save me from cheating businessmen, she thought.

"Every organism has limitations, Mr. Saladan," Kal said, and Trisk raised her eyebrows in surprise. "Those hairs are what make the T4 Angel tomato grow to such an amazing size without the cost of additional supports. Change that, and you remove the very traits that make your product both exclusive and desirable."

Which is a nice argument, but it won't matter to the lawyers, Trisk thought, wondering what Kal's game was. He'd been knocking on her door all this week, asking her to clarify things about her tomato and Daniel's virus that he already knew the answer to, but to defend her smacked of a plan within a plan.

"The GMO oversight committee has already ruled that self-seeding won't lower your profits in the commercial market or significantly impact sales in the private sector," she said. "No one starts their own tomatoes from overwintered seeds, and certainly not the farms and commercial outlets you're selling to. I'm sorry, Mr. Saladan, but if you're trying to get out of paying Global

Genetics your final installment to secure your right to the T4 Angel tomato patent, you'd better get your lawyers working a different angle, because my organism is perfect."

Saladan looked at her over his sunglasses. That move had bothered her once, but after she'd seen a demon do it, it had lost much of its punch. "I'm sick of uppity women where they shouldn't be," the man said suddenly, and Trisk's jaw dropped for an instant before she caught her mental balance. "Trying to do a man's job when they should be at home."

"To greet you at the door with a martini and bear your young," Trisk said dryly, her anger carefully hidden. "Such an outdated philosophy makes you charmingly quaint, Mr. Saladan."

"That was uncalled for," Kal said to Saladan, shocking her more than the gender slur had. "Dr. Cambri is one of the top genetic engineers in her field. That she's a woman doesn't impact her qualifications."

On a slow, deliberate heel, Saladan turned to Kal. His fingers were twitching but she felt no connection to a ley line to actually do a spell. He knew better. Not in the middle of a field surrounded by humans. He was probably just reaching for an absent cigarette.

"It's that attitude that's caused your family's failing, Kalamack," Saladan said as he took off his glasses and looked at Kal mockingly. "Broken not just in finances but also in genetic code, so degraded you can't engender a child with even a human anymore."

Trisk's eyes widened as Kal went white in anger.

"You are a *field manager*, Kalamack," Saladan said coldly. "Don't lecture me on social demographics until you have a hundred more years behind you." Tapping his sunglasses against his palm, he ran his attention up and down Kal. "And maybe a child or two. If you can manage it."

Kal's jaw tightened, and Trisk stiffened when the faintest tingle prickled through her aura. Kal might be stoically silent as he took the older man's abuse, but his fingers were twitching behind his back in a ley line charm. He was spelling, using the energy in his own chi instead of tapping directly into a line so it would be harder to detect. It wasn't a difficult skill, but she was surprised he knew about it. The technique would give his magic a stealthy finesse she hadn't expected from the elitist snot.

She took a breath to warn Saladan . . . then shut her mouth.

Clearly thinking he had them both cowed, Saladan smiled. It was as ugly as he was. "It's said the Kalamacks descended from the original slavers in the ever-after," he said as he turned back to Trisk. "They don't like to admit it, and they even changed their name when they migrated from the ever-after, but they'll never be anything other than flesh dealers."

Kal's eyes narrowed. His fingers had gone still, but his hand cupped a tiny, almost-not-there ball of glowing haze. It was a charm, his aura peeping between his fingers coloring it a pale purple and green.

Trisk arched her eyebrows at Saladan, long practice at swallowing insults making it easy. "That's nice," she said in a show of nonchalance. "Insulting me into giving you a free modification to your new tomato isn't going to work. If you'll excuse me, I have to write up my final report. Do you want a meeting between you and Rick or not?"

Saladan's lip twitched. He glanced at Kal when he snickered, then back at her. "Rick is an idiot, too," he said. With a sound of sliding gravel, he turned on a heel and walked off, yelling at the kids to get out of the field and back to the school where they belonged.

A tiny line in Kal's forehead showed, the only hint of the frustrated anger Trisk knew to be coursing through him. Under it was a growing embarrassment. "He built that school to keep them in the field, not out of it. Have you been to it?" Kal asked as he stared at Saladan's back.

"No."

"I have. It's amazing. I've never seen so much potential intentionally stifled to maintain a cheap workforce." With a flick of his wrist, Kal tossed the charm at Saladan. It was so small, it was hard to see it arcing through the low sunlight, but Saladan's entire aura flickered into the visible spectrum for half an instant as the spell sank in. Smirking, Kal turned to face her. "How have you been able to stand working with him for over a year?"

Trisk rocked into motion and headed for her truck, her steps slow enough so there was no chance of catching up to Saladan. "An egotistical, chauvinistic, hard-to-please bastard? I have no idea," she said, thinking the same words could be used to describe Kal. "I've never run into him outside of an arranged meeting, but I wanted to take some measurements of the woody stems."

Is Kal's family really on the skids? she thought as he silently paced beside her. The older families seemed to have been hit the hardest with the cascading genetic failure. Her line hadn't been affected as badly as most, prospering even with the occasional dark-haired elf showing up. Maybe because of it. Her mother had almost transparent hair, but had to marry into a lower house, Cambri, because of her dark eyes. In hindsight, it had probably given her children an unexpected vigor that marrying a blond, green-eyed godling would have lacked. Every child was precious, but some were more precious than others.

Saladan stalked into the field office, the door slamming shut behind him.

"He had no right to say what he did about you," Kal said, and she glanced up, surprised.

Her truck was just ahead, and she slowed even more. Seeing Kal in jeans and an open-collared shirt was giving her mixed feelings. He still had that insufferable confidence about him, but damn it if she didn't like the casual look on him better than the suit and tie. "Don't worry about it. I've been called worse by people who really mean something to me."

A grimace crossed his face. Without warning, he touched her elbow to bring her to a halt as she reached for the handle of her truck's door. She jerked back, startled at the twinge of ley line energy trying to equalize between them, tasting of ozone and power. "Trisk, I can't tell you how bad I feel about how I treated you in school," he said, and a bitter emotion flashed through her. She'd tried to set it aside and be the grown-up, but it had been there, coloring every chance meeting in the hall or request for information. "It's part of the reason I took this job."

Hand on her hip, she stared at him. "Really," she said dryly. *I am not going to let him cleanse his conscience and think it's all better.* "I thought it was so you could publicly find fault with my work."

He flushed all the way to his hairline. "I'm sorry," he said. "I was a total ass. I can see now that my family let me get away with it, encouraged it even. My dad . . ."

He hesitated, but her hot temper faltered as his breath shook on his exhale.

"It wasn't fair or right," he said instead, confusing her even more. "I think I tormented you because I was scared that if I didn't bring you down, everyone else would see what a loser I was, and I wasn't brave enough to be on my own the way you were."

"Let me clue you in to something, Kal," she said tightly. "I wasn't alone by choice."

"I can't change the past, and I don't deserve your forgiveness—" he continued doggedly.

"Damn right," she interrupted. He had hurt her, and though she liked who she was, she could do without the scars.

"But could we . . ." His words faltered and died when he saw the old anger rising in her. "This isn't coming out right," he said, hands gesturing for patience. "I was furious at you when I lost that job at NASA, but in hindsight, I'm glad it happened. I was a total jerk, and working at NASA would have only fed that. Trisk, I've spent the last three years at a tiny lab not much better than the one here. No one likes me or my ideas. My theories are going nowhere, and frankly, I had to take this job before they utilized the escape clause and fired me."

Poor baby, she thought, but she said nothing, intending to let him pour out his soul so she could gleefully stomp all over it.

"Saladan was right about my family," he said, the rims of his ears red as he looked at his hands and forced them apart. "They aren't dirt-poor, but they lost a lot, and I'm only now realizing how much they sacrificed for me in the hope that I could bring something back to them. Now that's not going to happen. It's probably what I deserve."

Trisk's anticipation faltered. *Damn it. I can't stomp all over him now.* She curled her lip, disgusted with herself as she heard herself say, "Your parents didn't spend their fortune as an investment. They spent it to keep you alive."

A faint smile brightened his expression. "For all the good it did," he said ruefully. "My family is going to end with me, regardless. I'm the very last one." He took a breath, focus distant. "In a very long . . . line."

He was sterile, then. It wasn't a death sentence, but in a society focused on bloodlines and family ties, it was more humiliating than dark eyes and black hair. Surprised at his candor, she fumbled, not knowing how to respond anymore. "They're making advances every day," she offered hesitantly. "You've got a hundred years left."

He looked up, and her breath caught at the vulnerability shadowed behind his eyes, the pain she'd never seen before, probably because she was too angry to look for it. "I didn't tell you because I want your sympathy," he said. "I told you because I'd like to think that I grew up a little over the last couple of years, and if you didn't know the reason why, you'd never believe it. I know you will never forgive me, and frankly, I don't blame you. But I'd like to be able to be nice to you without you thinking I'm working an angle."

Trisk leaned against her truck, arms crossed over her middle. School had been a misery. The only time she'd had any peace was when Kal had been absent for months at a time. Now she knew he'd probably been in the hospital undergoing rudimentary, painful gene therapy, but back then, his absence had only seemed like a gift.

"I'm not asking for a clean slate," Kal said as he saw

her resolve. "But do you think we could maybe just . . . not be at each other's throat all the time?"

"I found you poking about in my files, and you expect me to trust you?" Trisk said, and Kal bowed his head, looking almost contrite.

"I didn't think you'd simply let me do what the enclave sent me for, but you're right again. I should have asked. How can I convince you I'm not here to hurt you?"

"You can clear Daniel's work for use," she said, knowing he'd never do it. "Make sure he gets credit for it. I know the enclave will put his name on it if you ask."

"Done."

The one word shocked through her, and she stared at him, not appreciating the little quirk of amusement in his eyes. "Done?" she echoed, and he nodded.

"I have no idea what I'm going to do now," he said, focus blurring as he looked out over the green fields. "I came here expecting to have to fix your errors and use that as a way to get myself a new job, but you're right. It's his virus. His and yours. I'll let them all know tomorrow, and I'll be out of your hair by the end of the month."

Done? Trisk licked her lips, not sure she believed him even now. "I didn't do much."

"You made it safe for us," he said, rocking back on his heels and giving her a faint smile.

He turned as if to leave, and she exhaled, nervously rubbing her forehead. *I can't believe I'm doing this.* "Thank you, Kal," she said, the unusual feelings of understanding drifting through her.

Kal's entire body slumped. "You're welcome." His breath came in slow, and he exhaled. "Trisk, I know it's soon, but I wish you'd give some thought to coming back with me to Florida. Once NASA sees what you did with Dr. Plank's virus, they're going to want you."

Trisk's eyes widened, and she stared at him.

"Ulbrine said that he'd make the introductions," Kal gushed, his words falling over themselves in his effort to get them out before she shut him down. "I know at the very least they'll want to hear about your work in developing a universal donor virus. I can see hints of it in Daniel's work, and it can't be allowed to falter here in a human-run lab."

NASA? Trisk thought, shocked. Ulbrine would introduce her to someone in NASA?

From the office shack came a whoop of alarm, and then a clattering crash. Kal chuckled, and her eyes flicked from the direction of Saladan's continuing bellow of anger to Kal. His eyes were glinting with mischief, and she remembered that tiny charm he'd flicked at the witch. "What was it?" she asked as Kal ducked his head and hid a grin.

"Remember how clumsy you were your freshman year?" he said as he looked up.

Her smile vanished. "That was you?" she said as two field hands poked their heads into the office, then shouted for some help.

Beaming, Kal took her hands, almost pulling her off balance as he went down on one knee in a mocking, overdone show. He was being charmingly submissive, and damn it if it wasn't working. "I am so, so sorry," he blurted. "You have no idea. I was such an ass."

"Get up," she muttered, pulling him to his feet before the three field hands running to help Saladan could see. "I might forgive you if you teach it to me."

Kal gave her hands a squeeze before he let go and opened her truck door for her. "Maybe over dinner?"

he asked as she pulled the door shut with a familiar, rattling thump.

She felt safe there, liking the way he was looking at her. And she wanted to belong, liked hearing him say he was sorry. *Daniel is going to freak out that his name is going to be on his virus.* "Okay," she said, but even as he beamed, promising to pick her up at the office at six, she didn't believe him.

The scars went too deep.

10

Kal sat on the edge of the couch in the green-room, not comfortable consigning himself entirely to the soft cushions that had cradled an unknown number of nervous, sweaty guests. He knew his favorite suit made him look especially trim and as if he owned the world, but he wanted to look better than good for his first press release, even if it wasn't his product.

Trisk looked amazing in her gray business skirt and matching top, the silver threads running through it elevating her sophistication even as the gold helix necklace and metallic-tipped, blunt-toed heels she wore boosted her feminine charms. Her long hair, which she usually kept back in a loose clip, had been bound into a tight, no-nonsense bun that accentuated her cheekbones. But it was her calm that surprised him the most as she stood at the table and made him a cup of tea. To Kal, she looked better in her minimal makeup and honest beauty than Heather, the overpainted, over-accessorized host of the show.

Across the room, Rick flirted with the young sound tech, the man completely overwhelmed by the lanky vampire's charms. Saladan watched with thinly veiled disgust from the opposite corner, slumped in his chair with one thin ankle on the other knee. A cast poked out from the cuff of his black suit coat. Kal had watched him go through two cigarettes in fifteen minutes. Either he was as nervous as a cat in the dog pound, or he was using the smoke to block the vampiric pheromones Rick was pumping into the air as he toyed with the sound tech.

Kal's attention shifted as Trisk's heels clicked on the tile floor. "Here you go," she said as she handed Kal a mug with the station's logo on it. "You can give it a try, but honestly, I think the water has been sitting since morning."

"It can't be that bad," Kal said as he took a sip. The bitter tea hit the back of his throat and he forced himself to swallow. "On second thought, I don't need any caffeine," he said with a smile. "Not that badly." Shuddering, he set it out of his easy reach. "Thanks anyway."

Sighing, she sat down on the couch, surprising him when her weight almost slid him into her. The scent of cinnamon rose from her like a perfume. Only elves rich in power smelled like that. How had he never noticed before? But then again, it had only been the last few days that she'd let him get that close. Their bonding over Saladan's slights at the farm last week had led to six dates—six dates at the pace of a thawing glacier. Trisk wasn't cold, but she wasn't forthcoming, either, and he found he enjoyed the challenge.

"Any more caffeine, and I'll get the shakes," she said as she looked at the coffee-stained side table with its mugs and sugar cubes. "Daniel asked me out for lunch today afterward. You don't mind, do you? He wanted to talk to me about something." Her brow furrowed. "He should be here by now. He said he wanted to watch the show."

"No, I don't mind," he said distantly, wondering if the awkward man was going to try to make a last-ditch play for her. Maybe he should address that. "It's not like we're going steady." He hesitated for a telling moment. "Are we?"

Trisk visibly colored, clearly caught off balance. "Uh, I don't know," she said, then turned to Rick's infectious laugh.

"I can't keep track of the little thing," Rick said as he half spun, the cord from the state-of-the-art mic dangling from one hand. "I'm so sorry. Perhaps if I remove my jacket," he added as he handed the mic to the technician. Groaning sensually, he slipped his jacket off, stretching his shoulders and tossing his silky, wavy hair to make the tech blink in consternation. Clearly Rick was enjoying himself, and Kal smirked as Saladan watched in a high-eyebrow question.

"Dr. Cambri?" a second technician said, and Trisk stood, the first hint of nervousness showing as she ran the black cord under her jacket. Saladan, too, was being miked, and Kal rose when the tech finished with him and came over. Kal clipped the mic to his lapel and tucked the wad of cord into a pocket. He'd never been in front of the cameras before, but he wouldn't let any of them know that by a show of ignorance.

"I have one of your fuzzy tomato plants in my backyard, Dr. Cambri," the technician working with her said. His shoes were scuffed and his clip-on tie was askew, but he clearly knew his job. "Got it for free at the grocery store. It's grown almost as high as my garage. I've been giving tomatoes away all summer."

"They tend to do that when they're taken care of," Trisk said, her shoulders shifting as she felt the weight of the wire. "It isn't on yet, is it?"

"Not yet." The older man fiddled with a little box before timidly fastening it to the back of her skirt's waistband. "We'll plug you in before you sit down. No need to overwhelm the guys in the booth. Four guests at once is our tops. Have fun out there. And remember, everyone will forget what you said the instant the next segment comes on, so don't sweat it."

Trisk flashed him a nervous smile as she sat back down. "Thanks." Her knees jiggled as she fidgeted. "Come on, Daniel. You're going to miss it," she whispered as she looked at the door and then at the muted TV in the corner showing the current segment wrapping up.

Kal cleared his throat. "Where is Daniel taking you for lunch?" he asked. "Sander's is open this time of day. It's right on the river. You can get a mimosa."

"Champagne before six?" Trisk said good-naturedly. "That's a little early, isn't it?"

"Yes, well, I don't know about you, but I'm going to need a little something after this." He sat down again, and wincing, he forced himself to take another pained sip of that horrid tea. "Rick, are you up for lunch before heading back to the office?"

"I'm taking the rest of the day off," the living vampire intoned, his gaze heavy on the tech still lingering in the greenroom. "I may have other plans."

"Trisk!" Dress shoes sliding loudly on the tile floor, Daniel lurched into the greenroom. Behind him, his studio escort turned and jogged off. "I made it."

Kal's expression stiffened at the relief that spilled over Trisk's face as she stood. "I was starting to get worried," she said, and Daniel took her hands, holding her at arm's length to look her up and down in appreciation.

"I wouldn't miss this for anything." Daniel's smile

was just as wide. "Wow, you look great. A real credit to Global Genetics. Trisk, I'm so proud of you."

"I'm nervous," she admitted, touching her hair and fiddling with her necklace. Her vulnerability struck Kal, and a surprising feeling of jealousy cascaded through him. She was free with herself around Daniel, a common human, but with him, she was distant and politically polite—and that was on a good day. Seeing her tentative smile and the support she got from the man, Kal decided he didn't like it.

"You can't tell." Daniel tucked a strand of her hair back in place. "You'll be fine. Everyone loves their fuzzy tomatoes, and they're going to love that you made them."

Her gaze flicked to Saladan, who was stoically ignoring Rick sitting beside him, the vampire trying to draw him into conversation. "Yes, well, just wait. It will be you up there next year."

Still smiling proudly, Daniel shook his head. "I doubt it. The virus might have my name on it, but the government isn't going to advertise it. No press conferences for me."

Kal's eyes narrowed as Trisk gave Daniel a comforting half hug. Bothered, he unthinkingly took a sip of that awful tea. Spitting it back into the cup, Kal set it on the coffee table.

"Please tell me it's time," Saladan said faintly when a tech came in, the expression on the witch's long face as weary as Rick's was annoyingly upbeat.

But the tech shook his head, eyes on Trisk. "Dr. Cambri. I need to adjust your mic."

Immediately she turned to him with a helpful openness. Daniel went to get himself a cup of coffee, and Kal watched Trisk's confidence return as the tech fumbled with her mic, the man able to take liberties that most would get slapped for. Kal didn't like that, either.

Over the last couple of weeks, he'd gotten used to her dark hair, finding the silky strands in odd places to remind him she was around. Her strong cheekbones and narrow nose were far more attractive when she was smiling at him than when she'd been throwing curses, and her laugh was infectious.

With a start, Kal realized Daniel was watching him watch her, more than a sliver of jealous warning in the back of the man's eyes. *I've got time to take care of that,* Kal thought, his gaze flicking to the clock.

Kal stood. Horrid tea in hand, he ambled over to Daniel at the coffee bar. "I don't think I've said congratulations yet, Dr. Plank," he said as he set his mug down on the return tray.

"Thank you." Daniel looked at Kal's extended hand, then shook it. "It's odd, but now that the government has cleared it for trials, I'm as nervous as hell that it won't work."

Kal laughed, the pleasant sound filling the small room. "It will. It's a beautiful piece of work from what I understand."

"Thank you," he said again, but his eyes were on Trisk as he pushed his glasses back up his nose. "Dr. Cambri had a lot to do with it. Her name should be on it as well."

"No, it's your project. Your baby." Kal hesitated. "You're right, though. Trisk is talented. What she did with the T4 Angel is amazing."

Daniel nodded, both men still looking at her. "She's better than I'll ever be. If she were a man, she'd be my boss by now."

"Funny you should mention that," Kal said, stifling a

surge of satisfaction when Daniel stiffened. "I've been talking with NASA, and they think they might have a place for her. I keep asking her to put in her application now that her tomato has been sold, but she won't. She could shine there," Kal added, feigning obliviousness to Daniel's sudden disquiet. "If I could convince her to go, that is. I wouldn't mind the chance to get to know her again, either. NASA is just down the road from where I work."

"Seriously?" Daniel said, his voice rough. "She told me some of the things you did."

Kal's wandering attention slid back to Daniel, his lips tight as he lied. "Little boys often torment little girls to get their attention. I was a fool." He crossed his arms over his chest. "I will not be that same fool again."

"There you go, Dr. Cambri," the tech said, and Trisk straightened her skirt. "Gentlemen, we have five minutes," he added loudly as he checked his watch. "If you have to use the bathroom, now's the time."

"I'm fine." Rick stood before the long mirror and adjusted the drape of his suit.

"Can we just get on with it?" Saladan muttered, crushing out his cigarette.

Satisfied from the look of Daniel's tight jaw that his words would fester, Kal surreptitiously pushed his tie off-kilter. "I'm good," he said, then smiled at Trisk. "Do I look okay?"

"You look fine," Trisk said, reaching to fix his tie. Behind her, the head technician vanished. The door shifted closed only a few inches before stopping. Faint in the distance, Kal could hear the current segment, a good eight seconds off from what was playing on the TV. "How come you're not nervous?" she asked as she gave his tie a last tweak.

"I am," he admitted. "But it's not my baby in the beauty contest. I don't even know why I'm here."

"Are you kidding?" Trisk said as Rick sniffed his opinion, the vain man continuing to primp in the mirror. "You're a bona fide Florida geneticist. Everyone wants to meet you." She shifted slightly to put her back to Daniel.

"Kal, I can't thank you enough for clearing Daniel's virus for live trials last week," Trisk whispered. "And then making sure his name was attached to it. This is Daniel's life. Thank you."

Kal smiled, not a whisper of guilt in him. "Yes, well, he deserves everything coming his way. You too."

Her eyes dropped modestly, and they all turned to the door when the head technician leaned into the greenroom and said authoritatively, "Mr. Rales, you first, please, then Mr. Saladan, Dr. Cambri, then Dr. Kalamack. This way." They hustled down the hall after him, cautioned to be quiet before they stole out onto the live floor.

Under a bright spotlight surrounded by a moat of space where cameras swam like silent alligators, their host, Heather, chatted with the off-site reporter out at one of Sacramento's middle schools.

"Thank you, Tom," Heather said brightly as she beamed at one of the cameras pulling in close on her. "We'll be right back to talk to our own Dr. Cambri from Global Genetics and Mr. Saladan from Saladan Industries and Farms about how they're working to put an end to hunger overseas as well as boost the economy here at home."

"We're clear!" someone shouted, and the woman's smile widened.

"Good, good," she said, hand over her eyes as she

peered off set at them. "Wow. You guys look great. Don't they look great, Howard?"

"They look great," that same faceless voice said. "Three minutes."

"Well, come on up," she urged, waving them forward. "Let's get you plugged in. Here, Mr. Saladan, I want you beside me. Then Mr. Rales, Dr. Cambri, and then Dr. Kalamack all on the couch. Rose between thorns, gentlemen. Quick like bunnies, now!"

The warmth of the lights was pleasant, and Kal obediently sat where she'd told him to, wondering why Heather had changed their positions as the technicians plugged his mic in. Saladan took the chair beside Heather with a dignified air, clearly pleased to have the place of honor. Trisk gingerly sat between Rick and Kal on the couch. The living vampire was brimming with a sexually charged confidence in his tight, British-inspired suit, making Kal think Heather was trying to keep her distance. Her enthusiasm didn't seem fake as much as forced.

"You all look as if you should be on the cover of *Vogue,* not *Scientific American,*" the buxom blonde said as she touched her hair, wound up into a huge beehive. "I'm going to bring up a few things we talked about earlier, maybe delve deeper into one or two topics, but try to keep the science light. Our audience is a wide mix of housewives and professionals, and we don't want anyone feeling threatened by their lack of education. Good? Good."

"Five," Howard said from the darkness. "Four, three . . ."

Suddenly Kal felt like the mayonnaise on a triple-decker sandwich, a tiny part of a revolving system of guests and shows, to be quickly replaced and forgotten in the ever grasping need for ratings. Sitting straight, he adjusted his tie to knock it off-kilter again so it would stand out more.

Heather beamed at the camera, taking the last second to brush her front smooth. "It's all about fuzzy tomatoes this afternoon," she said warmly. "We have with us today Mr. Rick Rales, the CEO of Global Genetics, based right here in Sacramento. With him is Mr. Max Saladan of Saladan Industries and Farms, who just bought the patent on the new Angel cultivar. Also with us is Dr. Trisk Cambri, the woman geneticist who created that fuzzy tomato everyone is talking about. Beside her is Dr. Trenton Kalamack, who has been chaperoning its shift from commercial trials to full production. Thank you all for joining me and my watchers for our lunchtime segment."

Smiling, Rick took a breath to say hello, catching it when the woman steamrolled forward.

"I understand it's been quite a year at Global Genetics as the Angel tomato came out of the basement, so to speak, and was made available both internationally and here at home in an extensive live trial with Saladan Farms," she said, smile widening. "I hear it's already proved invaluable in helping to feed the third world. Quite an accomplishment for having been in general cultivation for only one season. I'm going to jump right in with the question that is probably on all our viewers' minds. Dr. Cambri, why is your tomato fuzzy?"

Confident and smiling, Trisk leaned forward. "Good afternoon, Heather. I'm glad you asked. The hairs are actually a big part of what makes the Angel so drought tolerant and are why we had to go through a second entire growing season trial period before finalizing the sale to Saladan Farms. There was a real concern that

the general fuzziness of the plant and fruit would prevent the T4 Angel from becoming anything more than
a farm crop," she said, glancing at Saladan's stiff smile.
"But this year has proven without a doubt that that
hasn't been the case. Orders are already coming in for
larger shipments next spring."

"My mother has one in her backyard," Heather said.
"She got it for free in a promotion. I don't think she'd
ever have bought one on her own, but after having
tasted it, I know she'd shell out some serious cash for it.
The plant is as big as her VW, and it won't stop fruiting."

Saladan stirred, uncrossing his leg and setting his
foot on the floor. "That's why I insisted on a widespread
general-populace test to justify the large price tag they
were asking."

Trisk smiled, but Kal could see her long-held frustration. "I designed the tomato to be equally at home in
a cultivated field or a backyard, as diversity is key to
a successful organism, and people seem to love growing the novelty. The hairs wash off easily, and oddly
enough, it's those same hairs that help give the fruit
the sweet tang in sauces and ketchup."

From the shadows, Daniel beamed, giving her a
thumbs-up.

Great, Kal thought, stifling his annoyance. The man
hadn't given up. "What Dr. Cambri did was amazing,
Heather," he said. "The hairs originate from DNA taken
from the international GTB, or genetic tissue bank,
modified and inserted into the tomato's genome."

Heather's brow furrowed. "There's human DNA in
my ketchup? Isn't that cannibalism?"

Rick gave Kal a look to shut his mouth. "Not at all,
Heather," he said smoothly, his dark voice mesmeriz-
ing. "The human genome is one of the best studied,

and we've found there's a lot of repeating blueprints for structures that appear throughout the biosphere, meaning we share a lot of DNA with other organisms from fruit flies to apples. To be honest, I'd get more human DNA in my body by nibbling on your ear than eating a bushel of Angel tomatoes."

"I see. Thank you for clearing that up," Heather said, then visibly shook herself of the obvious pull to him. "But I'm still questioning the prudence of having the last year of testing take place not only aboveground, but over entire continents."

"The final testing year was to prove the tomato's commercial viability," Saladan said sourly. "Not for safety. I wouldn't risk my workers with an untested product."

Chuckling, Rick leaned forward. "You're talking of the Cuban biocrisis, yes, Heather?"

She inclined her head, somehow looking both mischievous and no-nonsense. It was a fabulous expression, and Kal resolved to cultivate it. "You said it. Not me." The woman gave him an impish smile. "But since you did, yes. We all remember the lines at the airports, the travel bans, and those awful yellow body bags that came back to our shores to be burned. All because of a badly developed genetic product."

"That simply can't happen anymore," Rick soothed, and even Kal felt the force of his living-vampire persuasion telling Heather not to worry her pretty little head about it. "It's more than the underground testing grounds and rigorous quarantine procedures that take place at every genetic facility. We're actually working on a tactical virus at Global Genetics right now that has received military approval just this week. The Plank tactical virus, or PTV, has no host, no carrier, and will therefore die out after twenty-four hours to leave those afflicted to recover completely. So you can see why we're not concerned about a tomato designed to survive a severe drought."

"A tactical virus that doesn't kill people?" Heather asked, her eyebrows high. "How is that helpful from a military standpoint?"

Kal stifled a wince, sure that neither the government nor the enclave would thank them for talking about Daniel's virus, but Rick nodded even as Saladan stared at him in disbelief.

"Imagine three-quarters of Sacramento suddenly calling in sick," Rick said, leaning forward to give his words more impact. "Everything stops. The chaos will allow our troops to safely enter and take control of any situation, whether it be as small as a building or large as a city." He leaned back, smiling again. "And in twenty-four hours, everyone recovers."

Heather frowned, and in the shadowed area off the stage, Kal heard a whispered argument. "You have an antidote for our own men, yes?" she asked, ignoring the spinning teleprompter.

Rick's smile widened. "No, but U.S. troops won't enter the area until the PTV hits the top of its infection curve and is in decline. They'll never be fully exposed, and if they are, the worst that will happen is fever and perhaps a rash."

Kal thought it interesting that he didn't mention the racking cough that could tear lung tissue, the possible dehydration from vomiting, or that the rash sometimes left scars, but that occurred only with overdoses. Unlikely in controlled situations.

Suddenly Kal realized the current conversation could provide an opportunity to drive a wedge between Trisk and Daniel. "Heather," Kal interrupted, "you might be interested to know that Dr. Cambri actually worked on the Plank tactical virus as well."

"Is that so?" Heather looked down the long row of men to her, and Saladan sighed heavily, clearly not appreciating the topic shift away from his product.

Trisk's smile became stilted; she clearly didn't want to steal Daniel's thunder. "Yes, but only in a small capacity. It's Dr. Plank's work. He's here today, actually. Can we bring him up?"

"You worked on them both at the same time?" Heather asked, ignoring Trisk's obvious desire to get Daniel onstage.

"Uh, yes," Trisk admitted, and Kal jerked when she knocked his ankle a little too hard to have been an accident. "They share some of the same developmental techniques. The Plank tactical virus is one of Global Genetics' larger projects. Almost everyone had a hand in it."

"I see." Turning to the camera, Heather resettled herself. "When we come back, we'll head into the kitchen with Mr. Saladan to see how tasty these fuzzy tomatoes are."

Heather held her breath for three seconds, then stood when the tech with the clipboard pointed at them. "Four minutes!" he shouted. Immediately the three men rose as well, but Heather was already moving, unclipping her mic and striding toward the ring of darkness.

"Excuse me. I'll be right back," she said, and then the black took her. "Makeup! Where's my makeup?" she shouted, heels clicking. "I feel like a cow out there," she said distantly, and Kal stifled a smile. "I thought geneticists were dorks in black plastic glasses, but even the woman scientist has a better tan than me. Gwen! I need a touchup."

Rick unplugged his mic and handed it to the nervous technician who'd come forward. "Excuse me," he said faintly. "Heather?" Rick almost floated off the raised platform, following her. "You look fa-a-a-abulous, darling. Don't change anything."

Trisk stood, and the three of them edged off the stage as the lights dimmed and the camera and Saladan were chaperoned to the kitchen set. "Why did Rick bring up Daniel's virus?" she said, fingers touching a strand of hair that had escaped her bun. "Daniel should be the one to talk about it, not me."

Kal took her hand to stop her fussing. "Trisk, stop fiddling with your hair. You're one of the beautiful people."

She looked at Daniel watching the monitor playing eight seconds into the past. Her expression went blank as she saw her group next to the host. It wasn't so noticeable when they were in ones and twos, but with four Inderlanders under the spotlight with one human, it was obvious who was who. "It is Daniel's project," she said, her cheeks a soft red.

Daniel turned, his attention going from Kal to his fingers still twined with Trisk's. "I, uh, left my coat in the greenroom," Daniel said, then strode away.

"He should have been up there, not me," Trisk whispered, pulling her hand from Kal's.

"It was your day in the sun, Trisk."

"For my project, sure, but not his." Trisk took two steps after Daniel. "Excuse me," she said over her shoulder, her pace never faltering. "Daniel?"

Kal unclipped his mic and handed it to the waiting tech. Tension made his steps light and silent as he wove through the thick cords on the floor, finding he liked the silence and dark of the back rooms as he followed her. The door to the greenroom was open, and he hesitated, listening.

"Jeez, Trisk. I don't care that I didn't get a chance to talk up my virus. It will be forgotten in six months and Rick knows that. He's just grabbing publicity before the government slaps a gag order on him."

"Then why are you upset? Don't lie to me, Daniel. I know you better than that."

There was a silence, and Kal held his breath.

"Kal tells me he's pushing you to put in your application at NASA."

"And?" Trisk said, her tone holding a wary lightness.

"And I don't think you should. NASA is a fabulous opportunity, but I don't trust him. I've worked with men like him before. He's had everything handed to him, and he uses people like tissues."

"Did you know he was the one who convinced the government to put your name on your virus?" Trisk said hotly, and Kal felt a smile curve up the edges of his lips.

"It was my work!" Daniel exclaimed. "Thanking him for that is like thanking the man who pulled me from the rapids after he shoved me in! If he's pushing you to go, it's because he's working an angle to help himself, not you."

"So you're saying I'm not good enough to work at NASA? That the only way he'd recommend me is because he's 'working an angle'?" Trisk said, and Kal stifled a quiver.

"Trisk," Daniel said softly, persuasively, but Kal knew it was too late, and his palms tingled with anticipation. "I don't like him. Every time he makes you laugh, his eyes crinkle like he's moved a chess piece."

"You don't like him because he makes me laugh?"

"Can't you see he's using you? I thought you were smarter than that. Trisk, wait," Daniel pleaded, his tone suddenly changing, and Kal backed up several steps. Even so, Trisk almost ran into him as she strode out of the greenroom.

"Whoa! Hey. Did you find Daniel?" Kal asked, thinking she looked marvelous with her eyes snapping in anger—especially when that anger wasn't aimed at him. "Where are you going for lunch?"

"I lost my appetite," she said shortly, purse in hand and her color high as she began walking to the lobby, her steps quick and short. With a last look at the greenroom door, Kal followed, catching up to her easily. Trisk glanced at him, her brow furrowed as she pulled two clips from her hair and the bun fell completely apart. "I don't laugh too much, do I?"

Kal's eyes widened. "God no. I love your laugh." He put an arm around her, her hair pinched between them as he dared to tug her to him—a hint, nothing more. He quickly let go when she stiffened. "I'm sure he's fine. It probably didn't sit well that you got to talk about his virus and he didn't. Let me take you to lunch. You want to go to Sander's?"

He held the door to the lobby for her. Head down and hair hiding her eyes, she went through, stopping in the hushed quiet of glass and fake wood. It was a space of silence with the world of pretend on one side, the hard cement and blue sky on the other. Her breath shook as she exhaled. "I want to go to NASA," she said as she looked up at him, her eyes soft in hope. "I want to go to NASA, with you. We can work together on my universal donor."

Success slammed into him, making him breathless.

His knees threatened to give way, and he locked them. Not having to fake his excitement, he took her hands in his. "Really?" he said, beaming as he gave her a huge hug, right there in the lobby. "Trisk, thank you!"

"Kal!" she exclaimed, giggling as he picked her up and swung her in a quick circle.

"Felecia Eloytrisk Cambri, you've made me so happy!" he said, giving her another hug as he settled her feet back on the carpet. "This is going to be wonderful. I have to find a phone."

"But I can't leave until the enclave gets someone here to take my place," she said, her expression becoming serious. "Can you wait for me?"

He bobbed his head. "Of course." Daring, he gave her a kiss on her cheek, darting in and pulling away before she could react. "Lunch? We need to celebrate. Take the rest of the day off," he said as he turned her to the exit and the parking lot before she could see Daniel standing in the hallway, his expression riven with anger and grief.

"You've made me so happy, Trisk," he said softly. "You're going to leave your mark on the world, and I'm going to be right beside you."

Together they found the walk, his jaunty step luring her into a better mood.

Two more weeks. Easy.

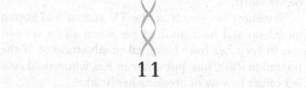

11

Daniel clenched the steering wheel of his black Ford Thunderbird, the big engine almost silent as it idled up the long drive to Trisk's house. A bouquet of white lilies sat beside him, gray in the dusky evening light. The lady at the flower shop said white lilies were a symbol of apology, even more so with the long streaks of brown pollen staining the white petals. "Tears," the shopgirl insisted, but Daniel had a feeling he'd been tricked into buying damaged goods.

Chocolate had seemed rife with tones of romance, jewelry was wrong for the same reason, and asking her out so he could apologize over a beer as he would anyone else felt worse. Waiting until tomorrow to meet her in the hall by chance smacked of insincerity, and so here he was, a bouquet of lilies that he hoped would stop her justifiable anger long enough so that he could say he was sorry.

For two weeks he had watched Kal slowly insinuate himself back into her life, moving with a sly confidence Daniel had seen all through graduate school, men working their way through the female student body as if women were perks the school had allowed in solely for their enjoyment. Trisk wasn't a fool, but of all the entitled, rich boy-men that he'd seen, Kal had to be the worst.

Somehow his words at the TV station had gotten mixed up and he'd insulted her when all he wanted was to keep her from being taken advantage of. If she wanted to leave, fine, but not with Kal, who would ruin her career by way of breaking her heart.

His gaze slid to the lilies. He didn't want her to think he was a kiss-up, or worse, trying to seduce her. Only now, when she was under attack, had he realized how important her steady, unassuming presence was to him. He didn't want to see her hurt, especially not by Kal.

Daniel squinted into the new shadows as he parked before the barn, sitting for a moment to gather his courage. The lights were on in the house and her car was parked at the front steps beside her worn farm truck. Music drifted out of the windows, opened wide to take advantage of the pleasant October night, the steady pop beat and vocals rising over the air heavy with sunset. *The Zombies*, he thought, and with a resolute sigh, he took the stained lilies and got out. They were all the rage, one of the many British rock bands storming the nation and pulling the hemlines higher.

Steps slow and methodical, he rose up the wide slate stairs to the expansive wraparound porch. *"Well no one told me about her, the way she lied,"* drifted out in time with his steps. Big wooden doors facing him, he halted to tug his shirt straight, hesitating as the bright lights of an approaching car passed over him.

"Kal," he whispered, and eyes narrowed, he dropped back, ducking behind a corner of the house and out of sight. *What am I doing?* he thought as he gripped his flowers tighter, wishing he'd never brought them.

But he cared, maybe more than if she had shown even a hint of interest. A lover he could find, but someone who understood him and his work, someone bright and engaging . . . that was worth risking embarrassment to protect.

His pulse quickened as a black Camaro came to a halt beside Trisk's car, the engine revving aggressively before it was turned off. But it wasn't Kal who got out. The man didn't see him in the shadow of the building as he strode up the walk with an eager confidence. His slacks were tight in the latest style, and his white shirt almost glowed in the dim light. Though he wasn't especially tall, his tightly muscular build made him stand out. A suit coat was draped over his arm, and he had a hat in his hand. His steps were eerily silent.

"Quen!" Trisk shouted as the music clicked off, and even before the man had a chance to knock, she'd flung open the door, clearly expecting him. "Right on time. How *do* you do it?"

"I skulk in alleys a lot," the man said, his voice markedly low and resonant for such a small frame. Clearly delighted to see her, Quen gave her a long hug, Trisk's long hair mingling with Quen's much shorter, softly curling version. *Brother*, Daniel thought, seeing the same dark hair and athletic build, though admittedly Quen's shoulders were wider and he stood a good six inches over Trisk. It was the hug that said sibling, though; there had been no kiss.

"I saw you on TV this afternoon," Quen said, then pushed her back to arm's length, his head cocked and a smile on his face as he looked her up and down in the light spilling out onto the porch. "You did great."

"I was nervous," she said as she touched her helix necklace, still around her neck. Beaming, she led him in.

"Thank you for the necklace. It went perfect with the outfit. It came yesterday, just in time."

"Yesterday? I sent it three weeks ago. I should have just brought it in my suitcase."

"You want some iced tea?" she said, voice going distant. "I baked yesterday. I've gotten pretty good at cookies, if nothing else. Is that jacket leather? I like it."

The door shut, muffling Quen's response.

Daniel slumped, the flowers in his grip now looking banal even as his resolution to give them to her strengthened. He'd give the two a moment, then knock, telling them he'd been in the barn looking for her. That it wasn't Kal was a relief.

"You look good." Quen's voice came out the kitchen window along with the familiar sounds of ice knocking into glass. "Not just outside, but inside. Have you met someone?"

"No," Trisk said, much to Daniel's surprise, but what sister tells her brother everything? "Daniel is starting to become a problem, though," she added, and Daniel froze. She'd talked to her brother about him? "He's wickedly smart. Quirky sense of humor. He respects me."

And that's a problem? Daniel mused, confused.

"He'd better," Quen muttered, the tinkle of something spilling over ice loud.

"I haven't encouraged him," Trisk said quickly. "But he's nice and—"

"The man you were sent to spy on," Quen interrupted dryly. "That is so classic."

Spy? Daniel eased deeper into the shadows, his flowers drooping to touch the porch.

"Stop it," Trisk protested, and Daniel could almost see her frown. "I'm not doting on him, but he's a good man, and I don't want to hurt him." The sliding sound of a plate scraped out into the night, then Trisk's voice, softer. "He thinks Kal is taking advantage of me."

"So do I," Quen said, ice clinking as he presumably took a drink. "How is that going? Your last letter wasn't very forthcoming."

"Because I don't trust Kal not to read my mail," Trisk said, and Daniel heard a chair being pulled out from under the counter between the kitchen and living room. "I had lunch with him this afternoon, and we already set up lunch tomorrow. The doofus thinks I'm eating out of his hand. If nothing else, dating him has helped with Daniel. Try one of the cookies. Good?"

Cold spilled over Daniel. Trisk was an industrial spy? Working at Global Genetics to steal methods and techniques for another lab? But she'd given information, not stifled it. She'd helped him with innovative techniques he'd never seen before. *Techniques no one had ever seen before. She has no published articles and a pretty face to open doors*, he thought suspiciously. Someone as good as her should be widely published. Unless she was trying to stay unnoticed.

"I'm sorry Kal put you in this position," Quen said, and Daniel looked past the edge of the building, drawing back slightly when he saw Trisk facing him, sitting at the tall counter with a plate of cookies between her and Quen, her angular face eager in anticipation as Quen ate one. Quen stood in the kitchen across from her, the cookie lost in his knobby hand. His back was to Daniel, every inch of his suit pressed and perfect and his dress shoes gleaming.

"Kal is a total jerk," Trisk said, her attention dropping into her half-empty glass as Quen obediently ate a cookie. "Everything coming out of his mouth is pure horse crap. But he can be surprisingly . . . fun." She winced in embarrassment. "Sometimes I go home at night—"

"Alone?" Quen interrupted, and she flashed a grin at him, dark eyes alight.

"Alone," she agreed. "I take a hot bath or sit in front of the fire as I remember all the nice things he said or did that day." Her smile faded. "I know it's fake, a game to him, but it feels good anyway. To hear those things from someone who once spit on your shadow."

Suddenly Daniel felt stupid. The woman was a spy, and he'd been worried Kal was trying to take advantage of her? Expression twisting, he dropped the flowers.

"He's been at me to put my application in at NASA," Trisk said, head bowed over her glass. "I said I would if he'd put his in, too. Come with me."

"I bet that put a sparkle in his step," Quen said, and Daniel drew back, holding his breath when Quen turned and his shadow spread long over the porch. From inside, he could hear the water at the sink run. "You're not going, are you?" Quen asked, standing right before the window.

"Are you kidding?" Trisk said sourly. "Talk about your boys' club. They'd have me washing their petri dishes and picking up their dry cleaning my first day. I'm putting Kal off with the excuse that I can't leave until the enclave finds a replacement for me here. By then, he will have signed off on the patent transfer for the T4 Angel, and with that, I'll have a successful product and can get a job anywhere. Meanwhile, I'm playing this stupid game of girlfriend. God! What a woman has to do to get credit for her own work."

Daniel frowned, more confused. She was spying on him for an organization called the enclave, but trying to make a name for herself? Perhaps she needed to in order to get into the more exclusive labs.

"I need to stay for a few years more at least," she said, and when Quen's shadow vanished, Daniel risked looking past the flat of the building again. "Someone needs to watch Daniel," she said, and his face warmed. "He's got a new line of tactical virus to play with and he shouldn't be left alone."

Left alone?

Quen moved to stand between him and Trisk, hiding her. "I don't like this game you're playing with Kalamack," Quen said as he sat, his elbows on the bar and his head down. "But I'll be there if you need me. Just promise me you won't let him sucker you into believing he's any different than he was three years ago."

"Yeah. Right." Trisk snapped a cookie in half. "I don't know what I would've done without you those last few years at school." She nibbled the cookie. "Needs more cinnamon."

Quen turned away. Trisk was busy wiping the crumbs off the counter and missed his expression, one so deep and enduring that Daniel suddenly realized that as much as they looked alike, this man wasn't Trisk's brother, though that same need to protect was there.

"So, how did you get time away from the Kalamacks?" she asked, oblivious to how deep the man's commitment to protect her went. "I was surprised to get your letter that you were coming out. It's almost six hundred miles. I haven't seen you since graduation."

Daniel dropped back as Quen looked to the window, his heart pounding. "I'm supposed to be in Kentucky looking at a horse for possible purchase for breeding stock," Quen said, his voice distant. "But I already know the animal is worthless. He's all pedigree, no drive. I'm going to suggest they buy him. They won't know he's a bad choice for at least two years, and by then, I'll be gone."

The man was at the sink again, and Daniel began to edge away. He could put his car in neutral, push it far enough down the road that they wouldn't hear when he started it. He wasn't sure who he was going to tell, but he knew he didn't want to be caught.

"You are incorrigible," Trisk said, the light play back in her voice. "How would you know if he's a good horse or not?"

"They speak to me," Quen said. "In little nickers and whispers. This guy? He wants to laze about in the field all day. Hey, if you ever want horses for your stable, let me know."

I can't leave the flowers, Daniel thought suddenly, turning to find them.

"Man, I've missed you, Quen. You have no idea."

Disgusted at his gullibility, Daniel bent to retrieve the lily bouquet. Blinking, he froze. There was a tiny, glowing woman standing in the petals, her hands orange with the pollen. "Holy shit!" he shouted, jerking his hand back.

The little woman looked up at him in shock, her gossamer wings a blur. "Son of a bitch!" she swore, her high voice clear among the crickets. And then she was gone, nothing but a silver trace of fading dust arching up into the rafters to say she'd ever existed.

"Did you hear—" Trisk said, but Daniel was staring at the eaves of the building, his heart pounding.

"Stay here," Quen said, a dangerous edge to his voice. "Someone is outside."

"It sounded like Daniel. Quen, wait!" she shouted, and then the door was yanked open, flooding the porch with a yellow light. "You don't know how much he heard!"

Shocked into motion, Daniel vaulted over the railing, landing badly and rolling down to the cars. Quen's Camaro still ticked with heat, and he scrambled up, dusty and disheveled. He turned to see Quen and Trisk silhouetted at the top of the porch stairs. Trisk was holding Quen's arm as if to stop him. He couldn't see their expressions with the light behind them, but Quen's stiff body language said it all. Daniel was up shit creek without a paddle.

Mouth dry, he dropped the flowers. "I, ah . . . I didn't hear anything," he said.

Quen slumped as he pulled away from Trisk. "I'm sorry," he said softly. "I'll make it painless."

"What? Quen!" Trisk shouted, rounding on him. "No!"

Painless! Daniel thought. My God, they were going to kill him. Hand up, he backed up into the Camaro. "I didn't see anything!" he said, and then his jaw dropped as that same eerie glow he'd seen about that tiny woman seemed to blossom in Quen's hands.

"*In es est,*" Quen said in regret, shoving it at him as if it were a dodgeball.

"I said no!" Trisk exclaimed, expression angry. "*Finire!*" she shouted, and Daniel stood transfixed as Trisk threw a second gold-and-green ball of light at the one streaking toward him. The two met with a ping he felt more than heard, and Daniel jumped, the sensation of having been pushed back filling him when the globes of light deflected to hit the earth to either side of him. The packed dirt spurted with an odd wet hiss, falling back to make a glowing crater.

Daniel's jaw dropped, gaze darting from them to the green haze and back again. "Y-you . . ." he stammered. "Who are you people?"

"You're not killing him," Trisk said, and Daniel froze. She was a spy. They both were.

"He heard everything," Quen protested as Trisk hustled down the stairs, shooting dark looks at Quen, tight behind her. "We can't let him break the silence."

"Yeah?" She stopped at the foot of the stairs, jerking Quen to a halt beside her. "He didn't break the silence, you did. So what if he heard us talking about Kal?"

Quen's fists slowly opened, his angry expression replaced by one of dismay.

Seeing it, Trisk nodded, her lips pressed tight. "This. Was. Salvageable," she said softly, poking him in the chest with a finger. "Until you went ape and threw a lethal spell at him. Good God, what have you been doing the last three years?"

Quen flushed. "Security."

"I can tell," she said sourly, then forced a sick-looking smile onto her face as she turned to Daniel. "It's going to be okay."

But it didn't feel like it as Daniel swallowed hard, the warm engine of the Camaro pressing into him. The keys were in the ignition. "I—I won't say anything," he stammered, but his thoughts kept returning to that tiny woman and the glow from her. It had been the same glow in Trisk's hand.

A memory slowly began to push aside the fear. *Finire.* He'd heard that odd word before. As Trisk and Quen argued, Daniel touched the back of his head, his eyes narrowing at the remembered bump from two weeks ago.

"There was a man," Daniel said, and Quen's forceful

argument about what to do stopped as they both turned to him. "In a crushed green velvet coat. In Angie's old office." His lips parted. "Blue glasses, ugly laugh. You threw me across the room without using your hands." Daniel stiffened. "How could I forget that?"

"How indeed," Quen accused, and Trisk flushed.

"Uh, I was going to tell you about that," she said to Quen, her shoulders hunched in embarrassment. "I found a stone in my grandmother's ashes with a name engraved on it."

"Trisk," Quen said, aghast.

"Daniel walked in on us," she continued, gesturing weakly.

"You didn't lock the door? Isn't that rule one in summoning demons?" Quen berated her, and Daniel started. *Demons?*

"I locked the door, okay!" Trisk exclaimed, and Daniel began to edge down the Camaro's side to the door. "I didn't know Daniel had a master bypass key. I spelled him into forgetting. I thought it would stick." Daniel froze when she turned to him, her eyes pleading. "Daniel, it's going to be okay. I promise."

Demons? Spells? Trisk thought she was a witch? *Thinks, or is?* he wondered in a growing panic as he looked at the still-smoldering pits. God help him, they both were. In a surge of fear, he fumbled for the door handle of the Camaro. Quen had tried to kill him, and Trisk had deflected the strike. With magic.

"I'm not letting you drive my car out of here," Quen said, and with a *thunk*, the doors locked on their own. Horrified, Daniel pulled his hand off the vehicle. *Magic . . .*

"And I'm not letting you kill him for my mistake," Trisk said, apparently not having a problem with the fact that Quen had locked the doors from ten feet away without touching the car.

But Quen shook his head, ignoring Daniel as if he were dead already. "I know you like him, but your charms aren't enough. Eventually he's going to blab, and then we'll *all* be dead."

"I *won't* let you kill him," Trisk said. "Don't push me on this, Quen," she intoned, but a horrible emptiness had taken the man's eyes, dark in the dim light.

"I'm sorry," he whispered. "You know there's no choice."

"There's always a choice!" she exclaimed, then turned to Daniel, making him jump. "It's okay," she said quickly. She was trying to smile, but it wasn't coming off as reassuring. "Quen won't hurt you."

"I don't care that you're spies. I won't tell anyone. I promise," Daniel said.

"Spies?" Trisk hesitated, an odd expression crossing her face. "No."

"Then who are you? *What* are you?" Daniel exclaimed.

"I'm the same person I was yesterday," she said, and Daniel shook his head vehemently as Quen sighed and pinched the bridge of his nose.

"Yeah?" Daniel pointed at the fading glow in the drive. "You can do . . . that. And *he* wants to kill me because I know about it? What are you people?"

"I'm not going to let him kill you," Trisk said, arms over her chest. "I'm not!" she said louder, looking at Quen. But Daniel could see the panic gathering in her eyes, the determination in Quen, his hands clenching into fists and his shoulders stiffening.

"You know forget curses aren't reliable," Quen said, and she nodded miserably.

"It would have been fine if I hadn't triggered the latent memory," she said, then louder when Quen took a breath to protest, "If my charms aren't strong enough, I know someone whose are."

Quen's expression blanked. "The demon?" he questioned, and Trisk nodded.

"The demon."

12

Daniel's breath came fast. Trisk had thrown a glowing ball of something to deflect the one Quen had aimed at him. And now Quen wanted to kill him. *This can't be happening.*

"We can do it in the barn," Trisk said, her voice low and her face hidden by her hair. "I'm not having that horrid smell in my house."

"Trisk, this is a bad idea," Quen prompted, and she rounded on him.

"If you don't want to help me, fine, but I'm doing it," she said, then spun to stride toward the barn. Her shadow vanished fast, leaving only the stars shining over the black hulk of the old building and the sound of her steps.

Quen frowned at Daniel as if everything was his fault. "After you, Dr. Plank," he said, gesturing sarcastically, and Daniel began to follow.

Fifty feet away, Trisk had reached the barn, her small shadow struggling as the door noisily rolled open. A moment later, light blossomed from inside, spilling out to glint on his car parked nearby. "I should have known Trisk wouldn't own three vehicles," Quen muttered.

A forget spell, Daniel thought. He wouldn't believe

it except he'd seen the glowing energy coming from both Trisk and Quen. *And what about that little woman in my flowers?*

He slowed as he entered the barn, glad to see the light was coming from a mundane gas lantern, hissing as it threw new shadows to the edges of the wide two-story space. "Where do you want him?" Quen said, and Trisk looked up from where she'd swept a wide area, the old boards shiny with age and polished by decades of straw.

"Daniel, why don't you sit there," she said, pointing to a bale of straw, and Daniel's jaw tightened. He was still wearing his scowl when Trisk turned to him, and he let it linger, angry something was going on, something he'd been kept out of—had been for a long time. He didn't think she was a spy anymore, but she was up to something. He wasn't sure if she was courageous or a whore. Maybe men were the bastards for making women have to choose between the two in order to get credit for their own work.

"I wish I could explain," Trisk said, but her evident guilt only made Daniel angrier.

"What's to explain?" he said flippantly. "You can do magic and you have to kill me to keep it a secret."

Beside him, Quen smacked a thick support post in agreement. "See?" he exclaimed. "Even he gets it."

"You are *not* going to kill *Daniel!*" Trisk shouted, then slumped. "I'm so sorry. We're going to make you forget. You'll be okay."

Okay? Trisk had been lying to him since he met her. How was that okay? "I'm not going to forget this," he said sullenly.

"You do, or I kill you," Quen said, his cool cracking as he looked at Trisk. "This isn't going to work," he said. "I promise I'll make it painless."

Daniel's pulse quickened, and he sat down fast, the straw poking him roughly even as the old bale threatened to split.

"No." Trisk turned away, her head bowed. "This is my mistake. I pay for it."

"Trisk . . ."

She shook her head, clearly unhappy as she poured a thick line of what looked like white sand in a large circle nearly six feet in diameter. Clearly disapproving, Quen stood and watched as she then set a candle in the middle and a dish of what looked like ash.

"Kind of big for a circle, isn't it?" Quen asked, and Trisk looked up, lips pressed.

"I'm hoping that with a larger circle, he won't be as eager to try to break it."

He? Daniel wondered, edging toward the open door. *Oh yeah, the demon.*

"It will make him harder to contain, too," Quen said, then louder, "Go ahead and run. She can't stop me from killing you if you're in a field of pecan trees."

"Quen," Trisk complained, but Daniel halted.

"This is foolish!" Quen exclaimed. "At least let me knock him out."

Trisk straightened from over her candle. It hadn't been lit a moment ago, but now the flame burned fitfully, finally catching to flicker in the draft from the door. Daniel would swear he hadn't heard a match being struck. "No," she said, and Quen's jaw clenched. "Will you give us a moment?" she asked.

"He won't remember it," Quen said, and she sniffed, expression miserable.

"I will."

Clearly peeved, Quen spun on a heel to leave, but he jerked to a halt before Daniel. "If you run, I *will* leave her to chase you down. If she then dies at the hand of her demon, I will still kill you, but it will be long and painful. Understand?"

Daniel looked past Quen at the circle and candle, not knowing if he should be afraid the demon was real, or that they believed he was.

"Understand?" Quen said louder, and Trisk frowned at them both.

"I won't run," Daniel said, but it was obvious Quen didn't believe it as he went to stand at the barn door, his shoulders tense in distrust as he faced away from them.

Trisk sat beside him on the bale of straw, her head bowed. She looked utterly alone, and feeling his own anger begin to dissolve, Daniel lost his frown. He could smell cinnamon and wine, but he'd swear she'd been drinking iced tea. "I'm sorry," Trisk said, her voice low.

"For what?" he asked. "That you can do magic or that your bodyguard wants to kill me?"

She looked up, her brown eyes catching the glow from the lamp as the sun went down and the light failed. "Quen isn't my bodyguard. He's my friend."

Daniel watched Quen's shoulders hunch, guessing that "friend" was not what Quen wanted to be, but that he liked her too much to risk ruining what he had. Daniel knew the feeling.

"I wish I could explain," she said, watching her fingers twist about themselves, "but it's not going to matter in a few minutes. We're only going to take away little chunks of time so you'll be safe. You won't remember this at all."

"This is not cool, Trisk—" he started.

"Don't," she blurted, clearly trying not to cry. "The law says you have to die to preserve the secret of our existence." She laughed bitterly. "*We* make a mistake, and *you* die for it. But not this time." Trisk raised her head, her breath steadying. "After this, I'm going to go to NASA."

Daniel felt his expression go slack. "Why? Trisk, you know they'll make you their collective assistant. You'll hate it there."

Her head dropped again. "Call it punishment. But at least my research will be acted on, right? And isn't that all that's important?" she said, voice rising. "That something I did means something? Who cares whose name is on it if it helps people," she finished, breath catching.

"Stay here," Daniel said, hating to see her so miserable. "We can—"

But she shook her head, taking his hands to force him to look at her. "If I stay, the memory charm will break apart again, even a demonic one. I have to go."

He sat back, his anger tightening his shoulders. "I wouldn't tell anyone you're a witch."

She started, and at the open door, Quen turned to stare at him. "We, uh, aren't witches," she said, and Quen cleared his throat in warning.

"Then what are you?" Daniel questioned.

Quen coughed. "He doesn't need to know this," he said, his voice tight in warning as he used his weight to pull the barn door closed and shut out the night. "We're wasting time."

"I'm sorry," Trisk said as she stood, her smile forced. "Stay here, and whatever you do, don't say anything. We're going to be dealing with a very dangerous person who uses knowledge like a weapon."

"You're telling him too much," Quen said tightly, and her shoulders stiffened.

"I don't care, *Quen*," she shot back, then spun to put

her back to both of them, staring at the candle flickering in the middle of her circle. "*Septiens*," she whispered, and without warning or fanfare, a shimmering wave of something sprang up from the sand, coming together at the top to form half a sphere. It shimmered like a heat wave, and Daniel would've gotten up to investigate, but Quen was glaring at him to stay put.

"Algaliarept," Trisk whispered. "I summon you."

Daniel's lips parted as a sudden haze in the middle of her circle solidified into . . . "A hippie?" he questioned, seeing a thick, somewhat tall man in baggy but exquisitely embroidered clothes. He wore a full-sleeved red shirt under a long vest. His dark hair was pulled back and his beard was thick. But then Daniel saw his eyes, and his breath caught. It wasn't that they were red and slitted like a goat's. There was anger in them—and a need to hurt.

"It's not a hippie, it's a demon," Quen said, grim-faced. "He looks like that to lull you into thinking he's safe."

"He doesn't look safe to me," Daniel whispered, and the man with his mix of casual disregard and brute strength gave him a knowing smirk as round blue-tinted glasses misted into existence, perched on the bridge of his strong nose. The scent of burnt tree sap grew cloying. Daniel stared, memory tickling the top of his brain. He'd seen this before . . . smelled it.

Trisk shifted from foot to foot, her shoulders up around her ears. "I like the Victorian dandy better," she said, and the demon looked down at himself, sniffing as he eyed his bare toes.

"You lust after dangerous subtext," the demon said, his deep, noble British accent familiar. "I can scratch that itch, little bird, scratch it until you writhe for more."

Smiling to show flat, blocky teeth, the demon tapped the barrier with a finger, and the haze between them dimpled. "You'd enjoy what I'd do to you. Promise."

My God. I remember this, Daniel thought as a feeling of vertigo cascaded over him. Pulse hammering, he tore his attention from the demon to look at Trisk, then Quen, in horror. It was all real. It hadn't been bluster, Quen really wanted to kill him! Buried-in-the-back-of-the-barn kill him!

As if pulled by his fear, the demon's gaze fastened on him, his thick shoulders cracking as he leaned closer to the barrier. Daniel swore he could hear a thrum of warning, and indeed, a wisp of smoke seemed to rise where the demon touched it, and the scent of burning sap became strong. "Two elves and a human walk into a barn." The demon grinned. "Sounds like a joke to me, Felecia Eloytrisk Cambri."

Elf, Daniel thought, looking at Quen and Trisk. Not witch. Would that make Kal an elf as well? They all went to the same school, apparently. *Why are they geneticists?*

"I need something," Trisk said, seemingly breathless.

The beach guru crossed his arms across his middle, eyes rolling. "Of course you do," he said, and then all three of them jumped when the demon lashed a fist into the barrier. Black smoke rolled up to show the curve of the circle, and with a start, Daniel realized the choking burnt-sap smell was coming from the demon himself.

"Trisk?" Quen exclaimed, and she waved his concern off, missing the demon's eyes flicking up to the rafters at a faint clatter. Daniel followed the demon's gaze, his brow rising when he spotted a tiny glow of light seeming to spill from the thick beams, dissipating before it fell more than a few inches. It was that tiny woman, and Daniel looked back down, startled to see the demon watching him, grinning wildly.

"You *need* something," the demon said as he ran a hand through the thin ribbons woven into his beard. "Seeing a human staring at me, I can guess." He hesitated, his feet in his rope-and-wood sandals spread confidently. "I like this. So sure of your skills that you summon me in a barn. Aboveground. Where I might see something other than the ceiling of your lab."

Trisk took a breath to say something, and again the demon jabbed out at her circle. White-faced, she took a step back, the barrier she'd made humming with a stronger force.

"Let me guess," Daniel said, ignored. "If he gets out, we all die."

"Only if you're lucky," the demon said.

"Ask him," Quen said, and Trisk stepped forward, an odd, stiff surety in her.

"How much for a memory charm?" she said, her mood an even mix of worry and frustration. "To cloud both the first time he saw you, and about an hour ago up to now."

Ignoring her, the demon blew the char from his burned knuckles to show new skin beneath. Head cocked, he looked at Daniel. "What is your name, little man?"

"Dr. Daniel Plank," Daniel said, peeved as he realized he'd been living in a world of magic his entire life, blind to it. Somehow, that made him angry.

"Don't," Trisk warned, but it was too late, and the demon beamed a great smile.

"She told you to be quiet," Quen warned, coming close to enforce his demand, and Daniel stood. That is, until Quen put a hand on his shoulder and shoved him back down again.

"No middle name, Dr. Daniel Plank?" the demon crooned, and Daniel's gaze dropped to the tiny bells chiming softly, sewn into the hem of his open, baggy vest. "Well, since you freely give me yours, I invite you to call me Gally," the demon said. "Though that's not my name. Call my real name, and I'll come kill you. Then kill everyone with you. Understand?"

Daniel nodded vigorously and Gally laughed. "I like you, Dr. Daniel Plank," he said, sitting down on a marvelously carved one-legged stool that materialized under him as he sat. "And just so you know, that's not a good thing."

Head cocked, Gally turned to Trisk. "And what will you give me for such a curse?" he said, eyeing her from over his blue-tinted glasses. "Your soul?"

Trisk waved Quen to silence. "A memory curse isn't worth that much."

"It is if you want it bad enough." Gally sighed dramatically. "If I don't give it to you, Dr. Daniel Plank dies, yes? And you will have to kill him yourself. Nasty work that. Killing someone you respect. Someone you would *die* for."

Pale, Trisk took a tiny step forward. "Showing me how to work the forget curse will make me a more valuable familiar. That should be worth something."

"A ghost's fart, maybe," Gally said, seemingly disappointed she'd suggested it. "I'm not in the habit of giving away anything, but we haven't known each other long. Still on our honeymoon, so to say." Gally made a show of thinking it over, but Daniel knew the demon was more interested in watching Quen fidget than in arriving at a price.

"How is your plot against Trenton Lee Kalamack going?" the demon said, the tiny bells on his hem ringing. "Badly? Is that why your . . . friend is here, your plans being overheard by clever, sneaky humans? I can get your name on your research, guaranteed. You should kill Dr. Daniel Plank and skip right to the good stuff of ensuring your species remains extant."

"Banish him," Quen said, clearly upset. "He's wasting our time."

"Hold up," Daniel said, trying to stand again, only to be shoved back down.

"I'm *not* killing Daniel," Trisk said, flushed. "And besides, if Daniel goes missing, Kal will know something is wrong."

"None of this matters if you agree to take my counsel," Gally said, posing dramatically. "Even your elven enclave is reluctant to allow a woman to succeed where a man has failed. Deplorable, really. *Our* only female demon is insane, but we still respect her."

Enclave, Daniel thought, rolling the word around in his mind. Trisk had used it, too. They were organized. *And going extinct?* he mused.

"Such a *noble* task you have before you," Gally continued, the lilt of his voice making it sound like a petty goal. "Let me help. Take a roll with Trenton Lee Kalamack. He's young. He'll go blind to everything if you involve his genitalia. No-o-o-o-o?" Gally drawled, and she turned her back on him. "Can't blame me for trying. Ta!"

"Wait!" Trisk blurted, and Gally's smile widened to make Daniel shudder as the demon confidently took an engraved box from the folds of his clothes. Opening it, he sniffed a pinch of something white, shuddering in what looked like pleasure before offering it to Quen, then Daniel. "All I want is a forget curse," Trisk said, flushed.

"My idea is better," the demon said. "Faster," he added, looking over his blue glasses at Daniel. "Fool-l-l-l-l-proof," he drawled.

"Forget spell only," Trisk said, breathless.

"It's a curse, not a spell," Gally said softly, and Daniel stifled a shiver at the heavy promise in the demon's voice. "And *you* will be the one carrying the smut for it, not me. And that's even providing we can come to some understanding."

Trisk straightened her shoulders. "Well?"

"This is going nowhere. Banish him," Quen demanded, and Gally stood, the stool vanishing as the bells on his hem chimed a warning.

"She won't banish me," Gally said, his goat-slitted red eyes glinting in anticipation. "She's going to give me everything I want. And it won't be long till she comes back for more."

Trisk stared at him, her pulse visibly pounding at her neck. "I want a fair price, or I'll send you away. Right now."

For three heartbeats, Gally seemed to weigh her need against her shaky confidence. "I give you a forget curse." He held up a finger. "If only to keep this little triangle of lies and anguish going," he added, and Trisk's brow furrowed. "But in return, I want a taste of the source of your power. Your donor virus."

"So you can sell it to Kal?" Quen said. "No."

Gally laughed at Quen, and the man flushed, angry. "No, dark buck. I wouldn't give it to him even if I had a discourse with Trenton Lee Kalamack and he asked for it. It's needful. If I'm to ensure that her name be attached to her research, I have to know what it is."

"But I'm not asking you to ensure my name is attached to my research," Trisk said. "I'm asking you to modify Daniel's memories. I can do the rest myself."

This is so unfair, Daniel thought, not liking that his world was spinning out of his control and that he was going to forget everything if Trisk got her way—or fight for his life if she didn't.

"I still say you should simply follow my advice." Gally leaned forward, jerking back in annoyance when his beard began to smolder. "Nevertheless, give me the price I ask, or I walk away and not only do you lose credit for your work when Kalamack nixes the patent transfer, but he will know you tried to play him and failed when your human talks."

"I won't say anything," Daniel said, ignored.

"I don't have it with me," Trisk whispered.

The demon's lips cracked into a wide, satisfied smile. "Not an issue," he said almost purred. "You can wear my mark until you satisfy our bargain, Felecia Eloytrisk Cambri. I have made it my goal in life to see that your name gets placed upon your great work. If it does not, you will owe me nothing."

"Trisk, don't," Quen demanded. "You'll have to summon him again to fulfill your promise. Even the professors at school knew better than to bargain with a demon."

Her lips pressed together in annoyance, and she looked across the barn at him. "They would if they had a summoning name," she said. "I know what I'm doing."

"Said every demon summoner ever," Gally mocked, his hands laced expectantly.

Daniel glanced at the barn's door, then at Quen behind him. He wouldn't forget. He would remember. And then, when Trisk calmed down and Quen was gone, he'd tell her, and they could live their lives with him knowing the truth.

"No, you won't, Dr. Daniel Plank," Gally said as if reading his mind, shocking Daniel to a heart-thudding silence. "So yes or no?" Gally asked Trisk. "Don't be tiresome. You called me."

"I'll wear your mark," Trisk whispered, and Daniel blanched at the quiver of excitement that rippled the demon's image. "You will curse Daniel into forgetting, and you will take your mark off immediately when I give you a sample of my work. Agreed?"

"Agreed." Knuckles cracking in anticipation, Gally looked at Daniel. "*Ut sementem feceris*," he intoned, his hand moving in what looked like sign language.

Quen jumped, backing up from Daniel with an almost comical haste. Daniel would have laughed, but the two elves and the demon were all watching him with expectant expressions. *I still remember.*

But then Trisk gasped, her face suddenly white. "Oh God," she moaned, dropping to a knee.

Daniel lurched forward, kneeling beside her and gripping her shoulder as Quen spun to the demon. "What did you do to her?" Quen demanded.

Trisk was cold under his hand, her breath shallow as she fought something Daniel couldn't see. "Trisk?" he whispered, and she shook her head, hiding her eyes.

"It's the smut," Gally said, explaining nothing. "I wanted to be sure she could handle it before I actually did the curse." Gally idly tugged at his vest to make the bells on it ring. "Very good, Trisk. You'll make a fine familiar when the time comes."

"It's okay," Trisk rasped, her eyes wide in pain when she looked up. "I can do this," she added, her attention going to Daniel's hand on her shoulder. "It's the payment for putting reality out of balance," she added, confusing Daniel more. "It's more than I expected." Her eyes rose to Gally. "I didn't know you could do that. Shift the smut from one to another."

"Of course we can, silly elf," Gally said imperiously. "That's what a familiar is for." Then he smiled, seeing the glint of awareness behind her horror. "You saw how I did it, didn't you," he accused, and she flushed. "Learning at my knee already? What a *splendid* familiar you will be."

"I'll take the smut for Plank's curse," Quen said suddenly, and Daniel stood.

"It's my curse. I'll take it," Daniel said, and Gally burst out laughing. Quen looked at Daniel as if he was a fool, and he flushed. *It's my curse, I'll take it* echoed in his thoughts, making him feel like an idiot.

"The bitch has it, and will keep it," Gally said, wiping tears from under his blue-smoked glasses. "Chivalry is not dead, but as usual, you have misplaced it." Still chuckling, he wiped his glasses clean and set them again on his nose. "Ahhh, men are morons."

"Where is it?" Trisk asked, looking at her hands, then shoving her sleeves up to see what she could of her arms. "Where did you put your mark?"

Gally simpered at her. "The bottom of your foot," he said, and Daniel could tell it was all she could do not to look right this moment. "I'd advise you to get Dr. Daniel Plank back in his bed before he wakes or the curse will be in danger of being picked apart. If not handled correctly, even *my* memory curses are susceptible to corruption, and after two thousand years of cursing Newt, I've gotten to be quite good at them."

Daniel's shoulders tensed. He didn't want to forget, and he looked at the door, knowing he'd never make it.

"Giving away information for free?" Quen mocked, and Gally's gaze flicked up and back down.

"Oh, it's not free." Gally watched him over his glasses. "She's a third of the way to being mine, and I take care of those who are mine. It's in my best interests. Is it not, little bird?"

The demon turned his attention to Daniel, and he paled. "I won't tell anyone," Daniel said, backing away. "Trisk, I promise. Please. Don't. I want to help you. Let me help."

She took his hands, the pain in her obvious. "I'm sorry," she said, her eyes spilling over. "Daniel, I'm so sorry."

"Oh my God. I think I'm going to puke," Gally moaned. "*Obscurum per obscurius!*"

"No!" Daniel exclaimed, sucking in his breath as the demon's voice seemed to shift from a sound to a feeling, coating him in a muzzy black blanket that tangled and weaved through his thoughts. *No!* he silently raged, feeling his body shut down and the ground rush up.

Daniel hit the floor with a shocking thud, the curse a split second behind. He could feel it slither over his skin, and slowly it began soaking in like black fire. He fought it, but the more he struggled, the more he opened himself to its touch, and eventually he forgot what he was fighting . . . and finally, he slept.

13

Kal wove through Global Genetics' parking lot, his Mustang easing into one of the back spots where the pine trees wouldn't drop needles or sap on it. The top was down as usual, and the wind making his hair bump around his ears had a decidedly damp feel for so early in the morning. Putting the car in park, he looked past the sprawling white building to the horizon. It was dark with clouds, and he paused, trying to decide if it was worth putting the top up now. If he didn't, he'd risk not being able to find Trisk's assistant and having to run out and close it himself if it should rain.

Sighing, he fell on the side of prudence, and after making sure the windows were down he found the right button and pushed it. Pleased, he sat where he was as the state-of-the-art car put its own top up. Things were progressing well. After yesterday's fallout at the TV station, Daniel was disenchanted and Trisk was his to sway. He might be home as early as next month.

His smile still held the pleasure of that as he glanced at the orange-and-gold orchid flower on the seat beside him. He'd harvested it this morning from his tissue-grafted stock to give to Trisk. Women liked flowers, and

Trisk would appreciate that this one was unique in all the world, oblivious to the fact that his attraction to her was as fabricated and engineered as the blossom itself.

"Kal!" someone called, and he looked to see Rick waiting for him on the walk. The living vampire pretending to be a British rock star with his tight suits and long wavy hair gave him the creeps, but Kal could always pin him in a circle if he got blood-amorous.

Still in the car, Kal gave him a wave before putting up the windows. Grabbing his hat and the orchid bloom, he got out, moving slowly in the hopes that Rick would just go in. Eyes on the line the white building cut against the dark clouds, Kal buttoned his suit coat and adjusted his tie. He couldn't wait until this would be done and the funding for Trisk's dangerous virus would be reappropriated into his safer theories and he could get to work on what truly mattered. Trisk would be cleaning his flasks and autoclaving petri dishes in a week, her techniques useful in moving his own research forward.

"Morning, Rick," he said, his pace slow as he tucked the flower into his lapel and wove between the cars. "How was lunch with Heather?"

The tall man hesitated, clearly searching his thoughts for her. "Ah, fine." Kal could almost see him dismiss the memory of her. "Do you have time this morning for a meeting?"

"Sure. What's up?" Kal smiled, but his expression stiffened at the barest clatter of pixy wings. *Orchid?* He'd sent her to watch Trisk, wanting to be sure the woman hadn't hidden any of her work at home. The pixy waiting for him in the parking lot didn't bode well.

Rick rocked forward, then back. "Wolfe wants to try out Daniel's virus in Vietnam, and we've got some number-crunching to do. Amounts of, dispersal of, that kind of thing. I don't have a clue if what Dr. Plank is telling me is right or not. I could use your input." He smiled a toothy smile. "A courtesy to the visiting doctor."

Kal slowed to a stop, a row of cars yet between him and Rick. "I'd love to. Why don't you go on ahead. My shoe unlaced, and I think I left my back windows down. It looks like rain."

"Will do," Rick said as he began to walk away. "Doughnuts. My office. Ten minutes."

"Be right there." Jaw clenched, Kal dropped down between the cars, hoping Rick didn't see him pull his lace free before he made a show of tying it up. "Orchid . . ." he whispered, relief spilling through him when the tiny woman flitted to him from under the cars. She was fine, her dust a little thin with hunger, but fine.

"Kal, she's got a demon!" the pixy said, her eyes so wide he could tell they were green.

"I know," he said, shifting so she could alight on his knee. "That's what that ring of fat is on my office ceiling." He didn't like that Trisk had not only found a demon name, but had the courage to summon one. By the looks of it, she'd almost been snagged. "Jeez, Orchid. Get under my hat before someone sees you. Are you hungry? I've got crackers in my desk."

But Orchid didn't move from his knee, her dust shifting suddenly to a bright red. "She's playing you for a fool," she said, wings blurring. "I heard them talking. She and some elf named Quen made her demon curse Daniel into not remembering what they said, but they didn't see me."

"Daniel?" he asked, then froze. *Quen is here?*

Alarm coursed through him, washing to a tiny pit in

his middle. Feeling like a ghost, he stood and scanned the outskirts of the parking lot as if the man was lurking in the trees.

"She doesn't like you," Orchid said, hovering in the shelter of the cars. "She likes Quen, even if she doesn't know it yet. Daniel overheard them talking, they broke the silence, and they made him forget so they wouldn't have to kill him. Kal, she's only pretending to like you until you sign off on her tomato patent. She's not going to go to NASA with you. Ever. You have to do something or you'll never be able to prove her theories are unsafe. Never ever."

He looked down at Orchid's last, plaintive words, and he knelt again, his shocked alarm shifting to an enduring anger. Quen was here. Daniel must have seen something bad if they had to ask a demon for a forget curse. *I wonder what a curse like that costs*, he thought as he took off his hat, wanting to ask Trisk if she had bought the demon's favors outright or if the demon had left a mark on her as a promise of payment. And would she lie if he saw it and asked what it was?

"Under the hat, Orchid," he said, and the pixy pouted as she obediently flitted to nestle in his hair. "We have to find you something to eat first."

He rose, feeling unreal and wanting to crush the flower he'd brought Trisk. He'd been convinced she was infatuated with him. She acted like every other woman he'd pursued and bedded. *Perhaps they've all used me*, he thought, anger tightening his chest. The bitches trying to find their way into the Kalamack family through his bed. Back stiff, he strode forward.

"She thinks you're trying to steal her work," Orchid said, her tiny whisper clear as she huddled under his hat. "Not prove how dangerous it is."

"The end result is the same, though, isn't it," he muttered, liking the new idea.

"Uh, Kal? Your aura is kind of nasty," Orchid said, and Kal hesitated in his reach for the door to the imposing building. He hadn't known pixies could see auras.

Exhaling, he calmed himself. He could keep the game alive. See how far she'd go. No one played him. No one. "Better?"

"Better," Orchid said, and he pulled the glass door open, his skin crawling in the ozone-scented air that leaked up from the lower floors where the computers lurked. His fake smile turned real—if somewhat mocking—as he saw Trisk and Daniel in the expansive lobby, arguing beside the elevators. At least Daniel was arguing. Trisk looked unusually awkward and submissive as she slowly rock-stepped away from him, trying to escape.

Curious, he drew upon his second sight and their auras wavered into existence. Daniel, he mused, had a bright gold aura, rare for a human, but Trisk's was a pale green, streaked with gold and black. She'd been summoning. Not only that, but she'd taken payment for something.

He dropped his second sight, steps slowing as he tried to piece it together. Forget curses were unreliable, even demon-crafted ones. If Daniel had seen something that broke the silence in a real way, she'd have to leave or risk eventually triggering his memory. A smile, wicked and devious, curved his lips up as a feeling of power dove to his groin. She had to leave Global Genetics to preserve the curse. If her tomato failed— and he'd make sure it would—Trisk's potential funding would shift to his work instead of her fast, chancy theories that had fallen short once already. He would save their species; Trisk would have nothing. No career, no prospects. Nothing. He had won.

"Alone?" Daniel said, one hand in his pocket, the other absently patting his lab coat to find his glasses in a front breast pocket. "You really expect me to believe that?"

Trisk's eyes were averted from Daniel. She hadn't seen Kal yet, either, his steps soft on the marble floor. He felt as if he were dancing. *How dare she try to con me.* He would hurt her, and hurt her bad. "I don't care if you believe it or not," she said. "Daniel, I have to go."

"I'm not blind, or a fool," Daniel said, his voice hushed but intent as he pointed his glasses at her. "If you leave with Kal, he will use you!"

She took another step back, her eyes pinched with heartache. "I have to go. Daniel, I'm sorry." But she froze when her attention flicked past Daniel and found Kal. Slowly she lost her hunch, shoulders dropping as the mask fell back into place.

Excitement spilled through him at the lost look she hid. She was his. "Daniel!" he called out, pretending ignorance. "Congratulations! Rick asked me to come up and help you calculate a drop. How exciting for you."

Trisk's brow smoothed as she made room for him before the elevator, her smile looking real as she adjusted Kal's tie. *How far, little whore, will you go in your lies?* "Morning, Trisk," he said, breathing deep to look for the scent of Quen on her. There was nothing but the tang of cinnamon and wine, another tell that she'd been spelling. "Have a nice night?"

"A little stressful, but okay," she said softly. "I have to talk to you. Do you have a sec?"

"Rick asked me to come up, but sure." She had a demon mark on her somewhere. He could sense a shadow of smut in her aura. *My little demon summoner. What did Daniel see?*

Daniel jabbed the call button again, his jaw clenched and his neck red.

"Mmmm. I wanted to ask you if you liked that wine we had at lunch yesterday," Kal said, smoothly taking the orchid from his lapel and handing it to her. "Bergen says he can get us a case for half price if we want it."

"Ooooh, that would be nice," she said as the elevator opened and Daniel took two steps into it, extending a long arm to hold the door for them. "But do you think we can get through an entire case before we leave?" she asked, waiting until Kal rocked forward and they entered the elevator together. "The last thing I need is more stuff to move."

Her hand was cold, and he brought her fingers to his lips and gave them a kiss, thrilling when, for the first time, she didn't pull away. "Maybe I can convince him to sell us half a crate," he said as the doors shut. "I told Rick I'd help Daniel prep his drop. It might take two weeks." He turned to Daniel. "How much mother virus do you think you'll need to expend?"

"Enough," Daniel said, and Trisk's head dropped, a slim finger tracing the outlines of the orchid he'd given her. "It grows fast in the lab. Unless they want to infect the entire city, we can have whatever we need by Friday."

"Half a case it is." Kal beamed, confidence buoying him up.

The doors opened, and Daniel held them, waiting for Trisk to get out first.

"I'm on my way down to talk to Angie, actually," Trisk said as she hit a lower button. "I only rode up to talk to Kal."

"I have to go down to the labs to get something for the meeting," Kal said, hitting a second button. Orchid was hungry. She came first. "Tell Rick I'll be right there."

Daniel stepped out, motions stiff. "Will do. I'll see you in a few, then."

Kal watched the pain cross Trisk's face as Daniel turned and paced quickly down the white and glass hall. She liked him, liked him enough to sell a part of her soul to keep him alive when he saw something he shouldn't, and now she was forced to leave lest she trigger it back into his memory. *What did he see, Trisk? Did you do something you shouldn't have?*

As if pulled by his thoughts, she turned to him, the pain hidden. "Thanks for the flower," she said, eyes fixed on it. "It's beautiful."

"You're welcome." The lift slowly descended, and his thoughts spun. She was hurting and vulnerable, unable to stay and forced to make good on her promise to go to Kennedy with her research. He'd make sure she got there with no credibility. All that funding would go to him and his safer, more viable research.

It's going to be an interesting end to the week, he thought, glancing at the numbers counting down. "Trisk," he said suddenly, taking her cold hands in his, "I can tell you're unhappy." He shook his head for her to be quiet when she took a breath to protest. "It must be hard to leave," he insisted, giving her fingers a squeeze. "You've made a place for yourself. You're respected. Your voice is heard. But I'm giving you the chance to push your research into the fast track. You can make a real difference. I promise," he said, almost believing the lie himself. "Just give it a chance, okay?"

Her head dropped, but she was nodding, and he let go when the elevator chimed and the doors slid open onto the ground floor again. "I want this to work," she said softly, and his breath caught. *Gullible to the end.*

"That's my girl," he said as she left the elevator, her shoes clicking. "Do you mind if I cancel on you for lunch? I have something special planned tonight. Just you and me."

Trisk lingered before the elevator, but he could see the lie in her tentative smile. "Sure," she said, hands clasped before her middle. "I'll see you later today, though, right?"

"It would be hard not to," he said. "Right after Rick's meeting. How do you get out of them?" he asked, shaking his head in mock dismay.

"It's in my contract. Bring me a doughnut?" Trisk said loudly as the doors began to shut.

"You got it!" Kal shot back. The doors closed, and he lost his smile.

"Thanks for taking me downstairs," Orchid said meekly from under his hat. "I'm starved, and it takes me forever to get there through the ductwork."

Kal loathed doughnuts, and he put his hands into his pockets and rocked back and forth. "She'll be at least ten minutes, knowing Angie," he said, adrenaline a slow burn as he felt the pinch of time. "You could forage in the field. That's better than crackers."

"Thanks." Orchid sounded subdued. "What are you going to do? Your aura is ugly again."

Kal's eye twitched as the door opened onto the flat white of the lower floors. "Something I should've done last week." He affected his usual pace as he walked to his and Trisk's twin offices. The thought kept surfacing: Had Trisk and Quen had sex? She and Daniel clearly hadn't, and he wondered just how far Trisk would play this game of girlfriend in her desire to salvage her career. The need to make her feel ugly was growing. She would feel shame. No—she would feel used when she found out he had known all along.

"Hi, George," Kal said lightly, and George absently waved him through, bent close over the hissing and popping radio, the connection weak at best down here as it faded in and out of the two-chord, long-running, psychedelic sounds of "Season of the Witch."

Kal's fingers punching in the code for his office were light, but his good mood faltered when his eyes were drawn to the ceiling as the lights flicked on. The smear of fat was still up there, a constant reminder that the woman had borrowed teeth—should she be willing to pay the price. And clearly, she was.

Must be careful. Sitting down in the rolling chair, he carefully took off his hat, tossing it to the nearby empty console.

"Thanks, Kal," Orchid said as she flew a subdued path to the entry pad and used her feet to punch in the code that opened the door to the subterranean green-house.

Kal absently waved his acknowledgment, glancing up only briefly at the flush of earth-tainted air. Her dust trail quickly vanished between the rows of waving green, and he turned to the terminal. Fingers fast on the keyboard, he brought up Trisk's tomato, asking the computer to do a search for a sequence that was commonly used as a marker for engineered linkage points.

His brow furrowed as he waited, imagining the spinning wheels and disks down below his feet, evidence of his coming betrayal, but his tension vanished when three sets of entry points into the tomato's genome flickered in yellow type before him. Trisk had put them among the genes responsible for the drought-resistant hairs. It wasn't in an area that would invite plant/human crossover, and he smiled. He could use this. In her effort to leave a way to tweak her creation, Trisk had all but invited tampering, made it easy.

But who would ever dream that the glittering science of the sixties, wonders that were meant to save the world and make life easy, could ever turn upon their creators?

Kal's attention flicked up as Orchid came back in, her dust thicker and brighter. Clearly she had been suffering, and he felt better that he'd been able to help her without tarnishing her pride. "Better?" he asked as she alighted on the console.

"Very much. Thank you," the little woman said primly, still eating from a ball of pollen she'd gathered. "I swear, parking lots are a study of why my people can't live near humans."

"Yes?" he said as he pushed his chair to the adjacent terminal. He needed a look at Daniel's virus. Fortunately Rick had given him the access codes for that as well.

"In two words, monospecies gardens." Orchid moved with him, bringing the acidic scent of tomatoes along with her. Trisk's tomato field was visible through her fitfully moving wings. "Grass and pine trees, pine trees and grass. And if the pine trees aren't pollinating, there's nothing to eat." Standing atop the console, she gazed down at the yellow text. "Whatcha doing?"

"Fixing things," he said distantly, surprised at how hard his voice came out. "Look."

Orchid followed his pointing finger, her tiny face screwing up. "You know I can't read," she accused, and he felt himself flush, embarrassed for forgetting.

"Sorry," he said as he asked the computer to print

out the screen. "These are engineered linkage spots on Daniel's virus. I figured he'd have them if Trisk worked on it. She put three just like them on her tomato in case she ever wanted to tweak it in the future."

Orchid hovered before the monitor, her pooling dust shifting color to match the text on the screen. "Isn't that kind of stupid? To have the same linkage on two things?"

"It would be if they were alike, but they aren't. See?" He pointed to the other screen, where Trisk's code for her tomato still glowed. Leaning to reach the other keyboard, he asked the computer to print out one of the linkage codes on Trisk's tomato as well.

Orchid dusted her hands free of pollen. "I'm not following. What are we trying to do?"

"Break the unbreakable," Kal muttered, and Orchid sighed, her dust shifting red. "Trisk made her tomato resistant to everything," he added. "I'm going to use Daniel's virus to kill it."

Orchid's mouth dropped into a little O of understanding, making Kal smile. "Her entire three years here will be discredited, tainting her work on her universal donor virus. I'll make sure all her funding goes to my studies, where it should have been in the first place."

Wings blurring into motion, Orchid took to the air, spinning to look out the wide window at the green field. "You said they wouldn't match up."

"Not on their own, no. I'm going to need to synthesize a link. A puzzle piece. A tiny piece of code that fits the virus on one end, the tomato on the other." He stood, leaning over the console to erase his actions. "QED."

"You can do that?" Orchid asked, still at the window. "How long will it take?"

Finished clearing the one terminal, Kal moved to the other. "If I were in my old lab, by lunch. Here, it might take a few days." He hesitated, his thoughts on his earlier plans of seducing Trisk into his bed. He was not letting go of that. "If I work through lunch, I might have enough by tomorrow to infect the cultures they're going to synthesize this week. They'd be incorporated right into the tactical virus's replicating DNA."

"And it will kill all her tomatoes?" Orchid asked. "What about everyone else?"

Unsure, Kal clicked his pen in rapid succession and tucked it behind an ear. It rubbed on the scar tissue where his ears had been docked to look more human, and he took it out. When his work was finished, he'd be able to change the elves' genetic code so they were born without the need to cut their children. "It can't kill people, Orchid. It can't even replicate outside of a lab. The only thing it can affect is the tomatoes." If he was lucky, it would decimate Trisk's entire crop from pole to pole, but he wasn't going to tell Orchid that. She liked growing things too much.

"But the enclave sent you to make sure it's safe," the pixy protested. "You have a responsibility—"

"Responsibility?" he interrupted, surprised Orchid even cared. "Trisk's work is dangerous. If no one can see that, it's my *responsibility* to put an end to it before it hurts anyone," he said, voice harsh. "Tell you what," he added when her wings drooped. "That's her seed crop out there. What if I infect that, and nothing else?"

"I suppose," she said reluctantly, and Kal smiled, thinking it would shorten his time in the lab as well. He straightened, his stretch to crack his back coming to an abrupt halt as his fingers closed into a fist inches from the smear on the ceiling. Sobered, he looked over the office, ready to pick up his copies at the printer and settle into a lab down the hall. If he were at Kennedy, his part would be done, but spending the day prepping strands of DNA was a small price to pay for seeing Trisk's helpless rage when her work was utterly disregarded.

"Coming?" he said as he scooped up his hat. "I have to hustle to get everything done for tonight."

Orchid turned from the window, her hands clasped at her middle. "You're still going to seduce her?" she said, her eyes becoming wide. "I thought you didn't like her."

"I don't." Kal's lips went tight in a mirthless smile. "She's playing me for a fool. I'm going to play her right back."

"Yeah, but Kal," Orchid protested, her wings a harsh clatter as she hovered right before his face, "you're talking about hurting her now, not just her work."

"That's right," he said, looking forward to playing the attentive boyfriend for as long as it was necessary. The payoff would be seeing her frustrated and angry, knowing she'd been used and discarded.

"But why?" Orchid asked, her wondering expression sending a stab of quickly stifled guilt through him. "You're going to get what you want with her tomatoes dead. Her work will be discredited. Yours will flourish."

The guilt rose again, swelling at the memory of Trisk's laugh at a shared joke, the way she had softened toward him over the last few weeks, how he liked knowing she was in the office next to his if he needed a second opinion—and how that opinion was actually worth something.

Then he quashed it with the thought that Trisk was lying to him, pretending to be his girlfriend to further

her career. She deserved it. *Those who live by the lie die by the lie.* "It all works together, Orchid. All or nothing. Now are you coming?"

Orchid's expression twisted into an unsatisfied frown. Seeing it, Kal mockingly doffed his hat in invitation. Her dust an odd shade of purple and green, Orchid flew to him, making a tiny huff before landing amid his fair strands.

But she *was* atop his head. Mood improved, he gently settled his hat over her. His eyes flicked to the ceiling one last time, and then he shut off the light, leaving the small room lit only by the glow of the underground field, green and waving in its artificial wind. Three days it would take to see if his "fix" was going to be effective.

Plenty of time to see how far Trisk would go.

14

The warm air was eminently pleasant, streaming through Trisk's long, unbound hair as she sat beside Kal in his Mustang convertible, top down to let the night flow over them. They wove through her twenty-five acres of tiny trees as if on ice, the motion smooth and unhurried, and she closed her eyes, surprised at how the ache of misunderstanding Daniel had left in her had been soothed by Kal's new stretch of silence.

Dinner had been casual despite Kal showing up on her porch in a suit and tie, his recently gained field tan and blond hair making him look as if he should be on a surfboard, not behind a lab bench. Even she had to admit they looked good together, with her in her new short dress and matching yellow knee-high boots. She wore Quen's helix necklace for strength, telling Kal her dad had given it to her when he remarked on it.

Kal had been attentive all evening, slowly pulling her from her funk. The waiters had fawned over them, and she'd caught Kal looking at her bare thigh more than once. It had gone a long way in helping her forget Daniel's angry frustration at realizing that not only was the world larger than he had known—but he wasn't allowed to participate. It bothered her. A lot.

Quen, currently lying low on the other side of town, hadn't been happy when she'd told him she wasn't going to break her date with Kal, and really, what choice did she have? Perhaps moving to Florida and working with stuck-up, chauvinistic pigs was a fitting punishment.

God, my feet hurt, she thought as the headlights bounced over her long, low-slung home and then the barn. The boots were new, and they pinched. She looked at Kal, a smile threatening when he jerked his eyes from her legs again. "Thanks for tonight," she said as she played with the metal helix around her neck, surprised to find she meant it. "I had a great time."

"You're welcome." The car came to a quiet halt between the barn and the house. "But it's not over yet," he said as he turned it off. "I've got a surprise for you."

Trisk dropped her necklace, her eyebrows rising as she followed his gaze. "In the barn?"

But Kal had already gotten out, his slim silhouette sharp in the car's headlights as he jogged around the front of the car to get her door. "Dessert is served, Dr. Cambri," he said with a flourish. "Jell-O made with champagne. You'll love it."

Her suspicions vanished in a wash of amusement and she grabbed her purse and got out. "You're kidding. You made Jell-O?"

Kal grinned, his expression almost lost in the dim light. "Uh, actually my cleaning lady did. She put pineapple in it, but you can eat around it if you want."

He took her arm as if they were heading into a four-star restaurant, not wobbling over the dried ruts to the rolling door. "I love pineapple," she said, head down to watch her step. "But why are we eating it in my barn?"

And then Kal shoved the rattling door open.

Trisk stopped, lips parted. It was dark inside, but she could see the cloth-covered bales of straw making a rude table and chairs in the middle of the floor where she'd summoned a demon. Hanging over them was her unlit lantern, and set to the side was one of the coolers from the lab used to carry temperature-sensitive samples off-site. A radio sat on it, and a bottle opener.

"When did you do this?" she said, not sure if she should be flattered or creeped out.

Still smiling, Kal escorted her in. "This afternoon after lunch. I was scared to death you'd come out here after work and see it before our date." His hold on her slipped away as he paced quickly to the make-shift table, his excitement infectious. "Music . . ." he said as he clicked the radio on, then winced as "I Got You Babe" drifted out. He straightened, clearly not happy as he turned to her. "Sorry. I can only get one station."

She came in a few steps, gingerly sitting down on the white-and-red-checkered cloth covering a bale of straw. "That's okay. I like Sonny and Cher," she said as she put her purse down. It didn't seem possible that she'd been here less than twenty-four hours ago summoning a demon, and she breathed deeply, testing the air for any sign of burnt amber. There was none, and her shoulders eased. Her trickery was hidden. Daniel was safe. *So why do I feel so crappy?*

"Ambiance . . ." Kal murmured, and Trisk jumped, startled when he flicked a tiny, aura-coated bit of energy at the dark lantern and it ignited with a whoosh.

"Impressive," she said, smiling at his obvious satisfaction. "I didn't know you could do anything other than break chandeliers and give bad luck to nasty, ornery witches."

Chuckling, he shot her a glance from under a lowered brow as he moved the radio to the edge of the straw table and flipped the lid up on the cooler. "You might be surprised what I can do," he said softly, almost a challenge as he lifted a mold of yellow gelatin from inside the box. "We have music," he said as he set it square in the middle of the makeshift table. "Jell-O with fruit . . ." He looked up at her, the question at the back of his eyes confusing her. "Would you like white wine or cognac? I brought both."

"Wine is fine," she said, still feeling the effects of the glass of red she'd had with dinner. The moon was low in the sky, visible through the open barn door. Not quite full, it was still beautiful, and her mood softened. *Quen loves a full moon.*

"White wine it is." Kal opened it with a pop, setting it aside as he produced two blue-and-white plates and silverware.

"I'll do it," she offered when he hesitated, probably never having served anything in his life, but he took up the serving spoon before she could reach it.

"My party," he quipped, and she sat back, the straw crackling under her as she put her elbows on her knees and felt useless. Her hair drifted forward around her face, and she brushed it back, not embarrassed about its color, but maybe . . . trying to diminish its presence.

The silence stretched, broken by the sudden clinks of the silverware as Kal fought the jiggling concoction. Her feet still hurt, and she ran a finger between her boot and leg. She was loath to risk Kal seeing her demon mark on the underside of her foot, but the raised welt in the shape of a circle with a line running through it was only the size of a quarter. She hadn't thought the demon would be so circumspect, but it still bothered her. "Do you mind if I take my boots off? My feet are killing me," she asked, and he looked up, his ears a faint pink of embarrassment at his inept attempts to serve the Jell-O.

"Go ahead," he said, finally managing to get an untidy slice on a plate.

His lack of polish made her smile. That he was sneaking glances at her legs as she took her boots off made her feel desired. The blanket he'd put down as a rug was surprisingly soft, and she stretched her toes, distracted as Kal set a plate before her.

"It's kind of wiggly, isn't it," he said as he took his suit coat off, carefully laying it aside before sitting down across from her. On the radio, the music shifted to "Mustang Sally," and Trisk smiled at his pained expression as he stared at the crackling speaker.

"It's fine, really," she said when he reached to turn it off, and he sat back, things clearly not going the way he wanted them to. "Mmmm, good," she added as she took a spoonful, finding it had indeed been made with champagne, little bubbles bursting in her mouth.

"Nothing but the best," he said, relieved. "I love stables. The only thing that could improve this more than better music would be an actual horse in here."

Trisk poked through the Jell-O for the fruit, wondering at the hint of wistfulness in his voice. "That's one of the reasons I bought it," she said, glancing over the dusty box stalls and empty tack pegs. "But I don't get enough free time these days to have a cat, much less a horse."

Kal reached for the wine, the shadow of his arm showing through his white shirt as he poured it out and handed her a half-full glass before dropping the bottle back into the cooler. "There's a stable within a ten-minute drive from my house in Florida," he hinted.

"That sounds nice," she murmured, wondering where this was going.

"It is." He took a sip and set his glass aside, eyes roving over the barn as if he were seeing it alive with the scents of horse and leather. "Believe it or not, some of my happiest hours were in the stables."

Trisk kept her eyes on her plate, suddenly uneasy. They had talked all night, but it was all surface. This felt close. Personal. "No kidding," she finally said. "I wouldn't have pegged you as an equestrian."

"Mmmm." Kal shifted, the straw under him sliding in a familiar hush. "My first horse stood only this high," he said, a bemused smile on his face as he held a hand out. "I was four. She was a real horse, not a pony, and I named her Cinnamon, because that's what color she was. I should have named her Ginger, because she had a snap that could come from nowhere."

Trisk laughed. "You sure she wasn't a pony?" Her smile faded. She liked this side of Kal, and she wondered if it had been there all the time, hidden under peer pressure. *School politics sucked.* She went quiet, remembering.

"There's something amazing about a good horse," Kal said, either oblivious to her mood or trying to shake her from it. "You both have the same need to run, and this massive, powerful animal is willing to take you to the horizon, jumping fences and logs as if you could fly."

She looked up, surprised, and he poked at his Jell-O as if embarrassed. "One with the horse, my mother would say," he muttered, eyes down. "Both my parents ride. They host a Hunt every year for the winter solstice."

His eyes had gone distant in memory, and Trisk

tucked her hair back and leaned forward. She'd heard there were a few families that still ran the Hunt, but it was harder every year with the population of humans growing larger. "A real Hunt?" she asked, and he finally looked up. "With hounds and a fox?"

He nodded, oddly silent. "Most times," he finally said. "We hunted a wolf once. It got away after mauling a handful of hounds. Every year my parents invite different people, but there's a core that doesn't change. Extended family, almost." He leaned back, glass in his hand. "They come from all over the world. If Christmas and a business meeting had a baby, that's the Hunt. People stay the entire week. I remember one year when the moon was full and the skies clear." He took a sip, gaze vacant. "Honestly, I could have ridden forever, hounds or not."

Trisk was silent, watching the memory ease his shoulders and soften his face. He was almost a different person. In her entire school career, she had exchanged perhaps no more than a hundred words with him. Why was he so different now?

"Do you ride?" he asked suddenly, jerking her back to the present.

"Sure." Head down, she wiggled a pineapple chunk free. "I got a horse for my fourteenth birthday," she said. "She was an old mare no one wanted, but she was mine. Before that, it was whatever was available at the stables, and trust me, no one offered me the easy horse."

She looked up, faltering at his wide-eyed expression. "I never had a favorite. I mean," she said to try to cover up her bitterness. "I like horses, but to be totally one with one?" She shrugged. "It never happened," she lied. It had happened. It had happened a lot, but with many horses, not one special one. They all needed her.

"Oh, that's too bad," Kal said faintly.

"Until I got Ruth, I'd always take out the most cantankerous horse," she said, uncrossing and recrossing her legs. The wind coming in the barn door was pleasant, and the wine had brightened her mood. "The one no one wanted to ride because it would try to brush you off on the trees or roll on you? Every stable has one."

"Why?" Kal asked, and she sipped her wine, thinking it tasted better with the pineapple.

"I felt sorry for them," she said, almost laughing. "Stuck in the barn while all the other horses got to go out with their little blond goddesses. I learned to read them pretty fast, but still, the stable's supervisor thought I was nuts when I kept coming back either without my horse or with scrapes and bruises—or both." Pineapple chunk in hand, she pointed at Kal with her pinkie. "But my *dad*. He told them to give me the horse I wanted. By the time I was twelve, I could ride every single horse in the stables." She slumped, an elbow on a bare knee. "It didn't make me any friends," she whispered. *Except for the horses, that is.*

"That settles it," Kal said, startling her. "You have *got* to come riding with me. Maybe for the Hunt. My parents would love to meet the woman who engineered the fuzzy tomato now feeding the third world."

Trisk froze, the memory of their cold looks, their disdain at presentation filling her as Kal topped off her glass. "I've met your parents," she finally said, and Kal's breath caught.

"Oh. Yes. Right. Sorry," he said, wincing as he rubbed the stubble on his narrow chin. "They didn't make much of a first impression, did they. Presentation is kind of stressful in the best of situations, and I did bust the chandelier." His expression pained, he stared at his wineglass. "They billed my parents. Did you know that? Seeing as the only magic residue was from Quen and myself, and Quen was officially working for my folks." He chuckled. "The charm on it was almost as expensive as my entire schooling."

Head tilted back, he downed his glass. "I don't think I ever hated anyone more than you that day when your dad gave you a hug, and mine gave me derision."

Shocked, Trisk fumbled, finally managing, "Sorry." She'd eaten all her pineapple, but she didn't want to take any more and look greedy. Fidgety, she rocked on the bale of straw as the silence grew, watching the moon through the open door and wondering how she could make a tactful exit. There was a ring around it. A storm was coming.

"I have something I want you to have," Kal said, his soft voice breaking the uncomfortable silence as he stretched for his suit coat and fumbled in a pocket. "I was going to wait—put it on a ribbon or something— but I want to give it to you now."

Trisk felt her expression become slack. "What?" she asked, the wine in her turning sour.

His mood was hard to read as he looked at his closed hand, head low. "This is going to sound weird, but I feel as if I've gotten to know you better in these last couple of weeks than I get to know most women after months. I don't want you to freak out, or think this means more than it does. Just. Here." He held out his hand, palm side down. "This is for you. If you want it. Maybe it will make you feel better about leaving Global Genetics."

Feeling unreal, she put her hand out. *Is he serious?* she thought, then blinked when a key fell into it.

"You can keep it until you want to use it," Kal said,

shifting to sit beside her, hunched and uneasy. "Or never use it. I just want you to feel welcome. That's all."

She looked at the gold key in her palm. The edges felt sharp against her fingers. It had just been cut. She could still smell the oil on it.

"You're not saying anything," Kal blurted. "Oh God. You think I'm a jerk."

She looked up, the vulnerability in his eyes giving her pause. "It's a key," she managed.

"To my house in Florida," he said, taking her free hand. "Damn it, I'm doing this all wrong. Trisk, I got you an interview at Kennedy, and you said yes, and I'm thrilled. But to be honest, I didn't do it just because you're one of the best genetic engineers I've ever had the privilege to work with. I want you to come back with me because I don't want to lose you."

Her pulse was fast, and she couldn't seem to wrap her mind around what he was proposing. "This is to your house?"

He nodded, inching closer. "It's set off the ocean about a mile or so, with a walled garden. It's not twenty-five acres, but it's nice, and like I said, there's a stable ten minutes away. Orchid will probably come back with us if she doesn't find a buck. Or she might bring him with her if she does. I don't know. Damn it, this wasn't supposed to be such a big deal," he said, his features pinched. "I just wanted to let you know you could move in with me if you were comfortable with the idea." He hesitated, his fingers falling from hers. "You want me to take my key back? Maybe I should go."

Trisk closed her fingers over the key. She had gone into this with the intent to hurt him, and though the pain was still there, it was getting harder to justify layering it on him in turn. "No," she said. She didn't know what she wanted to do anymore. *He wants me to move in with him?* she thought. If it had been a ring, she would have kicked him out knowing it was one of his nasty ploys, but this stumbling confession and awkward admission . . . "I'll keep it, if that's okay," she added, not knowing why, except that she was hurting, and this made the hurt less.

His expression was relieved when she glanced up, and she managed a smile.

"Sure. Yes," he said. "God, yes! That's why I wanted you to have it." Kal exhaled, looking at her hand but clearly not sure he had the right to take it. "Wow, that was awkward. I didn't mean for this to be such a big deal. Maybe I should leave."

Trisk touched his hand and pulled back. "Kal, it's fine." On the radio, the music changed to "Deep Purple," April Stevens's sweet voice mingling with Nino Tempo's in an innocent and charming expression of endearment, and Trisk smiled, curving her legs under her, up and off the floor as she tucked his key into her purse.

"It's just the key to my house," he said, as if trying to reassure himself. "Three thousand miles away," he continued, looking at the stables, wine, dessert, and her sitting there with her feet curled up under her on a bale of straw. "Just shoot me now, okay? I didn't mean for this to be so romantic. I simply didn't want to drive away and have the night be over."

She laughed, not wanting him to feel like he'd done anything wrong. "'Deep Purple'?" she said, kidding him. "That's your idea of romance? It might be romantic for my dad. I think it's older than him, for sure."

Kal sat glumly beside her, elbows on his knees as he stared at nothing. "Now you're poking fun at me."

"Am I?" she said, sipping her wine, feeling it ease the pain a little more.

"Come on. Stand up," Kal said suddenly, rising to extend a hand to her. "I'll show you how romantic 'Deep Purple' can be."

"Without shoes?" she said, eyes wide. "Besides, you can't dance to this."

"You can," he insisted. "Come on. Up. It's my party."

"Kal," she protested as he took her hand and pulled her to her feet. His slight build seemed a lot taller without heels, and she tensed, her eyes at his upper chest as he fitted his slim hand in hers and coaxed her into a box shuffle. His body was warm against hers, and she watched his shoes, nervous he might step on her. But he never did, and slowly she began to relax.

"See, I know romance," Kal said defensively, and she looked up, smiling at him.

"Okay," she admitted. "You can dance to it. I'll give you that."

But the music changed to something soulful and soft. Uneasy, she loosened her grip, but Kal tightened his, and her eyes shot to him as their motions slowed but didn't stop. She felt good here, the wine relaxing her, and the feeling of an old hurt being set aside was soothing, even if she would have to pick it back up in the morning. Beyond the open barn door, the moon rose higher, spilling light upon them.

Kal's chest touched hers as she took a deep breath, and she felt him breathe her in. Tentatively, carefully, she let her head fall against his shoulder. *What am I doing?*

"I'm sorry for everything I did to you at school," Kal said, his voice rumbling into her with the soft presence of distant thunder.

"Don't worry about it," she whispered, not looking up as they moved as one.

"It was wrong of me, all the way around. I'm sorry for being such an idiot. And I'm really sorry for spelling your hair white in fifth grade. That was cruel."

She looked up, stifling a shiver as his hand brushed across her hair. "I forgot about that years ago," she said.

"Liar," he said with a smile. "You have beautiful hair. Soft, silky." He ran his hand through it again, and she froze when he leaned in to kiss her behind her ear. "It's a crime to change this," he murmured.

They were no longer moving. An ache filled her, an ache to be accepted for who she was. "What are you doing?" she said softly, and his lips stopped.

"You're right." He pulled back, expression troubled. "I'm sorry. I didn't think—"

Trisk reached up and pulled his face down to hers. Excitement zinged through her as their lips touched, and she drew back, meeting his eyes. "Keep doing that no-thinking thing," she said as she leaned in to find him again.

Their kiss deepened, warm and tasting of wine and pineapple. She made a small sound of encouragement when his hand fell to touch her thigh, his fingers rising past the hem of her dress before lingering to send shivers through her. He didn't go nearly high enough, but her coming complaint vanished when his grip tightened and he pulled her into him with his other hand.

Her smile ruined their kiss, and she looked at him, knowing her gaze smoldered with heat. He was as domineering as she'd expected him to be, so she'd be just as demanding, and he grunted in surprise when she twined a leg around his, pressing into him while pulling his face to hers, lips hungry as they searched him out. *Why not? I'm a free woman. It's the freaking sixties.*

It had been so long, and even then, it hadn't been satisfying, as it had not been with the man she'd wanted. Chances were, this would end much differently.

Her hands brushed his shoulders, and she sent them lower, pressing the small of his back. Lips breaking from his, she found his ears, neck, whatever she could reach. His stubble pricked against her, and she delighted in it until he broke their kiss.

"I gave you a key, not a ring," he said, his eyes eager but cautious.

"And I've not yet told you if I'm going to use it. Why are you thinking again?" she asked, pulling him down to one of the covered bales of straw, sitting atop his lap to put their heights even. He kissed her, and she laced her hands behind his head, fingers in his hair as his hand traced a delicious path up her waist until he cupped her breast. His head dropped, and she moaned as he found her with his lips.

Passion raced through her, but he was going too slow, and when he returned to her mouth, she shifted her weight, grasping him and flipping him down onto the straw-bale table where she sat atop him. There was a clatter of the Jell-O mold hitting the floor, followed by the thump of the radio. The music turned to a static hiss, and she smiled at his surprise melting into anticipation.

"You might be shocked at what they teach you in Self-Defense 101," she said as she loosened his tie. She was intending to undo his shirt next.

"Trisk, this is my best suit," he complained, his hands gripping her waist sending a delicious tingle racing through her when he sent his fingers higher to find her breast, moving in ever-smaller circles.

She pulled the tie from him, looping it loosely around her own neck. "I never liked this suit," she said as she started on the buttons next. "You look better in the gray one."

"I'm not going to roll around in a barn in my best suit," he protested as he kissed her.

She moved her lips against him, their scents mingling with the heat of their bodies rising. Trisk shifted to his ear. "Then take it off," she said succinctly. Yes, he had made her life hell, but that he was here now, wanting her, was empowering. *And my God, he is so beautiful.*

His arm curved possessively about her, and she gasped when, with a sudden motion, he flipped her up and around, and their positions were reversed. Her shock vanished, and she smiled up at him. "Dr. Kalamack!" she protested coyly, but her hands were now free to tug his shirt out from his slacks.

"Don't give me that," he said, leaning over her. His kisses became savage, with gentle teeth worrying her flesh and sending jolts through her, making her gasp for more. Finally she got his shirt off, and she sent her hands over his smooth abdomen, wanting to feel him over her, in her, around her, suffusing her with feeling. *Mine, this will be mine,* she thought, wanting it all.

His hands slipped up her thigh, under her dress, searching. She rose up under him, her lips hungry at his neck as her hands found his belt, and then his zipper.

Kal sighed at his new freedom, then gasped, jerking when she ran her hand along his length as she let a whisper of ley line energy jump from her to him.

"Sorry," she said breathlessly, smoothly shifting her hands lower, cupping him, tracing his outlines. "I won't do it again."

Kal's head dropped, and she quivered when he

nibbled her breast again, lips both harsh and soft. She groaned in frustration when his mouth left her, only to play about her ear. "You surprised me is all," he said, his voice husky. "Most times, I'm the one with the ley line finesse."

"Is that—oh God!" she exclaimed when he sent a surge of line energy through her. Writhing, she shuddered as the connection faded. Breathless, she met his eyes, and they hesitated as they contemplated the options. Mixing sex and ley line energy elevated the experience, but if you didn't know what you were doing, it was also dangerous. It had been a considerable amount of power, and she was beginning to get a better idea of why all those women had followed him through school.

This, I have to have, she thought as a slow smile crossed her face, and she lightly traced his abs when he drew down the straps of her dress from first her left shoulder, then her right, pulling them low until the breeze from the open door made her shiver. She let the barest whisper of line energy flow from her moving fingers to him, and his eyes flicked to hers, having felt it. Sometimes it was the lightest touch that got the strongest reaction, and he trembled as her hands drifted up to clasp behind his head and she drew him to her. "Never been with anyone who's taken a four-hundred-level security course, eh?" she asked.

"I wouldn't go as far as to say—" His eyes widened, and he groaned as the slim trace of energy blossomed into a torrent that matched his own earlier wash. Gasping, his head dropped, his lips finding her again.

Her back arched as his energies flowed into her once more, the two patterns warring with each other in an exquisite pleasure/pain that blinded them to all else.

Wild with desire, she reached for him, almost frantic as she slipped her panties off and guided him in, even as they began to move together.

He was a glorious sensation suffusing her. She could feel him inside her, feel him over her, feel his energies mixing with hers in a delicious battle. His mouth on hers, they rose and fell, each straining for that perfect moment, knowing it was there, desperate for it.

Wild with need, she clutched him to her as their passions grew stronger, deeper, the energies more complex as they stirred them together, chiming to a still point.

"Now," she moaned, feeling the sharp edge of it. "Oh God. Now."

With a guttural groan of release, Kal clutched her, a wave of sensation spilling into her. Ecstasy washed over her, and she climaxed as well, wave after wave of it until the last ebbed to a soft hush and she could breathe again.

Kal's breath was fast as he held himself over her. Eyes open, she took him in during an unguarded moment, his expression soft. He smiled at her, and she liked what she saw. *What am I doing?* she thought, then answered herself. *Having a damn good time. Shut up, Trisk. There's nothing left for you here.*

Smiling peacefully, she laced her hands behind his neck and pulled him down to her. Slowly she took more of his weight, enough to feel he was real, solid. "You've had some security classes," she accused, knowing finesse like that came only with practice.

"Summer camp. My parents are proactive when it comes to safety." Kal gave her a sound kiss, then rolled off, sitting up beside her on the makeshift table. "Though we never practiced anything like that. This is no longer my favorite suit," he said as he kicked off his shoes, then his slacks. "You can keep the tie if you want."

"I'd rather keep the key," she said, seeing the tie on the floor beside her boots. *When did that come off?* The words had sounded real and convincing as she said them, probably because there was a kernel of truth to them, and she felt a moment of guilt. *My God, the man has skills.*

A smile quirked the corners of her lips up, lingering as she looked at the remnants of their date. Kal was nice when he wasn't being a jerk.

He reached past her, bringing up a corner of the blanket to cover her. He lingered, brushing the hair from her face, his eyes never leaving hers as he sent his hand lower, a tingle tracing from his careful fingertips. "I've never run into anyone who wasn't afraid to use ley lines like that."

She propped herself up on an elbow. "Is that what you call this? *Run into?*" She laughed to tell him she wasn't serious. "Did you just *run into* me, Dr. Kalamack?"

With a savage growl, he spun, eyes alight, and pinned her to the straw, delighting in her shriek, muffled as he kissed her again, bringing her alive once more. Her breath was fast when he pulled back, still holding her down. "It's been a while," he said as if apologizing. "Sorry that was so fast." He let go and eased down beside her, tugging the blanket up more until they were both under it. "It's early yet. More wine?"

Fast? It felt as if they had been dancing toward this for two weeks. Content, she spun to lie on her front so she could reach for the bottle of wine. "Yes. Thank you."

But then she almost dropped it when he ran a rough-smooth hand from her shoulder down to her backside, lingering suggestively until she quivered.

Turning to face him, she caught his eyes with her own, waiting until he saw her concern. "Kal, where do we go from here?" she asked, no longer sure.

He cupped her face and pulled her closer, his lips so light on hers they were almost not there. "I suggest you follow your own advice, Dr. Cambri," he said when he drew back. "The night is not for thinking."

No, it isn't, she thought as he kissed her again, his hands gentler this time while he began to explore her, unhindered by anything, anything at all.

15

The musty smell of her oldest books usually put Trisk into a content mood, but tonight, as she took them from her built-ins and stacked them in produce boxes, it only filled her with a heavy melancholy. It had been a week since she'd made plans to go to Kennedy and Kal had signed off on the Angel's patent transfer. It gave her freedom, but NASA was the only lab that had shown any interest in her résumé. That the enclave had found a replacement for her at Global Genetics so quickly didn't bode well, either, and her stomach hurt. She couldn't decide whether she was hungry or she'd eaten something that disagreed with her.

I'm never going to get these back out of storage, she thought as she consigned another armful to a box. She'd taken the day off with the excuse that she needed to pack, but the truth was she was avoiding Daniel. She hadn't realized how much their lives intertwined until she started untangling them. The real estate agent had said her place would sell better with the furniture. That was fine with her, but there was a dismayingly small pile of boxes beside the front door and in the bed of her truck to take to storage. *Three years, and nothing to show but twenty-five acres of sticks in rows.*

Depressed, she didn't look up at the soft scuff of sock feet on the smooth floors when Quen left the kitchen, his steps light as he came down into the sunken living room. "Three thousand miles away," he said as he set one of the two cups of coffee in his hands on the low table. "You sure you want to do this?" he asked, sitting on the couch with a sigh.

Ignoring the mug for the moment, she stretched for the packing tape. The *brrrp* of the tape grated on her, and she pushed the box aside and set an empty one in its place.

Elbows on his knees, Quen held his mug under his nose and breathed deeply. "I know why you're doing this, but I still think going to NASA is a mistake."

"Duh," she said as she carefully tucked a stack of paperbacks away. But the truth was she had nowhere else to go. Depressed, she sat back on her heels and picked up the coffee. She took a sip, her face scrunching. "This tastes awful. Are you sure you made it right?"

"I know how to make coffee, Trisk," he said darkly. "You want tea instead?"

She shook her head, her grip tightening on the warm porcelain. "No, this is fine," she said. "Bitter or not, I'll finish it," she added, thinking of her situation with Kal.

Quen was silent for a moment, then said, "You do know he's lying to you."

"Kal?" Not looking at Quen, she set the coffee down so she could put more books in the box. "Obviously." But she had to stifle a shiver at the memory of their night together in the barn. *Damn . . . the man had skills.*

"I can't believe you slept with him," Quen accused, and she looked up, annoyed.

"I never should have told you," she muttered. But he was staring at her in silent accusation, and in a burst of motion, she stood and went to the emptying shelves, her toes deep in the red shag throw rug.

"It was my decision, not his," she said, stacking more books along her arm. "Mine. And I didn't care if he was lying or not. It felt good to be wanted. I got to bag the cutest boy in school. Big deal. My body, my life." But it didn't feel as good as she'd thought it would, and she couldn't meet Quen's eyes as she came back, kneeling to let the books spill in disarray on the floor.

"I don't have much choice but to play this out until Kennedy fires me," she added, not liking his accusing silence. "It will be a cold day in the ever-after before I give them the keys to my research, but I will have found somewhere else to work by that time." *I hope.*

His feet moved, and her eyes flicked up, finding a grudging acceptance in him. "I'm not giving up," she said. "My research could save so many lives, but I can't develop it here."

"You really don't have a plan anymore, do you?" he said, and she shook her head, finding it wasn't as scary as she had thought it would be. It actually gave her an odd strength, and finding a sense of peace for the first time in days, she taped up the box and set it atop the first one. *All those trees, and I'll never see any shade, any fruit,* she thought as she looked at the darkness beyond the wide windows. It bothered her as much as leaving Daniel.

"You want those in the truck with the rest?" Quen asked, quickly rising to take the box from her.

"Yes, thanks," she said softly, watching as he easily lifted both boxes at once and took them out. Everything in the truck was going into storage. What she was actually taking to Florida was much less and already packed in her car. Her clothes, her music, a few pictures, and a locked box holding her grandmother's ashes and summoning supplies, never to be opened again.

Trisk's thoughts went to the raised circle of flesh on the bottom of her foot, an angry line slashed across it. It was a reminder of the debt she owed, and she refused to show even Quen.

"We have headlights on the road," Quen said loudly as he came back in, shaking her from her dark musing. "It's Daniel," he added as he lingered by the front door.

"Great." Stretching, she pulled her sneakers close and slipped them on to hide her demon mark. The raised welt bumped under her fingers, and she quashed the feeling of shame. But it was better than killing Daniel, and she lifted her chin defiantly. She'd do it again in a heartbeat.

"I'd recognize his T-bird anywhere after tailing him all week." Quen turned from the long window to give her a warning look. "Did you know he goes to the same bar every night to drink a beer and watch the news?"

"Gosh darn it," she swore mildly as she looked across the messy room to the phone. She'd taken the receiver off the rotary hook this morning when people kept calling, first to find out why she wasn't at work, and then later to tell her she was missing Daniel's results release party. As the guest of honor, Daniel would have been there, and she was doing everything she could to put space between them. It was more than making sure the curse stuck; seeing him made her heart hurt. "The curse is holding, isn't it?" she asked.

Still looking out the long window beside the door, Quen stepped back to remain unseen. "So far, but the more you talk to him, the riskier it is. You want me to get rid of him?"

She sat back on her heels, feeling unprofessional in

the jeans and black T-shirt she'd put on this morning. "No," she said as she took off the handkerchief holding her hair back and shook the long strands out. "I'll talk to him. You should go hide in the back. No reason to tempt triggering something with an introduction. Right now, he doesn't know you, and I'd like to keep it that way."

Quen nodded decisively. "Good idea," he said as he wove through the clutter of boxes. Jerking to a stop, he returned for his coffee, then his shoes, and finally his coat draped over the end of the couch. All evidence of him in hand, he hustled into the back as the doorbell chimed.

"When will this get easier?" she whispered as she got to her feet. Spending a night with Kal hadn't had the expected result of easing her heartache, apart from the few hours it had encompassed. Avoiding Daniel hadn't helped, either, and by the look on his face as he peeked through the window, he was still upset she was leaving.

Flicking on the porch light, she opened the door, saying nothing as she looked him over in his slacks, dress shoes, and brown tweed vest over his usual white shirt. The top two shirt buttons were undone, and he looked more relaxed than usual without his tie.

"Oh, good." He pushed up his glasses in an awkward show. "You're here. You weren't at the party."

There was a brown paper bag in his hand, and she hoped it wasn't cake. "Daniel—"

"You took your phone off the hook," he interrupted. "I was worried you might not be feeling well."

She hadn't been, but it was nothing she wanted to talk about. "What do you want?" she asked, wishing she could be honest with him.

He shifted his weight, scrubbing a hand over his five-o'clock shadow. "Look," he said, mood abruptly shifting, "I get that you have this thing for Dr. Kalamack. You're a grown woman, and I'm not your . . . brother," he said, and she wondered if he had been going to say *boyfriend*. "If you want to follow him to Florida to work with him, wash his flasks, and plan his dinner parties, who am I to say differently."

She blinked, lips parting. "Excuse me?"

"You probably want to start a family," Daniel said, his shoulders stiff. "And it's a good match. You'll at least understand what he's talking about when he sits down at the dinner table once they make you go home after you get pregnant."

Her jaw dropped, even though that was about all any woman had a right to expect, an elf in an elven lab or not. But it still ticked her off. "You don't have a clue what I want," she said hotly.

"Yeah, you're probably right," he said sourly. "I don't know why I'm even here, except that you have a problem in your seed field and Angie is out sick. I thought you might like to know before Monday, when everything is dead."

Her anger vanished, and she looked at the paper bag in his hand. "What's wrong with my seed field?"

"It's wilted." He held out the bag for her to take. "They're losing their hairs, leaves, and fruit, in that order. I thought you might like to see." She took the bag, and he looked angrily at the stacked boxes beside the door. "Good luck at Kennedy."

He turned to go, and the bag crackled in her grip. "Daniel, wait," she called, and he stopped on the stairs, silent as she fumbled for words. He thought she was giving up her career to cater to a self-indulgent, egotistical snot. It was more than her pride could take. "Don't tell anyone, but I'm not going to Kennedy. At least not permanently. I just can't stay here."

Daniel shifted to face her more fully. He was two steps down, and halfway gone into the dark. "Did I do something wrong?"

"No," she blurted. Hesitating, Trisk bit her lip, wishing things were different. "No," she said again, softer this time. "I did. It might take me a while to fix it."

He was silent, thinking that over and probably getting it wrong.

"How is the release going?" she asked, not wanting him to leave. "I'm sorry I missed it. Is everything hitting the right parameters?"

Daniel looked at his car, then back at her. "I don't get you, Trisk. I find you packing up your life, your career, and you ask me how my release is going?"

Worried that Quen might come out despite her telling him not to, she shrugged, shutting the door behind her and leaning back against it.

His chest moved as he sighed. "The government is thrilled," he said flatly. "The military got in and retook the building without a hitch. We need to adjust the dosage levels, though. It's having a wider effect than we expected. The entire city block is sick, not just the building." He hesitated, seeming to gather his resolve. "Is there anything I can do to help, Trisk?"

She shook her head, the guilt rising high. "Don't think badly of me," she said softly. "This isn't what I wanted to have happen."

Daniel took a step up, and she fumbled behind her for the doorknob. "No. I'm sorry," she said as she opened the door and retreated into the house. "I just wanted to know if your project was a success. You should go."

Jaw clenched, Daniel stopped. "It's not a failure to ask for help."

Miserable, she took another step in, almost peeking around the open door. "Thank you for telling me about my crop. I'll check it tomorrow."

Daniel took a slow breath as if to say something, but then he turned and walked away without a word, head down and hands in his pockets. Her eyes were stinging as she shut the door. "Damn it," she whispered as she turned, gasping when she almost ran into Quen. "I hate it when you do that!" she exclaimed, smacking his shoulder. "Don't you have anything better to do than sneak up behind me?"

"That poor, sad little man," he said, head shaking as the sound of Daniel's car leaving filtered in and his headlights flashed in the hall and were gone. "You're really hard on your boyfriends, you know that?"

Lump in her throat, she pushed past him, going to the couch and flopping onto it. She set the bag on the table and stared at her mug, wanting coffee but not when it tasted like that. "He was never my boyfriend, and you're not helping."

"I'd say the curse is holding," Quen added as he sat beside her and dragged the bag to him. "What's wrong with your tomatoes?"

"If Angie is out sick, she probably just forgot to water them before she left."

The paper bag crackled as he unrolled it, and Quen looked in, recoiling with a sudden jerk. "Are they supposed to smell like that?"

Brow furrowed, she reached for the bag. "They smell?" She looked in, seeing the clear lab-sample bag inside. It wasn't sealed, and a foul stench made her lips curl. She reached in to snap it shut before carefully lifting it out. The vegetation was coated in a black slime, falling apart in places. Daniel wouldn't have been able to put it in the bag like that, meaning it had decomposed over the course of a few hours.

"That doesn't look right," Quen said, poking the bag with a finger.

"It's not." Stretching, she reached for her phone and toggled the receiver button for a dial tone.

"Who you calling? Kal?" Quen asked, and she gave him a dry look as she dialed Angie's home number from memory. It rang twice before it was picked up and a masculine voice said hello.

"Hi," Trisk said, pulse fast as she looked at what was left of the tomato. "Is Angie there?"

"Who is this?" the man asked, and Trisk pushed herself up on the edge of the couch.

"Dr. Cambri," she said, rising to pace within the confines of the phone's cord. "Angie works with me. I wasn't in today, and I just found out she was home sick. Is she okay?"

"Dr. Cambri," the man said, his suspicion replaced by a heavy relief. "I'm glad you called. I'm Andy, her boyfriend. They wouldn't give me your number when I called this afternoon. Angie threw up this morning, but the fever wasn't high, so I didn't think anything of it. But she had a rash when I got home. It's all over her face and back. I think it's spreading."

Shit. Trisk gave Quen a sick look. Vomiting wasn't a symptom of Daniel's virus except in an overdose, but a fever and a rash were. *How did she come in contact with it?*

"We thought maybe she was coming down with chicken pox since the kid next door has it. But she's coughing up blood now. Dr. Cambri, is she okay?"

Trisk put a hand to her forehead, fighting the nausea. "I would think so," she said, not knowing for sure. "But it wouldn't hurt to take her into the emergency room."

"The emergency room?" Andy said, voice worried. "But it's almost after six."

"That's why they call it emergency," Trisk insisted. "Make sure they know she works at Global Genetics. Tell them I said to put her into isolation. Just as a precaution."

"Dr. Cambri?" His voice was higher, threaded with panic. "Is she going to be okay?"

She couldn't bring herself to say yes.

"Dr. Cambri?" Andy prompted again, and her jaw clenched.

"I think so," she said, soft so the lie wouldn't show. "It doesn't sound like anything we've been working with. I just want to be sure. Take her in right now, okay?"

"Okay. Thanks, Dr. Cambri."

The connection clicked off and she was left listening to a dial tone. Feeling unreal, she hung up the phone. Quen was watching her when she looked up, his eyebrows high.

"Aren't those the symptoms of—"

"Daniel's virus, yes," she said, brow furrowed. "But there was no way she could have come in contact with it. She never goes in his lab, and if Daniel brought it out accidentally, he'd be sick, too."

Quen's eyes slid to the ugly bag of black slime. "You don't think . . ."

Trisk shook her head. "It can't jump to a plant," she said, starting to pace a wider arc. "I've worked with both their genomes, and they don't mesh."

"But if they did?"

She stopped, gripping the back of the chair with a

white-knuckled strength. "Then Angie will be fine," she said, pulse slowing. "If she was exposed to Daniel's virus, she'll be fine. It can't reproduce outside of the lab." But that she'd come in contact with it was a problem.

Quen shifted farther away from the foul, black bag. "I didn't think coughing up blood was one of the symptoms."

"It is if you overdose," she said absently, wondering if she should call Daniel. "But she'd have to eat, like, a tablespoon of it," she finished, a horrible feeling of having been remiss settling deep in the pit of her soul as she looked at the remains of her tomato. Angie had taken one home Thursday. If Daniel's virus was attacking her plants, the toxins might build up to a lethal dose before the plant died.

Fingers shaking, she grabbed her purse and keys. "I need to go."

16

Kal pulled into Global Genetics, scanning the nearly empty lot for any sign of Trisk before bringing his car to a halt and turning off his headlights. It was just after six, the afternoon's results party long since over, but the lights were still on in the third-floor offices. A few cars were scattered about, support staff and late-shift security, mostly. Everyone who hadn't moved the celebration to Riverside Smokehouse had gone home.

"Except for Rick and Barbara," he mused aloud, seeing his Cadillac and her flower-decaled VW bug in their reserved spots. The thought of the two of them engaging in a tryst came and went. Rick was a living vampire, and for all his playboy tendencies and looks, he was obviously close to the top of the hierarchy in his camarilla or he wouldn't have gotten the job. That Rick would go to his early-fifties secretary to satisfy his mild bloodlust was ludicrous.

But odder things have happened, Kal thought as he got out. As expected, Daniel's virus had worked perfectly, the airborne dispersal downing an entire building in Vietnam and allowing the U.S. forces to move in safely and take it with minimal shots fired. Global

Genetics was celebrating, but Daniel had seemed distracted and uncaring that he'd just changed the world.

Smug, Kal strode to the main entrance, not needing to use his building pass to get in as it wasn't quite after normal work hours. The two-story reception area was empty, the front desk dark. The sound of a vacuum cleaner fought with loud music echoing into the lobby. It was coming from the largest meeting room, both mahogany doors flung wide. That was where the results party had been, and Kal headed for it. If anyone would know where Rick was, Barbara would.

Sure enough, the woman was there amid the streamers and containers of potluck food, looking odd but in control in her tall boots and overdone makeup as she organized the cleanup to the tune of "Wild Thing." "Dr. Kalamack!" she exclaimed when she saw him, her steps almost prissy as she went to take the arm off the record player. Smiling, she tugged on the vacuum cleaner cord until the man running it noticed and turned it off. "What brings you back? I think the interns moved the party to Riverside."

"That's where I've been, actually. I'm looking for Rick," he said, and the woman wobbled closer on her high heels, clearly having had too much to drink. She touched her hair to make sure it was in place. Even though her baby-blue vinyl dress was too young for her, her white calf-high boots and tall hair helped her pull off the look.

"I haven't seen him since he got that long-distance call and barricaded himself in his office," she said, flushed and fanning herself. "There was a miscalculation in the dosage, and he's taking hell for it." Barbara stopped before him, having to look up as she gave him her most fetching smile. "Phew, I'm tired," she said, gently rubbing her neck. "Just can't party like I used to."

She turned to the cleanup crew moving toward the open bar, and Kal's smile went stilted when he saw the beginnings of a rash on her neck. "Stay away from that booze until I get the cart over here!" she yelled, then turned back. "I'll find him if you like. He's probably still here."

"He is," he said lightly, inching away from her. "His car is still in the lot. If you see him, tell him I'm looking for him. I'll be in my office for a few hours."

"It's Friday, Dr. Kalamack!" Barbara said enthusiastically. "You should be at Riverside Smokehouse with the kids."

Kal glanced at the cake, CONGRATULATIONS DANIEL still legible in red icing. "No rest for the wicked," he said as he took a piece already cut and waiting on a paper plate. "Go home, Barbara. Someone else can clean this up."

"Soon as I get that alcohol back in Rick's office," she said, a thin finger moving between her neck and collar. "Have a nice weekend, Dr. Kalamack."

"Thanks, Barb. See you Monday." Careful not to spill the cake, Kal headed for the lobby. His thoughts spun as he strode to the elevator and hit the down button. She'd been exposed. But how? He'd only infected Trisk's underground field.

Curious, he thought as the doors opened and he got in. Barbara seldom went downstairs. Something or someone had brought it up. Daniel's clean-room practices were better than that, but the virus had gotten out somehow. *The tomatoes?* he wondered, seeing as they hadn't been clean-room protected in over a year. Hell, he'd seen Trisk's assistant put a basket of them by the front door yesterday for people to take home.

Frowning, he tried to recall if the basket had been empty when he'd passed it. He'd introduced Daniel's virus into Trisk's field three days ago. He'd never have thought that enough would remain on the plants to infect humans. But if it had, it would only hasten Trisk's downfall, and it wouldn't hurt anyone permanently.

The doors slid open, and he stepped out. George saw him immediately, rattling his newspaper as he turned to a new section. "Hi, George. Anyone bring you cake yet?" Kal called out as he lifted the plate in invitation.

"Barbara brought me a piece a couple of hours ago," the man said as he set his newspaper down in anticipation. "But I'd eat another. I thought you'd be at Smokehouse. It's Friday."

Looking for signs of infection, Kal smiled and handed him the cake. "Just a few things to wrap up before I call it a week," he said, his skin prickling as he tapped a line. "The party cut my day short."

"Thanks." George took the cake. "I hear you about the party. I could—"

"*Obscurum per obscurius*," Kal said softly, his now-free hand directing the energy the words had marshaled. "Whoops!" he added as George's eyes rolled up. Scrambling, he saved the cake from hitting the floor, but the man's head struck the desk as he collapsed. There was no sign of a rash that he could see, and Kal frowned. If anyone should be sick from an accidental release, it would be George.

"Sleep tight." Leaving the cake, he used George's master bypass key to open the door and slip through so there would be no record of him entering the downstairs labs. Immediately his nose wrinkled at the faint smell of decay, but that bothered him less than the bright yellow tape sealing off Daniel's area.

"Quarantine?" he mused aloud as he passed it. It was a rather extreme reaction for having miscalculated the dosage, and his concern grew as he continued on to his shared office space with Trisk and used George's key to open it to hide he'd ever been there.

Jerking back, Kal put a hand over his face when a putrid stench rolled out past the open door. *Shit, it's bad*, he thought as he flicked on the light. Breath held, he went in.

"My God," he whispered when he saw what was left of Trisk's tomato field. After three days, he would expect some wilting, perhaps the fruit dropping, but the field was nothing but a broken-stemmed black wasteland. It appeared as if it had been burned, puddles of black goo showing where there'd once been tomatoes, broken, smutty branches still standing like piked soldiers in a lost battlefield.

In a horrified awe, he pressed closer to the glass to get a better look. It was getting easier to bear the smell, but his brow furrowed. He would swear he hadn't miscalculated the dosage to infect the field. Something was working differently than he had anticipated.

But then his frown mutated into a satisfied smile. Trisk's tomato was an utter failure. As far as anyone would know, she'd made a toxic fruit and passed it off as the agricultural savior of the third world. Even better, anyone who ate one of the infected tomatoes would be in danger of getting sick from Daniel's virus. Trisk would be lucky to find a job as a sewage inspector.

"Her entire product line is destroyed," Kal whispered, fixated on the broken ruin.

"It's worse than you think," Rick said from the open doorway, and Kal spun, shocked to see him standing there, his tie loosened and his shirt almost untucked. His shoulder-length hair was in disarray, and he looked rattled. "What are you doing here?"

"I came down to see where the stench was coming from," Kal ad-libbed, and the living vampire nodded as he shuffled in and slumped into one of the rolling chairs, head in his hands to stare at the floor. "Rick?" Kal cautiously came closer. "Does Trisk know about this?"

His eyes flicked up and Rick leaned back. "Hell if I know." His eyes shut, and fear crossed his face, shocking Kal. Vampires were never afraid. Even when they should be. "I'm not a geneticist," Rick said, barely above a whisper, and Kal lurched to the door, looking down the hall to make sure no one was out there listening. "My master told me to come here. Make sure this virus of Daniel's wouldn't impact the vampire population or the human population—in that order. I told him it was safe." He looked up, expression riven. "And now I've got a fever," he said, holding his hand out to watch it shake. "I can't die yet!" he exclaimed, letting it fall. "I don't have enough set aside to retire or a place to stay out of the light. Or anyone to keep me alive." Panic widened his eyes. "My master will have to cull me. No one is allowed to turn if they don't have their scion already arranged."

Shocked, Kal stared at Rick's outright fear, realizing that the confidence, the sly power that all living vampires possessed, was a lie they told themselves so they could somehow survive. They knew what horrors awaited them at the end of their life, that they would become as beasts. Even when they were prepared, to die meant to become something they had both feared and loved all their lives.

"It's okay, Rick," he said, and the man's frantic gaze landed on his. "Daniel's virus can't kill Inderlanders. You're based on a human genome, so you'll get a rash and a fever, but you won't die. Even if you overdose."

"Are you sure?" he whispered, and Kal nodded.

"Absolutely," he said, smiling until the hard edges of fear left Rick. "Weres are so far from their human ancestry that they will hardly notice, and witches not at all. The undead, your master? He won't get sick either. He'll be pleased with you when you tell him, yes?"

Rick's shoulders slumped as he took a shaky breath. His eyes fell to his hands, his fingers tangled together, and he set them on his knees. That fast, he found his mask, the need to dominate and subjugate forcing his fear of his future back to the recesses where it would linger until the pressure of darkness and loneliness forced it bubbling to the surface again.

Tossing his hair back, Rick rose, the terror safely hidden. But Kal could see it. The living vampire fixed his tie, then his hair. "Then all I have to worry about is why a perfectly safe virus is spreading through Vietnam, killing humans like the black plague's evil twin."

Lip twitching, Kal glanced at the field of goo. "Killing? Impossible. I saw the dosage."

"Wolfe says the military docs say it found a carrier." Rick shuddered as he fixed his cuffs, the beginnings of a rash peeping past them. "It has a place to grow, somewhere acidic to multiply and condense its toxin. The government wants to send a focus group. I don't know what to tell them to do to avoid getting sick." He looked up, the fear still lurking at the back of his eyes. "If you see Daniel, tell him he's under arrest. I'm supposed to put him under quarantine." His eyes closed. "People are dying in the streets in 'Nam. It's spreading like wildfire."

"But it can't," Kal stated, and the fear returned to Rick as he realized Kal's earlier promise might be hollow.

"There's no pattern to it," Rick said. "Even when accounting for the Inderland immunity. Like an angel of God strolling through the cobbled streets, it's taking out entire human families, skipping others. No pattern, none at all."

"But not Inderlanders," Kal said, his shoulders stiffening. It shouldn't be killing anyone. And how was it spreading? *Trisk's tomato?* he thought, immediately dismissing it. He'd made her tomato susceptible, not a carrier and able to serve as an incubator. The dosage must be wrong. That would account for the utter destruction of Trisk's field as well.

Rick's face was haggard. "Inderlanders? So far, no reports of death," he said, taking his handkerchief and swabbing the back of his neck. "So far." He looked at the handkerchief, hand shaking as he saw little drops of blood on it. "Shit."

"I worked on the dosage calculations. It shouldn't have any effect outside the building," Kal said, and Rick laughed, a hint of hysteria in it.

"It's hitting the entire country," he said, rising unsteadily. "They've blocked travel in and out. The local Weres and witches are keeping the area together, setting up camps, keeping the food supplies, law in place. We're all going to die," he said, lurching to put his hand on the doorjamb. "Even if this doesn't kill us, we're all going to die."

"It can't do this," Kal said, but Rick wasn't listening, head down as he mumbled.

"Die," Rick said, stumbling into the hall. "I've got to find a hole. No one is going to bury me properly. I have to do it myself."

Kal looked at the decay-blackened field. He was sure he hadn't miscalculated the effective dose. The only answer remaining was that he'd accidentally made Trisk's tomato into a carrier. *My God. What have I done?* he thought, then shoved it down. No one knew it was him. No one ever would.

"Rick? Rick!" he called as he leaned into the hall, and Rick turned, staggering to hold himself up against the wall, though he couldn't possibly be that sick—yet. "Have you told anyone Trisk's field is infected?" Kal asked.

Fear flashed through Rick's eyes, fear at what his master would say when he found out Rick had failed to keep their people safe. "Not yet. I wanted to talk to her first."

Thank God. Kal steeled his expression. "I think it's Dr. Cambri's tomato, not an incorrect dosage, that's causing the deaths," he said, and Rick's eyes flicked to the office behind him. "The T4 Angel is a cash crop in 'Nam. You saw her seed field. It's putrefying. If Trisk's Angel tomato is a carrier, we have to eliminate it before it can spread any farther. Do you keep records in your office of who it's been sold to?"

"I don't know. Why?" Rick asked, and Kal stifled a surge of impatience.

"We have to burn the fields," he said, the rotting vegetation somehow smelling stronger in the hallway than in his office. "Starting with Dr. Cambri's seed field and ending with every field in the third-world countries. How long will it take to get a list of who's growing them?"

Rick looked better for having been given a task, and Kal realized how fragile vampires really were, abused children growing up weak and strong at the same time. "I don't know. I'll ask Barbara."

Wrong answer. "Wait. Rick," Kal called when the

vampire turned to go upstairs. "I need your help first. I don't have authority to sterilize the seed field. You do. We have to destroy Trisk's tomatoes before they make anyone else here sick."

"I don't know how to sterilize the seed field," Rick said, and Kal glanced back in through the open door to the ugly field beyond.

"It's in the computer," Kal said. "Just log in and ask it. The computer will walk you through it."

"Now?" Rick said as he came back, and Kal felt a wisp of relief. If it was Rick's name on the request, no one would come to him for answers as to why the field and most of the evidence had been destroyed.

"I can't take that stench any longer," Kal said as he darted back into the office and spun the chair around for Rick to sit in. "Can you do it? I need to go to the desiccator and destroy the seeds Angie set up yesterday."

"Sure." Rick sat, his fingers hesitant as he typed in his name and then a password.

"We can't let any of this out," Kal added, backing away as a list of instructions came up for how to hook up a tank of tissue dissolver to the sprinkler system. Not only would it cause any remaining cells to explode, as well as destroying the virus, but it was flammable, leaving a pristine, untainted soil in which to start the next crop if someone dropped a match. And someone would.

"Got it," Rick said distantly, and Kal gave his shoulder a reassuring touch before darting into the hall. But it was not the desiccator he went to, instead going to Daniel's lab and adjoining office, breaking the quarantine seal, and slipping inside.

Steps light, he made his way to where the active

virus was kept, using only the dim, ambient glow from the machines. He slipped two vials into his pocket, turning to smile at the large glass jugs of alcohol used for sterilization. "Perfect," he whispered, straining as he threw one across the room, where it shattered against a hood.

Warming to the task, Kal levered himself up onto one of the benches, stretching to the smoke and heat detectors. His fingernail split as he wedged the cover off, and after a moment of study, he delicately pulled out the power node. He did the same in the adjacent lab and office, the glugs of the alcohol and the cool sensation on his fingers seeming to foretell the clean fire that would soon sweep the basement.

It was obvious that his plan to kill Trisk's tomato with Daniel's virus had succeeded. But that he'd accidentally given the virus a way to spread . . . Damn, he hadn't wanted a full-scale plague. This had to be covered up.

The scent of alcohol was heavy as he backed his way through the offices and labs until he got to the door. Resolute, he tapped a ley line, harnessing the free energy and giving it shape. "*Flagro*," he whispered, throwing a ball of aura-tainted energy at the wet floor.

His eyes widened at the whoosh. There was no visible flame, but the cloying scent of half-burned alcohol rose, and he shut the door, satisfied the room would be an inferno in seconds.

Pulse fast, he jogged back to Trisk's office. It was empty.

Panic washed through him, but then he saw Rick in the field, his back to the window while he manually connected the flammable poison to the irrigation system, one hand over his face as he tried not to breathe.

Turning, Kal rummaged in one of the equipment lockers. It was dusty from disuse, but he found two masks. He put one on, then went out, grimacing at the stench. The mask hardly cut it, and he took it off, throwing it aside. "Can I help?" he asked, extending the remaining mask to Rick.

The man didn't look up as he fastened the canister of tissue destroyer. "You did this, didn't you," he said, his hands red and swollen, burned by the chemicals he was handling.

"Did what?" Kal said, but his arm holding out the mask dropped when he realized the rash on Rick's wrists and neck had ulcerated. The raw blisters oozed a clear liquid, giving his skin an alien-looking sheen. It looked terrifying and painful, and fear struck through Kal that this was his doing. *Unless I can make Trisk take the blame.*

"I'm not a scientist," Rick said, his watering eyes almost swollen shut, "but I know viruses don't jump from plant to human like that. You did this. Made this happen."

Kal pushed past Rick to get to the dispersal regulator. "Don't be inane. Why would I want to infect the world with this?" he said as he set the water to zero and the canisters to full.

Rick listlessly watched, his weight on one foot as he slumped. "I don't know. Maybe because you hate Trisk and want the shitload of funding headed her way."

Kal blanched, turning as he wiped his hands on his pants. His fingers burned from the residual tissue destroyer.

"Yes, I know about that." Rick seemed to regain some of his strength, pulling himself straight. "Ulbrine gave you a carrot, and you want the entire produce cart."

"I wouldn't threaten the stability of our numbers for funding my research," Kal said, but the anger in his voice was giving him away.

"Why not?" Rick rocked back, blood spotting his collar and cuffs. "Being a scientist doesn't grant you a golden moral compass, and you are broken, both your compass and your research. But it went wrong, didn't it," he accused, and Kal set the dispersal regulator aside, his steps wary as he headed back to the control room. "You didn't expect it to spread this fast," Rick said, stumbling slightly as he followed. "Did you. You son of a bitch."

Kal's lips pressed as he realized he was going to have to kill him. Rick would tell his superiors. They'd realize Kal was responsible. But if Rick died amid Trisk's failed crop with his name on the request for the burning protocol, everyone would assume Rick had committed suicide rather than face the accusations of creating a toxic tomato and infecting the world with it.

"Stop right there," Rick threatened, and Kal spun, pissed that it was falling apart around him. "I know what you did, and you will answer for it."

Kal stood with his feet firmly on the stained cement walk. "Not today," he said, pulling on a ley line. The splintered feel of it poured into Kal, giving him courage.

Rick's eyes were almost swollen shut, but the vampire snarled, his bleeding hands crooked to gouge. "You aren't leaving here alive," Rick promised, teeth bared.

"Funny." Breathless, Kal forced the incoming energy into his palms until they burned with the free force and flammable liquid. "That's exactly what I was going to say to you."

With a fierce roar of anger, Rick lunged. Kal fell back, eyes widening at how fast the vampire was. Kal slipped on the black slime, going down in an ungraceful pinwheeling of arms and legs. It probably saved his life as Rick's lash whispered over Kal's head.

"Burn, you bastard," Kal swore, still on the ground as he threw a ball of unfocused energy not at Rick, who was regrouping for another attack, but at the bags of fertilizer behind him.

Rick spun, sprinting to the distant door, but it was too late.

The green-tinted ball of energy hit the bags and exploded.

Kal cowered, his grip on the ley line strengthening. "*Cum gladio et sale!*" he shouted, gasping in relief as his circle sprang up. It was chancy and weak since the outline of it existed only in his mind, not scribed on the floor. It would do nothing to stop a bullet or demon, but it would hold for the instant needed for the fireball to wash over him.

Ears stunned, Kal looked up to see Rick thrown twenty feet, sliding to a halt in the black muck. Triggered by the blast, the sprinklers hissed on. Kal hunched where he was, jerking when the tissue destroyer, not water, pattered down against his circle, a foot above his head.

"My God," Kal whispered as he realized what was going to happen. He watched in horror as Rick stumbled to his feet, oblivious to the flammable rain pouring down upon him as he staggered toward Kal.

Kal's eyes flicked to the bags of burning fertilizer, then the door. He'd never make it if he tried to run. Swallowing hard, Kal scribed a circle in the muck with a shaky finger, a pure white showing against the black of decay. "*Cum gladio et sale*," he whispered again, strengthening his circle. But it wasn't against Rick this time.

With a little flick of flame, the spray caught. Kal watched, horrified, as it sped up and out with a whoosh. Rick screamed when it touched him, and then he became covered in flame, rolling to beat it out. But the ground itself was on fire, and his high-pitched agony rang against the bare walls, over and over as he tried to get to the safety of the office, failing.

Kal looked away, cold and shaking under his bubble, waiting for it to be over. Rick's voice finally ceased. One by one, the sprinklers ran out of propellant and stopped, little drips of fire falling from them. And still Kal sat, unable to move.

Slowly Kal realized a klaxon was ringing. He stood, his circle falling about him as he touched it. He gazed down, fixated on the disk of black goo he stood in, surrounded by pure, clean ash. Nearby, a lump of burned flesh lay smoking, but he didn't look at it. Rick wouldn't be needing that after-death plan anymore.

The air was fresher, and Kal's head rose as he lurched to the cement path. He left footprints of black decay as he walked away, but they grew fainter and fainter the farther he went, and soon, there was no trace of him at all.

17

"**G**et out of the way. Out of the way!" Trisk clenched her jaw, frustrated with the tractor-trailer full of tomatoes lumbering before her. That it had SALADAN FARMS emblazoned on the back didn't help as it spewed half-burned fuel and took up more than its fair share of the road as they went around a wide turn. Darkness made the road chancy, and unable to see around the truck to know if it was safe to pass, she hit the accelerator and sent her Chevy Apache 10 pickup truck bouncing onto the shoulder to get around him that way. The necklace Quen had given her thumped and bumped, and she held it against her as she jerked the truck back on the road.

The trucker blew his horn, and beside her, Quen clutched at the door handle.

"Problem?" she asked as she cleared the truck and sped toward Sacramento's hospital. Her car would have been faster, but it was packed to the ceiling.

"No." Quen's eyes were fixed on the car she was barreling down on, his right foot pressing into the floor-boards. "But is it going to matter if we get there five minutes later?"

Trisk said nothing, peeved when she was forced to

slow as they hit the outskirts of the city. It was Friday night, and it seemed everyone was out—getting in her way. She took the turn into the hospital so fast that the boxes in the bed slid, making Quen check to see they weren't on the side of the road.

Immediately she slowed, looking for signs to tell her where to go. The emergency department wasn't busy, and finding a spot in the visitor lot, she pulled in and threw her truck into park. Hair and necklace swinging, Trisk grabbed her purse and shoved the paper bag with the decomposing tomato plant under the seat. Brushing her hair back, she impatiently waited for Quen.

"You don't want me to wait in the car?" he asked, looking a little green under the bright security lights, and she shook her head, imagining what her field must look like. Breaking off a stem would hasten the process of decay, but it was likely she'd lose all her crop. *Saladan is going to be madder than a wet hornet.*

"No. I want your opinion," she said, not liking that the long sweater coat she'd thrown on as she'd walked out the door did nothing to elevate her jeans, black T-shirt, and sneakers.

"Why?" he said as he got out. "I wouldn't know if she's got Daniel's virus or not."

They walked quickly to the main door, Trisk's feet silent in her soft-soled shoes instead of her usual heels. Quen was taller than she was, and she felt his presence keenly as he awkwardly tried to open the door for her without touching it.

"You're not worried, are you?" she asked when he wiped his hands off on his slacks.

"I don't want to get sick," he said as they slowed, taking in the few people waiting and looking for the reception desk. There weren't many in the chairs surrounding the black-and-white TV. The kids seemed okay, but the parents, not so much. It was an odd combination, but in the corner, a small family of five sat in huddled misery, all of them appearing feverish and ill.

"There." Trisk pointed at the nurse behind the desk. Again wishing she was wearing something more professional, Trisk strode forward with an air of confidence. "Hi," she said, and the woman looked up, a tissue at her nose. "Could you tell me what room Angie Harms is in?"

"Angie Harms," the woman repeated, head down as she shuffled papers for the register sheet.

"With an H," Trisk added as Quen rocked to a halt behind her, his hands in his pockets. "H-A-R-M-S."

The woman flipped the page for the earlier entries. "I'm not seeing her. Are you sure she came in through emergency?"

Oh, God, what if she hadn't come in? "It would've just been within the last half hour." Trisk leaned into the counter, wanting to take the paper away from the receptionist and look herself. "Blond, about this tall." She put her hand up to indicate a few inches taller than herself. "Her boyfriend would have brought her in."

"Oh!" The woman behind the desk brightened as she reached for a different stack of papers. "I know the one. Fever and respiratory distress. She's probably still in exam room six. They haven't assigned a room to her yet as far as I know."

Trisk's relieved smile froze when she realized the woman had tiny blisters on her neck. "Thank you," she said, uneasy as she took her hands off the high counter. "Let's go," she said softly to Quen, not liking this. It could be that the woman simply had a rash, but Trisk didn't believe in coincidences.

"Ma'am. Ma'am!" the receptionist said, standing up

as they headed down the hall. "You shouldn't go back there. It's family and doctors only."

"It's okay," Trisk said over her shoulder, never stopping. "I'm a doctor."

"And I'm family," Quen said, not a hint of his lie showing.

With a tired wave, the woman sat back down. She was flushed, and Trisk looked at the people in the waiting room more closely. With a few notable exceptions, they were all showing the symptoms of Daniel's virus. *Or the common cold*, she thought, trying to clamp down on her panic.

"I'll wait in the hall," Quen said, and Trisk frowned, annoyed at his paranoia.

"My God," she whispered, wondering if the guy getting a soda from the machine was ill or if drugged-out hippie was simply his look. "I didn't know you were that paranoid. Even if it is Daniel's virus, it can't hurt you. It doesn't affect most Inderlanders. Elves, not at all." *Unless* . . . she mused suddenly, *he isn't 100 percent elf.* Until recently, there hadn't been a lot of options when a lethal fragment showed in their decaying code other than outsourcing to their nearest genetic relative. It muddied their ability to do magic somewhat, but that vanished by the second generation. Almost everyone had some human in them, and almost everyone pretended they didn't.

Quen flushed. "Great-great-grandfather," he said, lips tight when he saw her knowing expression. "My great-great-grandmother couldn't bring a child to full term. It was worth the genetic taint to try to save what we could of our line."

Trisk touched his arm to tell him she thought nothing less of him. "I'm glad they did."

He flashed a quick, grateful smile at her. "I don't mind being six percent human, but it makes me nervous."

"Well, you'd never know it now," she said, brow furrowing at the man slumped on a chair in the hall, his elbows on his knees and his head in his hands.

"Thanks," Quen said sheepishly, and she pulled him to a stop.

"Daniel?" she whispered, and the man she was watching pulled his head up. It was Daniel, and she froze, not wanting him to see Quen but needing to know why he was sitting outside Angie's door.

"Trisk." Daniel stood, looking haggard in the same weary slacks and white shirt he'd had on earlier. "How did you find out?"

Shit. Cold slipped into her, born from a hundred almost-thoughts. "What happened?" she asked as she hastened forward. "Is Angie okay?"

"She's dead," Daniel said bluntly, head down. "I . . ."

"No!" Trisk took his hands, shock making her breathless. "I just talked to her boyfriend half an hour ago. I told him to get her to the emergency room. He didn't say it was this bad!"

"I gotta sit down," Daniel said as he sank back into the chair. Trisk crouched beside him, not letting go of his hands. She watched his eyes, felt his aura, but he seemed okay, if a little in shock. Quen drifted away to make sure they wouldn't be disturbed, but she was sure he'd stay close enough to hear everything. "I don't know how, but it got out," Daniel said, his eyes haunted as he looked across the hall to the empty room. "Somehow it got out. This is my fault. I did this."

He was talking about his virus, and she squeezed his hands to get him to look at her. "No, you didn't," she said, voice hushed. "We made it perfect. It might put some-one in the hospital who's immune-depressed, but Angie was healthy. It was something else. Something new."

Daniel pulled out of her grip, his anger obvious. "I saw her, Trisk," he said bitterly, eyes on the empty room. "Blisters on her face and back. Out-of-control fever. Respiratory distress. Her body just shut down. They couldn't stop it." He swallowed hard. "They wouldn't let me in, but I heard it all."

"It can't happen!" Trisk protested, and his eyes came back to her.

"I think it found a carrier," he whispered. "It's gotten to your tomatoes, too."

Trisk's lip curled as she remembered the slimy mess under her seat. But they had made Daniel's virus per-fect. None of this made sense. Unless . . . Shit, what if it was her tomato that was the carrier?

Fear stabbed through Trisk, and she rose. Daniel looked up at her, and she almost panicked. She wanted to run, but she didn't know what to run to, or away from. "Stay here," she said, hands motioning for him not to move as if he were a horse or a dog. "I'm going to get you a coffee, okay? This is not your fault," she reassured him, knowing it to her core even if everything around her said otherwise. "We're going to wait and talk to the doctor, and see what really happened. She might have a heart condition or something we didn't know about."

Daniel nodded, his head dropping as his own thoughts took over.

"Ah . . ." she added when Quen arched his eyebrows questioningly at her. "This is my brother, Quen. I'll be right back."

Daniel smiled thinly. "Dr. Daniel Plank. Nice to meet you. Trisk never mentioned she had a brother."

"She doesn't talk about me much." Quen hesitated, a wry expression on his face. "I don't know why."

"You seem familiar." Daniel cocked his head, and Trisk hesitated. "It must be because you look alike."

Trisk and Quen eyed each other, but Daniel slumped back into his thoughts, and Trisk pulled Quen aside. *We look alike?* Trisk thought, never having given it much consideration, but it was better than Daniel remembering Quen helping her summon a demon.

"I need to find a phone," she said, voice hushed. "I have to talk to Rick."

Quen's eyes flicked back to her. "Rick? Why?"

Trisk glanced over her shoulder and to the waiting room. "Because he's the boss. Will you watch Daniel?"

"What if he remembers me?"

Trisk looked past Quen to Daniel, the man's expression stoic as he stared at the floor and watched his life crumble. "He's not going to remember you."

"Fine," Quen grumbled. "But I don't want to be your brother."

She pressed her lips together, frowning. "Just . . . I'll be right back."

Quen's heavy sigh seemed to echo as she went back to the lobby to find a public phone. There was one on a small table with laminated instructions on how to call outside the hospital, but she stopped dead in her tracks, staring at it, ashamed at her sudden reluctance to touch it. *You made that virus perfect*, she told herself, watching her hand as she reached out and picked up the receiver.

"Local only, please," the receptionist called loudly, and Trisk absently raised her hand. She was halfway through laboriously dialing Rick's office when the familiar silhouette of Global Genetics flashed up on the TV turned to the late news. Slowly she let the receiver drop from her ear. There were fire trucks and an ambulance. Trisk took a breath to ask someone to turn it up, her voice catching when a photo of Rick flashed up on the screen.

"CEO Rick Rales was pronounced dead at the scene," the woman was saying. "His body was found in one of Global Genetics' underground isolation field labs, suffering massive burns over almost his entire body. That it was after-hours is thought to be to blame for the freak accident. Drs. Daniel Plank and Trisk Cambri are wanted for questioning."

Rick is dead? They're blaming us?

Setting the phone back in the cradle, she turned. More people had come in, all with rashes and blemishes, all tired and looking winded. A woman in a nurse's uniform was sitting with the family in the corner. She seemed fine, but the faint scent of redwood told Trisk she was a witch. Distress crossed the nurse's face when the teenager ran for the bathroom and the sound of vomiting spilled out into the waiting room. The mother got up, staggering slightly as she followed her daughter in. At the coffee table, a crayoned picture of ghosts trick-or-treating drifted to the floor, forgotten.

Shit. Not only was Daniel's virus out, but it was spreading. Daniel was right. It had found a carrier. *Not my tomato. It can't be my tomato. I made it perfect.*

Wiping her hand on her jeans, Trisk backed away from the phone. Head down to avoid eye contact, she walked quickly to where Quen waited with Daniel. The man was still slumped in his chair. In contrast, Quen stood over him at parade rest, his stiff jaw and firm stance making him look military despite his longish hair and stubbled cheeks. His three years as Kalamack security were showing. "We have to go. Now," she said.

Quen's eyes shot to hers, drawn by her obvious fear. Daniel was slower, his focus distant as he pushed his glasses back up his nose. "The lab is on fire," she added.

Daniel's eyes widened. "What?" he asked, suddenly paying attention.

Clutching her purse in a white-knuckled grip, she looked up and down the hall. "Rick is gone. Burned to death in the fire. They think we did it."

"Us? Why?" Daniel said, bewildered, and then his expression became slack. "Before I left the party, I caught Rick in the hallway. He said the government was upset. That our calculations were wrong and their own people were being exposed. But how . . ." His eyes went past her to the sound of the kid vomiting. "Trisk . . ." he whispered, scared as he immediately made the same connection she had.

She drew him to his feet, and Daniel rose, obedient in shock. "We have to go." Trisk gave Quen a meaningful look, and he nodded. Pace even and unhurried, he started for the main door. His steps were light with tension and his arms swung easily. Trisk pulled Daniel stumbling in his wake.

"I don't understand," Daniel said. "Where . . . I don't have my car. I took a cab here."

She took a tighter grip on his arm as they passed through the emergency waiting room. It was starting to fill up. "We'll fit in my truck."

"Back to the lab?" Daniel said. "We have to find out what went wrong."

"What went wrong?" she said as they went out the door together. "Rick is dead," she said, relishing the clean night air. "They must think we killed him to cover up that your virus has gone rogue. If it's using my tomato as a carrier, it could be all over the world in a matter of days, springboarded by your trial in Vietnam."

Daniel stared at her, his thoughts almost visibly aligning as he put two and two together and got plague. "My God," he whispered, turning to look behind him at the emergency room, bright with light as they stood in the dark. "Your tomato is condensing the toxins to lethal levels. But how? They don't mesh."

"Tell me about it," Trisk said. "We need to find out for sure and see if we can stop it. But the last place we're going to go is Global Genetics. Not only is there nothing left of it, but even if there were, they'd throw us in jail."

Daniel swallowed hard, his steps holding the first hints of decisiveness as they stepped off the curb. "Where, then?"

Trisk looked at Quen. Her impulse to go to Cincinnati, where her father lived, rose and fell. There was no facility there. "Detroit?" she suggested, thoughts turning to the hidden elven labs scattered all over the U.S. Most were east of the Mississippi due to the fractured ley lines.

"Detroit doesn't have a biolab," Daniel said as they headed for the truck as one.

Arm looped in Daniel's, Trisk looked up at the moon as she paced forward. "As a matter of fact, it does."

18

The hum of her truck had become hypnotic, and the headlights illuminating the smooth two-lane road heading east seemed to push back the dark just enough for them to pass through before it swallowed the world again. Trisk was driving because it was her truck. Daniel sat between her and Quen on the long bench seat. Both men looked lost in their own thoughts, but neither was showing any signs of unusual fatigue, rash, or nausea. U.S. 50 had been busy up to Reno, but now, as they entered Nevada's deserts in earnest, the towns were smaller and the traffic almost nonexistent. It made her uneasy, and she couldn't exactly say why.

The radio hissed as Peter and Gordon's playful "Lady Godiva" ended, and Quen's hand shot out first, his careful fingers shifting the dial to bring the station's announcer in again. Sporadic news was being announced between British pop singles, and both men were listening with a morbid fascination. Sunset was only a few hours behind them, and Trisk's and Quen's elven metabolism made them both alert.

"Did he say they shut the border?" Daniel asked, and Quen nodded, his eyes never leaving the radio as it faded in and out. So far, Vietnam's sudden isolation was being blamed on the recent military action, not the likely thousands of dead who were being piled in mass graves or simply left where they fell. Closing the border wasn't going to help. The virus already had a foothold both in the U.S. and abroad, running rampant among oblivious populations.

Sick at heart, Trisk clicked the radio off as they came into a small town. Both men sat back in protest, but she couldn't take any more. "We need to fill up before we hit the desert," she said as she slowed, the engine sounding loud. Trisk scanned the dark storefronts and lighted stoops to see who was still open. It was dark, but not that late, the October night warm and clear.

"I could stretch my legs," Quen said, and Daniel nodded, rubbing his stubbled cheeks.

"Maybe grab something to eat," Daniel added with a yawn, and Trisk angled toward a gas station across the street from a diner.

"We should call the enclave," she said, and Quen's head jerked up in warning. "Sa'han Ulbrine has the clout to get the tomato fields burned," she continued, flushing for having mentioned the elves' secret cabal in front of Daniel. "If we bring it up, they'll slap us in jail and ignore it."

"Who's Saahan Ulbrine?" Daniel asked, and she winced.

"One of my instructors," she said, glad he'd focused on that instead of the more difficult-to-explain term, *enclave*.

Daniel looked ill as she pulled up to the pump and put the truck in park. "Trisk, it can't be your tomato. You know both organisms inside and out. It's just coincidence."

"What else would make the plants fall apart like that?" she said as Quen got out and made a beeline for the restroom sign leading behind the building.

Daniel followed him with his eyes. "It's my virus. Your tomatoes are perfect."

No one was coming to pump the gas, and she was feeling the need to use the restroom. "They were yesterday," she muttered, and Daniel's lips parted at the implied sabotage.

Impatient, Trisk grabbed her purse and got out, slamming her door to hopefully get some attention from the small garage. Her legs ached, and she stretched. On the other side, Daniel slowly slipped from the cab, his expression empty as he thought her last words over. "Maybe they're closed," he said, turning at the loud bang of the restroom door as Quen returned.

Trisk shrugged as she tried to see past the ads on the windows and into the garage. "Someone is in there. I'll go see."

Daniel jiggled on his feet, his attention going from the restroom door back to her. "I'll go with you," he said, eyes pinched in worry as she came around the front of the truck and headed in.

"Ah . . ." Quen stood beside the truck, fingers pressed into his forehead as he looked at the pump. "Either of you know how to turn this thing on?"

Daniel jerked to a stop. "You don't know how to pump gas?"

"I don't, actually," Quen said.

Trisk touched Daniel's shoulder. "I'll be fine. I'll make sure the pump is on."

Nodding, Daniel returned to the truck, and Trisk went inside. "Hello?" she called, smiling when a kid came out from the back. He was about fourteen, dressed in overalls and tatty sneakers. "Are you open?" she asked, and he nodded, seeming nervous as he looked past her to the two men managing the pump.

"I'm not allowed to pump gas," he said, voice cracking. "I'm the only one here, though."

"I think they have it," she said, glancing at a bucket of melted ice and bottles of Coke. "I'll take three," she said.

"Sure." The kid looked relieved to be doing something as he carefully rang up the bottles, waiting to total it out until he knew how much gas they took.

"Are you okay?" she finally asked, and his eyes darted nervously up at her.

"I was supposed to go home two hours ago," he said, fidgeting. "But Amos went home sick, and Evan never came in. I don't have a key to lock up."

Her smile froze. *How did it get here so fast?* "Well, that's good for us, then," she said. "Otherwise, we'd have to wait until morning to fill up."

He smelled faintly of redwood, and the wooden nickel he had on a cord around his neck was probably an amulet. He was a witch, and a knot of worry in her eased. He, at least, would be spared. "Do you need a ride somewhere?" she asked, and he shook his head, attention flicking behind her as Daniel came in.

"I can walk home, but if I leave the shop open, Amos will tan my hide."

If he survives, she thought as Daniel looked at the wet bottles on the counter. "We filled both tanks. It came out to seven sixty," he said. "You want to get some coffee at the diner?"

"And maybe something to eat," she said as the kid punched it in.

"Nine dollars and three cents with the soda," he said, and Daniel reached for his wallet.

"I've got this if you want to use the restroom."

"I'll wait for the diner's," she said. "You don't happen to have a phone, do you?" she asked the kid, now carefully counting out the change.

"Next to the restroom," he said, and Trisk gave Daniel a touch on his arm before going to find it. She didn't want to look like the chicken crying, "The sky is falling!" but Sa'han Ulbrine needed to know. Warn people.

Her sneakers were eerily silent on the old cement as she looked around the side of the building for the public phone. The light was out above it, but she could see well enough, and after spotting Quen reclined against the side of the truck, she dropped in a dime.

She knew his number by heart, and she turned, looking up and down the quiet street as the phone rang. The neon hummed over the bowling alley, but the lot was empty. Two cars and a semi lingered at the diner, but apart from that, no one was around. *Eerie*, she thought.

"Hello?" a nasal woman's voice said when the connection finally went through, and Trisk pressed the receiver tighter against her ear.

"I'd like to talk to Sa'han Ulbrine, please. It's an emergency. I'm calling long-distance. It's—Dr. Felecia Cambri," she added, hating the name but not wanting any misconception that might get her brushed off.

"Just a moment, please. I'll see if he's available. He might have left for the weekend."

"Please," Trisk blurted out. "It's an emergency, and I need to talk to him."

"I'll see if I can find him," the woman said again, and then there was a sharp click as the receiver was put down. The phone dinged for her attention, and she dropped in another dime. Daniel came out with the dripping sodas, and she turned her back on him, hoping he'd go to the truck.

She caught herself before she chewed on a fingernail, making a fist instead as she waited. The town looked empty, but it was hard to know if this was normal for a Friday night or if sick people were becoming sicker.

As she watched, a family pulled into the diner. Three kids boiled out of the long station wagon, then the dad, followed by the mom with a toddler in hand and another on her hip, cajoling the kids to behave. It looked like a slice of Americana, but she was betting they were Weres by the way the kids ranged out and back, the father watching the near area for trouble and the mother doing the same on the horizon. Though belonging as much as anyone else on the continent, they stuck out in a way they never had before, the slight differences telling with no humans to blur the lines.

Trisk's brow furrowed when the kids found the door to the diner locked. Her voice loud, the mother corralled them all back in the wagon while they decided what to do.

"Trisk?" came a low voice from the receiver, and she exhaled in relief.

"Thank God," she whispered, and then louder, "Sa'han Ulbrine. I think someone tampered with Daniel's virus. It's latched onto my tomato and gone rogue. If you can get on the news and tell everyone to burn the Angel tomato fields, we might be able to stop this. From what little I can tell, the tomato is condensing the toxins to a lethal level in humans."

Ulbrine swore. "Your tomato? Are you sure?"

Trisk nodded, not caring that he couldn't see the motion. "My lab assistant went from not feeling well to dead in less than twenty-four hours." A sudden lump filled her throat, and Trisk gasped, blinking fast as she walled the grief off. "She might have been exposed to a more massive dose than the general populace," she whispered. "But I don't—"

"Where are you?" Ulbrine interrupted, and Trisk looked at her truck under the garage's flickering streetlight. Quen was keeping Daniel busy and away from the phone under the excuse of checking the oil. Across the street, the Were family still sat in the wagon. The wind blew in off the desert, warm as it lifted her hair with the scent of dust and undisturbed eons.

"A gas station outside of Carson City," she said, eyes roving over the dark street. "Ah . . . Fallon, I think," she added, seeing FALLON LANES over the bowling alley. "We're trying to get to Detroit. If you can get us lab access, we can prove the tomato is the carrier."

"You don't know for sure?" Ulbrine asked, and she thought she could hear the scratching of a pen and the ripping of paper.

Trisk's jaw clenched. "I made that tomato perfectly, and my seed field is a black decayed mess. The emergency room was filling up with symptoms of Daniel's virus when we left. It's hitting people with no lab access. Kids. Entire families." *Oh, God, that family. . .* "I think Kal did it," she whispered, and Ulbrine grunted in surprise.

"I know you dislike him, but you can't blame Kal without proof. He's there doing a job."

"Yes, I can," she said, hunched over the receiver. "And I do. He's the only one who had access to both organisms." *Why the hell did I ever sleep with him?*

"Rick has access," Ulbrine said, and she pressed her fingers into her forehead.

"Rick is dead," she said. "Someone set fire to my seed field. He was in it at the time."

"That would explain the call I got a few hours ago from his camarilla," he said. "Damn. I was hoping it was just a rumor. But dead isn't always dead when it comes to vampires. His passing could be a way to push the blame for this on you or the elves in general. Vampires say they want everything to stay the same, but if there's an easy way to take out the humans and leave vampires as the apex predator, some uppity dead vamp might try in order to be king of the universe."

Trisk said nothing, the same thought having occurred to her. But it was Kal. She knew it.

"This is what I want you to do," Ulbrine said into the new silence. "Go to Detroit. I'll hop a plane tomorrow and meet you there with Kal. We'll look at it together, and if your tomato is the carrier, we'll make the announcement then."

"Kal? No." Pulling her hair into a ponytail, she let it go. "And why do we need proof before we start warning people?" she asked, her thoughts on Sacramento's emergency room.

"I *will not* start a panic that points fingers at the elves," Ulbrine said, and she swallowed her next complaint. "If it's the T4 Angel tomato, then of course we'll tell people, but not until we know for sure."

"Sa'han—" she said, unwilling to wait.

"Felecia, no," Ulbrine said, cutting her off. "If we announce that your tomato is the carrier, and then find out it isn't, the rest of Inderland will never believe it wasn't us. I don't want to go down as the species that exterminated the humans, do you?"

He thinks it might kill them all? "No," she said. "But we have to say something. It's fast, Sa'han. I don't understand how it's moving so quickly. Even a day is going to make a difference. I'm seeing evidence of it right now, in this little town, and we just got here!"

But her anger mutated to fear when a long black car pulled behind her truck, brakes squealing. Another boxed the truck in at the front. Big men started getting out as a third, smaller car slowly parked at the outskirts. "I have to go," she said, interrupting Ulbrine's demand that she keep her mouth shut until they knew for sure. "I'll see you in Detroit," she added as she hung up. Pace fast, she almost jogged back to the truck. "Quen!"

But Quen was well aware of them, the tips of his curling hair floating as he tapped a line and let it course through him. Trisk tapped the line as well. It slipped in with a startling quickness, and she staggered at the strength and surety that she'd been missing the last few years.

They were vampires, and it was obvious they were not happy as they ringed her truck, arms crossed over their middles or hands in their pockets. There was no expression on their hard faces, but the hint of bloodlust was enough to scare her. Some were tall and elegant, fair with youth and eager to hurt. Others were older, heavier and short with hard muscle held in check by an anticipation of dealing out pain. But they all stared at them in hunger. Mobs like this were not legal. It was too easy to lose control and potentially reveal themselves to the human race.

But she wasn't sure there were any humans left in this town.

Together, Trisk, Quen, and Daniel faced them, her truck behind them. Her skin prickled with the force running through Quen's aura, and she subtly shifted her strength so they would be more in tune. Her clenched jaw eased, but she still jumped when the door to a new, smaller car slammed. Her eyes darted to the narrow, thin man standing beside it at the outskirts. "We got them, Mr. Niles," one of the men said, and the small man tugged his suit coat straight and came forward.

Mr. Niles looked almost invisible in the flickering streetlight, a part of the shadows even as he moved closer, telling the ring of men to back off with a soft hand motion. His feet scuffed as he halted before them, his mood ambiguous on his long face as he checked an old-fashioned pocket watch and dropped it into his pocket. Exhaling a breath he hadn't needed to take, he assessed them.

Trisk's heart pounded. This was a true undead, and she glanced inside the garage, hoping the young witch was hiding. The Weres were still in their parked car across the road. There were no humans apart from Daniel, and it felt wrong and unreal. There were always humans. They were like the trees and the air—keeping Inderlanders alive, keeping them in check.

"The pumps are working, but the attendant is gone," Quen said, his low voice heavy with threat. "If you get back in your cars, I'll pump your gas and you can go."

The surrounding vampires laughed, and Trisk saw Daniel stiffen as he noticed the dead vampire's longer canines when he smiled. Niles's expression had no warmth, utterly devoid of emotion other than anger. "We are not here for petrol," Niles said, his voice carrying a faint Irish accent. "We are here for answers."

"Then ask," Quen said, and Trisk tightened her grip on her line, ready for anything.

A flicker of pain crossed the undead's face, making him almost human for an instant. It was a lie, though, a well-practiced act to lull them into thinking he might have compassion and understanding. The undead remembered love, but they didn't feel it anymore, or understand it.

"Rick was my child, my scion, my favorite," Niles said. "I sent him to watch you. Now he's horribly dead before his time."

"That wasn't our doing," Trisk said, then blanched when he turned his hatred to her.

"Yet he's unprepared and dead," he said. "Restitution must be made."

"If you're looking for restitution—" Daniel's voice cut off when the man shifted his gaze to him. "Holy shit," he whispered, suddenly ashen in the flickering overhead light. Quen scuffed his foot, and the vampire turned away, freeing Daniel before he could be enthralled.

"Look elsewhere for restitution," Quen said, and Trisk realized he had scratched a half circle in the packed, oil-soaked dirt. Foot moving slow, she scratched another segment. It was a start. She and Quen were good, but there had to be at least ten vampires here. "We didn't kill him," Quen finished boldly, and the undead vampire's fingers twitched.

"We didn't set the fire," Trisk said, drawing the man's attention so Quen could finish the circle. "We weren't even in the building at the time. I lost my research. So did Dr. Plank. What would we have to gain from killing Rick?" she added, but it sounded hollow. They weren't listening, just prolonging the anticipation.

"Humans are dying in my city," the vampire said, and Trisk's pulse quickened. *His city?* He was the freaking head vampire of Sacramento? No wonder Rick was so confident—had been confident. "My child suffered. Saladan seeks restitution as well, but all he wants is money.

My child's needs take precedence over his greed. Someone is responsible. I blame you."

"Humans?" Daniel whispered, then louder, "There was an accident."

"Shut up," Trisk hissed as the vampires circling them began to inch closer.

The master vampire looked again at his watch. "An accident," he echoed. "Yes. Good idea." He flicked his fingers, and that fast, his men sprang at them. "Take them. Alive."

"Down!" Trisk shouted, simultaneously throwing a ball of unfocused energy at the vampire leaping for her and pushing Daniel to the pavement. Quen dove into a roll, rising up before them and shoving a ball of force at the nearest attacker. "Quen!" she exclaimed, eyes widening at the three vampires coming at them. "Get back in the circle. Quen!"

"Invoke it!" Quen dove clear of an attacker and flicked a tiny ball of light that exploded in the vampire's face. The incensed man fell back screaming.

Stupid male ego, she thought, pulling heavily on the line. "*Septiens!*" she shouted to invoke the circle, and it sprang up.

"Hey!" she yelped, cowering as three vampires suddenly hammered at her and Daniel, held off by the strength of her barrier. Daniel looked up, his foot pressed into the base of the circle. If she touched it, her aura would cause it to fall. If she threw a spell through it, her aura holding the charm together would break it as well. As long as she made no contact, it would be like clear steel.

"My God," Daniel whispered, touching the barrier to find it give slightly under his fingers. Then he jerked, shocked at the three men circling them, slavering almost. "A shield?" he guessed, eyes wide. "How did you do that? Who are you?"

Trisk grimaced. *You should have stayed in the circle, Quen.* "I'm the same person I was yesterday," she said. "Just as dumb and foolish." She jerked when one of the vampires punched at her, the strike ending inches from her head. He smiled at her, teeth wet with saliva. "Just like that stupid Quen!" she shouted, frustrated. If she'd known he was going to take them all on himself, she never would have even helped draw the circle.

But Quen was still standing, flicking orbs of raw energy between spelled ones that blew the attacking vampires back. Trisk tensed, wanting to help but pinned down by her need to protect Daniel, even as he stared, his odd expression making her wonder if he was remembering watching Quen do the same thing a week ago.

"Finish this!" their master shouted. "I have to be home by sunrise!"

"Quen!" she called, frantic as they all fell on him at once. Three men in suits were thrown back, and then Quen was gone again, hidden by a pile of bodies.

"Get off," Niles said gruffly, picking his men off one by one and flinging them to the side. "Let him up. Let him breathe. I want to see him. I want him alive."

Daniel got to his feet, awkwardly hunched to keep from hitting his head on the top of her circle. "Who are these people?" he asked, and Trisk felt heartsick. Regardless, if they survived this, Daniel, and even herself, likely, would end up dead at the hands of the enclave. Letting a human know they weren't alone on the earth was not a forgivable mistake.

"My guess?" she said, giving up on fixing this. "Rick's family."

"Rick was in the mob?" Daniel said, getting it utterly wrong and utterly right at the same time.

"Let him up," Niles said, head cocking when three of his thugs wrestled Quen upright. He was bleeding from his lip, and his once-white shirt was filthy, but his eyes were bright with unspent fight. Eyebrows high, the master vampire turned to her. "Come out. Or he dies. Right here."

"You wouldn't dare," she said, hands shaking. "Not in front of witnesses."

The master vampire scoffed, looking at his men leaning against their car and tending their sundry hurts. "Humanity is dying, Dr. Cambri. Soon, there won't *be* any witnesses." His lip twitched as her breath caught. It couldn't be that bad. "Get *out*!" he shouted, gesturing at her as if she were a reluctant child. "We need to make an accident."

Quen gasped, his struggles surging into a frantic motion that cut off with a pop of his shoulder. Trisk reached at his sudden cry of pain, stifled in a groan. "Stay in there," he ground out through his clenched teeth, head down as he knelt before them, his arm twisted at an unnatural angle. "I'm going to die anyway."

But letting that happen wasn't an option, and pulse fast, Trisk touched her bubble, breaking it. "You stay off—" Then she shrieked as someone grabbed her bicep and yanked her from Daniel. Quen looked up, his jaw tight in pain, but behind it was regret. Daniel was silent in the grip of a third vampire.

The master vampire before them grinned, liking Daniel's shocked reaction when he showed him his long canines. "You really should let the professionals do their job," he said, nose wrinkling when he motioned to his men, and they enthusiastically began sloshing gas on, in, and over her truck. "Accidents can happen."

Again he smiled, and Trisk's anger mixed with fear in an unreal slurry. He was going to burn them alive as Rick had been burned. *Son of a bitch . . .*

"No," she whispered, channeling a wad of unfocused energy into the hand holding her.

The vampire gripping her arm jerked. She was free. For one glorious instant, she was free.

"Trisk!" Daniel shouted, and then he gasped.

Trisk spun, the unfocused energy balled in her hand sizzling. Daniel was in Niles's grip, his head pulled back, his pulse pounding just under his skin, inches from the vampire's teeth.

"You are going to die," the vampire said. "I want you to burn, but this one, I could make an exception for. He could take years to die with my children, a decade with me. You choose."

Daniel was terrified, his eyes wide as his world was rearranged with a savage suddenness and he knew he was no longer the apex predator. Daniel was prey.

"Let him go," she whispered, hand aching as she reabsorbed the freed energy. "Let him go!" she shouted when Niles hesitated, and he flung Daniel at the truck with an angry petulance.

"Daniel!" she exclaimed, lurching forward, but he hit with a thunk and fell, out cold.

One of the vampires yanked him up, bundling him into Trisk's truck and gesturing with a macabre graciousness for her to follow.

Jaw clenched, she got in, her hands tingling from her charged aura sparking against the spilled fuel. Quen was shoved into the other side, and the door slammed shut. The handles were twisted off, locking them in.

"Shame to waste you," Niles said as he checked his watch. "It's going to become hard to find a way to satisfy everyone, soon. But this holds satisfaction. You burn my child, I burn you."

"We didn't start the fire!" Trisk exclaimed, but he turned his back on them and gestured for his men to get on with it.

Daniel slumped between them, still unconscious. It would be more merciful to let him stay that way. "We filled both tanks," Quen said, eyes pinched in pain. The keys were gone. They couldn't move, even when the cars blocking them backed up. "It's going to make one hell of a bang."

"Shit, shit, shit," Trisk whispered as the vampire standing in front of them took a long drag on his cigarette and dropped it into a puddle. The fumes caught, and a yellow glow spread out and under her truck.

"Got any ideas?" Quen said, his nose wrinkling at the smell of half-burned fuel.

"Circle?" she said, pulling more strength into her.

Quen winced, his arm cradled in his lap. "We'd have to sit here with the truck burning around us until it was done. I don't think we can last that long. The air is going to get hot, not to mention the fire will use up the oxygen."

"Two circles," she said, breathless. "Us in the center, and a larger one around the truck to contain the blast. It burns up the oxygen in one swoop. Like a backfire putting out a forest fire."

Quen's eyebrows rose, his attention flicking back to her from the flashing lights coming down the road. They were too far away. "I'll take the outer circle."

"*I'll* take the outer one," she said, imagining it in her mind. "I've got more practice."

"I know how to make a circle," Quen said dryly, dabbing at his lip.

"The size of a truck?" Trisk turned, watching the vampires run to their cars. "One strong enough to hold a demon? I take the outer circle."

Between them, Daniel stirred, his head down. "One of you better do something," he slurred. "I think I heard the tank just catch."

"*Septiens!*" Trisk shouted, the energy streaming through her prickling as she felt Quen's protection spring up tight around them.

And then her ears exploded as the hand of God reached down and slapped her.

Too fast to cry out, she was shoved forward. She hit twice, hardly noticing the twin bumps of first Quen's circle, and then the hard dash, before she was flung through the front window, the harmless shards hitting her like snowflakes as she tumbled through, over the hood, and onto the hard-packed dirt.

She gasped for breath as she rolled, feeling as if she were drowning, and then she hit her own, larger bubble. It fell. Behind her, the fire whooshed up, making a second flash of heat to crisp her hair.

"Quen!" she shouted, her ears numb and her skin hot. Hip aching, she sat up, turning to look at her truck, engulfed in flames. "Daniel! Quen!" *Oh God, were they thrown clear?*

"Ow," Daniel said, and her head whipped around. He was behind her, flat on his back and holding his head as he stared at the floating ash of her burnt books drifting down.

"That didn't work as well as I thought it would," Quen said, and she looked to see him standing over her, his hand extended to help her up.

Thank you, God. She shook her head, trying to clear it. "We're alive, though." His hand fitting into hers was warm and calloused, and she felt the prick of tears as he hauled her up. "How is your shoulder?"

Pain creasing his brow, he shifted it. "Slamming into your circle popped it back in place," he said, turning to the four cop cars now racing up, lights and sirens going. "We have to go."

"How?" She gestured at her burning truck, her long hair swinging. "We'll just explain what happened. I'm sure they'll understand."

"What they'll understand is that you're wanted for questioning in a murder," Quen said, but she hadn't done it, and for some stupid reason, she thought that mattered.

Both Trisk and Quen turned when the door to the garage was flung open and the kid came out, his eyes wide and round. "Are you okay? I called the cops!"

Quen pinched the bridge of his nose, but worried about Daniel, Trisk held one hand against her sore hip and limped to him. He'd managed to sit up but was still blinking as if in a daze. "Maybe they won't recognize us," she said as the thump of a car door echoed. Men were getting out, their hands at their hips as they crept closer, skirting the burning truck.

"Dr. Trisk Cambri?" the biggest officer said, and she winced.

"Or not," she whispered. Giving Daniel a pat on the shoulder, she rose up beside him. "That's me," she said louder, determined to see it through. "And this is Dr. Plank, and Quen Hanson. Did you see those yahoos? They set my truck on fire."

The cop came closer, weapon unsnapped. "Thanks for the call, Casey," the gruff man said to the kid. "Go on home now. You know you're not supposed to be working here alone."

"Okay, Officer Bob. My mom wants to know if you're coming over Sunday for dinner."

Officer Bob grimaced, motioning to his men to check out the building. "You just get home now. I'll call your mom later." Putting his hands on his knees, he peered at Daniel as he sat on the ground, head down. "You okay, son? You know where you are? What day it is?"

"I'm okay," Daniel rasped, squinting through one eye up at them.

"Good, good," Officer Bob said, and one of his men reached down and helped Daniel to his feet. "If everyone is okay, cuff 'em and stuff 'em."

"What!" Trisk spun, immediately regretting it as everything began to hurt. "They attacked us! Ask Casey. Hey!" she yelped as someone jerked her arms behind her and cuffed her. "We didn't do anything!"

There were humans here. A show of magic would be disastrous, and she watched Quen go from tense to pliable as he realized it, too. His face twisted in frustration as they shoved him into one car and Daniel into another. The man propelling Trisk to a third car had a rash, and one of the men at the outskirts was vomiting. They were all human. Every last one. "They attacked us!" Trisk exclaimed as she was pushed into a car. "Why are you arresting us?"

Officer Bob stood beside her open door, making sure her foot was safely inside. "You and Dr. Plank are wanted for arson and questioning in the murder of Rick Rales. We're arresting your friend until we know who he is."

"We didn't start the fire." *Damn it, I hate it when Quen is right.* "I was at home packing my stuff. Look, it's in the truck," she said, then jumped when the cop car's door slammed shut.

"Let's go!" Officer Bob shouted, voice muffled. "José, stay here with the fire trucks."

Trisk sat forward on the edge of the seat, the need to do something filling her. Her stuff in the truck was still burning, ignored. Slowly she sat back. Being arrested for Rick's murder was going to put a real crimp in her travel plans, even though if the police hadn't shown up, the vampires would have killed them.

But as she watched the ailing officers and recognized the earmarks of Daniel's virus in their flushed faces and lethargic motions, the idea crossed her mind that being stuck in a cell might not be any better.

19

The early-morning news was on in the living room of Kal's uptown apartment, muted to a pleasant murmur that almost hid the thread of panic stringing the woman's words together. Kal had felt domestic this morning, and since sleep had eluded him, he had decided to make his own breakfast even before the sun had come up. It was unlikely that Lilly, his housekeeper, would be in today. The instructions on the box of blueberry muffins had said it would make twelve, but he must have done something wrong because he'd filled all the tins and had some batter left over.

Kal came up from the oven, having peeked in at the rising muffins. Throwing the empty box away, he stood in the apartment's tiny kitchen and watched the woman reporter from across the room. "Muffins from a box. Amazing," he said as he ate the leftover batter with a spoon.

Sacramento was currently under Accidental Release Protocol, which was very much like a voluntary martial law without the military. The story was that Global Genetics had undergone an accidental release due to yesterday's fire. Residents within the drift area had been advised to stock up, sit tight, and boil their water. Hanging a towel in a front window would bring help, as the phone lines were no longer working. People were being asked not to come into the hospital, as care was likely better at home. Red Cross wasn't expected until later today, but government troops were setting up outside the perimeter and would start a door-to-door sweep at sunup. Employees of Global Genetics had been told to remain home and wait for instructions until it was better understood what had been released. Incidences of sickness had popped up in Nevada as well as San Francisco, and even Las Vegas, but so far, only Sacramento was under quarantine.

Licking the last of the batter from the spoon, Kal checked his baking again. "Ten minutes?" he guessed aloud, setting the bowl in the sink and taking his coffee into the living room. There was a toy horse on the coffee table, and he shifted it to make room for his feet. He'd bought it for the boy downstairs, currently under house quarantine with the mumps and bored out of his little-boy mind. Kal could sympathize, having endured a childhood that often had him in the hospital and away from friends. It was a strong, dark, mane-flaring horse, and he hoped DJ liked it.

His smile widened when Orchid slipped in through a side window, her wings clattering and a faint yellow dust slipping from her as she stopped short upon seeing him. "You're up early," she said as he settled in front of the TV. "It's not even sunup yet."

"No need to adhere to a human clock today," he said, marveling at her wings as she carefully cleaned the dew from them. There was a basket of clean laundry at his feet, his clothes from yesterday washed and dried in the communal laundry downstairs. It was unlikely that his laundry service would be functioning anytime soon, and letting them molder about with decayed tomato and accelerant hadn't been an option. He'd left them for Lilly to iron and fold.

I should probably at least fold them.

Orchid landed on the rim of the basket, and his eyes shifted to the TV. It was black and white. He missed his color TV. "So," the small woman prompted, "whatcha doing today?"

Her disapproval was obvious in her sickly green dust and in how her hands were set on her hips. "Taking DJ that toy horse I bought him," he said, his lip twitching as he remembered Rick's twisted body, moving even as he burned. "Waiting it out," he added, his eyebrows rising when he noticed the announcer had a rash, badly hidden under pancake makeup.

Orchid rose up, shifting to his shoulder. "It's spreading fast," she said, her dust turning yellow as she saw the rash as well.

Kal nodded, taking a last sip of his coffee before he set it aside and pulled the basket closer. Orchid darted off, but she didn't go far. "Faster than I'd expect," he admitted. His clothes smelled pleasingly clean, and he searched out the socks, making a pile on the couch to fold last.

"You think it's airborne?" Orchid asked, and he shrugged, setting his shirt aside to iron.

"Perhaps." He frowned in thought, remembering George's clean skin. "Not everyone in Global Genetics seems to have caught it. But it's popping up in odd places."

"Like Carson City." The pixy dropped to the basket, tugging until one of his socks came free and she ferried it to the pile on the couch.

"Trisk could have taken it there," he admitted. "But

San Francisco?" Kal's brow furrowed. It was as if healthy tomatoes, those picked weeks ago, had been exposed to the virus and suddenly become toxic. Had he erred in using the hairs as a connection point? Was the virus attacking the picked fruit as well as the plant? Fruit that could then acquire the virus while it sat on produce shelves or a truck driving through town? "And Las Vegas?" he questioned softly as the reporter was replaced with a map of the western U.S., ominous red dots showing where signs of the virus were now appearing.

"All roads lead to Vegas," a bitter, masculine voice intoned, and Orchid darted into the air, inking a bright red in shock.

Kal spun, rising to his feet when he saw the shadow of a man in his front entry. "Saladan," he blurted, recognizing the unmoving figure in his black suit and white shirt.

"I'm sorry, Kal," Orchid gushed, clearly embarrassed. "I didn't hear him come in."

Saladan removed his sunglasses and dropped them in a shirt pocket with a pointed slowness. "I didn't want you to."

The faint purple glow about his fingers was mirrored on the door handle and lock, and incensed, Kal felt his eyes narrow. "You broke my lock with magic—" Kal yelped, dropping to the floor when Saladan flicked an aura-laced ball of energy at him.

"Hey!" Orchid shouted, the tiny woman pulling her garden sword and hovering over Kal. "You got a problem, stinky britches?"

"Not with you," Saladan said, and Kal froze when a room-wide bubble snapped into place. It shrank even as Kal sat up, slithering over him with an icy feeling. Orchid darted up, then to the left, then down as the bubble condensed until she was trapped in a globe the size of a beach ball. It was an incredible show of finesse, and Kal's jaw dropped.

"Let me out!" Orchid demanded, her dust pooling up to show the bottom of the sphere as it slowly drifted.

"What do you want?" Kal said as he got to his feet, then blanched when Saladan turned to him. Anger etched the witch's face, his fingers hazed from the energy from the ley line he was channeling. Seeing Saladan's shoulders hunched in anger, Kal suddenly realized that in trashing Trisk's reputation, he'd utterly destroyed the man's product—the one that Saladan had mortgaged his entire family's wealth on.

Thin lips pressed into a line, the tall, dark witch pointed at Kal. "Tell me why."

Power dripped in sparkling purple threads from Saladan's fingers, and Kal retreated deeper into his living room, forced back as Saladan came farther in. "It was Trisk," he lied. "She holds a grudge longer than any person I've ever seen, and she was tired of you trying to weasel out of the patent transfer."

"You blame your failed schemes on a *woman*?" Saladan exclaimed. "You *coward*!"

A flicker of anger in his eyes gave Kal bare warning, and he dove to the side as Saladan sent a hissing, tangling curse at him. The black threads cored with purple twisted and writhed like dying snakes until one touched the leg of the couch. With a soul-stealing keening, the arms of the spell fell upon the couch and tightened. There was a crack of breaking wood, and in three seconds, his couch was twisted into a shredded pile of upholstery, wire, and wood.

Holy shit. He knows black magic. Aghast, Kal backed up, hands raised even as he tapped the nearest ley line.

Energy limped into him, slippery from the frequent quakes. *I can't best black magic*, he thought, his eyes wide as he deflected another ball of energy. The two forces struck, and Saladan's spell pinwheeled onto the table where Kal's orchids were set to catch the morning sun. With an ugly, wet splat and snapping, his entire body of work was gone, reduced to torn blooms and wet bark. Anger flashed through Kal, smothered by the fear of self-preservation. It could have been him.

"Was this a personal vendetta for you, Kalamack?" Saladan said as he came in another step, fingers twitching in another ley line spell. "Or is destroying my family something the enclave wants?"

Still angry, Kal held a hand out, trying to reason with him. "Do you honestly think I'd hang around here if I was trying to swindle you? For God's sake, Saladan, I gain nothing by your downfall."

The older man's lip twitched. "Neither does Trisk," he almost growled. "But the enclave might. *You* are the enclave's representative. *You* signed off on the patent. Everything I own was tied up in those damned tomatoes, and my fields are nothing but black goo and my workers dead in the field. And I will know *why*!"

"I don't know," Kal said, then, gasping, flung up a protection circle around himself as Saladan threw another spell at him. "Will you stop it!" he exclaimed as a purple haze coated his circle, trying to eat its way in. "That tomato was perfect. If there'd been a problem, I would have seen it. She changed it to bring me down by framing me for gross negligence. If you want revenge, get it from her!"

Saladan made a quick, almost unnoticed motion with his left hand, and the sizzling evil eating its way into Kal's circle crawled into itself and vanished. Relieved,

Kal darted a glance at his demolished orchids, then met the man's eyes in the new quiet. "I don't believe you," Saladan said softly, and Kal pulled himself to his full height, anger buoying him up.

But the witch had stopped trying to kill him, and Kal let his protection circle drop even as he continued to pull ley line energy into himself. "I'm making muffins and watching TV," Kal said, glancing at the kitchen. Orchid's bubble had drifted into it, and the pixy was doggedly trying to pierce her way out of the floating sphere, her dust an angry black. "Trisk has fled the city and is under suspicion for murder. I have nothing to do with it. Any of it."

Saladan's expression blanked. "How do you know she's fled the city?" he said.

Kal's eyes widened. "Ah . . ." He scrambled for a reason, but they all sounded false.

"The demons were right," Saladan said, the glow strengthening around his hands. "You should all die. Down to the last pointy-eared newborn."

"Saladan," Kal started, then backpedaled. "Hey!" he shouted as an icy thread of purple-cored blackness spun through the air toward him. Fast from panic, Kal marshaled his energy into his hand, narrowly throwing the unfocused energy at the incoming spell. The twin powers hit, and the black coil writhed, overcome by the gold haze. Kal took a relieved breath and looked up.

Saladan was on him.

In a tangle of legs and arms, they hit the floor. Long, thin fingers twined around Kal's throat, choking him. Kal dug at him, his nails going slick with blood. Panic was an icy wash, and he lashed out, hitting hard flesh.

"No one swindles me, Kalamack," the old witch said through his gritted teeth, his bloodshot eyes inches from Kal's. "And not some upstart elven whelp from a dying line."

"Get . . . off . . ." Kal rasped, flooding them both with ley line energy.

Saladan's fingers twitched, and Kal got in one good breath before the more experienced ley line practitioner flipped the polarity and it all rushed back into Kal in an agonizing flood. He couldn't scream, couldn't breathe. Racked with pain, he felt himself begin to fall unconscious. *Trisk is going to laugh her ass off*, he thought.

And then Saladan was gone, his fingers ripped from Kal an instant before the flood of ley line energy flickered and died.

Retching for air, Kal knelt on the floor, trying not to throw up as the sound of something heavy hitting the wall echoed in the small apartment. Still gasping, Kal wiped the spittle from himself and looked to see a vampire, his hundred-dollar dress shoes set firmly amid the remnants of the couch. With the casual indifference of the undead, the man watched Saladan slip down the wall and fall into a heap of black cloth and pale limbs.

"Mr. Niles," Kal rasped as he recognized Sacramento's master vampire. "Thank you," he said as he sat up, hands still on his neck. "I can't thank you enough. He's off his rocker."

The well-dressed, unconcerned man turned from Saladan. "That remains to be seen," he said in his slight brogue.

Shaky, Kal got to his feet, not knowing if Niles was talking about Saladan being off his rocker or Kal being unable to thank him enough. *Maybe he meant both.*

"Kal. Kal! Let me out!" Orchid demanded. "You touch one hair on his head, and I'll lobotomize you in your sleep, I promise you!" she threatened Niles.

Kal's reach to break the bubble hesitated. She was safer in there. Uneasy, he looked at Saladan. It took a tremendous amount of skill to hold a circle while unconscious. Kal was lucky to be alive. He looked at the blood under his fingernails and hid them in a fist. *So far . . .*

"I have no quarrel with you, winged warrior," Niles said to Orchid. "But I will talk to your charge before sunup."

Shit. Something's gone wrong. Pasting a pleasant smile on his face, Kal tried to slow his pulse. He knew Niles could sense it, and fear would only encourage the vampire to act. "You got my message, then?" Kal asked, his head hurting when he tried to tap a line and found his synapses were singed. With a grimace, Kal let the line go. He had nothing if he had to defend himself again. And though the sun would be up soon, Niles wouldn't be standing in his front room if he didn't have enough time to get belowground. It was likely his apartment building had an opening to Sacramento's vast underground, dug out by a generation of Asian immigrants. *Son of a bitch, I should have checked for those.*

Niles turned to him, and Kal's fist tightened, hiding the blood. "I've had a disturbing evening," Niles said, eyes roving over Kal's apartment. "It's better now that I'm home, but I don't like being forced to leave."

The vampire was here alone. Could be good. Could be bad. Kal's eyes slid to Saladan and back. "You didn't find them, then?" Kal asked, trying not to show his fear. If Trisk blabbed, it would be twice as hard to shift the blame for the rogue virus to her or Rick.

"I did."

Kal exhaled slowly, cursing himself when Niles's eyes met his, recognizing his relief.

Eyebrows high in thought, Niles went into the kitchen. "They weren't hard to find. Your suggestion that she was fleeing was correct," he said as he used a dish towel to open the oven door. "But before I burned her, she said something that concerns me. I think your baking is done. Let me take them out for you."

"You burned her?" Kal asked as Niles set the tin on the stove to cool.

"I'm not sure." Niles breathed deeply of the moist steam, eyes closing. They were pupil black when they opened, and Kal edged around his shattered couch, reaching for a tissue with which to clean under his nails. "Her truck exploded," the vampire said as he carefully folded the dish towel and draped it on the oven again. "But she and those with her might have escaped. We had to leave before checking for bodies, and you elves are tricky bastards." He turned to face Kal, and Kal threw the tissue away with a wary quickness. Sunup couldn't get here fast enough.

"She said she wasn't in the lab when my child was burned," Niles intoned. "She said it with such conviction that I believe her." The undead vampire looked pointedly at Saladan, still not moving. "Why should I *not* believe her . . . Kalamack?"

"She's a good liar," Kal said, his head nearly exploding as he touched the ley line and filled his chi despite the pain.

Niles hesitated, clearly knowing Kal had teeth. "Tell me, Kal, did you know that the undead—and our living kin, to some degree—are able to see emotion after the person creating it is gone?" His attention shifted behind Kal to the brightening windows. "Your auras leave stains, and though we can't suck them up like banshees, we can see them, sense them. At least until the sun rises and bleaches them out. It helps us find the vulnerable, the weak, the susceptible. They make me think she was telling the truth. It's you, I believe, who is lying."

Don't move, Kal told himself, feeling as if he was walking a thin line. "I'm not the one running away," he said, and Niles lifted a hand and inclined his head in a gesture of acceptance.

"That's what you told Saladan. Perhaps she still lives and can tell us if she is running away from or running to something." Steps soundless, Niles moved to the door. "It's become obvious that you don't know what is going on, but Dr. Cambri? She knew less. Her confusion was more." He hesitated. "Is more?" he questioned, grinning as he put Trisk into present tense.

"You think she's alive?" Kal asked, cursing himself when the vampire's eyes went black again at his faster pulse. But the sun was threatening, and for Niles to remain aboveground would mean light poisoning and his death.

But still the vampire lingered, his feet spread wide upon Kal's welcome mat. "I think my attempt to end her life was less than successful," he said. "And that has become an unexpected pleasure. What's more, I expect you and the enclave to clean up after yourselves instead of baiting me into doing it for you. If Dr. Cambri is indeed dead, you've put yourself in my debt, Dr. Kalamack. Think on that, and perhaps hope that she is alive."

Kal's shoulders stiffened. Seeing his understanding, Niles stepped back through the threshold and into the hallway. "If I see the need to call that debt in, I will kill you, Dr. Kalamack. Not fast, and certainly not without pleasure, but I will kill you."

Saying no more, Niles left, leaving the door open behind him.

Lip curled, Kal strode forward, not daring to look into the hall before he slammed the door shut. His hands were shaking, and with a sigh of frustration, he frowned at Saladan, still unconscious on his floor. "Kal?" Orchid prompted, and with a soft thought that moved his headache to the front of his skull, he broke Saladan's connection to the ley line and the bubble holding Orchid fell. Saladan shuddered and went still. Kal knew he should check on the man, but frankly, he didn't care.

"You okay?" Orchid said as she hovered beside him, her dust an ugly yellow-green.

His couch scattered about his feet, Kal stood in the middle of his apartment, his plans ruined, stinking worse than Trisk's decaying field. "We have to go," he said flatly, too angry to think straight about the details yet. "Right now."

"No kidding." Orchid darted to the window. "So much for riding it out here. Nothing like a master vampire wanting to come to you personally when his main food supply goes bad."

"That's not it," Kal said as he strode into his bedroom to pack a small bag. Most undead had a bevy of living vampires they fed upon, but if they all fell sick, there'd be a span of time when the undead might go ranging for the uninfected, and unwilling, blood of witches, Weres, and elves. Even so, he wasn't running from Niles *or* Saladan.

No, he had to find Trisk and prevent her from exposing the truth, for as Sa'han Ulbrine had said, if humanity was indeed on its way out, he couldn't allow the elves to be the reason for it lest the rest of Inderland rise up and wipe them all out in turn.

20

Trisk lay on her cot, aching from having hit her truck's dash and rolling over the hood and onto the road. One arm across her forehead, she stared at the ceiling, knowing exactly how many wads of gum were stuck to it and the exact rhythm of the faucet drip in the cell across the aisle. The smell of the cotton cot mixed with the oil and grime from the gas station on her clothes, making her ill. There were no windows, but she could tell by the utter silence that dusk had fallen. The sun hadn't set yet, but it was close.

And I'm alive. Stretching where she lay, she winced, a hand going to her middle. Alive, yes, but she didn't feel well, hungry and ill at the same time. Lunch had been spaghetti, which Daniel had missed entirely since he had been at the hospital getting his possible concussion checked out. The thought that she'd caught Daniel's virus flitted through her, easily dismissed. Even if Kal had made the virus more virulent, he wouldn't allow it to infect elves, and not through spaghetti sauce canned a year ago.

All afternoon, they'd listened to the sporadic talk coming from the front offices of possibly transferring them to Reno, but that apparently had fallen through.

So had dinner, as lunch had been their last meal, Daniel getting someone's meatloaf sandwich instead. The phone had rung a few times, going unanswered. That they hadn't seen anyone since Daniel had been brought back didn't bode well. It was utterly quiet, not even a radio anymore. Daniel was asleep on one of the benches in the cell across from her, but Quen, in the cell with him, stood at the bars, his head down as he listened.

"Do you think anyone is out there?" she whispered, and his eyes flicked from the open door to the offices to her.

"Alive? No." Sighing heavily, he sat down right where he was, legs crossed and head thumping gently into the bars. He looked tired, his heavily stubbled face reminding her of their late-night study sessions.

Tugging her blanket tighter around her shoulders, she stood and hobbled closer on her sock feet. Everything complained as she stoically sat down as close as she could get to him. The cold from the cement floor seeped into her like an ache. Her hand, still raw from a burn, rasped against the rough wool, and she hid it behind the fabric before he could see in the dim light the officers had left on for them. "I don't know about you, but there's usually copious amounts of alcohol and loud music before I wake up in jail," she said wryly.

Quen's head came up, and he showed her a smile before it vanished in worry. "I haven't heard any movement in the front offices for hours. Not since someone threw up. I haven't heard anyone leave, either. We might be in trouble."

"You think they're dead?" she asked, not sure what horrified her more: that the cops might be dead, or that if they were, no one would know the three of them were in here.

He didn't answer as he looked toward the silent front offices. "We should probably start thinking about how we can get out."

Trisk watched Daniel, his face to the wall as he slept. It would be easier to escape if they were free to do magic. "Do you think he remembers?" she said softly.

"That you can do magic?" Daniel said loudly, clearly not asleep as they had thought.

Trisk froze, her lips parting as Quen turned to stare at the man as he sat up on the bench, tugging his blanket up against the cold and putting his stocking feet on the floor.

"That you summoned a demon in your barn?" Daniel said, squinting. "That *you* wanted to kill me?" he added, scrubbing a hand over his face to feel the bristles. "Yeah, I remember."

His hair was a mess, and his dress slacks and shirt wrinkled and dirty. But he was alive, and Trisk closed her eyes in heartache. "I'm so sorry," she said, and his gaze shifted to hers.

Quen's expression darkened, and Trisk's pulse quickened. "Sit your butt down, Quen," she barked out, angry at him, angry at the world, angry at being in jail. "You're not killing him now. Besides, by the end of the year, I don't think there are going to be any humans left."

Quen didn't look convinced as much as willing to wait. "You think it's going to take that long?" he muttered as Daniel shuffled to the washbasin and splashed water on his face. "How is it moving, Trisk? If it was airborne, he'd be sick," he said, gesturing at Daniel, who now had his face in the sink and was running water over his hair.

"I don't know," she said softly. But she was willing to bet Kal was responsible.

Finger-combing his wet hair, Daniel edged closer to Quen, his attention alternating between them. "Who are you?" he asked bluntly.

His expression stoic, Quen stood and turned his back on them as if by ignoring the question, he could pretend she wasn't about to break the most important rule of all, the one that had kept all of Inderland safe for two thousand years.

Trisk bowed her head. "My family is from Europe," she said as she tried to make him understand. "We lived on the same land for eight hundred years. Before that, I don't know."

Quen went to the far end of the cell. "Hey! Anyone alive out there?" he shouted, but only silence came back.

"Yeah, okay. But what are you?" Daniel asked, his hands going into his pockets.

She tried to smile. "There was a problem with a girl. It escalated, and my great-great-something grandfather fled to America in the 1820s."

Anger crossed Daniel's face, furrowing his brow. "You aren't human," he accused, his weight shifting to his other foot.

"He started a farm," she tried again. "And then went back to get the woman he loved." Her smile turned real. "He stole her away in the night. I'm named after her, actually. My family has lived here ever since. I grew up in Cincinnati. My dad still lives there."

Daniel grasped the bars. "Trisk," he prompted, and she stood, heart pounding.

"Before I say, you have to understand. We've been here all the time," she pleaded, and Quen sighed, his wide shoulders moving as he fiddled with the lock. "All of us. Your society is our society. We helped make it as much as you. We've died in the same wars, fought the same battles, suffered the same economic depressions. There is no them and us, and we don't want things to change."

An angry light in his eyes, Daniel waited, and she fidgeted, pulse hammering. "I'm, uh, an elf," she said, feeling as if she had betrayed the entire world.

Quen's shoulders hunched as he reached through the bars to lay his hands atop the metal lock. "*Quis custodiet ipsos custodes*," he whispered, trying to break it.

Who guards the guardians, she thought, but the common phrase to unlock doors probably wouldn't work on the cold steel. Not because it was made of metal, but because the door itself had probably not been imbued with the spell to open it in an emergency.

Daniel's eyes slid to Quen, then back to Trisk. "He's one, too?" he said, letting go of the bars and backing up in distrust. "And Kal, and Rick?" he guessed, and she shook her head, wishing they had let her keep her shoes. The cement was freezing, making the demon mark on her foot seem to burn.

"*Quod est ante pedes nemo spectat*," Quen said, the back of his neck red as he used magic in front of Daniel.

No one sees what is before them, she thought, but that didn't work, either. It was a more elaborate charm than the first. He was going the wrong direction. "Rick is a, uh, living vampire," she said, deciding he might as well have it all. "It's only the dead ones that have the long teeth and light restrictions. But he's got a lot of charisma." She hesitated. "Did. Niles was a dead one. You can see the difference."

Daniel frowned. "Vampires? If you're going to lie, at least make it convincing."

She pressed into the bars, hating the distance

between them. "But you have to admit you saw the difference, yes?" she insisted. "You don't hear about vampires because the dead take the blood they need to stay undead from living vampires, who enjoy it. The living vampires don't need blood at all, though I've heard they do practice a lot between themselves. Keep it in the family. It's all very civilized."

And it had been for a long time, the infrequent lapses put down fast and hard by other vampires. But if the master vamps suddenly found themselves surrounded by fear and death, that might change.

Worried, she paced the small space of her cell. The sundry hurts were easing with movement, and the need to get out was growing. "Try something to unlock, not open," she suggested since Quen was still fiddling with the door.

Quen took a tighter hold on the lock, a faint haze of green aura hovering over his hands. "*Reserare*," he said softly, but that, too, failed. Slumping, Trisk grimaced. If it didn't open with that, it wouldn't. They'd have to find another way.

Daniel edged closer. "An elf. Like Santa and the shoemaker?" he asked.

"No, those are just stories. The reality is a lot more mundane. Daniel, we're not that different from you," she said, but he was watching Quen's hands, the energy from the ley lines so thick his aura was visible. "We can even have children together, with some help."

"You mean magic," Daniel said flatly.

Quen pushed back from the locked door in frustration. "And now we have to kill you to keep it a secret."

"Knock it off!" Trisk shouted, fed up with his bloodlust, even if it had been a joke. Catching her anger, she glanced at the silent front office area, then back to

Daniel. Five feet and a world of misunderstanding were between them. "We can't let anyone know. That's why we cursed you to forget and I had to leave, because eventually you'd remember if I stayed. I didn't want to." Her jaw clenched, and she looked away. "Still don't," she finished softly.

Daniel seemed to lose his hard edge, but he was still angry. "You turned my virus into a killer," he said, and Trisk shook her head.

"I made it safe," she insisted. "That's why I came three years ago. To make it safe."

"Safe for vampires and elves, but not humans," Daniel accused, and Quen eyed him.

"Your *goal* was to make people sick," Quen said dryly. "Trisk made it safe for elves, witches." He sighed as he sat on the cot. "Weres, trolls, pixies, and fairies. Banshees. Gargoyles." Stretching, he tapped his toe on the bars. "Do you have anything to melt metal, Trisk?"

"Not that hot, no," she said, thinking that talking about magic in front of Daniel was almost titillating. If caught, they could all be put to death for it. Not that it mattered anymore.

"Gargoyles?" Daniel said, eyes wide. "You're kidding, right?"

"They are a minority, but they exist," Quen said as he leaned back to put his head against the wall. "After this plague, you might be the minority."

That'd be a switch, she thought wryly. They could come out of the closet if humanity was the endangered species. Humans wouldn't have the strength or organization to protest, much less mount an attack. Even the most backward would realize if the Inderlanders were wiped out, so would be their TV, cheap gas, and easy food supply.

"No . . ." Daniel drawled, his head moving in denial. "How could an entire species, several species, exist without anyone knowing?"

"Well, we knew." Trisk went to sit on her cot and rub her cold feet. The bump of her demon mark was startling, and she tucked her feet under her. "We've had a couple thousand years to blend in. You changed to match us as much as we changed to match you. Most of us mimic you really well by now, but I'll admit those who don't are dying out. It's not easy to make a living when you have to hide all the time."

Again, that hard look came over Daniel's face. "Hence the plague," he accused, and Quen's eyes opened.

"It wasn't her, okay?" he muttered.

"The plague is not my doing," she said, frustrated. "I can't even figure out why it's affecting some more than others. I mean, look at you. You made the stuff. Why aren't you sick?"

Quen sat straighter. "Yes, why aren't you sick, Dr. Plank?" he accused. "Been doing a little self-inoculating in your lab?"

Daniel's look of surprised shock melted into a sudden guilt. He hadn't, at least not intentionally, but maybe multiple accidental exposures while it was in development had given him some resistance. God knew he wasn't an Inderlander. She would've been able to smell it on him. He might look like an elf, but he wasn't one.

Head bowed, Daniel turned away. "I thought it was ready. This is my fault."

"It was ready," she cajoled, wanting to reach through the bars to touch him, but she wasn't sure he'd accept it even if she could. "We made that virus perfect. If you want to blame anyone, my money is on Kal. God knows he had the time to modify it. Why, though, is beyond me. He was the best genetic engineer in our class."

"Except for you," Quen said. He had stood and was testing every bar. Giving up, he smacked at them.

Trisk gave him a brief, mirthless smile. "If Kal did this, we can fix it. It will be harder without the sample in my truck, but if we can get out of here and reach Detroit, I imagine we can find an Angel tomato along the way."

Daniel glanced past Quen to the silent, unseen offices. "I'm sure we'll run into someone sick with my virus as well," he muttered. "Though I'd rather work with a sample from my lab. Unfortunately, that's not an option anymore."

Quen turned, his face ashen. "Trisk," he whispered. "Your virus is gone."

"My what?" she said. It was Daniel's virus, not hers.

"Your universal donor," Quen said, coming right up to the bars. He looked scared in a way that he hadn't been when telling Daniel about Inderlanders. "You had it in the lab's computer system, right? The fire dropped the entire floor of your lab onto the computers. Everything in them is gone, along with your research. How are you going to pay Gally back for the forget curse?"

"What virus?" Daniel asked, and Trisk's flash of worry vanished.

"Don't worry about it," she muttered, but Quen gripped the bars of the cell, clearly upset.

"You have a demon scar!" Quen said, and she nervously flicked a look at Daniel. "I can see the smut on your aura, Trisk."

It sounded ugly when he said it like that. Grimacing, she hunched into herself, feeling filthy. "I said, don't worry about it," she repeated, louder.

"Demons," Daniel said dully. "I knew he wouldn't be able to make me forget."

Trisk nodded, a sudden idea making her stand. "Yep. Maybe I should get my money back."

"Whoa, whoa, whoa," Quen demanded, clearly knowing why she was looking at the floor. "No. Trisk, it's not worth it."

"Why not?" she said, embarrassed and resolute. She had no chalk, no salt, nothing. But she did have blood, and that would make a fine circle. "I want that mark off my foot. His curse didn't stick. He owes me. He can get us out if nothing else."

"You're not getting a second mark for us." Quen stood against the bars, his worry obvious. "Besides, you don't have a sample of your virus to give him."

"What virus?" Daniel said again tiredly as Quen began to pace.

"Trisk has developed a universal donor virus that has the potential to introduce healthy genetic code into failing elven infants. It will save our species. We're in a catastrophic genetic meltdown. A parting gift from the demons when we left the ever-after two thousand years ago."

"Oh, well, if that's all," Daniel said flippantly as Trisk scanned the cell for something to cut herself with. It was intentionally sharps-free, but there was a burr of metal on one of the screws, and jaw tight, she gouged her finger. Blood slowly seeped out, and she crouched, pushing her blanket aside as she scribed a small circle. Her sock feet seemed small on the cement floor, making her feel as if she was being foolish.

"That's why you're all geneticists," Daniel said, and she looked down at the tiny circle. Gally wouldn't like its size, but seeing her in jail would probably make up for it.

"Or businessmen," she said as she smeared the rest of the blood off her finger and backed up. Her pulse quickened. Summoning demons was a rush, and she hoped Quen never guessed how much she liked flirting with the danger.

"I can get us out of here," Quen insisted, expression twisted in worry as he gripped the bars between them. "We don't need his help."

She stood well back from the circle. If Gally got out, he'd kill them all, the bars that held them meaning nothing to him. "If I'm going to die in a cell, I don't want a demon mark on my foot."

"Trisk!" Quen reached through the bars of the cage, his arm dropping. "You don't have a candle, ash. Nothing. I forbid it. Someone might see you!"

We should be so lucky. "You forbid it?" she said, eyebrows high. "They're all dead, Quen," she said, pointing at the silent offices. "No one knows we're in here. If we don't get out, the entire human population is going to vanish. I don't want to be responsible for that. Do you? We can stop it. I intend to."

Breathless, she tapped a line and sent the cool energy to fill her circle. Her pulse quickened at the different feel to it as it rose, tainted with her aura. It was a blood circle, heavy with intent. Gally would show if only to know why she'd drawn one.

Quen stood silently at the bars, knowing she was right, knowing she was risking all their lives. Beside him, Daniel watched in unexpected anticipation, not a lick of fear on him.

"Besides," she said as she steadied herself, "I don't think we're going to get to Detroit. Sa'han Ulbrine wants proof? I'll give him proof." Taking a deep breath, she exhaled.

"Algaliarept, I summon you."

21

Breath held, Trisk watched the smoky black haze fill her circle. Her instructor had told them it was the demon looking for any weakening of will or unexpected conduit either above or below ground that could be exploited. She'd drawn blood circles before, but never actually used one to contain anything. It felt different from a chalk line or salt circle: deeper, with more intent.

"Holy crap," Daniel whispered as the haze thickened, shrank, and finally coalesced into the familiar but unsettling figure of Algaliarept.

"This is different," the demon said, his lip curled in distaste as he poked at the tight confines. It was a relief that he hadn't shown up as Kal or that unsettling "beach guru" but in his crushed green velvet frock, lace, white gloves, shiny boots, and the round blue glasses he liked to look over at her to make her feel stupid.

Unmoving because of the close confines, Gally shifted his head to see Quen and Daniel. He jumped when his elbow hit the inside of her circle and a whiff of burnt amber grew stronger. "Just because you are in a cell doesn't mean I should be. This is *barbaric*."

Barbaric, perhaps, but the circle was holding, and

her breath slipped from her in relief. "My finger wasn't going to bleed long enough to make it bigger."

Again, his nose wrinkled as he took her in, eyes lingering on her helix necklace in interest. "Perhaps you should have chopped it off. It would bleed then. Why do I smell . . . dead human?"

"Because there are some in the room next door." Quen's shoulders were tight around his ears. Daniel just looked shocked—at the demon, not the dead-human comment.

A wide smile came over Gally's face as he leaned to look toward the open door, and he beamed, showing his flat, blocky teeth. "You are in a delightful pickle. Come for another favor, Felecia Eloytrisk Cambri?"

Trisk frowned. "There should be a 'doctor' in there somewhere," she muttered, and Gally inclined his head, laughing at her.

"That's him!" Daniel pointed a shaky finger, and Gally sighed heavily, clearly too tired and blasé to play the evil demon tonight. "That's who I saw in your barn."

A new anger pulled Gally's his brow tight. "No," he said, wide shoulders hunched. "I will not reimburse you for the purchase of a memory curse."

"That's not why I summoned you." Trisk shifted her weight to ease the ache in her hip.

"You maintained contact with . . . *Doctor* Daniel Plank," Gally said tightly. "I outright *told* you that would break it, and therefore you invalidated any implied warranty."

Trisk pulled her blanket tighter about her shoulders. "I want the mark off my foot."

"It was your *own stupidity*!" the demon exclaimed, jerking when his forehead hit the circle and a ribbon of smoke rose and vanished. "I am *so weary* of people not treating curses with enough respect. I am an *artist*!" he shouted, stomping his foot where he usually would have flung an expansive arm. "You can't use a flower to cut a steak." He hesitated. "I suppose if you flash-freeze it you could, but honestly, if you want to preserve the anonymity of your species, you *kill* the offender, not soften them to ignorance with forget charms." Gally leaned toward the barrier between them, leering. "Especially if you *like* them."

Flustered, Trisk glanced at Daniel. "Uh, I called you to give you a sample of my donor virus," she said. "I want the mark off. As agreed."

Gally lost his anger, the quickness of it making Trisk think he never had been upset at all. "Truly?" Gally drawled, flicking nonexistent fuzz off his sleeve with his white-gloved hands.

"And maybe you could analyze Daniel's virus," she said, knowing the likelihood of them making it to Detroit to meet Sa'han Ulbrine was slim at best. "See what went wrong with it. I think I caught it, and that's impossible." She'd been feeling ill all day, tired and nauseous. It was better now, but she was afraid to push up her sleeves to see if there was a rash.

"I knew it!" Quen pressed into the bars of his cell as if trying to phase through them. "Why didn't you tell me you weren't feeling well?" he accused.

Trisk shrugged and pulled her blanket tighter. "What good would it do?"

"What good!" Angry, Quen smacked the gate with the flat of his hand, a growl of frustration coming from him. "Damn bars!" he finally shouted.

Gally watched Quen pace, the elf's hands fisted. "Cages," the demon said slowly. "More fun than a kraken in a bathtub, eh?" Shifting his shoulders, he turned back to

Trisk. "You called me to exchange one mark for another? How am I to access the sample?" A wicked smile lit up his eyes as he looked over his glasses at her. "You'd free me to fetch a sample myself? Fun. I might even do that for free."

"My God," Daniel whispered, sitting down right before the bars.

Trisk wished she could tell him it would be okay, but she wasn't sure she believed it herself. "The sample is in there with you," she said, and Gally looked at his feet, inches from the circle she'd drawn.

"Your blood," he said flatly, as if disappointed. "Well, if you have contracted it, it will be there. What about the donor virus? The one you so *desperately* want your name attached to?"

Trisk glanced nervously at Quen. "Uh, it's in there, too," she said softly.

"What!" Quen exclaimed, his face flashing red. "You infected yourself with your virus? When did you do that?" he asked, clearly appalled.

Her shoulders lifted and fell. "I wasn't going to have it in a vial where anyone could steal it," she said, both embarrassed and resolute. "It's harmless. That's why Kal wants it."

Daniel's head came up, lips parted and looking pale. "That's brilliant," he said, clearly meaning it. "Whenever you needed it, it would be there. Is it contagious?"

She shook her head. "With a blood transfusion, sure. But not casually." She turned to Gally, not liking that she had to give this up. "Go ahead and look. If I've caught Daniel's virus, it will be there, too."

The demon's eyebrows were high. "Felecia Eloytrisk Cambri. You might just be clever enough to survive. Excuse me a moment. I'll be right back. It takes a second or two."

With an audible whoosh of inrushing air, he vanished.

"Is he gone?" Daniel whispered, and Trisk shook her head, eyes fixed to the rising haze. Not gone, just analyzing the residue of the circle.

"We should be so lucky," Quen grumped, hands on his hips as Gally solidified, his gloves absent and a red smear between his fingers.

"Well?" Trisk took a step forward, her pulse hammering as the demon began to smirk. She put a hand to her stomach, feeling ill. "I've caught it, haven't I," she whispered, and Quen pushed forward into the bars.

"No!" he protested, almost frantic. "How can she be sick when *he* isn't?" Quen said, looking at Daniel. "It's his virus!"

Gally's smirk extended up into his eyes. "Well, well, well . . ." he drawled, breathing deeply of the red smear between his fingers. "Isn't this interesting?"

Trisk swallowed hard, tugging the blanket tight around her shoulders. She hadn't been feeling well, but she'd been so careful. "How did I mess up so badly?" she whispered, and Quen looked at her helplessly. She would have sworn the virus was Inderland-safe. Kal might tweak it to kill her tomato out of spite, but why would he make it break the species barrier?

"I don't understand," she said, fumbling behind her for the bench and sitting down. "I made it perfect."

"*You* made it perfect?" Daniel accused, and Trisk looked up.

"*You* made it perfect," she amended. "I just made it unable to infect anyone but humans."

"Yeah," Daniel muttered, "I can see that."

She knew that nothing she could say would take that betrayed expression off his face. "And it shouldn't have made anyone so sick they'd die," she added. "Even if my tomato is allowing it to multiply outside of a lab."

Gally's hand dropped, again encased in a white glove. "That would be my guess."

"Guess?" Quen scoffed. "You don't know?"

Goat-slitted eyes narrowed, Gally stared Quen down. "My guess is better than a year's worth of your research. Plebeian," he said dryly. "For all your skills and advances, you are scratching in the dirt. Who do you think had the knowledge to send your genome into a catastrophic crash? Not my great-ever-so-great ancestors, but us. Me and mine. And I guess . . . you are correct that your tomato is responsible." He turned to Trisk. "*Doctor* Felecia Eloytrisk Cambri."

Quen turned away, a hand held up in acceptance, and Gally sniffed, brushing off his sleeves. "The Angel tomato is condensing the virus into lethal doses," the demon added, apparently mollified. "Eat a tomato, and you die. Death by BLT." He chuckled, but Trisk felt ill, her side aching where she'd hit the truck and then the road.

"That's impossible," Daniel said, still sitting on the floor of the cell. His face was white, and Trisk imagined he was doing the same thing they all were: going over what he had eaten the last couple of days. *Spaghetti*.

"The virus couldn't have possibly been in our lunch," Quen said, more to Trisk than Gally. "It came out of a can. Those were last year's tomatoes."

"Probably." Gally tugged his glove down, finger by finger. "But it's just as likely that they were Angel tomatoes, the *savior* of the third world and the *boon* to the Midwestern farmer." He clasped his hands behind his back, rocking on his boots expectantly. "It's all you people plant anymore," he said lightly. "All over the planet, acres and acres of monospecies gardens." Gally shook his head as if chastising a stupid child. "Why take a canary into your coal mine if you don't listen to it sing? Sometimes I wonder how you have lasted even this long. And now, since the virus is attaching to the hairs, which are in everything from ketchup to . . . spaghetti sauce, was it? The virus multiplies like botulism, spreading with a gust of wind and a produce truck running west to east." He smiled. "Giving a virus the characteristics of a bacterium? Inspired, lovey. I applaud you. What a marvelous way to infect large numbers of people quickly."

Quen sat down heavily at the back of the cell, head bowed as he whispered, "That's how it's moving. It is airborne, but it goes from tomato to tomato, not person to person."

"Tomato, hell," Daniel said, white-faced. "It's going product to product."

Quen's head came up. "I've been exposed, too, then."

"Bad luck, chap," Gally said as he rubbed the red smear between his fingers, the digits going misty for a moment. "Curious . . ."

"I don't believe it," Trisk said, unable to accept she had left an opening that large. "Even Kal wouldn't be so stupid as to change the species barrier."

Gally blinked. His expression went utterly blank for an unreal three seconds before a wide, evil grin settled onto his features. "You little trickster," he said as he snapped his fingers, the blood vanishing and the white glove taking its place. "Perhaps you should sit down, Felecia Eloytrisk Cambri. A woman in your condition can never be too careful."

"I am sitting down," she whispered. God help her. She'd killed them all. There would be no one left but perhaps pixies and fairies.

"Why, so you are. Don't be too hard on yourself, lovey," Gally said as she tried not to hyperventilate. "These things happen to the best of us, though you have been particularly stupid." His laugh made her shudder, and she hunched deeper into her thoughts. "I'm glad you have taken my counsel," he said slyly. "For a time, I thought it might be difficult to get your name on your research, but you, my little whore, have done the hard part for me."

"Hey!" Daniel said, affronted, his harsh cry shocking through her.

Trisk lifted her head, arms wrapped around her middle as if to hold her together. "I haven't taken your counsel. I never agreed to anything. You just started talking." She pressed her fingers into her forehead. "I can't believe Kal would break the species barrier to put us in danger of infection."

"But you are not in any danger, lovey," Gally said merrily. "The species barrier is still intact. You're not ill because you carry Daniel's virus. You are ill because you are pregnant."

The worried frown slid from Trisk's brow in shock, and her jaw dropped. "Excuse me?"

Gally's laugh exploded from him, long and deep. "You've got a bun in the oven," he said, delighting in the look of horror that flooded her. "Flunked the rabbit test. Enrolled yourself in the pudding-of-the-month club. Let me be the first to congratulate you and your little bastard."

"Pregnant!" Quen exclaimed, his eyes going to Daniel.

"Don't look at me," Daniel said grimly as Trisk sat unmoving in shock. "I'm not the one who's been following her around the last couple of weeks."

Trisk felt herself go pale as they both turned their

accusing eyes on her. *Kal*, she thought as they all figured it out together. "I think I'm going to throw up," she whispered. Oh God, she'd gotten herself pregnant? By a *Kalamack*?

Gally was still laughing, apparently not caring that he was singeing his elbows and knees.

"How?" Trisk said, then waved a hand for him to shut up when he took a breath to answer. "I know how," she amended. "But it's so difficult for us to become pregnant at all." Her pulse quickened. "Is it a viable fetus? Can you tell?"

"From your blood?" Gally said, glancing at Daniel when he got to his feet. "I'm good, but not that good. By the amount of hormone coursing through you, I'd say chances are good you'll carry to term if you stop rolling over truck hoods. Tell you what. I'll let you all out of your cages if you give it to me on his or her sixteenth birthday."

She swallowed hard, hand on her middle. "Go to hell."

"Is that an official banishment? Come on now. Do it properly," he coaxed, knowing that wasn't what she'd meant.

"Trisk." Quen stood before the bars, hands helplessly at his side. "He's a loathsome, prejudiced bastard! How could you have a child with that jackass?"

"Back off, Quen!" she shouted, embarrassed. "*Don't* lecture me on morals. With men holding all the keys, women don't have a lot of choice but to whore themselves out for their bodies or whore themselves out for their minds." Her face warmed, and she stared Quen down, seeing his understanding but not finding any joy in it. "So what if I did both at the same time for the chance that my work might stand as *my* work and not someone else's." She slumped, feeling the tears prick. "Maybe it was a bad idea," she whispered. "But I'm tired of not being allowed to make my own life." Besides, it had been damn enjoyable, so enjoyable that the thought of it kept popping into her mind at the most inopportune moments.

"That's not what I meant," Quen said, and her head snapped up.

"Then what did you mean?" she said bitterly.

"This is just *delightful*," Gally said, wiping tears of laughter away with a gloved hand. "Truly, I will take the unwanted child off your hands. I'll give you three wishes for it. A dozen."

Unwanted? Trisk's attention flicked from Quen to Gally. "Why don't you leave?"

The demon looked affronted. "What about your foot?"

"Get out!" she shouted, rising to fling a hand at him. "Take your mark and go home! Now!"

Gally frowned, his hands clasped quietly behind him as his expression fell. "Bad dog, eh?" he grumbled. "Fine. But I own you, Felecia Eloytrisk Cambri, and if I take you while you are pregnant, that child is mine, too, by association."

That fast, he vanished with an inrushing pop of air. Trisk shuddered, reaching down to rub a cold hand under her even colder foot. It was smooth. His mark was gone. But her tension didn't ease. His grip on her felt stronger, not weaker.

"Trisk?" Quen said, and she turned away, not wanting to deal with anything right now. There was nothing left in her circle, and she let go of the line. Flickering, the energy holding the circle vanished.

Unwanted? No, it wasn't unwanted, but his or her

appearance was really bad timing. Shuddering at the thought of a child raised by demons, she vowed not to call Algaliarept again. It was too dangerous. *No wonder my grandmother hid his name on a stone she swallowed.*

"Trisk," Quen said again, and thinking she heard recrimination in his voice, she put up a hand to stop his next words. Damn it, she couldn't go to NASA now. They would never hire her. Not with a child to care for. She could hide a pregnancy for a time, but how responsible was it to work in a genetic lab with a developing fetus?

"I'm sorry, Trisk," Quen said, and she bowed her head, shaking as she shuffled to her cot and sat down. "I didn't mean—"

"Not now, Quen," she said as the springs gave way under her.

"I promise, it's going to be all right," Daniel said softly, and she glanced up, relieved there was no reproach in his eyes. It only seemed to make it worse.

"How is this going to be all right?" she said as she lay down, facing both the wall and her uncertain future. With a sinking sensation, she realized Kal had won, because she could not in good conscience allow her work to lie fallow for the decade it would take before she would be allowed back into the workplace. And that was even assuming they would let her. A viable child was almost a mandate to make more. *How could I have been so stupid?*

But it was what it was. Calming, she breathed in and out as her world realigned, her lifetime mind-set of *I* shifting seamlessly into an unshakable *we* with the unstoppable force of those who came before her. She blinked, shocked at how fast it was, how unexpected.

Slowly Trisk put a hand to her lower middle. *A child?*

22

The quiet sounds of Quen's frustrations were growing louder, but Trisk pretended to be asleep as he tried to pull the sink apart for the thin shaft of metal he thought was in the drain. The foul stench from the front room was getting stronger, and his need to get out of the cell was almost palpable in the late-morning air.

"There's nothing in this cell to break out with!" Quen whispered loudly.

"That's the intent," Daniel said dryly, and she rolled over to see the two men at the sink. Quen had his fingers down the drain, Daniel standing so close he was getting in the way. "Why don't you bring that demon back," Daniel suggested, leaning closer. "We can't give him Trisk's baby, but there must be something he'd take in exchange to open the door."

Quen straightened, angrily rubbing his cramped red hand. "You offering your soul?"

Daniel blinked, probably trying to decide if he was joking or not. Frowning, Trisk sat up, tired of doing nothing. "We can't summon Gally unless the sun is down," she said, and Daniel spun to her. "Something about the energy in the ley lines moving the wrong way."

Hands in his pockets, Daniel shifted to the bars. "Really?"

She stood and stretched, feeling different although nothing had changed. *A child.* "Ley line energy moves like tides with the sun. Energy from our world is what's keeping the ever-after, where the demons live, intact."

"So wouldn't that mean they owe you something? If our world is keeping their world alive?"

For someone who hadn't known magic was real twenty-four hours ago, he was becoming comfortable with it unsettlingly fast. "That's not how they see it, since they were the ones who scraped the ley lines into existence." Shaking her blanket out, she draped it over her shoulders.

Giving up, Quen sat back on the bench, elbows on his knees as he massaged his palm. "I'm about ready to chew off my own finger to make a lockpick. Do you have any ideas, Trisk?"

Daniel shifted impatiently. "You said you can't melt the bars, but what if you focused the energy on the lock itself?"

Quen looked up past bangs clumped with sweat. "You don't think I tried that?"

"How about making the metal brittle, with cold?" she suggested, and Quen's focus shifted to her, his brow smoothing.

"Sure," Daniel said, voice holding excitement. "If you can shrink the workings of the lock enough, they might slide apart. At the very least, you can repeatedly warm and chill them until fatigue breaks something."

"Worth a shot." Quen stood and moved to the lock. "Might take a few hours."

"A few hours, we have," Daniel said as he followed Quen to the door, eager to see some magic in action.

Quen's hand took on a hazed glow as he tapped the nearest line and pulled its energy through him. But the faintest click in the outer offices struck through Trisk like a shot. "Wait!" she exclaimed. "Someone is out there," she added, and Quen jerked his hands away, the pain of having drawn the charm back furrowing his brow.

Trisk grasped the bars and leaned toward the open office. "Hey! We're locked up here!"

"There's no one there," Daniel said. "It's just the bodies settling."

Which was ugly all on its own, but adrenaline surged when the clatter of pixy wings sounded clear and true. "Orchid?" Trisk called, not believing it. "Is that you?"

"What would Kal's spy be doing here?" Quen said sourly, making Trisk regret ever telling him about her, and grimacing, she pressed closer into the bars. If it was Orchid, Kal wouldn't be far behind.

"Kal! We're back here!" she tried again, breathless. "Please," she whispered.

With a wash of dust, the tiny woman stopped short right in the middle of the open door. Orchid's face was flushed and a bright silver spilled from her in uncertainty. "Kal said it would be okay if Daniel saw me," she said, twisting the hem of her dress shyly. "Are you sure? This feels wrong."

Quen strode forward, startling her into darting back. "It's fine," he said. "Where's Kal?"

"It's you," Daniel said, his eyes fixed on the pixy. "I knew I saw you before."

"Before!" Quen barked as he turned to him in anger, and Orchid colored.

"You were erasing his memory. No harm done, right?" Orchid said as she flitted to the lock and bent to look into it. "This is so weird. I've never let a human see me on purpose. But Kal said you're probably going to be dead in a week, so it doesn't matter."

"Daniel is not going to die," Trisk said, surprised when the pixy woman stuck her entire arm into the workings of the lock. "The virus is condensing in the Angel tomato. Avoid that, and you don't get sick."

"Then one of you is going to have to kill him," Orchid said, distracted. "Because I'm not going to be the one giving us away."

"No one is going to kill Daniel!" Trisk exclaimed, but then the lock clicked open, and everything left her but the need to get out.

Quen pushed past the bars. Striding to Trisk's door, he waited impatiently as Orchid hovered before her lock, the tiny woman biting her lower lip as she fiddled with it. Her dust shifted green, then red, and the lock finally disengaged. "Thank you," Trisk said, taking a huge step forward, then blinking in surprise when Quen pulled her into an unexpected hug. Giving her a quick, confusing smile, he set her back on her feet and went to check out the front offices.

"You're beautiful *and* amazing," Daniel said, and Orchid rose up, glowing in pleasure.

"No one ever thought I was amazing before," she said as she landed on his shoulder, shocking the man still.

"Well, I do," Daniel stammered, trying to see her and afraid to move all at once.

"So do I," Trisk said. Shedding her blanket, she threw it into the open cell. "Where is Kal?" she asked as she followed Daniel to the lockers.

"Looking for you." Orchid darted up to the high window and peered out. "I took the abandoned buildings," Orchid continued as Trisk sat to put on her shoes.

"He's hitting the hospitals, searching among the survivors. There's a lot, actually."

"That's good to hear." Daniel checked his wallet and tucked it in his back pocket. "I don't want to be the last human on earth."

He clearly meant it to be in jest, but Orchid made a rude noise. "I meant surviving vamps," she said. "Humans are another story."

"They can't be all dead," Trisk whispered. "It can't possibly be moving that fast."

Quen came back from the front office, his eyes haunted. "Stay left. Don't look around," he said as he grabbed his shoes, putting them on even as he shepherded the group to the front.

"They can't be all dead," Trisk said again, then reeled, hand over her face as she left the cellblock. *Head down. Stay left*, she thought as her feet scuffed on the dirty tile. But when she saw someone's foot, she couldn't help but look up. Swallowing hard, she averted her eyes. It was one of the younger officers, still sitting at the desk he'd died at. His face was covered in welts and blisters, his eyes swollen shut even with the blood pooled in his feet.

"It's spotty." Orchid flew beside her, tiny fingers delicately pinching her nose shut. "The news says big cities are handling it better, but smaller towns don't seem to have enough Inderlanders in them to keep services going and information flowing. Stay here. I'll go get Kal."

"In the street, maybe," Trisk said, gagging at the smell.

Zipping up his boots, Quen harrumphed. "I'll come with you."

Orchid looked him up and down, her eyebrows high. "You can try," she said, then darted off. In three seconds, she was gone.

Quen hesitated, watching her dust settle. "Damn," he grumbled. "They're fast."

"They'd have to be to keep out of sight," Daniel said, his eyes carefully down as they wove between the desks. "I can't believe they've been here all this time, and no one knew it." He hesitated, adding softly, "No one human."

Trisk felt her gorge rise, and she reached for the wall for balance, sickened.

"You okay?" Daniel said, and she looked up when Quen opened the front door.

"I don't know," she said, relishing the fresh air slipping in. Maybe the entire plague was her fault.

"We'll get you something to eat and you'll be fine," Daniel said. "Your blood sugar is low. Look. Your hands are shaking."

She made fists of them, embarrassed. Her knees were wobbly as they went out, and she hid her hands in her pockets while she teetered down the wide, shallow stairs to the sidewalk. "I'm just glad we didn't have to call on Gally."

"Me too," Quen muttered, taking in a deep lungful of air as the door clicked shut behind them. "Where do you think we are? That's not the interstate."

Daniel squinted at the street signs. "Downtown," he said shortly. "The hospital they took me to is up that way. I don't know if that's really where we want to go, though."

Trisk shook her head, uneasy. The buildings were taller here than just off the main road—three stories, maybe—solid and made of stone. The street itself was wider. There were birds and the sound of the wind in the awnings. The noise from the nearby interstate was sporadic and light. The noon sun was warm, driving out the chill of their cells. Still, it was obvious all wasn't right. There was a sour smell, and something was burning in the distance, plumes of black smoke rising into the air.

"There's a diner two blocks up. It might be open. Trisk needs to eat something," Daniel said as he looked up the street toward a gathering of cars.

Nodding, Trisk fell in beside him, Quen on her other side. If Orchid found them once, she could find them again. *Damn. Kal.* "Hey, can I ask you guys not to say anything to Kal about . . ." She took a breath, reluctant to say it aloud. "You know," she finished, feeling her face warm.

Quen glanced askance at her as Daniel murmured, "Of course."

Her flush deepened. "I'm not ashamed," she said, wishing her face weren't red. "And I *will* tell him, but not until I know if it's healthy. Unless he's responsible for the plague," she added, but the need to have viable children was so strong that his causing a plague might not even matter to most elves.

Quen's stiff shoulders eased. "Sure. I get that," he said, gaze roving over the empty streets. Curtains were being flicked aside as people watched them, and Trisk wondered if it was as bad as Orchid had led them to believe.

"Besides," Trisk said, feeling better in the sun with the motion easing her muscles, "I want to make sure it's true. Gally could've been trying to get me to make a mistake."

"I won't say anything," Daniel said, angling them to the diner.

But it seemed unlikely that Gally had been lying if he had offered to exchange a dozen wishes for a child that might not live long enough for him to take. The shadows of bodies moved behind the glass, and nervous, Trisk tried to fix her hair, aware that she smelled like oil and gas. Still, it was comforting not to be alone anymore. She could tell Daniel was feeling the same way, a worried eagerness in him when he lurched ahead to yank the door to the diner open. "Thank God they're not closed," she said as Daniel hesitated just inside, looking for an empty table. She ran her fingers through her long hair again, trying to get it decent.

"You look fine," Quen said stiffly, then took her arm, drawing her back into the sun a moment longer. "I'm sorry," he said, and her eyes shot to his. "For judging you," he added, gaze dropping. "Your decisions, while not those I'd choose, were made with sound reasoning. I'm a total jerk," he added, lips pressed and focus distant.

She flushed as she remembered the passion between her and Kal. There'd been no reason, just emotion. "No, you're not," she said, a faint smile crossing her face. She took a breath to say more, but Daniel leaned out the door.

"Uh, I have a table," he said, and Trisk nodded, suddenly a hundred times hungrier.

"I look like a disaster victim," she said softly as she followed Daniel in, feeling self-conscious when the locals looked up. "On second thought, I fit right in," she added, seeing the weary expressions, tense with doubt and fear. There was a radio set to the news blaring from behind the counter, and it was obvious that was why most of them were here.

Quen's hand on her shoulder was comforting, his confidence and attitude of protection welcome as he raised his hand at the cook's inquiring glance and called loudly over the radio, "Can we have three hamburgers, sodas, and fries?"

"Sit where you can," the cook answered back, and Quen angled them toward a side booth, where Daniel anxiously waited. Her eyes darted over the clientele, clusters of them oblivious as they wove between the tables.

"Everyone here is an Inderlander," Quen said, leaning to breathe the words in her ear.

"I noticed," she whispered back, smiling thinly in case anyone made eye contact. There were mostly witches, evident by their amulets and dexterous fingers when seen all together. A table of Weres was in one corner, the alphas suave and cool, mingling freely with their rougher subordinate kin. Their tattoos set them apart. In the back were living vampires, every one of them model perfect, every one of them scared.

Trisk slipped into the booth, sliding down when Daniel sat beside her. Eyeing everyone sourly, Quen took the seat across from them, the flats of his forearms on the table to make his fisted hands obvious.

"My God," Daniel said as he read the headlines on the paper someone had left at the table. "China is gone. Borders closed, no communication."

"You didn't drop anything on China," Quen said.

"We didn't drop anything here, either," Trisk said, elbowing Daniel when the server approached with their drinks.

Daniel looked up, folding the paper and tucking it away with a guilty quickness. Trisk eagerly reached for her glass, eyes watering when she gulped the soda down, the bubbles making her eyes burn. "Water, please," she asked before the woman left, and Daniel held up two fingers. Quen sipped his drink, his eyes never leaving the gathered people.

"Don!" one of the patrons called. "Turn it up. They're talking about Sacramento."

The cook wiped his hands off on his apron and fiddled with the radio behind the counter. It crackled and popped, and then cleared. ". . . Global Genetics, which is now closed and barricaded behind government forces, is being blamed," the announcer said, clearly caught halfway through his newscast. "Early numbers indicate that the tactical virus affects almost half the population, with a quarter of that succumbing."

The sweet bubbles bursting in her throat went flat. Someone swore, quickly hushed. "Both susceptibility and immunity appear to run in families, and people are advised to stay at home until it's discovered how the virus is being transmitted."

Trisk pushed her drink away, her fingers cold from the glass. Someone was crying.

"Turn it off," another man demanded, standing to get out of the way of the sobbing woman who was being helped out by an older man. "We have to make a decision. Right now, before things get uglier. I know this hurts. Everyone here has lost friends, and I'm sorry that we can't give everyone the proper burial they deserve, but if we don't do something, by tomorrow we will be fighting not just this new disease, but everything else decomposing bodies bring with them. We need to do a house-to-house check at the bare minimum."

"Mass graves are barbaric, Sid," one of the better-dressed Weres said, causing heads to bob and a soft agreement to rise.

"So is a polluted water supply," one of the vampires shot back. "That's where we're headed if we do nothing."

"I say we try for Reno," someone at the table of witches said. "The higher populations are handling this better. We don't have the resources."

Loud agreement came from the shadowed back

where the vamps had congregated, but the Weres and most of the witches didn't want to leave. As the arguments grew loud, Sid raised his hand, ignored. Lips pressed, he stood up on a chair. "Listen!" he shouted. "I'm all for Reno, but we can't leave rotting corpses. It's not right!" Eyes bright, he waited until it grew quiet. "The way I see it, we can make one common plot for every family. Luke, you know how to work the digger. We can use Phillip's field. It's close to town, has that pretty little church across the road. He's not likely to protest, seeing as he's down with whatever the hell this is."

"And who is going to dig my grave?" a Were called out. "We can all see what's happening. It's taking out the weakest first. I say we go now, while we can still drive!"

"Who are you calling weak?" a flushed vampire exclaimed, and it started up again. Sid tried to shout them down, but he'd lost control. Shouts rang out and tempers frayed, pulled apart by fear as the threat of plague ran rampant.

Trisk's pulse pounded. "No!" she called out, but no one heard her. "You're safe!"

Quen stared at her. "What are you doing?" he whispered, but she couldn't stay silent.

"You're not going to die," she said, standing up at the booth and awkwardly putting her knee on the seat for balance. "Vampires might get the pox since they're the closest to humans, but they'll recover. It's only humans who are so susceptible."

Silence fell, everyone shocked to stillness as she openly named them. It had likely never been done before, and she suddenly felt exposed, nervous.

"And you know this how?" Sid said as he got off his chair and faced her.

"Ixnay on the objay," Quen muttered.

People were dying. She couldn't stop it, but she could help. Even so, a little lie wouldn't hurt. "My husband works for the government," she said. "He said the virus only affects humans."

"Does this look like nothing?" a frightened vampire said as he pushed up his shirtsleeve to show red pustules.

"It's okay," she said as everyone but his family moved away from him. "It's not contagious. It's a toxic reaction, not a disease." But then she started, lips closing as Sid approached, his hands aggressively on his hips.

"I saw you on TV," he said, his eyes on her necklace. "You work at Global Genetics."

Quen grimaced, his hands clenching on the table. "Way to go, Trisk."

Flustered, she gripped the double helix to hide it. "Listen. It's in the tomatoes," she said, but it was getting noisy. "Don't eat them, and you won't get sick. Humans, either."

"Time to go." Quen stood. In the back, the vampires had gotten to their feet, murderous expressions on their faces as they found someone to blame for their fear.

"You made the tomatoes. You did this!" Sid shouted, and Quen pushed forward, getting between him and the table so Daniel and Trisk could slide out. "You damn elves think you're better than everyone!" Sid shouted, eyes bright with zeal as people backed him up. "You're trying to kill everyone but the elves, aren't you!"

"No!" Trisk exclaimed when Quen grabbed her arm and dragged her to the door.

"Get them!" came a shout. "If we turn them in, the government might help us."

"There is no medicine for this," Trisk said as she

jerked out of Quen's grip. "It's not supposed to kill anyone. Will you listen? We're trying to help."

"Stop them!" Sid shouted, and Trisk gasped when an
ugly, strong hand gripped her wrist.

"Hey! Let go!" she said, jolting the man with a flash
of ley line energy. He fell back, eyes wide, but it only
made things worse. As a mob, they came forward, their
fear spilling into action.

"Plan B!" Quen pushed her and Daniel toward the
door. "Fire in the hole!" he exclaimed.

Trisk dropped, yanking Daniel to the ground with her.
Breath held, she snapped a protection bubble over them.
Someone beat on it, once, twice, three times, his face ugly.

And then Quen opened the gates of hell.

"*Dilatare!*" he shouted, and Trisk cowered at the
heavy bang of air slamming everyone toward the walls.
It was a white spell, but the quickly expanding bubble
of air could do a lot of damage in an enclosed space.
People pinwheeled back, tables slid, and plates crashed
to the floor as cries of fear rang out. Then it was quiet.
Someone said "Ow" and then a moan of pain rose.

"Let's go," she whispered. Finding Daniel's cold
hand, she stood. Her bubble shivered to nothing as she
touched it. Around her, people groaned as they picked
themselves up. A large open space surrounded Quen,
the tables shoved to the edges and tangled with broken
plates and spilled food.

"Out." His expression angry, Quen pushed them
to the door. Trisk went, still dragging Daniel, his neck
craned to look back over his shoulder at the destruction. They hit the sun-drenched sidewalk together,
stumbling as Quen shoved them toward the police station. Behind them, shouts became loud, confused at
first, then angry.

"Plan B?" Daniel questioned, still trying to get his feet under him.

Trisk tightened her grip on his arm. "Quen and I always paired up in defense class."

Behind them, the first people spilled out of the diner, pointing as they caught sight of them. "Can you make us invisible?" Daniel asked, and Quen yanked them into an alley, his expression grim. "Forget I said that," Daniel panted, breathless as they were forced into a run.

The damp walls rose up tight and tall around them, the sound of their steps out of sync and somehow threatening: Quen's slow, solid thumps, her rapid patter, and Daniel's hesitant gait. A brighter light beckoned at the other end of the alley. Trisk had no idea where it led, but it didn't matter, and the first real fear slid through her. They had nowhere to run to.

"I'm not going back to that jail," Quen muttered when they reached the end.

"Where are we going?" Trisk asked, and Quen yanked Daniel back as the man looked out.

"Anywhere they aren't. Keep moving."

Quen's hand on the small of her back jostled her forward, but she hesitated, head going up at a familiar clatter. "Quen, wait," she said as the bright silver dust of a pixy caught the light. "Orchid!" she shouted, and the tiny woman did a quick stop.

She stared at them for a moment, the dust slipping from her shifting to a muted gold, then back to silver. Trisk shrugged at the woman's irate look, and then Orchid zipped off. Slowly her dust shifted into a sunbeam and was gone.

"Is that a good thing or a bad thing?" Daniel said, and then the people from the diner found them, spilling into the far end of the alley in an angry mob.

"*That* is a bad thing," Quen said, pulling them out into the street.

Again they ran, and the crowd's noise redoubled. Memories tumbled over each other, shoved to the front of her head: memories of torment, of running from classmates, of being pinned down and having worms draped over her until she beat them off, of sitting outside the principal's office, punished for using magic when her tormentors got off with a token wrist slap.

"They're catching up," Daniel panted as he pounded the pavement beside her, and she readied herself, drawing on the nearest ley line to defend herself as best she could against a mob of vampires, witches, and Weres.

But then her heart stuttered when the roar of an engine rolled over them, and with a pebble-popping wave of heat, Kal's Mustang rocked to a halt beside them. The top was open, his almost-white hair shining in the sun. "Get in!" Orchid chimed out as she flew over them, urging them to hurry.

Daniel cried out in relief, surging ahead to close the twenty feet between them. Quen, though, slid to a halt, his lips pressed into a thin, angry line. "Are you kidding me?" Trisk said, grabbing his bicep to drag him forward. "It's a ride. Let's go!"

Quen didn't move, and Trisk stumbled, catching her balance. "I'm not getting in a car with him," Quen said tightly. "He tampered with your work, ruined it."

Save me from fools and male egos. "Fine. You want to stay here?" she said, pulling the hair from her eyes as she glanced at the oncoming mob now shouting obscenities.

Eyes narrowed, Quen looked at Kal impatiently revving the Mustang's engine. Daniel was in the back, arm stretched, reaching for Trisk. "We don't know if this was Kal's fault or not," she said, and Quen grimaced.

But finally he moved, and Trisk exhaled in relief. "It is," he muttered as he lifted her up and set her in the back beside Daniel. "And you know it."

She did, but Kal had a car, and there was an angry mob behind them.

"Get in! Get in!" Orchid shrilled, and Quen calmly went around the front of the car, vaulting into the front passenger side even as Orchid slipped under Kal's hat and the man floored the accelerator. They took off in a cloud of dust, spitting pebbles at the people chasing them.

Trisk turned, watching their instinctive, collective cower become rage and a shout to get to their cars. They weren't out of this yet, and they'd been lucky that it was so ingrained not to use magic openly. It wouldn't happen a second time.

Tense, she held the seat ahead of her as they jostled back to the interstate. Kal drove confidently, one hand on the wheel, the sun on his face and his expression stoic as he concentrated on the road. The thought flashed through her that he looked amazing . . . and then she quashed it. Quen's neck was red, the man holding firm even when Kal took a tight turn to run parallel to a railroad track. A slow-moving train was on it, and Kal raced down its length, looking for the engine and a chance to cross and be gone.

"Where are we going?" she called out over the wind, and Kal turned to her. There were little red marks on his neck as if from fingernails.

"Does it matter?" Kal said, and Quen's expression stiffened.

"It does to me," Quen said. "You tampered with Plank's virus. You created a bridge between it and Trisk's tomato. This is your fault."

Kal took his foot off the accelerator. The car came to a quick, head-bobbing halt right in the middle of the road. "Is that what you think I did?" he said, and Quen's eyes narrowed.

Daniel looked behind them, the *click-click, click-click* of the moving train an ominous metronome. "Uh, can this wait until we outdistance the mob with torches and pitchforks?"

"You're responsible, Kalamack," Quen intoned. "And you will swing for it."

Kal's lip twitched. "Get out."

"Whoa, whoa, whoa." Trisk scooted forward to push herself between the two men. Her pulse was fast, and she could feel both their energies prickling against hers. "We can do this later. Kal, drive. Please."

Kal's eyes found hers. "Do *you* think I did this intentionally?"

Trisk's lips parted. She didn't know if Kal knew her well enough to see a lie.

Daniel stood up, hand on the car for balance. "They have cars, now. Can we go?"

Kal's eyes slid from Trisk, and she took a slow breath. "Not until he apologizes."

"Me?" Quen's face reddened. "You threw the entirety of Inderland off balance and will be responsible for killing a quarter of the human population in the name of job advancement."

"Out. Now," Kal insisted, and Trisk looked behind her to the plumes of dust racing toward them. Daniel slowly sat back, his expression frightened.

"Stop it, both of you!" she said bitterly. "Kal, make this thing move or I'll call your mother and tell her what you and I did in the barn last week. Quen, we don't know it was Kal. I want to hear you say it." Neither man looked at the other. "Now!" she yelled, and Kal twitched.

"I have no proof that it was you," Quen all but growled.

Brow furrowed, Kal put the car back into drive, the *click-click* of the moving train lost in his angry peel-out. Trisk let the inertia push her back into the seat, where she stared at the backs of their heads. Beside her, Daniel heaved a relieved sigh. "I'm too much of a lab geek for this," he whispered, but she heard it over the wind regardless.

"It wasn't me," Kal said, still racing the train's length. "It was Rick."

"Rick?" Quen spat. Trisk thought he was lying as well, but she was willing to overlook it—for the moment.

"Why else would he commit suicide?" Kal said, his posture easing. "He said it himself. He's not a geneticist. He tried to shift the Inderland balance for his master, make a few less humans so they could come out of the closet and safely enslave what was left, giving them a net increase. I don't think an outright plague was what he had in mind, but watching him was why the enclave sent me."

Trisk's eyes narrowed. Daniel, though, was nodding. "We thought you were here to stop Trisk's patent transfer," he said.

Kal's hands clenched on the wheel. "I was watching Rick. But you're right. It's my fault. I didn't watch him well enough."

Lies, lies, lies, she thought, but he had a car, and once they joined Sa'han Ulbrine, Kal couldn't hide behind them any longer. "We need to get to Detroit," she said. "Once we prove the tomato is involved and how it's functioning as a carrier, we can make a public announcement and end this." She looked behind them at the town. "Or at least slow it down."

A shudder rippled over her despite the hot wind. There had been no one human left in Fallon except Daniel, and it had felt wrong, unsafe. There hadn't been enough infrastructure to take care of their weaker kin or figure out what was going on and perhaps prevent some of the deaths. She only hoped it was different in the larger cities. Maybe things would be normal in Detroit.

Quen was silent, a fisted hand to his mouth as similar thoughts probably skated through him. "How did you know where to look for us?" he asked, and Kal lifted a shoulder in a shrug.

"I ran into Rick's master," Kal said uncomfortably. "He said he tried to kill you in Fallon but wasn't sure he had succeeded. I had to know for sure."

"We can't drive all the way to Detroit," Daniel said. "They are following."

"That's why we aren't." Glancing at the slowly moving train, Kal slid his car onto the narrow shoulder and stopped. "We're taking the train," Kal said with a grand gesture, and Quen scoffed, the soft sound obvious in the still air.

"You mean this train? Right here?" Trisk asked, the creeping cars suddenly looking faster now that she was faced with possibly trying to jump onto one. "It's a freight train."

"You and Plank will be recognized if you try to take a passenger train," Kal said as he got out of the car. "The schedules are pretty simple. It's going east. We get off at Detroit. QED."

Quite easily done? Trisk thought sourly, but Daniel's eyes were pinched in concern as he looked behind them to the growing plumes of dust. Their pursuers hadn't given up. "This could work," he said as he gave Trisk's hand a squeeze and opened his door. "The trains run right into the edge of the city. They won't shut them down, not in the middle of the desert. It only takes a few people to move thousands of tons of product."

Nervous, she looked at the handholds on the passing cars, wincing. "Fine," she breathed. "We take the train. Just one problem. If those wackos find the car here, they'll know where we're going. One call, and they'll be waiting for us."

"It's a risk, yes," Kal said as he watched the passing cars, presumably looking for a suitable one.

"One we don't have to take." Quen stepped between Kal and the moving train. "Keys. I'll lead them away."

"What? No!" Trisk exclaimed, scrambling out of the car. "Quen, no."

Face expressionless, Kal took his keys out of his pocket.

"You're kidding, right?" Daniel said, clearly loath to put their trust in Kal.

But Quen's jaw was set. "Get to Detroit," he said, moving Trisk toward the train. "Do what you need to do. I'll find you. I promise. I'm not a geneticist. You don't need me there."

"I need you there," she protested, but he had turned to Kal.

"If you hurt her, I will find you. Understand?" he said, and Kal's expression went stiff. "Now, next week, next year, forever."

"I'm not leaving you here to get caught by those butchers," she said, then gasped when Quen picked her up, heaving her into a slowly moving car. "Quen!" Scrambling, she righted herself, her hands feeling the rough floor as she crawled to the open door. "Damn it, Quen!"

Her eyes widened, and she flung herself out of the way as Daniel half scrambled, half fell into the car. Kal was next, his stumbling lurch looking almost graceful.

"You are unbelievable," she said, pushing around him to get to the door. "Let go. Let go!" she shouted, but Kal's grip on her arm only tightened. "I said . . . let go," she intoned, letting the barest hint of ley line energy slip from her to him.

Lips twisting, Kal released her arm.

Her eyes had almost adjusted to the dimmer light, and she squinted when she staggered into the doorway and looked back at the car. They'd moved far more than she would have expected, and her heart dropped.

"Quen!" She sat down to slip off. He was already in the car, not even looking back.

A thin hand landed on her shoulder, and her first impulse to hit Kal faltered when she realized it was Daniel. His eyes were pinched in heartache behind his dirty glasses, giving her pause. "Let him go," he whispered, and she took a breath to protest. "Trisk." Daniel crouched beside her, his hand never leaving her shoulder. "He's infected. Let him go."

Infected? Trisk's breath seemed to go stale in her, and she exhaled. She sucked in the air, but the dry heat had robbed it of any oxygen. His neck had been flushed. Had it been the beginnings of a rash and she hadn't realized it?

"No," she whispered, leaning to look out again, but he was gone, heading out into the desert like an old cat to die. "No," she said again, spinning where she sat, lurching awkwardly to her feet to move to the other side of the car. But she couldn't see him from there, either, and she closed her eyes, letting her head thump against the hard wood. Why hadn't he said anything?

But the answer was obvious. She would have stayed to see him through it, slowing her down and possibly resulting in never getting the word out about how the virus was spreading.

The rumble of movement vibrated into her. She took a breath, then another. Somehow she kept breathing. Daniel was still holding her elbow, and she tugged free of him. "I won't jump out," she said, and he rocked back, awkward and unsure.

"Trisk, come over here out of the wind," Kal said, but she didn't move, refusing to let him see the depth of her pain. Quen would be okay—if he could slip Fallon's population, hell-bent on retribution. He was only 6 percent human. He'd survive. *Please, God. Let him survive.*

"Come out of the wind, Trisk," Daniel said, and she numbly let herself be led to a pile of blankets. It was only then that she realized they were not alone. Two families, human by the look of it, were huddled on the other side of the boxcar between pallets of goods headed east.

They had to have come from Reno, and as Trisk tried to smile at the little girl watching her with wide, frightened eyes, she wondered if anyplace was safe.

23

Trisk sat with her shoulder against the open door, her legs stretched out before the edge. She'd braided her hair back, and the stray strands tickled her neck. It was cold now that the sun was down, but the air was decidedly fresher at the edge, and she could ignore for a moment the awful truth being played out in the dark boxcar behind her.

A pale light still lingered in the sky, washing out all but the strongest stars. The steady *click-click, click-click* had long ago retreated to a background noise, but the feel of it vibrated through her like a massive heartbeat. They were traveling through spacious fields of cultivation, and Trisk pulled her blanket closer against the damp rising from the night-cooled earth.

A racking cough drew her attention to the shadowed end of the boxcar. Daniel had helped the boys, both between the ages of six and ten, to build a makeshift hearth on the floor of the car out of a huge glass bowl. The slat-wood box the bowl had come in was currently being burned within it, the fitful flames lighting the tired, blister-marked faces surrounding it. Hunger and cold had pushed them into becoming thieves as they searched for something to eat. That Quen might be huddled alone somewhere gnawed at her, and she played with her necklace, missing him.

The back of her head seemed to itch, and she turned to see that Kal was watching her from his far corner. Eyes narrowed, she let go of the worked gold and looked away before he mistook her glance as interest. He'd been there from almost the very moment they'd pulled themselves into the moving car, settling his pristine black slacks on a piece of cardboard to try to keep himself clean. He'd slept most of the day while the sun was high, but she figured his traditional elven sleep pattern was more about avoiding any questions she might ask rather than the opportunity to slip from a human schedule to the elves' natural crepuscular rhythm. Pixies were the same way. Trisk couldn't believe he'd blame Rick and the vampires, but there was enough possibility of it being true to make her keep her mouth shut. Sa'han Ulbrine could decide.

Vampires were known to be bat-shit crazy, especially the older ones, and the younger went along with them as if their word was God's. Besides, it had been hammered into Trisk from an early age that her opinion held very little weight, even with the facts to back it up. Sa'han Ulbrine had the clout to make a difference, while her words would be dismissed as those of a crackpot.

The harsh ripping of cardboard pulled her attention back to the paper fire. Daniel was using his short lab knife to open up one of the more promising boxes. His brown trousers and soft tweed vest made him look almost frumpy compared to Kal's sharper image, and she smiled when he pushed his glasses back up his nose and brushed his blond hair back, making room for the two boys when they clustered close to pull out the packing paper and see what was inside. A little girl with dark hair was right in the thick of it, her arm clutched around a hard plastic doll with white hair, an impossibly thin waist, and an equally impossibly big chest.

The girl watched the boys pull out the paper stuffing as if it were Christmas. But then her expression fell. "Oh no," her high voice rose in complaint when it turned out to be another cheap decorative knickknack piece of glass.

"That's okay, April," Daniel said, his hand consolingly atop her head as the boys began enthusiastically dismantling the box. "It just means more paper for the fire."

Nodding, April looked to the edge of the light where they had stacked a row of boxes to give the sickest some privacy. Behind it, someone was crying.

Uneasy, Trisk drew her long sweater coat close. Apart from her, Kal, and Daniel, all but two of the adults in the car were showing signs of the virus, and she was proud of Daniel's bravery as he made sure those who were sick were being tended and that the kids were distracted.

The scuff of a shoe brought her attention back to Kal, and she pulled her knees to her chest, startled when he sat down beside her with a heavy sigh, casually dangling his feet out of the car.

"Do you think he told them the toxin is coming from a tomato?" he asked softly, and she looked past him to the cluster of people. One of the men was vomiting out the far side of the car, his wife standing beside him, her arm over his back as she silently wept. Daniel was doggedly trying to keep the kids distracted, but Trisk was sure their bright voices as they played with the fire were only an act so they could pretend nothing was wrong for a few hours more.

She shrugged, feeling her throat close at the pain she could do nothing to stop.

Kal scooted closer. "It doesn't matter. I don't think any of them will be alive tomorrow."

Trisk stared at him. The tips of her toes were almost touching him, and she fought the urge to shove him out the door. "You are unbelievable," she said, her thoughts going to Quen and that rash she had seen but hadn't recognized. She wished there was a way to contact him magically, and she ached to know if he had escaped or if he was lying in a field somewhere, dying.

"Why?" His eyes were on the field in evaluation. "Because I don't worry about things I can't control?" Kal glanced over his shoulder at the two families, then, as if satisfied, he lifted his hat a bare inch. Orchid slipped out, dropping the few feet to the car's floor.

"This is the last of it," Kal said as he took a leaf-wrapped ball of what looked like pollen from his front shirt pocket and handed it to her. "I'm sorry. I didn't expect we'd have to leave the car. I think your food stocks are halfway to Colorado by now."

He is such a dick, Trisk thought. Worried one of the kids might come over, she inched closer to Kal to make a more certain barrier, hiding the pixy.

"I'm not your responsibility, Kal," Orchid said, her wings slowly moving as she unfolded her provisions and began eating the soft cake. Like magic, the blue dust falling from her began to brighten. "Besides, it's dark now. I can slip out. Do some foraging. Catch up."

"Orchid . . ." Kal whispered, and Trisk eyed him, shocked at the depth of his worry.

Smirking, the tiny woman rose up, cutting her motion short when she remembered they weren't alone. "Relax. The train isn't going that fast. I can find something to eat in a cornfield."

Without another word, she swan-dived off the platform, her wings catching the wind and zipping her out into the open field. "I should have planned for this," Kal muttered, and Trisk wondered if he'd forgotten she was there as he chewed on his lower lip and peered out into the night, probably for a trace of pixy dust among the dark plants.

"I'm sure she'll be fine," Trisk said, and Kal started.

Clearly embarrassed to have been caught unawares, he shrugged, taking his hand away from his face where he had been scrubbing his thickening bristles in worry. "She's not used to having to think about pesticides," he said in explanation. Moving surprisingly gracefully in the swaying car, he stood, holding the open door for balance as he waited for Orchid's return.

Trisk frowned up at him, thinking he looked different as his eyes searched the dark for any sign of trouble. She had no doubt he'd jump from the train if Orchid showed any indication of distress, making Trisk wonder how he could care so much for the pixy and nothing for the people behind him dying.

Her hand strayed protectively to her middle. She'd said that she'd tell Kal, but not until she knew if Gally had been lying. And even then, she wasn't sure if she wanted him to know. Conceiving was never easy between elves, and the idea that she and Kalamack were so genetically compatible that a one-night stand left her in a family way was . . . icky.

Holding her knees to her chest, she watched the kids feed their little bonfire. She couldn't tell if their skin was red from the heat or a coming rash. "Do you think they'll be okay?" she whispered, her gaze lingering on the little black-haired girl, her eyes solemn as she watched the flames from the security of her mother's side. *Four?* she wondered. *Five?*

Kal never took his eyes off the night. "I don't know," he said, but what she heard was *I don't care*.

Angry, she gathered herself and stood. "Excuse me," she said coolly.

"What?" he protested as she pushed around him to go help Daniel open another box.

"What can I do?" she asked, and Daniel smiled, looking good surrounded by the kids.

"I could use a few more boxes," he said, and the two boys darted off before she could move, their voices loud as they said they wanted the very top ones.

"Hold up," she said as she went to get them, reaching over their heads to carefully pull down one, then another. At the edges, the parents watched, heartache and grief in their eyes, as they knew they were dying. Their blisters were obvious, the oozing pustules growing as they crept down their arms. *They are not contagious*, she thought, putting an arm around the smaller boy to keep him from falling in the swaying car as he made his determined way back to Daniel and dropped the box at his feet with satisfaction.

"Well, let's see what we have," Daniel said, and Trisk pulled the boy back, gently holding him to her and out of the way of Daniel's knife. "More paper for the fire," he said, and they reached in, giggles sounding and then shouts as the boys ran off, eager to play with the flames they'd been forbidden to touch until tonight.

"Why didn't we hop a produce car?" Trisk whispered.

"Good question." Head down, Daniel unrolled a wad of paper from around yet another piece of glass. But then a smile threatened. "April? Come and see what I found."

From the far side of the impromptu fire, the little black-haired girl sat up from beside her mother. Absently scratching her neck, she stood, her mother's blistered hand steadying her. The woman's eyes were red from crying, but her voice held love as she urged her daughter to go see.

"Is it something to eat?" the little girl said, her pure voice cutting deep into Trisk. *Shit, she's got it*, Trisk thought when she saw the beginnings of a rash on the little girl's neck.

Seeing it, too, Daniel forced his smile to brighten. "No." He knelt, a glass figure in his hand. "Better."

April's eyes widened. "A horse!" she exclaimed, the knickknack looking huge in her tiny fingers. Shoving her gangly plastic doll under her arm, she took it.

"Close." Daniel shifted, giving her something to lean against so she wouldn't fall in the swaying car. "It's a unicorn. A magical horse that only little girls can ride."

She beamed up at him, and Trisk's throat tightened. It was as if all the beauty from the years she would not have was suddenly condensed in her. "Thank you, Uncle Daniel," she said, holding it close as she gave him a hug.

Daniel's expression froze, her thin arm wrapped around his neck. For an instant, he held her, his grief open and honest. "Go show your mom," he rasped, and April cheerfully ran to her.

Trisk unrolled a second unicorn and dropped it back in the box. The paper was more precious. "'Uncle Daniel'?" she kidded him, trying to get that awful look off his face. But behind the makeshift wall, a woman was crying softly as another unseen voice tried to convince her that they'd be in Detroit in the morning and everything would be okay. But Trisk knew nothing would help them if they had received a killing dose. There was no broad-spectrum cure for a toxin. It had to run its course. *April, I'm so sorry.*

"It wasn't supposed to do this," Daniel whispered, his motion to unwrap another figurine faltering. "I made this to prevent death, not cause it."

A lump filled her throat as she gave him a sideways hug. "I know," she said, turning to Kal with an evil glance. He was still standing at the door waiting for Orchid's return. If this was his fault, she was going to strangle the man with his own intestines. "They're going to be okay," she lied. "I don't think the boys have it." She hesitated, watching them play with the fire and send their little paper balloons of trapped heat to the ceiling. "Have you told them that it was in the tomatoes?"

He shook his head. A haunted expression lurked at the back of his eyes. "I didn't see the point," he said, voice so low she almost missed it. "Maybe tomorrow, when we get into the city."

She could almost hear his unspoken thought: *If they're still alive.*

His frustration twisted his lips, and he kicked the box out through the open door, his arms pinwheeling. There was a crash of glass, and the kids turned. Seeing Daniel slowly sink to the floor, they went back to the fire, their bright mood broken for a moment.

"Daniel, I'm sorry," she said as she sat beside him to tug him sideways into her, but he only shook his head, pinching the bridge of his nose as if to stave off any hint of emotion.

"Do you know how they got here?" he said, head still bowed. "Into this train car?"

She shook her head. A few feet away, the boys opened the second box, throwing the glass birds it contained out the door in a mimicry of flight.

Daniel looked up, his expression desolate. "Government trucks were slated to come through their neighborhood to relocate anyone who'd had a death in the house."

"That's awful," she said, and Daniel pulled one of the boxes to him, clearly needing something to do even if it was only finding more paper to burn.

"If anyone died or was clearly sick, the entire household was forced onto a truck," he said as he wrestled the box open. "They were only allowed to take what they could fit in a suitcase, made to go to a quarantine area to die."

She remembered the angry, numb-looking expressions at the diner as good, everyday people were faced with the awful need to find a way to bury their neighbors that was both respectful and fast. It had to be better in the big cities. It had to be. "I'm so sorry," she said.

"April's parents were already on the pickup list because their oldest daughter had died in the hospital the day before. They didn't want anyone to know they were still alive and maybe try to follow and find them, so they dragged their dead neighbors into their own house so everyone would assume it was them. Soon as the truck left, they jumped the train. The other couple with the boys saw them and followed along with the husband's brother."

She gave his shoulder a squeeze. "This isn't your fault."

"No?" he asked, then he laughed bitterly as he unwrapped a jar of hard candy, ready for the store shelves. "I killed them all, and all I can do is give them a jar of candy."

"Daniel . . ." she pleaded, but he had turned away.

"Hey, I found something to eat!" he called out, and immediately the two boys scrambled up, taking a jar. April took another to her parents, holding it carefully between her arm and her body so she wouldn't have to let go of the glass unicorn.

"Kal?" Daniel said, his anger barely veiled. "How about some candy?"

"I'll have one," he said, and Daniel threw a jar at him. Hard.

Kal caught it, taking one candy and tucking it in his shirt pocket before setting the jar aside. It was for Orchid, no doubt.

"How about you?" Daniel asked as he opened the last jar. "I know it's not much."

"Thanks." Her stomach hurt, but she took one anyway, the crisp plastic crackling in a clean sound. *Lemon drop*, she thought as the tart flavor made her more hungry, not less.

Beside her, Daniel crunched through his and reached for another. Taking a handful, he put the top back on the jar and set it aside. Kal was still staring out into the night, and Daniel watched him, reluctantly saying, "You haven't told him yet, have you."

"Told him what?" she blurted, then realized she was holding her middle protectively. "Oh. No," she said, eyes down. "How can you tell?"

Daniel smirked, sighing as he settled himself more firmly on the floor in the middle of the car. "Because he's over there, and you're over here. If he knew, he wouldn't let you sit over here with us sick humans, worried that you might endanger his baby with a possible infection."

Her eyes slid to Kal, then back to Daniel. "He doesn't strike me as the protective kind," she said, though his concern for Orchid was considerable.

"No? Well, no one will blame you if you don't tell him. Ever." He hesitated, then asked, "Why is Quen sick? I thought he was . . . like you."

"He is," she said, listening to the kids' voices become more cheerful with the sugar and the prospect of no bedtime. "But humans and elves can, uh, you know." Daniel's eyebrows rose, and she felt herself warm. "Before we had gene therapy, the only way to bolster our failing genetic code was to bring in different stock."

"The chromosomes match up?" he asked incredulously, and she looked at Kal, wondering if he was listening.

"With a little help from magic." She shifted to find a more comfortable spot. "Some say it's indicative that we share an ancestor, but I've seen the math, and it's not easy, just possible."

Daniel ran a hand over his face in thought. "And it doesn't create a sterile mule?"

She chuckled. "I did say there was magic involved." Her gaze went past Daniel to April and her family bedding down for the night, both parents struggling with how to say good night knowing they might not wake up tomorrow. April was petulant, wanting a story, and Trisk could see the grief in their eyes. *God, save me from such a fate.*

"Quen had a human ancestor in his great-greats," she said softly, unable to watch anymore. "He'll be okay. Even if the tomato has condensed the toxins." But she didn't know for sure. No one knew anything for sure.

"It wasn't supposed to kill anyone," Daniel said again, making a tight fist. "It was only supposed to make you sick. That's it. Sick."

She reached over and gave his hand a squeeze. "It's going to be okay. Once we get to Detroit, we can get the word out, and we can stop it. Sa'han Ulbrine will be there. They have to believe him. We might even be able to come up with an antitoxin."

But they both knew it was a one-in-a-million shot.

The two boys quietly tended the fire, somber as they no longer had anything to distract them from the hacking coughs of the adults. "But Mama, I'm not sleepy," April protested. "I want to play with my magic horse."

Trisk watched April's mother's grief as she tried to settle her daughter, and she wondered if Kal could love a child with black hair. "April, do you want to hear a story?" she asked suddenly, and the mother's frightened eyes shot to her.

"It's okay," Trisk said, wondering if the woman thought she was going to steal her final moments with her daughter away. "Come sit with me for the story, but you have to promise you'll go right to sleep afterward."

"I will," the little girl said, clearly used to bargaining for "just one more."

Trisk smiled, then blinked when April plopped down not beside her, but in her lap. Startled, Trisk snuggled her in, wrapping them both in the worn blanket. "This is a story about a young girl," Trisk said, smiling when she noticed even the two boys were listening. "A princess. Just about your age."

"Can she have a magical horse?" April asked, her attention on the fire, and Trisk nodded.

"It's a true story, and yes, she did have a magical horse that only she could ride. The little girl's name was April," Trisk said, tweaking April's nose to make her giggle.

It was as if the happy sound drew Orchid in from the dark, her wings' clattering lost in the clack of the wheels as the pixy vaulted into the shadowed roof slats, hiding. Kal turned away from the door, his worry gone as he made his steady way back to his corner.

"Princess April liked to ride her magical horse in the

woods," Trisk said, her arms feeling more natural as they curved around the little girl. "She liked to ride in the spring, when the trees sent their tiny flowers out to test the air before the leaves dared show. She liked to ride in the summer, when the insects sang and the wind whispered secrets to the leaves. And she liked to ride in the winter, when the snow made the world into a pristine black and white and she could go for hours without seeing anyone but a sly white fox and her friend, the otter."

Her eyes half-lidded, April sighed, content as she galloped her unicorn down Trisk's arm.

"But Princess April's favorite time to ride was the fall, when the dry leaves coated the ground in a wash of gold to make the world look upside down, and the squirrels hid the falling acorns as if they were the trees' whispered secrets and hopes made real."

Even the boys had quieted, and no one but Trisk and Kal saw the faint slip of silver dust drifting down from the roof.

"Princess April lived with a nice family who looked nothing like her," Trisk said, and April twisted in her lap, looking up at her.

"Why not?"

"Because her mother and father had found Princess April in that very same woods. And because they loved her more than the child they couldn't have, they built a little house among the trees and raised her as their own. They even taught her how to use her great and awful gift so it would never hurt anyone, and she was happy, and they loved her."

April's eyes widened at the thought that a girl, a princess even, had a power that no one else did. "What was it?" she whispered, lisping slightly.

Trisk leaned closer, whispering, "She could start a fire with her hands."

From his corner, Kal snickered, guessing correctly that the girl in the story was an elf or witch. "No matches?" April asked, her eyes even wider.

"No matches," Trisk echoed. "No lighter, nothing. Just by wishing it. Everything was beautiful in April's world, and she grew up to be a beautiful woman. Her horse carried her far and wide, and she met other people, far away from the tiny house in the woods, but she always came back to be with her mother and father and her friends.

"Until," Trisk said dramatically, "one day, a prince from a far-off city heard of her. He came to see her on a big black horse whose hooves were shod with metal." April shivered in her arms, imagining it. "His horse's nostrils flared when he was angry, and his ears? His ears showed his mood, which was mostly bad, so they lay flat against his head."

April clutched her glass unicorn to her. "Did he hurt April's horse?" she asked.

Trisk shook her head, and even the boys at the fire relaxed. "No. Princess April wouldn't let him, but the prince wanted her to come with him. He gave her presents, and food, and kittens. And when she still refused to leave her house in the woods, he got angry and cut them down."

"No!" April cried, horrified.

"He did." Trisk held her closer, her heart breaking at the little girl's blisters, easy to see now on her neck. "He cut down the woods to the last tree. Right to the ground for miles and miles. Even the two old oaks in her backyard. And then he stole her away while she wept."

The two boys had crept closer, even their incessant

jostling ceasing. "What did she do?" one asked, and Trisk arched her eyebrows wisely.

"Princess April waited until the prince took her back to his city, and then she used her great and terrible gift to burn his city to the ground. Prince and all."

Kal grunted in surprise from his corner, but Daniel was grinning as he unpacked another box for the paper to keep the fire going, throwing the useless glass out the door.

"What about the people?" April asked, and Trisk rocked her gently.

"The people ran away. Far, far away and never came back."

"Did she go home?" April asked next, her eyes on her unicorn.

"She did," Trisk said, and April sighed, happy. "It took a long time because her horse was lame, but yes. April went home to find that her parents were gone along with the trees. There were no leaves whispering secrets, no squirrels hiding acorns, no sly fox to teach her sly wisdom, and even her otter friend was gone."

Lips pressed in disapproval, April ran her unicorn a prancing path down Trisk's arm.

"That's a dumb story," one of the boys said, and Kal grunted his agreement.

"It's not over," Trisk said tartly. "Princess April searched her backyard and found enough acorns to fill a basket. She took those acorns and planted one at the base of every broken stump, hoping that when they were again tall and strong, her parents would return." Trisk took a slow breath, loath to let April go. "And that is the end."

"That's sad," April said, her high voice clear with the truth of it.

"Most fairy tales are." Bowing her head, she kissed the top of April's head. "Go back to your mother now. Dream about what you want to be for Halloween, okay?"

Solemn, April rose, grabbing the shoulder of one of the boys when she wobbled on her way back to the shadows. The soft sounds of their mother-daughter conversation evolving into silence dug at Trisk, and she held herself before the paper fire, wishing things were different.

His exhalation soft, Daniel sat down beside her. "I don't know what you're worried about. You're going to make a great mom."

Trisk blinked fast, refusing to cry. From the far side of the car, Kal turned his back on them, rolling over and pretending to go to sleep. Saying nothing, she wadded up another sheet of paper and tossed it on the flames. "Maybe someday."

"That was a true story, wasn't it?" Daniel said, and she nodded.

"Except for the princess part," she admitted. "She was a dark elf raised by dryads sometime in the early part of the twelfth century." Leaving a dark-haired baby in the woods to die of exposure was not allowed anymore. Even her genetic diversity had value.

"Tree spirits?" Daniel whispered, leaning close to hide his lips. "They really exist?"

"They used to. I don't think there are any alive in the U.S. anymore." She tossed another wad of paper on the fire, thinking it was ironic. "It's said that some of England's old-growth forests might still be alive, but dryads are sensitive to pollution. They're probably extinct."

Daniel silently looked at the quickly burning flames. "Together, you outnumber us. I would've thought you could do something about it."

A bitter frustration rose from nowhere. "We don't have a lot of options when it comes to saving at-risk species."

Her eyes went to Kal at the faintest clatter of pixy wings as Orchid dropped down to sample the hard candy he'd saved for her. The dryads were probably long gone. Pixies and fairies were next on the list as human and Inderland populations grew, pushing the softer species into smaller and smaller pockets, and she looked from Kal to the humans dying among their blankets and misery. She couldn't help but wonder why their human existence was more valuable than the dryads or pixies. Maybe if the weaker Inderland species came out of hiding, humans would modify their behavior to save them.

But then again, vampires, witches, Weres, and elves were just as bad about creating air pollution and toxic waste dumps.

Not any closer to finding an answer, Trisk huddled under her blanket, cold and hungry when the last of the paper fire flickered and went out, leaving only the *click-click* of the wheels and a square of lighter darkness to mark the horizon.

24

It was the gradual cessation of the *click-click* that woke her, more than the gentle bump as the train ceased moving. Cold. It was so cold. Trisk opened her eyes, her focus on the brighter reflected bands of light on the ceiling of the boxcar, now flooded with the frigid glow of dawn. *Quen*, she thought, hoping he was okay, her heartache colored with a flash of anger that he'd left so she could not see him suffer, not knowing if he was going to live or die.

One of the boys was crying, his sobs bracketed by the low voice of his uncle consoling him. Rolling toward the open door, she saw Daniel sitting on the floor of the car as he put his shoes on. His exhaled breath was gold in the sun, and she tugged her blanket tighter about herself.

"The boys lost their parents last night," Daniel said softly as their eyes met.

Trisk's brow furrowed in sorrow. "Oh no." She sat up, her attention going to the corner where April had fallen asleep with her mom and dad. There was nothing to see but heaped blankets. Behind Daniel, the boys' uncle had lurched out of the boxcar, his shoes grinding on loose rock as he helped the boys down one at a time.

"They don't show any signs of illness," Daniel said as the man exchanged a word with Kal standing beside the tracks before turning to give them a wave good-bye and silently herding his new charges toward the nearby buildings, bright with new sun in the chilled air. "I told them to stay away from tomatoes. They should be okay."

But Trisk didn't think anything would ever be okay again. Knees hurting, she got up to check on April and her family. She was slow and stiff from the hard floor, and grimy from too long without a shower, and cold from exposure. But everything paled when she realized there was no sound coming from the blankets, no coughing, no soft movements. "April?" she called, and Daniel's hand landed on her shoulder, stopping her.

"Don't."

Trisk shrank from his gentle touch, her flash of panic evolving into a frantic need to do something. It couldn't be too late. It had only been a few hours. But then a small noise struck through her. April was still alive.

"Trisk, please," Daniel said again as she lurched to go to her, pulled back once more.

His eyes were dark with sorrow as they met hers, and anger flickered. "I'm not leaving her like this," Trisk said in affront.

Daniel's hand fell, his expression terrible in his grief. "You can't help her," he said, voice low, and her breath quickened. "You heard what they're doing in Reno. What they're doing everywhere. Leave her here with her parents. Don't take her from them, even in death."

"I'm not leaving her here to die alone," she whispered harshly, angry with him—angry at the world—and with a final sniff, she pushed past him.

But her hope twisted into heartache when she

saw April's flushed face, her breath fitful as she slept between her dead parents, her mother's bloodless white hand still protectively covering her.

"Oh, sweet pea," Trisk whispered, falling to a kneel to gather the little girl up in her blankets. "We're here now. We can get you some help. Make you better." But even as she said it, she knew it was too late. It had been too late the moment the virus had been released.

April's eyes opened at the clatter of pixy wings, and her expression lit up in wonder when Orchid hovered at Trisk's shoulder. A glittering blue dust sifted down, flashing silver where it touched April's face. She smiled, her innocence and wonder heartbreaking.

"Are you an angel?" April asked, her cheeks flushed to make her eyes look eerily bright. "Are you going to take me and Mommy to heaven?"

Trisk's throat closed. "She sure is, sweet pea. Go to sleep. Dream of angels."

April's smile lingered as she blinked fast and closed her eyes. Daniel eased up beside them, silent as together the three of them watched April's breaths go shallow and finally stop.

"She had such a pale green aura," Orchid said, wings slowing as she landed atop Trisk's arm to peer at the child. "Pretty. I thought I'd like it better if there were less humans, but I don't know anymore. She called me an angel."

"I'll take her," Daniel said, and Trisk's grip on April tightened. But she knew he was right, and while the helpless tears slipped down, she felt April's weight leave her as he took the bundled girl into his own arms.

Empty and cold, Trisk stood in the middle of the boxcar as Orchid and Daniel gently nestled April back between her parents. They lingered over them, one in curiosity, the other in what looked like a prayer. Trisk didn't know if it was for the family or for himself.

"Wait outside," Daniel said, head bowed and voice rough. "I'll be out in a minute."

Arms wrapped around herself from grief, Trisk scuffed to the open door, sitting down to slide out. The jar of meeting solid ground echoed through her and up into her spine, and she paused to unhook her long, open sweater coat when it caught. The air was chill, and she sucked in huge lungfuls of it, trying to find her composure. Orchid had let April see her, and April hadn't been scared. She had been charmed—for what little time she still breathed. Maybe it had been a mistake to keep their existence from humanity. No one could be afraid of pixies or fairies, but it had been thought if people knew of the smaller Inderlanders, they would recognize the darker, larger, and more dangerous ones in the shadows.

Quen, please be all right.

Wiping any hint of tears away, she turned to Kal. He was doing calisthenics in the sun, his limbs toned and his motions deliberate against the backdrop of the city. The boys and their uncle were gone, swallowed up by the shocking silence. There was no roar of traffic and nothing in the sky. Trisk's eyes narrowed as she saw the skyline. "That's not Detroit."

Kal came up from a stretch, a hint of annoyance furrowing his brow. "It's Chicago."

Lips parting, she faced him squarely, the boxcar holding a guilty silence behind her. How could she have ever slept with him? The man was a toad. "We have to get to Detroit. That's where Sa'han Ulbrine is." It was obvious that the train wasn't going to move again. Either it hadn't been going where they thought it was or the rails had been shut down.

Kal glanced at her and then away, focused on his stretch. "I know that."

"You said you knew the schedules," she insisted, though to be honest, they would have gotten on any train at that point.

"What I said was the schedules are simple." Kal's motions became sharp.

Arms still over her middle, she cocked her hip. "You can't say it, can you."

He came out of his stretch, shaking himself to resettle his clothes. "That I'm sorry?" he said, his flush making his baby-fine white hair stand out. "Sure I can. I'm sorry. I thought the train was going to Detroit. Clearly they stopped all traffic. You're going to blame me for that?"

"You are such an ass."

Daniel carefully lowered himself to sit in the open door. His blond hair, catching the light, was mussed, and his sweater-vest was filthy. His jaw was set, though, and his eyes were determined as he slid out and down, his dress shoes scraping on the scree. His broken humanity made him somehow more attractive than Kal. "That's not Detroit," he said.

"It's Chicago." Trisk shot an ugly look at Kal.

The train yard was quiet and empty. The only motion came from the sparrows hopping among the cars looking for grain. Daniel ran a hand over his thickly stubbled cheeks and stared blankly at Chicago's buildings. "Do your people have a lab in Chicago, maybe?"

"No," Kal said, his gaze following Daniel's, the barest hint of worry on his face.

"Someone will have a working phone," Trisk said as she put the toe of her shoe up on a wheel to retie it. "The police, maybe. We can call Sa'han Ulbrine. Tell him where we are. Get a government transport to Detroit." She dropped her foot, shoe scuffing on the loose rock. Her eyes went to the absolutely empty skies. Not a plane anywhere. *God, it's quiet.* "At the very least, we can get the word out that infection is caused by eating tomatoes."

"We need to find a phone," Daniel said, arms clasped around himself. "And maybe a coat. Wow, is it cold out here."

Kal's expression darkened as he pushed ahead to take the lead. "We agreed we couldn't tell people the plague is spreading by way of the tomatoes until we know for sure. I'm not starting a panic over a tomato engineered by an elf."

Trisk jerked to a stop. "Excuse me?" she said, hands on her hips.

Kal turned. "We don't *know* it's the T4 Angel," he said with an exaggerated patience that said he thought she was being a child about this.

"Bullshit." Daniel's face reddened at the foul word even as his expression hardened.

"And even if it is," Kal said, "the vampires caused the plague, not your tomato. The virus was their weapon, the tomato their delivery system. You really want to be on their hit list?"

Daniel's jaw was clenched, and Trisk looked between them as the tension rose. "It wasn't vampires. It was you," he said softly, and Trisk put a warning hand on his shoulder. "You had access, the knowledge, and the motive."

"So did Rick." Kal turned. "Let's go. We have to contact Sa'han Ulbrine."

You are a cold, callous fish of a man, Trisk thought as he walked away. The years since graduation hadn't changed him. And he was lying. She could tell now. It was in his eyes.

"Rick didn't do this," Daniel said, unmoving beside her. "You did."

Kal stopped short. Trisk's heart pounded when she felt him tap a ley line and turn. "Don't be absurd," Kal said, and Trisk's anger hesitated, slipping into what might be fear at how far Kal would go to hide his guilt. He'd already killed one man. "We need humans to keep everything functioning. But the vampires . . ." He stopped, head bobbing. "You get a crazy one, and they think they can rule the world." Lips pressed, he looked past them to the boxcar. "Orchid!" he shouted. "Let's go! It's too cold for you out here."

The pixy flew out of the car, her dust an alarmed red. She didn't land on his shoulder, instead alighting on the top of a nearby car, looking unsure and unhappy. Kal's expression tightened into an angry grimace upon seeing her reluctance.

"Maybe it's not about saving your species," Daniel said. "Maybe you're sick enough to kill the world if you can blame it on Trisk. Maybe your pride led you to think you were smart enough to tweak the virus safely, but you were dumb enough to screw it up. That's my working theory until I find a better one. *Dr. Kalamack*."

Trisk flushed, not moving away from Daniel. Kal was petty and self-serving, and with an ugly certainty, she decided none of Daniel's suggestions were beyond him—especially the one about pride. All this might be because of a grudge. *God, please. Anything but that.*

"Is that what you think?" Kal said, and hearing the warning in his voice, Trisk eased a thought into a ley line, praying he didn't notice and that there was no one around to see.

"Let me tell you what I think." Daniel pointed an accusing finger, his outrage warring with his professional need to get along. "I think you tried to discredit Trisk by killing her tomato with my virus, and when Rick found out that you accidentally made a carrier for the PTV, you burned him to death in Trisk's field to destroy the evidence as well as Rick. That's what I think."

Wire tight, Trisk watched Kal's hands, not his eyes.

"You shouldn't have told those people your virus was in Trisk's tomatoes," Kal said, and a wash of heat took her. Shit. It really was him. Not only that, but he wanted the virus to spread.

"You bastard," Daniel whispered, and before she could stop him, he went for Kal.

"Daniel! No!" she shouted.

Kal's hands twisted, and a green-tinted ball of energy vaporated between them. It was ugly, larger and deadlier than the spell he had thrown at her on the presentation floor. This smacked of black magic, its only purpose to hurt or kill. If Kal was responsible for the plague, he'd have no problem killing her, much less Daniel, to cover it up.

"*Septiens!*" she shouted, imagining a circle around Daniel to deflect and protect him. It was undrawn, and therefore vulnerable. Exhaling, she pushed more energy into it until the molecule-thin barrier flashed with an instant of stability. Her hand flared in pain, and she funneled more through her, burning. Daniel, intent on reaching Kal, hit the inside of her circle, bouncing back with a grunt of surprise and falling in the loose rock between the tracks.

Kal's energy hit her bubble at the same time, ricocheting away with a ping and an evil-sounding hiss, the black-and-green haze corkscrewing into a distant box-car, where it burst in a shower of gold sparkles.

Her circle failed, and the power of the line rushed to fill the void the deflected energy had made, swirling toward it like water down a drain and vanishing. It hurt, but she wouldn't let go of the line, and Trisk held her throbbing hand to her middle.

Daniel blinked, surprised to find himself on the ground. Kal stared at him for an unreal three seconds, trying to figure out why the man was down and not withering in whatever spell that had been. But then Kal's gaze shifted to Trisk, his eyes narrowing as he saw her, shaking in anger as she stood protectively over Daniel.

"You will be held accountable for this," she promised Kal, her hand aching as she pooled the spent energy from the circle into a mass of unfocused magic in her good hand. "You will be held accountable!" she exclaimed, thinking of the dead family behind her, of April, who would never smile at pretend again. "I will make sure the entire world knows it was you," she vowed.

Kal backed up a step and her confidence swelled, feeding her anger.

But then he laughed, becoming again that prideful snot she'd grown up with. "Who do you think they're going to believe?" he said in a show of confidence that was just that—a show. "You or me?" he added. "It was your project. I was sent to find the flaws, and boy, did I find one." Saluting them with a casual finger, he turned his back on them and walked away, sure she wouldn't have the guts to throw the energy pooled in her hand.

"You little bastard," Daniel said as he scrambled up.

The world will thank me, she thought. But knowing

that if Kal died, so did the only way to prove her and Daniel's innocence, she warped the energy not with a curse, but something else, something she hadn't known was possible until last week. It was a black magic; she didn't care.

Perhaps Gally is right about me, she thought, her only emotion one of satisfaction as she threw it, the scintillating sparkles pulling off and away from her with the sensation of drawing a glove off inside out. She shuddered, feeling both clean and filthy at the same time. Coated in black, her spell sped toward Kal's retreating form.

"Kal!" Orchid shouted, and the man turned, his toe elegantly sketching a circle like a figure skater. A whispered phrase of Latin, and a circle sprang up. Her spell slammed into it, slivering over the entire barrier like black lightning, little flashes of gold looking for a way in.

Kal's fear showed for an instant, and then he stood from his instinctive crouch, a demeaning smile on his face when her energy seemed to spend itself and vanish into the earth.

"Looks like I'm not the only one doing a little correspondence study," Kal said, and with a scoffing laugh, he let his circle fall and beat a hasty retreat, slipping between two cars and out of her sight. "Orchid!" he shouted, and the pixy rose up, hovering indecisively for a moment before darting after him.

This time, Trisk let Kal go. Shaking, she looked at her hands, still feeling the pinpricks of the spent energy. She was breathless and a little ill, and she swallowed hard, determined not to throw up. What Kal didn't know was that her charm *had* reached him, sliding underground and then through an open pipe buried in the ground to cross his circle and gently settle into his aura like a second skin.

"It worked," she murmured, looking at her hands and seeing no difference. It hadn't been a spell or charm to hurt or kill, but one to mark. After seeing Gally move his curse's smut onto her, she'd figured out how to then move it to Kal, coating him in her smut. It was a curse without actually cursing him, marking him so the demons could find him. It might be tomorrow, it might be in eighty years, but when one got out, he would sense the blackness on Kal like a lighthouse in the night and take him for his own, thinking Kal had earned the smut honestly.

"Are you okay?" Daniel asked, and she pulled her head up, resolved to carry the shame of it with no regrets.

Nodding, she took a deep breath and shouted, "You hear me, Kalamack! Something will come for you in the night. I promise you!" Falling back into herself, she gingerly rubbed her burned hand. She'd broken the most sacred rule of magic. You *always* pay for the dark you do. Forcing the smut on another was the darkest sin, one she'd walk away from with no one the wiser. It made her fouler than Kal. It made her akin to a demon. She didn't care.

Much. "How about you?" she said, feeling unreal. "Are you all right?"

Daniel looked at the cars, his head drooping. "Fine. What was that you threw at him?"

Trisk gripped her elbows. Her aura was spotlessly clean, and she'd never felt so dirty. "Regret," she said, though she'd do it again in an instant. *And I'm going to raise a child? Our child? Quen, what have I done?*

Her longtime friend's moral compass would never

understand why she'd done it. Unexpected tears threatened, and she clenched her jaw, refusing to cry. Seeing it, Daniel tugged her into a sideways hug—which only made things worse. "It's okay. The thing right now is to get to a phone and let people know you can avoid getting sick."

She nodded, throat tight. Her thoughts still on what Quen would say, she turned to the boxcar for one last look. Her grip on the ley line strengthened, and with a flick of thought, she sent the entire car into flames.

Daniel stumbled back, his eyes wide as they shifted from her obvious misery to the engulfed car, burning hotter than any normal fire. She wouldn't leave them half-burned and foul; she wanted them cremated. Bones would remain, but little else.

"Let's go," Daniel said softly as the heated metal began to creak and ping. For all the fury of the flames, Trisk knew they wouldn't catch anything else on fire. Head down, she fell into place beside him, thinking that she didn't deserve any kindness when his arm went over her shoulder.

She watched their feet, her sneakers beside his sensible office shoes, now scratched and marred into a bland gray, as far from their original shiny black as she was from the innocent woman she'd been two weeks ago. Slowly the uncomfortable rocks turned into flat dirt, then an echoing, empty wheelhouse. The gates were locked, but they used a Dumpster to get over the wall, and the two of them came out onto the streets proper, their first eager steps faltering as they took in the empty silence.

"Where is everyone?" Daniel whispered, and she shrugged, angling them toward the taller buildings. A megaphone blared in the distance, and a heavy diesel truck rumbled. Without comment, they went in the opposite direction. Twitches of curtains balanced the pervading scent of new death. The city wasn't deserted, and it wasn't dead.

"I think everyone is hiding," Trisk said. "How much change do you have?" she asked as she saw a pay phone outside a gas station.

"Few dollars." He searched his pocket as they crossed the road. Someone was coming. Not that big diesel truck, but several cars by the sound of it. "Maybe we should find a phone off the main street," he said as they passed two abandoned vehicles in the parking lot.

She didn't have even a dime, and she lifted the receiver to find a dial tone. "Oh, thank God," she whispered, loath to leave it.

"Uh, Trisk, it's the cops," Daniel said, and she stumbled when he pulled her into the chancy shadows to leave the receiver swinging.

Ahhh, shit, she thought, but it was too late and the lights flashed and the siren whooped once to tell them to stay put. "Oh, man," she whispered when five cars stopped tight in the parking lot, almost pinning them against the wall of the building. Men dressed in combat gear spilled out, yelling at them, and she put her hands up. Her thoughts went to her hair, her clothes. She looked a mess. They'd never believe her story. *Quen wouldn't have made a mistake like this. I should have been more careful.*

Silent, Daniel raised his hands, his fingers spread as two men approached, pushing him into the wall and cuffing him.

"Hey, we're the good guys," Trisk protested as one manhandled her, cuffing her hands behind her. "We know what's causing the plague. We need to talk to someone in Detroit."

Daniel stumbled, grunting as they pushed him into the wall of the gas station again. "I don't think they care," he said, lips pressing when someone told him to shut up.

Ticked, she reached for a ley line, her eyes widening when she realized the cuffs were made of charmed silver. It was probably standard practice in a big city where it was easier to treat everyone as a witch, vampire, or Were until proven otherwise—whether the humans on the force knew it or not. "We haven't done anything wrong," she said as an officer patted her down.

A thin man with a hint of a mustache looked up from where he stood at a car, a radio in his hand. "You're breaking curfew," he said. Though not the oldest cop out here, he was clearly in charge, his soft wrinkles falling into themselves as he tossed the radio into the car and came over.

Immediately she recognized him as a witch, his long fingers made dexterous from spell casting and a faint scent of redwood emanating from him. His close-cut salt-and-pepper hair gave him a distinguished air, but his lumpy nose ruined it, and feeling an unexpected connection, Trisk fought a lifetime of conditioning to not blurt out that she was an elf.

"We didn't know about the curfew," Daniel said over his shoulder. "We just got here."

The captain hesitated a good eight feet back. It was telling, and her unease tightened into a hard knot. If you were fast, eight feet was enough time to react to a magic assault as well as a vampire attack. "And how would you have done that?" the man said as he looked down at a sheaf of papers one of his men handed him, the wrinkles about his eyes bunching up. "The roads are barricaded."

"We came by train," Trisk said, and then upon seeing his doubt, added, "Freight train."

The man beside him fidgeted. "Captain Pelhan, we've been asked to investigate a fire in the train yard," he said, and his eyebrows high, Pelhan waited for an explanation.

"Ah," Daniel said, eyes darting to Trisk as he turned to put his back to the wall. "That was us. We set fire to one of the cars to contain any sickness we might have brought."

The officer, Trisk realized, was a witch as well, and in a sudden flash of hope, she decided everyone out here was either a witch or Were. They were probably the only ones on the police force that were reporting for duty. *But no vampires*, she mused, thinking that odd, as living vampires were drawn to the power that came with a badge. Not to mention being on the force made it easier to cover up a master's mistake in taking a lost human.

"It was me," she said, knowing they'd go out and find the bodies. "I wasn't going to walk away and leave them to putrefy. The fire won't spread. I made sure of it."

It was all she could do to not openly say she was an elf, but Captain Pelhan's brow rose in understanding when she made a small finger motion as if making a spell.

Hesitating, Pelhan tapped his papers against his hand. Behind him, his men came back from searching the nearby area. "The government is asking everyone to hunker down," he said. His voice was softer, holding the hint of understanding.

"We really need to get to a phone," she tried again, not liking the feel of the cuffs around her wrists. "We were trying to get to Detroit and ended up here. Sa'han

Ulbrine is waiting for me. We might know how to stop this. I have to talk to him."

The captain's eye twitched at the openly Inderland term, his gaze going to Daniel, then to her. "No one can stop this." He took a slow breath, as if divorcing himself from what was to come. "He's not sick!" he said loudly to his men. "Tom, take him to the stadium."

"Hey! Wait a minute!" Daniel exclaimed when they began to pull him away. Trisk stiffened in protest, and the man beside her put a heavy hand on her shoulder in warning.

"He's with me," she said, but she wasn't sure if that was going to help him or not. If she wasn't going to the stadium, where was she going? "Daniel!"

Captain Pelhan came forward to take her arm, the tingle of a ley line, promising hurt if she should try anything. "All humans breaking curfew go to either the hospital or containment centers. Everyone else goes to jail."

Humans? she wondered, but he had said it softly enough that only the nearest officers could hear. At least they knew *she* wasn't one. "He's a scientist, like me," she said, stumbling as she looked over her shoulder at Daniel as they were led to different cars. "I need his help. It's the tomatoes, the T4 Angel tomato. That's where the toxin is. Even stuff that's been on the shelf for a year."

Pelhan stopped at the car, waiting as one of his officers opened the back door. "The fuzzy tomato?" the younger man asked, and the captain gave him a look to shut up.

"That's the one," Trisk said, breathless, glad someone was listening. "The virus is using it as a host, condensing the levels into toxic range. I need to get to a phone. If I can convince Sa'han Ulbrine, he can get the word out, and we can stop this."

Pelhan chewed his lip, thinking that over. Beyond him, Daniel was shoved into a car, but it didn't drive away, and she waited, heart pounding.

"Captain?" a man called from a third car, a radio in his hand. "They match the descriptions of the two geneticists from Global Genetics. They're wanted for questioning in a murder, sir."

Trisk's eyes shot to Pelhan's, her first flush of fear settling in for a long stay. "We didn't kill Rick. One of my colleagues, Dr. Trenton Kalamack, killed him to cover up that he was the one who allowed Daniel's virus to attach itself to my tomato. He's here. Somewhere. Please. We're trying to stop this. If I could just talk to Sa'han Ulbrine. I need to get to Detroit."

At that, the captain seemed to come back to himself. "Detroit is gone," he said as he put his hand on her head and all but pushed her into the car.

"Gone!" Inside the car, she stared up at him, quickly putting her leg outside so he couldn't shut the door. "What do you mean, gone? Like no communication?"

Pelhan bodily put her foot back in the car, warning her with a frown to leave it there. "No, gone, as in wiped off the face of the earth, taking everyone with it. It was the vamps and the witches, and we're by God not going to let that happen here."

And with that, he shut the door.

25

The police station smelled like angry dog and spicy redwood. Overlaying it was the musky scent she'd always identified with vampires, and Trisk's nose wrinkled as the officer holding her elbow escorted her deeper into the facility. It was busy with cops and a few harried secretaries in trim uniforms who never saw the street, and she wondered whether she was smelling her fellow Inderlanders so strongly because there were no human scents to mask them, or if they were just really stressed.

"Captain Pelhan!" one of the officers hailed as he caught sight of them coming in, his short red hair making him stand out. His arm was in a sling, and the metal charm around his neck disguised as a St. Christopher medallion made her think he was a witch. Telling the kid at his desk to stay put, the officer stood, grabbed a folder, and wove through the open offices toward them.

"Thanks, Randy." Wrinkles in his forehead bunching, Captain Pelhan slowed as he took the papers, but he didn't stop. "I'll sign these later."

"Uh, sir?" the officer added to make Pelhan's eyes crinkle, and the tired man rocked to a halt, his narrow shoulders slumping. "I've got a kid at my desk I don't know what to do with. He says he's a minor, but he won't tell me his name because he's more afraid of his mom than us."

Together, Trisk and Pelhan looked around Officer Randy. Trisk's eyebrows rose. The kid looked too tall to be a minor, but his face was baby smooth as he slumped in the stiff-looking chair, his head lolled to make his red dreadlocks hang down his back. She'd never seen hair like that, but it kind of went with his orange bell-bottoms, yellow shirt, and rope sandals. *Witch*, she thought, seeing the plethora of wooden charms around his neck disguised as beads.

Pelhan winced, running a quick hand over his short graying hair. "Please tell me he's dressed like that for Halloween."

Officer Randy grinned. "Nope. He says he's part of a band, which checks out since there's a bass guitar and drum set in his van. We're running the plates to find out who he is, but it's from Ohio, and . . ."

"Everything is down," Pelhan finished for him as the kid pantomimed playing a guitar. The scent of redwood grew, and Pelhan rubbed his forehead in defeat. "We can't put him downstairs with the vamps. Cuff him to a table in the break room."

"Yes, sir."

"Wait." Pelhan eyed Trisk dryly, the wrinkles at his eyes deepening. "Cuff Dr. Cambri in the break room. I'll talk to the bass player right now."

"Yes, sir." Officer Randy took her arm, and Trisk stiffened.

"Now, wait a minute—" she began to protest, her anger cutting off when a young man dressed in a powder-blue suit and wide tie spilled into the lobby, his long blond hair flying everywhere as he waved a knife as long as her arm.

"Where is he!" the man shouted, his eyes pupil black as he flipped a desk over and stood in its place, papers scattering and the typewriter hitting the floor with a dull thud and ting of its bell. "Let him go, or I'll rip this place apart looking for him!"

"Oh God. We've got another one going ape," someone said, and then the room seemed to shift all at once as six uniformed men launched themselves at him.

The man with the knife bellowed, brandishing it as if it were a sword. His lips curled back from his teeth to show his slightly larger canines. He was a living vampire, and he was totally freaked out as he flung the attacking officers off him.

"Holy crap," she whispered, unable to look away as Officer Randy pushed her back. The vampire had totally lost it, wild and screaming as a mass of men piled on top of him. The knife was sent skittering across the floor. It was quickly followed by a howl of anger, and she heard Captain Pelhan shout, "Got 'im!"

The men atop the vampire fell off, and the incensed man rose like a vengeful god. His suit was torn, and his hands were cuffed. Fury spilled from him in a roar, spittle flying as he lashed out at anyone who came near. The men circling him knew to keep back. Suddenly Trisk realized almost every officer in the room had a bandage or limp.

"Easy, now. We have your master downstairs," Pelhan said, his hand raised in placation. But the living vampire's expression twisted into frustration, and Trisk's eyes widened when the cuffed man stared down at his bound hands and his shoulders tensed.

"Uh, those aren't going to hold him," she said to Randy.

"Captain!" Randy shouted, but it was too late and the cuffs broke with an echoing ping.

"Dude!" the kid at Randy's desk exclaimed, his eyes wide as again Trisk pressed back, the charmed silver cuffs on her wrists preventing her from even protecting herself, much less helping.

"Where is he!" the vampire shouted, lashing blindly out at the captain.

Pelhan took it right on the jaw, reeling backward as officers fell on the vampire once more. "Son of a bitch," he said, feeling his face. "Get him down. Now! And no weapons!"

"But sir—" someone complained.

"No weapons!" Pelhan bellowed, his brow furrowed as he watched the vampire struggle under six men. "We hurt this loon, and we pay for it through the nose. Someone find out who his master is so we can get him in the right cell!" Still holding his jaw, he bent down over the pile of men, his face inches from the incensed living vampire. "Who is your master?" he asked. "You can't take him out of here now anyway. The sun is up."

"Let him go!" the man in the powder-blue suit raged. "You have no right to hold him! You have no right to hold me!"

"Tell me who he is, and we'll take you to him," Pelhan said patiently, but the man twisted and bucked, trying to escape.

A woman in uniform inched closer, a mass of stapled paper in her hand. "I think I heard him ask for Ormand, Captain."

Pelhan sighed and leaned back on a desk. "Do we have Ormand here?"

"Yes, sir." The woman studied her papers.

"Well, we can't take him down like this," Pelhan said,

and with a roar, the vampire made another bid for freedom. Three more men fell on him.

There has got to be a better way, Trisk thought. "Hey," she said suddenly to Officer Randy, still standing beside her. "If you uncuff me, I can circle him."

Pelhan's eyes lit up. His sharp whistle brought everyone's attention up. "Tex," he demanded. "Circle the bastard."

"Here?" A thick man disentangled himself, breathing hard as he pulled out of the pile-on.

"I don't see any humans, do you?" the captain said, glancing at the kid with the amulets and getting a thumbs-up. Shrugging, Tex pricked his finger with the sharp point of what looked like a pen but was probably anything but.

Immediately Trisk knew it had been a mistake when the scent of the blood hit the living vampire, and with a bellow, the man rose, throwing everyone off him.

"Now, Tex!" Pelhan shouted, and the officer wiped the drop of blood on a wooden disk he'd taken from his pocket, tossing the charm at the vampire and shouting a word of Latin.

Trisk shuddered as the circle rose up around him, the earth magic both alien and familiar as the witch used the magic of plants and his blood to do the same thing she could do right from the ley line. The vampire slammed into the circle, falling back in a hunched rage. He was caught, and his threats cycled down to an eerie, rocking anticipation that was somehow more disturbing.

There was a collective sigh as everyone picked themselves up off the floor, inspecting new hurts and righting desks as that kid swore and laughed. Someone went for a mop, and the people who had clustered at the doors to watch quickly found something else to do. Trisk looked at Officer Randy still gripping her bicep, clearing her throat for him to ease up. "You should have circled him with a ley line charm," she said as Pelhan watched his people reorganize with a tired patience. "Avoided the blood issue. Don't you have any ley line witches on your payroll?"

A hint of embarrassment colored Pelhan's stubbled cheeks. "We do, but we like to keep them in research and development."

She tugged out of Randy's grip. "You should give them guns and put them on the street. At least temporarily."

Nodding, Pelhan turned to one of his more intact officers. "Get me downstairs on the phone, will you?" he asked, and a thick black receiver was almost immediately shoved into his hands. "Hey, it's Captain Pelhan. I need to talk to Mr. Ormand. One of his children is up here causing bloody hell and we want to bring him down."

Trisk watched the vampire seething in his circle. It had taken nine men to subdue him. If he'd been an undead vampire, it would've been near impossible. Magic, though, was the great equalizer, gaining respect from the most violent Inderlander. She could almost sense a new pride and confidence among the battered and bruised officers now shaking Officer Tex's hand and giving him back-slapping congratulations. *There's something here*, she mused, but it eluded her, distracted when Captain Pelhan pushed himself up off the desk.

"Yes, sir." Pelhan inclined his head in respect to a man who wasn't even in the room. "One of your children is asking after you," he said, and an officer tending a scratch snickered. "I'd like to bring him down, but he's distressed and I'm reluctant to move him until he's calm."

The captain listened for a moment, his eyes flicking back to the vampire now brushing the street dirt off his suit. "He failed to tell us, but he has long blond hair. Tall. His nose is crooked, and he's wearing a blue suit with a white tie." A relieved expression came over Pelhan's face. "Thank you, sir," he said, yanking the cord of the phone to get more slack. "Jake," he said authoritatively, and the man in the circle scowled.

"You've no right to hold him," Jake said. "Or me. I've done nothing wrong."

Pelhan yanked more slack from the phone cord and came closer to the humming circle. "Jake, you know your master can't leave until the sun sets. He wants to talk to you."

Jake's expression shifted, the anger vanishing into a sudden unease. "He's here against his will," he said, the severity of his pupil-black eyes behind his straggly hair beginning to ease. "You can't care for him. You're going to kill him."

Captain Pelhan nodded. "That's why we need your help. Ormand needs your help. But I won't let you out of the circle when you're angry." He held the phone up, unable to just hand it in. "Okay, sir," he said loudly.

Officer Randy had taken Trisk's arm again and was trying to lead her away, but she dug her feet in, wanting to hear, and they both stopped when a low, cultured voice with a precise accent seemed to flow from the tiny speaker. "You allowed fear to make your decisions," Ormand said, and Jake shuddered, suddenly looking frightened.

"They're holding you against your will," Jake said, his voice trembling in fear that he might have done something wrong. "I came to free you. The others fled. Cowards," he spat.

"Jake," Ormond said lovingly, but Trisk knew it was a lie. Ormond had no soul. It had gone before him, and if the light ever touched him, his mind would realize that and he'd walk into the sunlight, killing himself to bring his mind, body, and soul back into harmony.

"They were afraid," Ormand said, and Jake fidgeted, brushing his suit clean again. "It's not a crime to be afraid. You will make a powerful undead, Jake, but not yet. I need you as you are. Tell the officers you'll stop this so they can bring you to me."

Jake's eyes flicked up, the hint of quickly smothered worry striking through Trisk. Living vampires both loved and feared their masters; loved the emotions they pulled from them along with the blood the undead needed to survive, feared because deep down they recognized it for the abuse it was, all the while knowing that if they were lucky, they'd become the very thing they hated.

"Yes. Okay," Jake whispered, and the captain placed the phone back at his ear.

"Thank you, sir," he said, but Trisk could already hear the dial tone. Ormand had hung up. Grimacing, the captain set the phone back in the cradle. Facing Jake, he put his hands on his hips in evaluation. "Well?"

Jake squinted at him for a moment, then squared his shoulders, fixed his tie, and even pulled a comb from his back pocket and ran it through his hair. Tucking the comb away, he faced Captain Pelhan squarely. "I apologize for my behavior. I was distressed, but that is no excuse."

Trisk's eyebrows rose, but Pelhan smiled as he gestured to Officer Tex. "Let him out."

She could almost feel the room take a hesitant

breath as the charm broke and the energy dissipated. "This way, Jake," Officer Tex said. "I'll take you down."

With a last condescending look at those he had fought off, Jake fell into place beside the man. "Am I under arrest?" the living vampire asked, his voice surprisingly meek.

"Not officially, no," Tex said, sounding almost cheerful. "They'll explain downstairs, but your master is in no danger. If you have others you think he'd like to see, write down their names, and I'll get word to them."

"That would help, yes, please," Jake said, his voice going faint. And then they were gone.

Captain Pelhan exhaled. With a surge of sound and motion, the room began to get back to normal. "It's going to be one hell of a Halloween tomorrow," he said, then his expression went grim. "Randy, I asked you to take Dr. Cambri to the break room. I have to finish a few things, and I'll be right in."

Trisk pulled out of Randy's new grip on her with a jerk. "Am I under arrest for breaking curfew or for murder, Captain?"

Pelhan's narrow face smirked at her even as he dialed a number by heart, one slow digit ratcheting around the dial at a time. "That's what I'm looking into," he said as he listened to it ring. "Unless you want to follow Jake down to holding?"

She shook her head, not liking the idea of being six feet underground with who knew how many vampires. But he'd already turned back to the phone, waving them off in dismissal.

"This way, Doctor," Randy said, and she obediently followed him, appreciating that he wasn't trying to manhandle her anymore. Silent, they went deeper into the building, passing dark offices that spoke of missing colleagues. The scent of angry vampire eased, and she shook off her feeling of angst. "Has that been happening a lot?" she asked, and Randy shrugged.

"Enough that we're having a meeting tonight on how to handle aggressive vampires," he said. "It's almost easier without humans around." Randy shook his head ruefully. "I never thought I'd say that."

She frowned, not liking the idea of a world without humans, or that some people might want it that way. "Why?" she asked belligerently. "It just gives them the go-ahead to be as ugly as they want. You can't tell me Jake would have done all that if he knew there was a human watching and he might be punished or killed for giving us away."

"True." Randy nodded. "But it's easier when you can openly use magic. You saw how many people it took to down him physically compared to one circle."

"So . . ." she hedged, feeling marginally better, "it's not the humans being gone that makes it easier, just that you can do magic?"

Randy slowed at a wide archway. Beyond it was the break room, the tall windows showing sparkling bright day reflecting off the surrounding buildings. "What's the difference?" he asked as he gestured for her to go in.

But she thought there was a lot of difference, and she scanned the small room, wrinkling her nose at the coffee slowly thickening on its burner. Coffee sounded good, but not the sludge at the bottom of that pot. There was a hand-lettered sign over the coffeemaker saying if you didn't know how to work it, ask Sarah.

"Ah, if you leave me uncuffed, I'll make a fresh pot of coffee for everyone," she said. *And clean the counter. Sweep the sugar off the floor.* It looked as if no one had been in here to clean in days.

"Sorry, Dr. Cambri." Officer Randy cuffed first the table leg, then her hand. She volunteered her burned one since she didn't want to use it anyway, hiding the red skin behind her curled fingers. "If the captain doesn't show up in an hour, just start yelling."

"You're kidding, right?" she asked as Randy gave her a mirthless smile and hustled out. "Great, just great," she muttered, pulling at her cuff and feeling it clink.

26

Trisk sat at one of the long break room tables, her head pillowed on her folded arms as she waited for Captain Pelhan. The scent of tuna rose from the wadded-up paper that had been wrapped around a sandwich someone had gotten for her, but she was still hungry. She had a feeling it might be a while before the captain showed, the efficient man clearly taking on more than he was used to and too married to protocol to delegate until he knew the men he'd assign new duties to would be good at them. Still . . . it had been an hour.

A scuff at the door pulled her head up, and she flushed when the incoming officer stopped short, his eyes on her cuffs. "Morning," she said, pulling herself up even straighter.

"Are you supposed to be here?" he asked as he went to the coffee counter, blanched at the ugly sludge, and went for a tea bag instead.

Like spots on a tiger, she thought. "Captain Pelhan wants to talk to me."

Nodding, the man poured the stale hot water over the stale old tea leaves, and she shuddered at the imagined stale, nasty taste of it. "So he cuffs you to a table in the break room?"

She smiled cattily. "He's the captain," she said brightly.

The officer snorted his agreement. "Can I get you something? Tea? Coffee?" he asked, his shoes grinding the grit of sugar on the tile floor.

"Water?" she suggested, and the man set his brewing cup of tea down to find a water-spotted glass in the cupboard and fill it. The lukewarm feel of the smooth glass in her hand made her suddenly ten times thirstier, and she slammed it even before he'd taken his tea up again. *Great. I'm going to need to use the ladies' room in about twenty minutes,* she thought as she wiped the last drops from her lips. "Thanks," she said as she held it out for him to refill, and the man gave her a hesitant smile as he took it.

"Hey, is it true you set fire to one of the boxcars at the railroad? They can't put it out."

"That's what she told me," Captain Pelhan said loudly, startling them both as he walked in. "Smith, they could use your help downstairs. Try not to get enthralled, okay? We don't have enough staff right now to give you a week off."

"Yes, sir." Hunched in embarrassment, the man took his tea and headed for the door.

Captain Pelhan eased down across from her, a heavy sigh spilling from him as the bench took his slight weight. His eye was twitching, and he looked as if he needed sleep—a lot of it.

"Sorry about the fire," she said. "It will go out when the sun goes down. I couldn't let them sit there and putrefy."

He held up a hand as if asking for patience. "I'm not worried about the fire." Pelhan scrubbed his hand across his bristled face, making her wonder if she was in worse trouble than being wanted for questioning. "And no one is accusing you of foul play," he added, seeing her sudden worry. "I wish everyone could be as mentally capable of seeing that sentiment doesn't interfere with health and safety."

"I didn't burn them because of health and safety," she said tartly.

Pelhan chuckled, making her flush in anger. "Mars must be in retrograde," he said. "I'm not getting my ideas across at all. I'm simply saying that it's a mess out there right now. Someday, though, someone will want to know if their kin is alive or dead. If you have names, I'd like them." His smile faltered. "I'm sure their family would appreciate knowing that they were taken care of respectfully and not tossed into one of those mass graves they're turning the parks into," he finished, a city's worth of worry on him.

"Oh," she said, wondering if he might be Chicago's senior employee right now, the man with whom the buck started, stopped, and circulated around. "Ah, it's kind of funny, but we never got to last names. The little girl's name was April, though." Her chest hurt, remembering her beautiful smile at Orchid before she closed her eyes for the last time. "Two boys and their uncle survived. They'd probably know."

Pelhan grimaced. "I'll keep an eye out for them, but it's likely that another family saw them in the streets and took them in before we could." He exhaled loudly, narrow shoulders slumping, the weight of the day falling on him now that he wasn't moving. "The word has gone out to avoid anyone in a car or uniform. Even the sick hide, afraid of dying in a mass grave."

He was silent, and she didn't know what to say. He clearly needed more people. At least he wouldn't get sick, being a witch. Trisk began to fidget. If they didn't have her here because of the fire she'd set, then she was here because she was wanted for Rick's murder. She was worried about Daniel, worried about Quen, and worried what Kal might be doing. "I didn't murder my boss," she said, and Pelhan's eyes met hers. "You should be looking for Dr. Trent Kalamack. He's on my shortlist. He's got motive, means, and opportunity."

"I don't think you murdered your boss, Dr. Felecia Eloytrisk Cambri."

He sounded like a demon when he said it all like that, but relieved, she held out her left hand because her right was cuffed under the table. "Well, in that case, it's a pleasure to meet you, Captain Pelhan. Call me Trisk."

His eyebrows rose as they awkwardly shook. "Trisk?"

Her shoulder lifted and fell, a faint warmth on her cheeks. "Childhood trauma," she said, and he thought about that for a moment before a faint smile lightened his mood.

"Boys can be idiots," he said, then sighed heavily. "God, what a day."

"I bet mine was worse." If she wasn't being detained for murder, then why?

"I wouldn't take that bet." Pelhan's head tilted to the side. "Just how sure are you about this tomato thing?"

She sat up straighter, hope sparking through her. "Very. Kal—"

Waving a hand, he cut her off. "You're lucky. Sa'han Ulbrine is alive. I got word he's on his way here, though I don't know how. Nothing is moving." A rueful smile crossed his face. "He's why you're cuffed, by the way. If I lose you, I'm out of a job."

She eased up to the edge of the seat, cradling her

bad hand. "Did he say anything about the virus?" she asked breathlessly.

Pelhan nodded, and she exhaled in relief. "He corroborates your story about the tomatoes, but he asked me to keep you away from the press and for me to keep my mouth shut until he can address it personally."

"How long is that going to take?" she said, suddenly unsure. People needed to know now.

"Tomorrow, maybe next week." Pelhan's eyes crinkled and his wrinkles deepened.

"Next week!" she exclaimed. "Every last human could be dead by next week. We need to burn the fields and bury everything tomato-based now! Spaghetti sauce. Tomato paste. Ketchup." Her voice went soft as the magnitude of that sank in. "Can't they charter a plane?"

Mood pensive, Pelhan got up and went to the coffee-stained counter. "It's not simply an issue of transport," he said as he dumped the sludgy coffee and threw out the grounds. "He was in Detroit when it was extirpated."

Trisk took a breath to protest, then caught it back in alarm. They had *erased* Detroit?

"He has to survive his own inquiry first," Pelhan said, his back to her as he made new coffee. "A million and a half people, gone." He gave a rueful scoff. "Inderland and human alike." He rinsed out the pot and added cool, fresh water to the coffeemaker. "I suppose we were lucky to have an elven representative there at the time to make the vote legal." Taking the grounds from a cupboard, he looked at her. "I'm curious. Just how many of you are out there, anyway?"

She swallowed. "Ah . . ." She tried to grasp the power needed to end an entire city—and why the powers that be saw the need. It felt wrong to be talking about Inderland matters in public, where anyone could be listening, but she'd seen no humans in the entire building. "Few hundred thousand, mostly in the U.S.," she said, and he nodded, focused on measuring out the grounds. "It's easier if we stay on the same continent. What happened in Detroit?"

Concentrating on the new gadget, Pelhan carefully pushed the start button. "Vampires got out of hand," he said, satisfied when the machine began making gurgling noises. "That's why we've been bringing them in here. Detroit has always had a disproportionately large vampire population. Never many witches or Weres to balance them out. When the plague began to impact their living kin, the undead panicked and began taking the healthy but unwilling from the street."

"My God," she whispered, truly appalled.

"As few as they were, the witches began to try to force the undead vampires back into the shadows before something happened that couldn't be explained. Some fool master vampire began taking witches instead of humans when it was realized they never got sick. That," he said with a sigh, "was a mistake. Witches fought back and the magic couldn't be explained away, especially when even more undead masters began to surface in an effort to regain control."

"They broke the silence?" she said, shocked, and Pelhan nodded.

"I'm sure they tried to get as many out as they could, but everyone caught within the area is dead." He hesitated. "They're blaming it on the plague."

Trisk swallowed hard, trying to wrap her mind around what had happened. They had killed the innocent and guilty alike, human and Inderlander, as an object lesson in self-patrol: keep your neighbor in line, or you yourself might pay the cost.

The rich scent of the coffee began steaming out of the machine, and Trisk put a hand to her middle, feeling ill. *Damn morning sickness . . .*

"Hence the reason for us trying to relocate all humans to a central place," Pelhan said as he got two mugs down and wiped them out with a clean towel. "Not just for their safety, but ours in case of an accidental use of magic. We're taking no chances, jailing the master vampires with their children to prevent a spread of plague to the living vampire population as well as help keep the masters calm. You don't see many right now, but Chicago's Weres are out patrolling, especially at night. They can take a lot in wolf skin, and if anyone sees them, the first thought is abandoned dog, not werewolf."

"I didn't know you could jail a master vampire," she said, still not liking the idea of human camps. It was better than having your city razed because the vampires lost control, though.

Pelhan poured coffee into the two mugs and came over to set one down beside her. "It's more like house arrest within their own domicile. It's only the nastier vamps, the ones more inclined to ignore the rules, that we have down in the basement lockup with their children." He took a sip of coffee, visibly relaxing as it slipped down. "We've asked them to come in voluntarily, but most are too agitated to think clearly." He chuckled, feeling his jaw. "I don't know how many more *voluntary* vampires I can handle."

Ormand is a nasty vampire? she thought. But it was said that the nicer they were in the day, the uglier they were in the dark. She slipped her hand around the warm porcelain, drawing it closer to her but not drinking it. It smelled wonderful, but her stomach was in knots.

"As it stands, all the major cities except Cincinnati are in lockdown. The Cincy vamps rebelled the same time Detroit did, but the city had a larger population of Weres and witches, and with a little creative encouragement, the master vampires quickly directed the fear into keeping the city running. The vampires still own the streets, but their incredible need to protect the weak was somehow clicked on instead of their incredible need to dominate, and the city is under control. From what I understand, they even have shops open."

"Thank God," she said, thinking about her dad. "It's all about the balance," she added, and Pelhan looked at her as if she'd said man would someday walk on the moon. "Don't you see?" she asked. "When there's a good balance of Inderland species and humanity, the fear is contained. When humans or witches and Weres are low in numbers in comparison to the vampires, the vampires try to take control and cause their own destruction. We need a moderate population of witch and Were to balance out the more aggressive vampire, and we need humans in sufficient numbers to keep the vampires' fears, irrational or otherwise, under control."

His eyes held a heavy doubt and she added, "We can't wait for the elven council to approve of the announcement. We have to start telling people before more, human and Inderland alike, get sick from eating ketchup on their hot dog and send the vampires into a freak-out."

Pelhan shuddered. "Why would anyone put ketchup on their hot dog?" Eyes lifting from her untouched coffee, he pushed back. "Dr. Cambri, there's nothing more

I'd like to do than give you access to our public TV station so you can tell the world about your theory, but the witches' coven of moral and ethical standards and a member of the elven enclave just eradicated Detroit, taking Inderlanders, humans, and little brown dogs with it. I'm not risking they do the same here to shut you up. I'm sorry, but you are stuck here until I hear different. I don't want to put you in a cell, but I need some kind of promise that you won't try to leave."

Her lip curled. The cuff was more than confining, it was insulting. "I won't be any trouble," she said, and Pelhan twisted to reach his keys in his pocket.

"I'm glad to hear that," he said as he opened the cuffs and she rubbed the cold feel of metal off her wrist. "I don't have a lot of places to put you anymore." His gaze lingered on her red and slightly swollen palm as he stood. "Is that a sensory burn from the fire you set?"

She followed his attention to her hand, curling her fingers to try to hide it. "No. I was trying to stop Kal from leaving," she lied, determined not to feel guilty about coating him in smut. He'd caused the plague, and for what? Because he was jealous and stupid enough to think he could control her science? "It's just a focal burn."

"You should be more careful," he said as he stood over her with his cup of coffee. "They still don't know how large amounts of energy affect a developing baby."

Wha-a-a-at . . . ? she thought in shock, her hand instinctively going to her middle. "How?" she asked, and his gaze went to her untouched coffee.

"My sister went off coffee when she was pregnant. Seeing your face, I just guessed." Smiling, he put a finger conspiratorially to his nose. "And your aura tends to shift when you're carrying. Kind of condenses in certain areas."

"I didn't know that," she said, worried. Crap, how was she going to keep this a secret if people could just look at her and see?

"Don't worry about it," he said as he went to top off his mug. "I only knew about it because my sister is a midwife. I hope everything goes well for you."

"Thank you," she said softly. "Captain, about Daniel. Is there anyway you can get him out of containment?"

He turned, head cocked. "Is he the father?"

She felt her face warm. "If he is, will it get him out?"

Pelhan chuckled. "No."

Trisk slumped, determined that Daniel wouldn't stay there long. "He's just going to tell everyone there not to eat tomatoes," she muttered.

"Which is exactly why I'm going to pretend I didn't hear that." Pelhan looked at his watch. "I'll have something sent over from the deli across the street. Any diet restrictions? I don't know a lot about elves. We seldom bring any in, and when we do, they're usually released in an hour on some technicality no one has ever heard of."

She drew herself up, hope a faint ribbon pulling through her. He *wanted* the word to get out, but his hands were tied by the elven and witch councils. "No tomatoes," she said, giving him a grateful smile. "And thank you, Captain Pelhan."

He nodded, pleased she understood. "I want you to stay here," he said. "I mean it. My ass is on the line. You're welcome to nap in one of the empty offices. Some have couches. I'll try to get you a cot tonight. If we're lucky, Ulbrine will be here tomorrow."

"I'll be good," she said faintly, and with a last look, he walked out.

Standing, she stretched and went to the window

to gaze out at the river. The street below was empty, and even as she worried about Daniel and Quen, the thought crossed her mind that the earth might appreciate a few less people on it. Still, if Sa'han Ulbrine didn't show soon, she was going to get out of here and find Daniel. She'd take this right to the enclave in DC if she had to, and if they wouldn't listen, she'd go to the elven religious council, the dewar. One thing was sure: it wasn't going to end here, and not with Kal running free.

27

It was the noise that first struck Daniel as wrong as he was escorted to the arena floor, a Red Cross comfort pack under his arm. It wasn't the roar of the crowd living vicariously through athletes playing out their strategies with elegance and grace. There was no rise or fall to make the sound a living, breathing thing. No, the clamor spilling into the hallway to push against him was the muted thunder of a thousand conversations, of coughs and baby cries, of laments unanswered, all merging into a din without meaning. It was a sound absent of intent . . . but one heavy with the promise of no way out.

He scuffed to a halt as he emerged into the light, gazing at the court in a moment of shock. His grip tightened on his cot assignment, and as he looked over the humanity sprawling out of the neat rows designed to give order to chaos, he wondered if he could ever go to another basketball game and not see cots in columns.

B-12, he thought as he looked at the number the man had given him along with a thin pillow and blanket, and he blinked fast when he sent his gaze over the malaise. He was reluctant to step down into it, afraid that if he did, he'd be swallowed up, his ability to change the course of the future—gone.

Why did they send me here to die? he wondered, his thoughts going to Trisk and her expression of anger and fear when they'd shoved her in the back of that cop car. But the answer was clear. Global Genetics, or perhaps the entire elven community, was going to make her into the scapegoat for Kal's actions. Blaming the plague on a poor, stupid human was not as believable or satisfying as blaming it on an upstart woman. She'd go down easy, her defense written off as a weak attempt to sway when everyone knew she shouldn't have been trusted with such a monumental task to begin with.

The bitterness swelled, showing in his expression.

"Looking for your cot?" a voice at his elbow said, and he jumped. The noise beat again on him, and he turned to the man beside him with a laminated STAFF badge and a clipboard. "Single men are to the right, single women to the left, and families are in the middle," the man added, pointing in case Daniel didn't know his right from his left.

"It's just me," Daniel said as he showed him his cot assignment. He couldn't help but wonder if the man was a criminally optimistic human or a witch who knew the virus had been engineered to not even see him. Witch, he decided, though he couldn't say why.

The man frowned at the small slip of paper and handed it back. "Down the stairs. About four rows in, cut a right. You're near the basket."

"Thanks." Daniel shifted his care package and started down the stairs. He was in the red zone. How appropriate.

The noise changed as he descended, and he stifled a shudder when he reached the court and was immersed in chaos. Immediately he stopped trying to make eye contact. There was no privacy apart from what you could find behind a draped blanket. Signs of his virus were everywhere, hidden like guilt itself.

He turned right, walking sideways and feeling as if he was intruding as he slid between the cots where people played cards or dice or just lay covering their faces. No one looked at him. His head lifted when he came under a blue canopy providing a little relief from the open aspect of hundreds of people in one spot, and he slowed when he saw the empty cot. *B-12.*

There was a big, dark-complected man in slacks and a white button-down shirt reclining on the cot to one side of Daniel's, reading a paper so used it was almost like fabric. A skinny young man in a tee and jeans sat on the cot to the other side, coloring his sneakers with a black marker. They both looked up when Daniel cleared his throat. "Hi, I'm—"

"Don't want to know," the ragged-looking man with the marker said, his gaze lingering on Daniel's care package. "The last man to have that cot lasted four hours. He shouldn't have been allowed in, but they say you can't catch it by touch."

Daniel leaned to follow his gaze, now focused under his cot, an ugly feeling filling him as he saw the dead man's belongings still there.

The big man sat up with a weary sigh. "Can it, Phil," he said as he extended his thick hand across the empty cot. "I'm Thomas. I teach fourth grade math and history."

Daniel shook his hand gratefully, appreciating the solid strength of it. "Daniel. I'm a . . ." His words faltered. He couldn't tell them he was a geneticist. "I'm nothing at the moment," he decided on, getting a rueful head bob from Thomas and a "Hell yeah" from Phil.

He let his things slip from his arms to land on the

cot, and after a moment, he sat down, appreciating the canopy even more. The sound of the kids playing cowboys and Indians in the stands was incongruous with the man weeping nearby, and Daniel quickly looked away. Thomas had gone back to his paper, and Phil to his shoes. Daniel's stomach rumbled. "Did I miss lunch?" he asked.

Thomas kept reading, even as he said, "No. Meals are three times a day. Women and kids first, then the men."

"They take us into the back to the kitchens," Phil said as he capped his marker and wedged it between the mattress and the cot frame. "Try not to look sick. That's when they pull out anyone showing signs of it. If you stay at your cot, you're gone when the rest of us get back."

"So we suggest you go even if you're not hungry." Thomas slowly turned a page.

Phil scooted closer to the edge of his cot. "Women have the home showers, men the away. Don't go through your care package too fast. They won't give you a new one. I tried." Phil stretched, making him look even thinner. "I've got three care packs if you need something. They leave 'em when someone gets taken out. I've got shavers for two weeks."

"Phil," Thomas intoned tiredly as he went back to his paper, shaking it out to all but hide behind it. "Shut up."

But Phil leaned across the narrow space, whispering, "Tom's wife and little girl died yesterday."

The paper hiding Thomas's face trembled. "Phil. I swear I will reach over there and pull out your tongue. Shut the fuck up."

Expression dark, Phil pushed back and settled silently to stare up at the blue canopy.

"I'm sorry to hear of your loss," Daniel said as he

took his shoes off, blanching when he saw another man's loafers under the cot.

Thomas sighed. The paper dropped, and he looked toward the sound of the boys now flying balsa wood airplanes down the bleachers. "I still have my son. His cot is with my sister and her two boys. I think he's pretending it's a sleepover and the world hasn't gone to hell."

"I'm so sorry." Guilt was thickening, and lunch, as Thomas had said, was yet to be served. The women and kids ate first. What kind of a man would he be if he did nothing as they died from a pizza? "Ah, I'd be willing to bet your son doesn't like tomatoes," he said hesitantly.

Thomas chuckled, the sound a mix of rueful parenting and pride. "He hates them. I can't tell you how many times my wife tried to bribe or bully him into trying them. She did love her tomato sandwiches. A little salt. A little pepper . . . I'm with my boy. All that slime."

But then Thomas's expression of heartache shifted to one of questioning, then anger. Moving slowly, he sat up, carefully setting the paper at the foot of the cot. "What are you saying?"

Daniel dropped his eyes, torn between telling him and saving the few lives that he could here, and keeping his mouth shut in the hopes that he could get out and spread the word to a wider audience. The first would save lives, but as soon as the police realized he was talking, they'd shut him up and the truth would end here at Chicago Stadium.

"How do you know my son and I don't like tomatoes?" Thomas said again, his thick hands clenching.

But as he saw the man's grief, Daniel knew there was no choice. The authorities might realize they'd made a mistake and haul him off at any moment. He would do what he could.

Head down, Daniel leaned forward. "The plague is carried by tomatoes," he whispered.

"No way!" Phil plopped down on Daniel's cot beside him.

"A virus that kills humans carried by a plant?" Thomas said quizzically, and then his expression went empty, horror flitting behind his eyes as he probably mentally reviewed his and his family's diet the last few days. His focus suddenly cleared, hard as it found Daniel. "Why is this the first we're hearing about this?"

Phil scooted closer, his bad breath washing over Daniel. "Is it the Soviets?"

"No," Thomas said, glancing at his newspaper. "They're in worse shape than we are." But then he seemed to go still, his dark eyes narrowed as they found Daniel's. "You," he said, voice accusing. "I've seen you before. Yeah. A few days ago."

Daniel put up a placating hand, his pulse quickening. "I'm trying to fix this, but I can't do anything stuck here. I have to get out or the truth dies with me."

"You can't leave," Phil said as Thomas stared at him. "The only people who get out are the dead."

"You're from that company on the West Coast that caught on fire, aren't you," Thomas said, and Daniel stood, jerking when he bumped into a third man who'd come over to listen. "Dr. Plats." Thomas snapped his fingers three times in thought. "No, Plank. Dr. Plank," he said, pointing at him. "I saw you on TV. You're wanted for killing your boss." His eyes narrowed. "You let something get out, didn't you."

"No. It's not like that." Daniel edged around his cot, but more men were coming, angry with loss and frustrated. "I can stop it, but I need to get out of here."

"My Amy is dead because of you!" a weary red-faced

man shouted, held back by a boy in his teens, the wisdom of an old man already in his eyes.

"No. Will you listen?" Daniel said, then stumbled when someone pushed him. He flailed, going down on one knee in the tight confines. Someone's foot lashed out, and he lost his breath when it slammed into his middle. Eyes watering, he curled into a ball as more feet struck him.

"I'm trying to help," he gasped out, thinking that perhaps humans deserved to die out if they couldn't think past their grief and pain to the hope beyond it. But this, probably, was why the authorities weren't worried he'd talk. If he did, he'd die that much sooner. *I am a fool to have thought otherwise.*

"Get off!" someone shouted. "Mathew, I said get off!"

It was Thomas, and Daniel blearily looked up to see the teacher standing over him.

"I'm the king of this death camp, and no one is going to get lynched on my watch," the man said, his grief obvious in the new, deep wrinkles at his eyes. "You hear me? Get back before someone comes over here and sees Mathew has the rash and takes him away. Go on, now. Get back!"

They retreated with muttered threats and promises, and Daniel hesitated when Thomas extended a hand to help him up.

"It's his fault my kids are dead!" the rash-marked man was shouting, half in tears. "It's his fault." Shaking, his finger pointed at Daniel and Thomas. "And you aren't big enough to stop me, Thomas. I'll get him. I'll get you both!"

Phil had set his cot back up, wadding the bedding up and dumping it on the foot of the bed. Uneasy, Daniel sat down. Mathew had the rash. He wouldn't have time to "get" him or Thomas. He'd be joining his family by morning, dead.

"I'm sorry," Daniel whispered as he brushed the grime off his pants. His side hurt, and he held it. "It wasn't supposed to be lethal. It wasn't supposed to be able to multiply outside of the lab at all. That was the beauty of it. It couldn't kill. I designed it that way."

"So why are we dying?" Thomas said, and Daniel shook his head, silent as he felt his ribs, wondering if one was broken. Trisk wouldn't have lied to him. Daniel's hands clenched, and he forced them to open. Others, like Kal, would lie to her, though.

"I'll kill you! I'll kill you and everyone in that company!" Mathew shouted, held back by three other men who looked as if they wanted to let him go.

Thomas grunted and sat down across from Daniel, their knees almost touching in the close confines. "Someone shut Mathew up!" he shouted.

"This isn't what I had planned," Daniel said, and Thomas laughed without mirth.

"You think?" Thomas eyed Daniel, his desire to throttle him clearly just in check. "Start talking, or I'll let Mathew force-feed ketchup to you."

Daniel exhaled long and slow. "It was only supposed to make people sick," he said. "A new way to help the military avoid lethal action. You get sick, and in two days, you're back to normal. It couldn't spread or replicate outside of the lab. It was perfect."

"So what went wrong?" Thomas asked, and Daniel finally looked up, reading in him the need to understand outweighing the need to make someone pay for it—just barely.

"Someone tampered with the safeguards," he said, not sure how he was going to handle this. He couldn't blame Trisk, which also might be why the authorities had dropped him here, thinking he'd sell her out to save his own skin. They'd call him a crackpot if he said elves had done it.

"That's not going to wash, Plank," Thomas said, his own hands clenching. "Why should I believe anything that comes out of your mouth when in all likelihood the simple truth is that you didn't make your weapon safe and it got out of control?"

Daniel grimaced. His knees were shaking, and he couldn't stop them. "It was perfect," he said, not wanting to bring Trisk into it if he could avoid it. "A researcher sent to check its safety made a link between it and one of our experimental tomatoes as a way to destroy a rival's reputation. I don't think he had any clue that it would multiply like it did. I will not believe that this plague was intentional." He swallowed hard. "Not that it makes any difference."

Thomas just looked at him as if he was one of his students, trying to force a confession of truth from him with guilt alone.

"Look," Daniel said, nervous as Mathew began sobbing, five men standing protectively over him. "If I can't get out of here and start telling people how not to get sick, no one will."

Thomas frowned even as he relaxed, apparently willing to believe him until proven otherwise. "I'm listening," he said sourly.

"Dr. Cambri is the only one who can prove how it's being spread," Daniel said. "She's the one who designed the tomato, knows the adhesion points and how it's condensing the toxin to lethal levels. She and I can show how someone intentionally created a bridge between the two. The people responsible are trying to keep it quiet until they can find a way to blame it on me and Dr. Cambri. I can't let that happen. The longer I sit here, the more people are going to die. I need to try to stop it, but I can't do it here."

Daniel winced as Mathew shouted, "Force his mouth open. Pinch his nose. Get me some ketchup!"

"I'm trying to help," Daniel said, knowing if he couldn't convince Thomas, no one else would believe him, either. "If I can't get out of here, they'll just keep covering it up until every last person susceptible to it is dead. Why do you think they dumped me here? They want me to die."

Thomas shook his head, clearly not believing him. "I've seen people eating tomatoes who didn't get sick. Entire families," he said. "We had tomato soup last night. Are you saying everyone here is going to die tomorrow from tomato soup?"

Daniel glanced at Phil, then Thomas, emboldened now that they seemed to be listening. "It's . . . genetic," he whispered, trying to stick to the truth and still hold to Trisk's precious silence. "Some people get sick and recover, as it's supposed to work. Others it doesn't affect at all. And it's only the Angel tomato that can carry it, so if the soup wasn't made from an Angel tomato, it's perfectly safe."

"Which would explain why you're not sick," Thomas said, thick arms crossing over his chest in accusation. "Is there an antibiotic?"

"For a virus?" Daniel blurted, then reminded himself that not many people outside the medical profession knew the difference between viruses and bacteria. "No. And it's not just this year's crop you have to be aware of. Anything canned or frozen can pick it up once it's thawed or opened."

Thomas rubbed a hand slowly across his clean-shaven cheeks. "How can something processed last year have your virus in it?"

"It's the hairs," Daniel said. "I can't be sure because I need lab access, but if the virus is attracted to the hairs on the tomato, anything containing them can condense and pool the toxin. Once there, it multiplies."

"Sweet Jesus," someone swore behind him, and he turned to see that a semicircle of men had gathered to listen. "How do you survive that?"

"You don't eat tomatoes," Daniel said, relieved they were listening. Not only that, but they believed him. And even more important, they weren't trying to kill him anymore. "That an old product can become toxic is probably why we're seeing some people eating something that ends up infecting someone else," he said to try to obscure the fact that it was only humans who could die from it. "It takes a while for the hairs to attract enough virus, but once they do, it multiplies rapidly. And like I said, it's only the Angel tomatoes. Any other kind is okay."

"I gotta tell Margret," a sallow-faced man said, bumping into people as he turned and tried to force his way clear. "Margret!" he shouted, and Daniel tensed, not wanting the authorities to know that their secret was coming out lest they shut him up. Permanently.

Thomas rose, the big man seeming to have found his strength again. "No one else is going to die here," he said, and for the first time, it didn't sound like a prayer but a promise. "Go get the word out about what to avoid. Phil, go after Fred and make sure he and his wife keep this quiet. No tomatoes or tomato products, and don't tell anyone you aren't sure about."

"Sure about what, Thomas?" someone asked, and Thomas chuckled.

"Sure they aren't the government," he shot back. "Go."

They scattered, and Daniel dropped his head into his hands to take a long breath, keeping it shallow because of his hurt ribs. Startled, he realized his nose was bleeding as well, and he wiped it on a cotton handkerchief that Thomas handed him.

"Thank you," he said, still shaky from the knowledge that it could have gone the other way. "I have to get out of here. I'm not letting the man responsible force me and Dr. Cambri to take the blame."

"And who is responsible?" Thomas asked, waving his hand to tell Daniel he could keep the handkerchief.

"Dr. Trenton Kalamack," Daniel said, the hatred and bile in his voice surprising even him.

Thomas nodded, his gaze over Daniel's shoulder where a man sobbed, "I shouldn't have given them the pizza. They ate it and got sick. I thought it was the old mushrooms. I hate mushrooms, otherwise I would have eaten it, too."

Guilt slithered back, coating Daniel's feeling of relief with a black haze. "Soon as they realize you didn't kill me for them, they might send someone to finish the job."

"Not to mention you have to find that lady scientist," Thomas said, and Daniel's fear for Trisk redoubled.

Phil sat back down on the edge of Daniel's cot as if it belonged to him. "I'm telling you, there's no way out. Only the sick and dead leave."

"Then maybe I should be dead," Daniel said in desperation. *Maybe I should be dead . . .* he thought, his eyebrows rising in hope as he met Thomas's eyes.

Thomas started at his expression, then catching on, he began to smile as well. "Phil," he said as he casually reached for his shoes and began to put them on. "Go find Betty Smitgard for me, will you? She worked in the entertainment industry and knows her makeup."

"Betty?" Phil questioned, and then grinned in understanding. "You got it," he said, dashing off.

"Don't worry, Daniel," Thomas said, dropping a heavy arm across Daniel's shoulder in a show of shared strength. "We'll have you sick and out of here tonight for sure."

28

It was cold, but not enough to bother Kal. He was more uncomfortable with being in the same slacks and shirt he'd put on Saturday morning. Orchid, though, had him worried, the tiny woman shivering under his hat as he stole through Chicago's curfew-emptied streets looking for a working phone. The sun was nearing the horizon, and the wind funneled through the tall buildings, skating down the river to blast him with a wall of lake-scented air.

"Let's try this way," he whispered as he took a right to get out of the wind and perhaps find something for Orchid to eat, and the pixy tugged his hair in agreement. He was reluctant to start knocking on doors, as he'd been dodging patrolling packs of what looked like Weres both in fur and on two feet, bringing in anyone who wasn't where they were supposed to be. The chance that a random door might lead to an unwanted confrontation was too high.

But there were plenty of closed businesses downtown that showed promise, and he slipped into an alley, appreciating the still air as he crossed to another street.

Feeling small between the buildings, Kal picked his way past the Dumpsters and burn barrels, wanting to

get Orchid somewhere she could warm up. It didn't
escape him that his overwhelming concern might be
because he'd begun to identify Orchid's plight with
that of his own species. Pixies were failing because of
a lack of territory due to their need to hide. The elves
were failing because they lacked resources due to a
need to hide as well.

The fading light brightened as he reached the end
of the alley, and stumbling on the trash, Kal caught his
balance against a damp building. He hesitated, looking
carefully out onto the seemingly empty street. A traffic
light blinked from yellow to red, but there were no cars
except those abandoned at the curb. The shops were
smaller here, and he felt a hint of hope when he spotted a pharmacy across the street with only one window
broken.

"Wait," Orchid said as he rocked forward to check it
out, and he immediately halted.

"What are you doing?" he asked, one hand going
to his hat when she pushed it up and took to the air.
"Orchid, it's cold."

The tiny woman frowned at him, almost no dust
slipping from her as she held her arms about herself
and shivered. "It's not that bad," she said impatiently.
"I smell Were."

Kal pulled back into the shadows, but Orchid was
looking behind them, down the alley. Frowning, he
pressed back tighter against the rough brick, feeling his
back go cold. He held his breath as a silhouette of a man
and what looked like an enormous dog hesitated at the
far end.

"Shit," Kal swore, wondering whether they'd been
following him or if it was dumb luck.

"Stay here," Orchid said, and his eyes widened when

she shot straight up, her dust almost nonexistent as she vanished back the way they had come.

Immediately Kal's attention dropped from the sunset-bright clouds to the pair of Weres. They were looking down the alley, and he suddenly felt naked without Orchid beside him. He held his breath when they spun at a loud shatter of glass . . . and then they ran off, following it and leaving him undetected.

He slumped in relief, his mood easing even more when Orchid arrowed down the long alley to him, shivering as she dropped right into his shirt pocket. "Oh, man, that wind is bitter," she said, voice muffled, and Kal held his hand to his chest, trying to warm her even more.

"Thanks, Orchid," he said, reluctant now to step out into the open street. "I don't know what I'd do without you."

"That wasn't me," she said, her tiny body feeling like a cold stone against him. "We're not the only ones skulking around, but we are the stealthiest."

"Only because you're so smart," he said, eyeing the street for any movement. "I'm going to try that pharmacy," he added as he inched out of cover. "If we're lucky, they'll have a working phone. If we're really lucky, there'll be something to eat."

"I'm fine," she said faintly, but he knew the short flight and the low temperature were taking their toll. If she got too cold, she'd fall into a torpor that might last until spring. Ideally he would wait until dark to move, but Orchid needed to eat, and he had to contact Ulbrine. The plague could not be allowed to be blamed on the elves.

He crossed the empty street, taking care to keep his feet from scuffing. Pulse fast, he stepped up onto the opposite curb, feeling as if he'd passed enemy lines somehow. Frowning, he eyed the broken window, deciding that no one could have gotten in that way, but then he tried the door and found out why. It was unlocked. With a last look at the street, he pulled the door open, reaching for the door chimes in a panic when they began to clink.

"Way to go, Kal," Orchid muttered, and he slipped inside, breathing a sigh of relief when he looked out the glass door and saw no one.

"It's warm," he said, and Orchid pulled herself up, standing in his pocket to poke her head out the top. "I think the heat is on."

"Thank God." With a clatter of wings, Orchid levered herself out, hovering beside him as they looked over the conspicuous gaps on the shelves. The long counter with its swivel stools was strewn with straws, and a sticky syrup dripped from one of the nozzles behind it. Kal's nose wrinkled at a sour smell, and he could guess why the place wasn't entirely looted. "Oh, gross!" Orchid exclaimed as she darted behind the counter to sample the syrup, only to rise up with her fingers pinching her nose shut. "Kal, don't come back here."

"No problem."

If there was a phone, it would be in the back, and Kal headed that way while Orchid enthusiastically stabbed a sugar packet left forgotten by a desiccated cup of coffee on the counter. Seeing her dust brightening made Kal feel marginally better, and he peered at a stale slice of chocolate cake decorated with Halloween ghosts under a glass dome. It looked okay, so he lifted the lid, crumbs spilling to the tile floor as he ate it. Feeling better, he continued to the back to find the offices.

"Kal, if I package up some of this frosting, will you

carry it for me?" Orchid asked, her tiny voice somehow reaching him.

"You bet," he called out, smiling as he found a phone in the first paper-strewn office. He knew Ulbrine's number by memory, and the ratchet of the dial was familiar as he cycled through it. Listening to it ring, he felt himself relax; the decaying smell wasn't as strong back here, either.

No one answered, and looking at his watch, he hung up and immediately dialed again, hoping that the practice of making two calls in quick succession—an age-old code for an emergency—would trigger a lingering secretary to pick it up. Sure enough, the line clicked open, and a terse voice said, "Sa'han Ulbrine's office is currently closed. If this is an emergency—"

"It is," Kal interrupted. "This is Dr. Kalamack. I'm calling long-distance, and I need the number where I can reach the Sa'han in Detroit."

"I'm sorry," the woman said, not sounding it at all. "He's not in at the moment. I can take a message if you like."

Kal pinched the bridge of his nose in annoyance. *Did I not just say he was in Detroit?* "I know he's not in," he said patiently. "All I need is the number where I can reach him. I have information about the plague, and I need to talk to him."

"Sir," the woman said somewhat snidely, "I can't give you the number where he is in Detroit, because Detroit is gone. Sa'han Ulbrine is unavailable, en route to Washington to give his deposition concerning his part in Detroit's extirpation."

Kal's jaw dropped. *Extirpation?* he thought in shock, looking at Orchid as she darted in. Her pale gray dust gave evidence that she'd heard as well, her pixy hearing much better than even his. "Extirpation?" he said, the word feeling alien on his lips. "Why? What happened?"

"The fool witches broke the silence when those moronic vampires started taking witches as unwilling but healthy blood donors," the woman said, the sound of shuffling papers in the background. "He was there, and the witches' coven of moral and ethical standards asked him to help since they couldn't get one of their members out there in time."

"They destroyed an entire city?" Orchid whispered as she landed on a bookshelf full of smiling troll dolls, and Kal nodded, not believing it himself. The only other time that had happened was more than two thousand years ago. That was when they'd begun to self-police themselves.

"Do you want me to take a message?" the secretary said, clearly trying to get him off the phone. "He's in transit to Chicago to meet with Dr. Cambri before shuttling to Washington and his court date."

Because Trisk is here, he thought, but it was good to know some planes were still flying. "No," he said, remembering the woman had asked him something. "I'm actually in Chicago myself. Where is he meeting Dr. Cambri? I'll try to hook up with him here."

"Just a minute." There was a second or two of silence, and then a weary sigh. "The police station on Adams Street."

"Thank you," Kal said, immediately hanging up.

Orchid hovered before him, her dust pooling on the desk cluttered with papers and survival pamphlets. "The witches destroyed Detroit? They can do that?"

Kal nodded grimly, wondering if the dead man behind the counter had invested in a gun. "If it was their people who broke the silence, then they'd be required to, yes. From what I hear, Detroit was mostly humans and vampires." He hesitated. "Do you smell cigarette smoke?"

Orchid's eyes widened, and they both turned to the hall and the irate sound of someone clearing his throat. "And that there were no elves killed makes it right, then, doesn't it?" a dry, sarcastic voice said as Saladan took a step into the doorway.

"Saladan!" Kal blurted. The tall man looked formidable in a black coat that ran all the way to the floor. His hat was pulled low over his short black hair, and a lit cigarette hung in his grip. His long face looked even longer with his thin lips in a frown.

"Damn it!" Orchid swore, rising up on a column of red dust. "He snuck up on me again!"

"I can fix this," Kal said, hand raised as he backed deeper into the office until he stumbled into the rolling chair. *Saladan followed me? Halfway across the country? The man is crazy!* "I can fix this!" he said again, louder as the man came farther in. "That's why I left."

"You *left* me for dead," Saladan said, and Kal fumbled for a ley line, watching the tips of Saladan's black hair float from the force of the line he was holding. "All you do is lie, Kalamack. All you elves ever do is lie."

Stay out of this, Orchid, he thought, but the pixy was hovering at his shoulder, her bare garden blade in hand. "Trisk is here," Kal said. "And Daniel."

Saladan's hand twitched. Kal's breath came in with a gasp. Adrenaline pulsed, and he ducked, flinging an unfocused ball of power at whatever nasty spell Saladan had thrown at him. Stumbling, Kal went down, arms pinwheeling until he fell into the rolling chair. Saladan's charm hit the ceiling, where it stuck, little tendrils of black questing out like Fourth of July snakes.

"Trisk and Daniel didn't ruin the T4 Angel, you did," Saladan said as he paced closer, lips in an ugly snarl.

"Leave Kal alone," Orchid said, then she yelped, darting away when he flicked his cigarette at her.

"Hey!" Kal protested, only to fall back into the chair when Saladan lunged for him. "Sa—" His words were choked off as Saladan knocked his forming spell aside and grabbed him by the throat. An abiding anger narrowed the witch's eyes, inches from his own as the older man pinned him to the chair. Above them, Orchid stood on the top of Saladan's circle. Kal hadn't even seen its construction, it had happened so fast. Her sword was out, and she was using it like a pick, trying to force her way in like a little demon.

"You made my product worthless. Leaving me for dead I can forgive. Leaving me broke I will not," Saladan said, and Kal choked, his breath cut off.

Then Kal screamed, arching his back in agony when ley line energy poured into him, burning away every thought except escape. "Not my intent," he rasped, sucking in air. "Give me the chance . . . to fix it." The flow ceased, and he gasped, relishing the lack of pain. He was shaking, feeling his synapses smoldering from the overload, and he scrambled for a charm, a spell, anything to break him free of Saladan's tight grip as the man leaned closer, the warmth of his hand under Kal's chin a warning that worse was coming.

"I'm not going back to my son and telling him that the money is gone," Saladan said. "That an elf brought us down."

Kal's foot twitched. "I can fix this," he got out again, and then screamed as fire lit through him, bursting from his chest to race through his body, rebounding at his fingers and toes to cycle back on itself and cause more pain. It was a phantom agony, but it would leave a real mark on his mind, and for the first time, panic filled him as his mind began to burn, ley line energy crisping the delicate patterns that allowed him to use magic.

"They're here!" he exclaimed, hearing his voice as if outside his head. "Kill me, and you get nothing!"

Again the fire vanished, and Kal stifled a moan, vowing that if he survived, he'd never be hurt like this again. Money was power, but magic made you a god.

"I'm not killing you," Saladan said as he adjusted his grip. "I'm softening you up, then I'm going to sell you to a demon. Rumor is they'll give a lot for a Kalamack. Your slaver past catching up to you. It might be enough. It might not. But either way, I'll feel better."

"No!" Kal screamed as another burning wave crashed over him, and with a resolve he never knew he had, he grappled with the pain, studying it until he found its pattern. Not knowing if it would work or simply kill him, Kal shifted his aura to match the incoming flow.

With a shocking suddenness that was almost a misery in itself, the energy poured into him cleanly. It was the resistance that was causing the burn, and with a gasp of relief, Kal opened his eyes, fixing them on Saladan.

"Get off me," Kal intoned, shoving the energy right back at the distasteful man.

But Saladan had felt the shift of flow and had let go, pushing Kal and his rolling chair into the back of his circle as he stood up.

For three heartbeats, they faced each other. "Who taught you that?" Saladan said, nervously reaching for a cigarette.

"A little bird," Kal said, but his voice was shaking, and he wasn't sure he could stand yet. "If you're through with your tantrum, I have a proposition for you. I can get it all back, and more. I only need some time."

Saladan's thin lips twisted, and he lit the new cigarette with a pop of magic. "If I had a dollar for every gambler in my father's casino who said that," he said. "No, wait, I do. Or did."

"Stop," Kal said, hand raised when Saladan reached to choke him again. "Just stop," he added impatiently as he sat up, not liking the impression of cowering in a chair. "Hear me out, and then if you want to sell me to a demon, fine, but Dr. Cambri has in her head the holy grail of genetic fixes."

Saladan growled something inaudible, and Kal added, "Why do you think I was at that lame excuse of a lab? To sign off on a tomato patent?" he said. "The enclave sent me to find out if it was real, and it is. Her universal donor virus can change the world."

Saladan blew smoke at Orchid, the pixy still standing atop his circle. The tiny woman looked confused, and Kal frowned. True, his original intent had been to shut down Trisk's research as dangerous, but the plague pretty much settled that. She'd never set foot in an elven lab again, and it left her donor virus curiously—and unexpectedly—vulnerable. It would be like cheating off her test. Easy, and if there were issues down the road, he could blame them on her.

Looking even more troubled, Orchid darted away as the gray smoke curled up and against the inside of the circle to show the limits of Saladan's power. "Change the world?" Saladan said dryly. "More than killing a substantial portion of its population has?"

Kal straightened his tie, only now seeing how filthy

it was. *I need to do something about that.* "Everything, Saladan. Not just for elves, but for whatever humans survive this. Witches. Weres. We all benefit. And they will pay whatever we ask because we will hold the keys to everything they want."

Orchid was frowning at him, her slight figure looking even slimmer as she stood between two troll dolls, hands on her hips and shedding a bright silver dust. A spark of hope lit through him when Saladan's eyes narrowed in thought. "You think getting rid of diabetes was significant?" Kal asked. "Give me a year in a lab with Trisk's donor virus research, and we can stop heart disease, leukemia, sickle cell, Down syndrome, or any genetic disease there's enough people afflicted with to show a profit. All I need to do now is make sure the blame for the plague lands on Dr. Plank."

From the shelf, Orchid frowned at him, her dust turning into black sparkles.

Saladan's eyebrows rose. "How does blaming a human for Dr. Cambri's mistake give you control over her other work?"

Kal shrugged, not letting the man's eyes go so he'd believe the lie that it was Trisk's fault. Besides, most of it was true, and didn't the world spin on what was mostly true? "Because even if everyone else thinks otherwise, the enclave will know it was her error, and trust me, they will want someone to take her other work to completion. We can both benefit, me with the product, you with the manufacture and distribution."

"Kal, you said it was dangerous!" Orchid exclaimed, and he frowned. That had been before he realized the potential. The profit outweighed the risk, and he knew what he was doing.

Unfortunately, Saladan never let greed overrule his

suspicions, and his thin lips pressed as he flicked his cigarette away. "I'd rather give you to a demon."

Kal stood, lurching to put the rolling chair between them. "Damn it, Saladan. You're not a fool!" he exclaimed. "There's no risk here for you other than letting me live this side of the ley lines. It's all on me. If it fails, you can sell me to a demon then."

Saladan eyed the faint glow about Kal's hands, clearly knowing it would be harder now to down him with magic. "You can shift the blame to Dr. Plank?"

"The enclave will do anything to keep the elves out of it," Kal said. "Alive or dead, Daniel will take the brunt of the blame. It's his virus. Trisk was working in a human facility, so covering up that the tomato was elven crafted will be as easy as ensuring that she never sees a lab bench again. Even the enclave will want her discredited to help hide that it was her tomato that spread the virus." He smiled, inclining his head with his best boy's-club smile. "Someone will have to take control of her research."

The flicker of magic wreathing Saladan's hand went out. "And you will be more than happy to do so, eh?"

He nodded, his grip on the back of the chair easing. "The enclave will give it to me, calling it incentive to keep my mouth shut."

Saladan laughed, but it was an ugly sound. "I'm beginning to see why your family is still in existence, Kalamack." His posture shifted. "I don't trust you, though."

"Good." Shoulders easing, Kal came out from behind the chair. "You tagging along with me will be useful."

Saladan backed up into his circle. It fell with a sliding wave of color, and Kal took a deep breath, not liking having to breathe that foul, smoke-scented air that Saladan had been expelling. Immediately Orchid dropped down from the bookshelf. Saladan eyed her cautiously, and the pixy flipped him off before landing on Kal's shoulder.

"Kal, you said her work was dangerous," she whispered.

He shook his head, wishing she'd shut up. "In her hands, yes, but not mine."

"But Kal," she protested, "you can't blame Dr. Plank. They might kill him."

"It's going to happen, Orchid," he said brusquely, not wanting Saladan to think he didn't have control over her. Guilt made his words harsher than he intended, but he couldn't explain with Saladan listening.

Orchid pursed her lips, staring at him with her hands on her hips and her wings a blur of motion. "Fine," she said saucily, then flew out the door, making Saladan duck as she clattered past his head and into the hall.

Kal watched her go, not liking the gray and red colors of her dust. "Do you have a car?" he asked Saladan, not believing the man was lighting up again.

"No, why?" Saladan asked as he gestured for Kal to go first.

"Because we have to get to the police station and I'm tired of dodging Weres. That's where Trisk is, and where Trisk is, Daniel will be. We'll shove a tomato down his throat, and it will be done."

Saladan's steps were eerily silent behind him, and Kal grimaced when the smell of the dead man grew strong. Muttering about the stench, Saladan took a long drag, the glow of his cigarette bright in the gloom. Outside, it had gotten dark, but Kal was confident that with Saladan beside him, he'd reach the station without being caught. "Orchid!" he called as Saladan looked out at the empty street, but she didn't show.

"Where is your pixy?" Saladan said, and Kal felt his face warm.

"She's probably running vanguard," he said, knowing Orchid would find him when she got over her tiff. He couldn't wait here for her, though. She'd have to catch up.

29

"Stop making that face. You're giving yourself creases," the woman sitting before Daniel said, but the perfume in the makeup was tickling his nose and the light touches on his neck itched. With a sudden spasm, he sneezed.

"Whoa, back up," Phil said as he leaned out of the way, and Thomas, sitting on the edge of his cot, exchanged a nervous look with Betty. It made Daniel wonder what he looked like, but the little compact mirror was out of his reach.

"Hold still," Betty demanded again, and Daniel forced himself not to move as the older woman in her tie-dyed poncho and army boots leaned in and patted on some more. There were six compacts and eight eye shadows arrayed on the cot beside him, but none was the right color. The only other option was the red pen Thomas had, stuck in one of his books, and even Daniel knew that would look suspect.

"I don't have the right products," Betty said, the wrinkles around her eyes deepening. "If I was at my studio . . ."

Thomas made a rueful sound. "If we were at your studio, we wouldn't have to do this."

Betty stopped dabbing, frowning as she leaned back. "That looks like cat barf," she said sourly. "It's only fifteen minutes to lights out. Let me ask around tomorrow. Someone might have something in their handbag. We'll get you out then."

Daniel's brow furrowed. His face felt caked and uncomfortable. *How can women wear this stuff?* "Tomorrow is too late," he said, fighting the urge to touch it. Last time he had, he'd gotten his hand smacked.

Head down, Betty began collecting the compacts into her poncho. "I'm sorry, but that looks awful. Go wash it off. I'm embarrassed."

Daniel reached for the compact, starting when he saw his reflection. He moved the mirror around to get a better idea, but even seeing only tiny bits at a time, it was obvious it was a bad job. The overall complexion was too red to look convincing, and the dots of color that were supposed to be blisters looked fake. *I can't sit here and do nothing.* "It's fine," he said as he set the mirror down. "I'll just stay wrapped up in a blanket. They aren't going to look too closely if I'm sick, right?"

Betty looked old as she stood, the makeup held tight to her chest. "Go wash it off."

"She's right," Phil said. "It looks like shit."

Desperate, Daniel looked at Thomas, but the big man shook his head. "Wash it off. Lights out in ten minutes. You want to be back here by then."

Ten minutes. Daniel sat, frustrated. He'd wanted to be covered in pox and carted out as sick on the hospital's evening truck. But no one was saying anything as they looked at him, and so he finally stood. "Excuse me," he said stiffly as he wove between the cots, embarrassed at the obviously fake blisters and rash.

But as he made his way to the locker room, he realized something had changed among the people here. They were meeting his eyes now. It was more than them knowing who he was and what he was trying to do. There was hope again. Even as they cared for the last of the people dying from his virus, they believed there would be no more, that they had a way to fight it. He could see it in the way they held themselves. The heartache and pain were still there, but the hopelessness and abandonment were gone.

He couldn't fail them.

Stiff-arming the locker room door open, he went to the rows of sinks, leaving his glasses on the shelf before turning on the water and bowing his head over it. He hit the soap dispenser, appreciating the grit as it helped to scrub the makeup off. He was alone this close to lights out, and the ratcheting of the cotton cloth he pulled from the cycling roll echoed in the hard space. Depressed, he dried his face with the rough fabric before pulling a clean section out for the next person.

"I have got to get out of here," he whispered as he leaned toward the mirror and eyed his reddened skin. Tomorrow would be too late. Who knew what they were railroading Trisk into?

A familiar, distinctive clatter caught his attention, and his eyes darted to the corner of the room through the mirror. "Orchid?" he whispered, then ducked to look under the stalls for legs.

A tiny *harrumph* pulled him up, his head almost smacking into the tiny woman hovering at eye height. "Do you think I'd be in the *men's* locker room if there was anyone in here but you?" she said tartly, a faint pink dust of embarrassment slipping from her.

He fumbled for his glasses, shocked to see her. "What are you doing here at all?" he said in a harsh whisper, and then his expression hardened. "Are you spying for Kal? Going to go back now and tell him the poor human is stuck with the sick and dying?"

Orchid dropped in altitude, brow furrowed. "I nearly froze getting here, and you think I'm spying?"

"I'm sorry," he said. "The last I knew, you and Kal were like peas and carrots."

With that, her expression fell, her tiny hands wringing the hem of her gossamer dress. "Kal is a moss wipe," she said, her dust shifting to a bright red to match her face. "I'm not with him anymore. I thought he was trying to prove Trisk's research was dangerous so he could help his people, but he thinks he can make a *profit* with it now, hide that it was his fault your virus made her tomato toxic. He said the enclave has to kill you so the elves won't be blamed, and I—" Her words cut off as she lit upon one of the sinks, slipping on the wet porcelain and catching her balance.

Kill me? Well, that might be why she was here, and Daniel shifted to get between her and the door in case someone came in. "Are you hungry?" he asked softly.

"No, thanks," she said sourly, a hand to her middle. "Halloween is tomorrow and the kids have candy."

His eyes widened. "You haven't been . . ."

She laughed, the tiny chiming sound going with the sudden silver dust spilling from her to the floor. "Letting them see me? No." She coyly swung back and forth, playing with her dress. "But I think one of the girls heard me. She left some milk out for me on the bleachers. I'm going to go get it once the lights are out."

Daniel's lips pressed. Children talking about fairies in the bleachers could be rationalized away, but it still made him uneasy. "Maybe you should leave," he said as he used his sleeve to try to get the makeup off from behind his ears.

"I don't want to leave," she said petulantly as she took to the air again, hovering so she could watch. "And you can't make me. Kal is an ass. His need to succeed has gone beyond the bounds of you and Trisk and him, and he hurt the world. It was my fault. I could have stopped him. But I didn't know it would be this bad, and now he's trying to make a profit on it. Besides, there are kids here."

He started when she landed on his shoulder, bringing the scent of wildflowers to him. "You missed a spot," she said, lifting off and hovering backward when he carefully cleaned it.

"Thanks."

"Betty was right," she said, hands on her hips as she hung before him, watching. "That stuff looked like cat puke."

"Thanks," he said again, more dryly. But he couldn't help but feel special having her with him, like a powerful secret. "I have got to get out of here," he said softly as he ran the water and tried to scrub the makeup off his sleeve. "You're small. I bet you know all the ways out."

"For me? Sure," she said, inspecting the other side of his neck and giving him a thumbs-up. "For you?" She shrugged. "Hitching a ride on the truck headed for the hospital is still your best bet."

"Not if I look like Frankenstein's monster," he muttered, eyeing his smooth face. He'd shaved only an hour ago so Betty would have an even surface to work with. Luxuriating under the locker room showers had been a welcome relief—until he realized he had nothing to put on but the same tired clothes, worn from surviving exploding trucks and hopping a train.

Orchid's wings hummed an odd sound. "Do you trust me?" she said suddenly, and he raised an eyebrow. "Oh, don't be a stick in the mud," she cajoled, making him smile as she hovered before him, twin pixies facing him in the mirror. "I can help."

Images of Kal waiting outside to kill him so they could blame him and Trisk for the plague drifted through his mind. Trisk was probably in jail, waiting for the same fate. He had to get her out. "I trust you," he said warily, and she clapped her hands, her wings shedding a sudden gray dust that she waved into his face.

"Hey!" he said, coughing as he stumbled backward, eyes tearing and waving the dust away. "What am I supposed to do now?" he said sourly as he looked at her through his watering eyes. "Think happy thoughts and fly away?"

"You're such the smart-ass when you're depressed, you know that?" she said, apparently pleased with herself. "Give it a minute."

"Give what a minute?" he said, then rubbed his neck where his collar met his skin.

Smirking, Orchid hovered right before him, a sassy half smile on her face. "If you take your shirt off, I can pix your back and chest, but seriously, you might want to just stick with your face. It looks like you might be sensitive to it."

Daniel brushed the last of the dust off. "Sensitive to what?" he said, but the back of his neck was itching, and he rubbed the sensation away.

"Pixy dust," Orchid said proudly.

He looked at her, then his reflection. There was a faint rising of skin where he'd scratched it. "You're joking," he said, angling to get closer to the mirror.

"Nope." Orchid laughed. "Betcha didn't know that

we can change our dust. I can put out fires with it, or make them more intense. We can even pix people coming near our homes. It's one heck of a passive deterrent. Most people think it's poison ivy and never come back." Hovering beside him, she slowly landed on the glass shelf under the mirror. "Most times," she said, clearly remembering something sad.

Daniel drew back, concerned. "Your family?" he asked, and she shrugged.

"It happens," she said. "You can't pix a bulldozer."

He ran a finger down the faint red patch, shocked when a series of swellings popped up. He couldn't help but wonder if things would be different if people knew of pixies, if that would stop a bulldozer or money-hungry developer. Probably not. Knowledge never stopped them from destroying beaver dams or wildflower banks that fed bees, not to mention polluting streams with frogs and trout. But if the wildlife had a name, perhaps, and could smile and sing. And cry.

He looked at Orchid, not seeing the harm in people knowing about her. Maybe it would make a difference. Maybe bands of people would unite together. Flower power, they could call it.

"Go on, give it a good rub," Orchid said as he gingerly touched the faint welts. "See what happens."

Giving in to the faint itch, Daniel used his nails. Head down, he scrubbed at his neck and jawline until the initial relief slowly turned into something almost painful. Exhaling, he swung his head up, hands on the sink as he leaned in and looked at his reflection.

"My God, it's almost perfect," he said as he turned his head one way and then the other. It was beautifully ugly, even if it was starting to itch again. He didn't look like he had the plague, but it was vastly better than the makeup. "How long until it goes away?" he asked as he and Orchid looked at it together, a new hope filling him. He would not let Kal get away with this.

"If you're sensitive to it, it can last for days, but if you leave it alone, morning?"

"Fantastic," he whispered. "Orchid, you are amazing," he said, and the tiny woman blushed. "This is going to work. Can you come with me, or should you stay here with the warmth and a food source?"

"I'm coming," she said as she rose up to find a perch on top of a stall. "Besides, I haven't found a husband yet."

He strode to the door, hesitating. He didn't have a hat to hide her, and there was no guarantee that one would stay on his head if he was playing sick. "Ah . . ." he hedged.

"I've got this," she said as she hovered near the ceiling, waiting for him. "You lunkers never look up."

"If you're sure," he said as he opened the door and the sounds of the arena slipped in to draw him out. He went back to his cot with a new sense of hope, nodding at everyone who met his eyes. Thomas, Phil, and Fred were all there, their heads together as they talked in urgent tones. Thomas noticed him first, and he drew himself up, his expression pinched with worry.

"Daniel, I don't . . ." Thomas hesitated, his eyes lingering on the welts. "Good God," he said, and the two men with him turned to see. "What happened to you?"

Daniel grinned, the satisfaction almost unbearable as their frightened expressions turned to wonder, then relief. "I think I'm allergic to something in the soap," he lied.

Thomas stood, using a finger to shift Daniel's chin and carefully eye the welts. "They don't look exactly the same," he said as he let go and dropped back, smiling. "But this is a lot better than what we were going to do."

"Which was?" Daniel looked across the arena to the clock. It was almost time.

Phil chuckled. "Beat you up so bad they'd have to take you to the hospital in the morning. It's too late for the regular run. If you want out tonight, you have to play dead and try for the morgue."

Daniel laughed, then sobered when he realized they were serious. "So now what?" he said, nervously fidgeting. Orchid would find him. She was a clever woman.

Phil gestured grandly at the cot. "Your chariot awaits," he said, and Daniel settled on the bed, feeling awkward as he took his shoes off and set them beside the pair of loafers already under there. "I'll go get 'em," the young man added cheerfully, then jogged across the arena to the communications desk, weaving between the cots as if they were the back streets of his town.

"The morgue," Daniel said, not looking forward to trucking out among the dead. But for Trisk, he could do it. It felt as if he was starting on a trip, and he scratched his neck as he settled back beneath the blanket to play dead. "Thank you for everything," he said, staring up at the blue canopy. "If this works and I get out of here, I'll put an end to this. I promise." Seeing Thomas's worry, he stuck his hand out and the larger man took it. "I'll try to find you when this is over. We can have a beer."

"I'd like that," Thomas said, letting go and moving to shake his pillow free from the case. "I just wish you could have stopped it before it started. Here they come. Take off your glasses and try not to blink when they uncover your face. Shallow breaths. If they don't get you on tonight's truck . . ." He hesitated, his pillowcase in hand to drape over Daniel's face. "You'll get on tonight's truck. It always comes after the hospital van."

But it wasn't a sure thing, and Daniel tucked his glasses in his pocket and closed his eyes, trying to hold his breath as the case settled over his head. He could hear Phil coming closer, the man jabbering about how he wanted the cot sterilized.

"I'm telling you, that cot is cursed," Phil said loudly. "That's the second man to die in it in two days. Can I have a new assignment? I won't be able to sleep beside that. No way!"

Daniel forced himself not to move when someone shook his arm and then pulled the shroud off. "Sir? Sir, are you awake?"

"He's dead," Thomas said bitterly. "Could you do us a favor and take him before his bowels let go?"

"Good God, yes," a higher voice said. "Rob, run back and keep the truck from leaving."

"You got it," a third voice said, and then there was the sound of sneakers on the court.

Daniel let his arm sag as they picked him up using the blanket he was wrapped in, and he figured it was Thomas who tucked his arm back, giving it an encouraging squeeze.

"What about me being moved?" Phil questioned.

"You're lucky you're even in here," one of the men carrying Daniel said. "Shut up, or we'll put you in with the women."

"That's okay with me," Phil said, his voice going distant as the rhythmic thumps spoke of Daniel's passage through the arena. "They don't fart or spit or snore."

Daniel stifled a nervous smile, hyperventilating while they were moving so he could hold his breath longer when they were not. He listened to the silence spread out from them as they passed through the compound, and he stifled a shiver, wondering how many more "new" cases might crop up tomorrow in an attempt at freedom. He'd given them hope, and his heart swelled. They had something to aim for, something to strive toward, and he was proud of their resilience.

"Hold up," one man said as they stopped, and then louder, "Rob! Some help here?"

"Just a sec!" came a distant voice, and then the rapid patter of footsteps. "I got the truck to wait, but he says he won't take him," Rob said, and then came the squeak of the gate opening. Again they moved forward, and the fence clanged shut. Never would Daniel have thought that bars meant to keep people out would be used to keep them in, and he fought to remain slack and passive.

He could smell fresh air and hear the sound of a diesel truck. "Adric!" the man at his feet shouted, grunting from his weight. "Hold up. One more for you."

"Look, I already told Rob. This is my last stop. I don't have time for the paperwork."

"Then we're all in luck," the man holding Daniel's feet said, and Daniel tensed as they began swinging him back and forth as if to throw him. "This guy," he said between swings, "doesn't . . . have . . . any!"

They let go on the last word, and Daniel shuddered when his stomach dropped and he fell on the squishy, firm feeling of a person. They were treating him like a chunk of wood, and he gritted his teeth, eyes closed as he heard a tarp pulled over them all.

"Just take him to the park with the rest, will you?" someone said. "One more body isn't going to kill anyone."

"He's not even in a bag," the driver of the truck said,

but the voices dropped in volume, and before long, the truck revved its engine and they jostled into motion.

Daniel shifted, rolling to get off the person under him and to the edge, where he could look out through the open slats. The road changed and their speed picked up. He sucked in the new air, relishing the coolness even as his sock feet became cold. He wouldn't look behind him at the bodies, the uniform black bags doing little to ease the horror of what they contained. "Orchid!" he whispered, but there was nothing.

He was alone in Chicago, in the back of a morgue truck, but he would find Trisk if it was the last thing he did.

30

Shocks squeaking, the morgue truck trundled through the streets of Chicago. There was no traffic, and no one stopped them. Daniel began to shiver, and he wondered if the driver would have a heart attack if he banged on the panel between them and asked if he could ride up front.

Fortunately, they kept to the surface streets, and Daniel tensed as he saw the sign directing traffic to the Adams Street police department. At the next red light, he slipped to the back of the truck's bed, climbing over the gate and rolling out under the tarp. It was a long drop to the pavement, and he hit awkwardly, his breath hissing in when his ankle gave a twinge. Adrenaline rising, he lurched to the curb, tucking in behind a mailbox on the corner when the light changed and the driver smoothly shifted gears and drove away.

His back against the cold metal box, Daniel sat on the sidewalk and fumbled to put his glasses on. He felt naked without his shoes, cold without a coat. There was no traffic, no TV blaring, no voices raised in anger or conversation, no heels clicking or low men's voices rumbling in the dark. The curfew or plague had silenced it all.

"Orchid!" he whispered, his relief shocking when the pixy dropped down, her dust looking like fog in the dim streetlight over the intersection.

"Nice drop and roll," she said, hovering before him with a scrap of candy bar wrapper around her as if it was a shawl. "I told you I could get you out."

"That you did," he said, even as he knew the memory of hitching a ride out with the dead would stay with him forever. "You want to warm up in my pocket?" he asked as he reached behind his sweater-vest to pull his shirt pocket open, and she dropped in to settle like a little mouse. "I think we're just a few blocks from the station," he added, surprised at the need to protect her. Sock feet cold on the sidewalk, he shook his head ruefully and started walking. "I should've thought this through a little more. I have no idea how I'm going to get in and out of there with Trisk."

"Leave that to me," Orchid said, her voice rising from his pocket.

But Daniel hesitated at the sharp bark of a dog and the sudden sound of feet and a clanging pipe. *Damn it to hell*, he thought, knowing it was too late to hide when a group of eight men and two dogs walked boldly down the street. He couldn't take his eyes off the dogs, unleashed and roaming free. They were huge, looking more so next to the men, who were all kind of . . . short. "Orchid?" he questioned, and she poked her head out of his pocket, swearing prettily.

"Bluff it out," she said, dropping back down.

Bluff it out? he thought. *Easy for you to say.* But knowing she was with him, even if all she could do was dust different colors, he was able to pull himself together, waving at them to try to be both unassuming and in charge at the same time—in stocking feet.

"Hey, hi," he said, uncomfortable when they circled him. They didn't look like a gang, even if all of them had conspicuous tattoos, some sharing the same design though they were not on the same patch of skin. Their hair was long and their clothes worn, and he'd say that they were hippies except something didn't fit—the wide range of ages, perhaps. There was no show of weapons other than that pipe the smallest was dragging, and the two dogs were not overtly aggressive even as they sniffed him. It was obvious who was in charge: the older man wearing a fisherman hat and sporting a grizzled beard. The younger men surrounding him jostled one another and cracked jokes about early trick-or-treating.

"You're breaking curfew," the old man said, and Daniel held up a hand, ducking his head as if it were all a big joke. He was the tallest man here, and it felt odd.

"I know. I'm sorry. My wife is pregnant, and you know, when the lady wants pickles, she wants pickles." He stiffened when one of the dogs made a weird, chortling laugh and trotted off. No one called the dog back, and when he spotted the same eagle tattoo in the dog's ear, he realized they were werewolves. All of them.

Fear spiked through him, and he quashed it, forcing a smile when the remaining dog cocked his head at him in question. These were not the werewolves of the horror stories, he told himself. They wouldn't kill him or bite him to make him one of their own. They'd been quietly living in Chicago since the city had been founded, most likely, and probably had as much to do with its success as the humans living beside them.

"He's got the blisters," the kid with the pipe said, and Daniel's hand rose to cover them.

"This? No. That's razor burn," he said, and the old man in the hat sighed.

"Mister, we can do this easy or hard, but you're going to the hospital. It's your choice if it's on your two feet or carried between us."

"Really, I'm okay," Daniel insisted, not liking how they were circling behind him. "I wouldn't even be out here but I have to get to the police department."

"You said you were getting pickles," the man next to the remaining dog said, and Daniel's anger spiked. He didn't like lying, less getting caught at it.

"What I'm doing is none of your business," he said, a hand over his pocket to keep Orchid safe. Someone grabbed his arm, yanking it free of his chest. "Hey!" he shouted in affront, but they all froze at an attention-getting yip.

The sound of cans rolling into the street echoed, and they all turned to a boy, scared as he tried to put the cans back into a paper bag and skirt back into the shadows.

With a curt gesture, the alpha male sent three of his men to get him. "Is he yours?" the man asked.

Daniel's eyes narrowed. "They're all mine," he said, and then kneed the man holding his arm—right in the groin.

He was free. The Were fell to kneel on the pavement with a pained, whining yip of a groan. "You stinky, flea-bitten hippies!" Daniel shouted, then turned to run.

"What are you doing!" Orchid shrilled.

"Making this up as I go along," Daniel said, a weird, delusional smile growing as he pounded toward the police station, all the Weres in tow. The kid, at least, would get away.

"Well, make it up faster," she said as she scrambled out of his pocket and flew up and out of sight. It was none too soon, either, as with an aggressive bark of warning, one of the dogs ran right in front of him, tripping him.

Gasping, Daniel went down, rolling and bruising his shoulder. He panicked when sharp teeth clamped onto his arm, and he curled into a ball, hiding his face. "Uncle! Uncle!" he yelled, praying it really was a person under all that fur. "You got me!"

"Son of a bitch!" someone said, and Daniel clenched, waiting for the expected kick in the ribs, but it never came. "Alvin, get off him!"

Daniel took a grateful breath when the dog let go, an odd guffaw coming from it as it sat back and looked for all the world as if it was laughing.

"That was stupid," the old man said as he hauled Daniel to his feet, letting him go with a little shove when the rest of them arrived. "Get in the truck," he said, pushing him again. "Now."

Daniel stumbled, his sock feet cold on the hard pavement. "You're making a mistake," he said, thinking Quen should have stayed with Trisk and he should've gone into the desert to die.

"Hey!" Orchid shrilled, dropping down to make everyone gasp and back off. "Get your hands off my person, you mangy mutts!"

"Holy shit!" the youngest Were exclaimed. "Is that a pixy?"

"That's right, puppy." Orchid poked the kid in the nose with a tiny sword, darting back when he tried to smack her away. "And if I'm with him, then you know he's not a human, and therefore not getting in that truck." With a clatter of wings, she landed on Daniel's shoulder, shivering from the cold. "Go away. Bad dog."

"I told you I smelled pixy," the youngest man said in excitement, never taking his eyes off her. "Didn't I say I smelled pixy?"

"Yeah, you did." The old man pushed past him, standing with his hands on his hips.

"I'm not sick," Daniel said again. "I have to get to the police station. Please."

"You're blistered," the Were he'd kneed said, and Orchid shivered her wings, shedding a thin green dust that spilled down Daniel's front to pool on the pavement.

"He's blistered because I pixed him," the tiny woman said, clearly proud of it. "It was the only way to get him out of the pen they put the humans in."

"I need to get to the police station," Daniel said as they all cringed at the word *human*. "They need to know that eating tomatoes causes the plague. As far as I know, there've been no vampire or Were deaths from the pox, and even humans won't get sick if they don't eat anything with tomatoes in it."

They exchanged nervous glances as he threw their secret around so casually, not even hearing what he was saying about the source of the plague.

"Keep it up," Orchid whispered in his ear. "They know you're not a witch, vamp, or Were, but you're acting like an Inderlander, and they don't know what you are."

"It's in the tomatoes," he tried again, desperate to get them listening. "Vampires who eat them get sick, but we won't die like humans do. Just stop eating tomatoes."

"You're kidding," one of them said, absently touching the second dog as it trotted up and sat beside him, and Daniel felt his shoulders ease.

"And how come you know this and no one else does?" the alpha male asked suspiciously.

"Because I've been stuck in a cage, that's why," Daniel said belligerently. "You're the first people I've seen since rolling out of that morgue truck."

The dog whined and pawed at his nose, and Daniel stiffened when the man he'd kneed leaned close, his eyes narrowed as he took a big sniff. "He smells human to me," he said.

"Duh." Orchid pressed against his neck, clearly cold. "Did you not just hear him say he was in a truck full of dead humans?" But they weren't going for it, and Orchid took to the air. "Do you really think I'd be seen with a human? He's an elf, and he's helping me find a buck. Have any of you seen one? Just one?"

Her plaintive question brought a smile to the older man's eyes, and seeing it, the rest of them relaxed as well. "No, little warrior. More's the pity," he said, and Daniel heaved a slow, hidden sigh of relief. "Fine, you can go," the man added, and the circle around him broke up. "But be more careful. Especially with that pixy rash. We heard about what happened in Detroit, and we're not letting it happen here. If any other pack finds you, they might not listen."

"I will," Daniel said, his mood brightening when one of them handed him a pair of shoes with peace signs drawn on them. He smiled his thanks at the werewolf in fur who nuzzled him to put them on. "What happened in Detroit?"

No one said anything, and Daniel looked up from slipping the shoes on to see haunted expressions. One by one, the men fell back into the dark until only the old guy and one of the dogs were left. "I haven't heard a radio broadcast or read a paper in days," he said, suddenly uneasy. "What happened in Detroit? I was supposed to meet someone there."

The alpha male grimaced, his eyes on his pack as

they gathered under a nearby light. "The vampires freaked out. Started taking witches. The witches used magic to fight back. Detroit was wiped out to preserve the silence."

"My God," Daniel whispered. "Are you sure?"

"That's why we're keeping the streets clear," the old Were said. "Living vampires breaking curfew go to the police to be locked up with their masters, humans to the hospital, morgue, or containment area. I don't know what to do with elves."

Daniel would have said the Were was exaggerating— you couldn't just destroy an entire city—but Orchid's dust had turned a dismal blue. And then he wondered at the many other societies that had vanished suddenly and without explanation. Maybe there was a reason after all.

Daniel's pulse quickened, and he scuffed his feet more firmly into his borrowed shoes. "I'll be careful," Daniel said, and the man nodded.

"Chuck, go with him." The dog stood, ears pricked.

"Uh, thanks," Daniel said as he moved Orchid to his shirt pocket, "but it's just up the street."

Orchid poked her head out. "I'm watching him, you mangy dog," she said belligerently, and the man smiled, his hand on the top of the dog's head.

"I bet you are." With a final nod, he turned and walked away with Chuck, the dog who wasn't a dog. Daniel watched as they rejoined the rest of the pack, and quicker than he would have believed possible, they were gone. He was alone.

"Maybe we should be more careful about you being seen," he said. His shoes were a little tight, but he wasn't going to complain.

"That might be a problem," Orchid said, and he peeked in at her, huddled in his pocket.

"Just stop moving your wings. You don't glow then," he said, and she shook her head, looking up at him with a mournful expression.

"No, I mean that kid with the cans? He heard the entire thing and is following us."

Daniel sighed, and Orchid pulled herself up, hanging half out of his pocket. "You have to take care of this," she said. "I'm not going to be responsible for another Detroit."

Daniel eyed the dark alleys between the buildings. "Maybe we can bribe him into silence," he said, taking a slow right into one of the alleys.

"What's your plan here?" Orchid asked as he put his back to the wall.

"Plan?" he whispered as he crouched to find a rock. "Shhh. I think I hear him." Daniel's pulse quickened as the silhouette of a small boy showed at the top of the alley. Daniel flicked the rock to clatter farther in, and convinced, the boy followed.

"Now!" Orchid called, and Daniel grabbed him, shocked at how small he was. Six? Seven?

"Let go! Let go!" the boy shouted, wiggling as Daniel wrapped his arms around him.

"Hold still," he said, grunting when a little elbow hit his nose. "Hold still, or I'm going to do something you will not live to regret."

"Oh, like that's going to convince him," Orchid said, glowing a bright yellow dust as she alighted on the top of a burn barrel.

Catching sight of her, the kid stopped, entranced. "You're a fairy," he whispered, and Daniel let go apart from an iron grip on his wrist.

"A pixy," Orchid said, hovering before him. "And you're in trouble, little man."

Immediately the kid tried to jerk away, stomping on Daniel's foot.

"Hey! Knock it off," Daniel said, but the thrashing just got wilder. "I don't know, Orchid," he added, chin high as the kid hammered at his middle like a pint-sized boxer. "He doesn't want to know how to stop the blisters."

Immediately the boy lost all his fight, staring up at them with wide eyes. "I don't want my mom to get sick," he warbled, and Daniel's heart just about broke.

Giving Daniel a dark look for making him cry, Orchid dropped down to hover before the boy, her glow shining on his tears. "What's your name, kid?"

"Johnny," he said, and Daniel eased his grip slightly.

"Okay, Johnny," Orchid said. "My name is Orchid. We'll tell you how to keep everyone you love from catching the plague, but you have to keep quiet about me."

Johnny wiped his nose on his sleeve. "What about the werewolves and vampires?"

Orchid's brow furrowed. "Have you seen any werewolves and vampires?"

"Just the werewolves."

This wasn't good, but Daniel was seeing an interesting pattern, and he let go of the kid and dropped down to kneel before him. Johnny was taking everything at face value. He was scared, but it was the kind of scared you were about the bogeyman under the bed, a fun scared that held no real fear. Maybe Inderlanders coming out wouldn't be such a bad thing.

"Johnny, pixies and vampires and werewolves are a really big secret," Daniel said, and the boy looked from Orchid to him. "And if you tell anyone, everyone you save is going to die anyway. Do you understand?"

Big, helpless tears rolled down his face, making Daniel feel like a jerk. "I don't want my mom to die," Johnny sobbed, and Daniel took him in a hug, feeling his tiny body shake.

"Does she have the blisters yet?" Daniel whispered, and Johnny pushed back as if suddenly remembering big boys didn't cry.

"No," he said, wiping his nose on his sleeve again, and Daniel smiled.

"Then I can tell you how to save her, but if you tell *anyone* about vampires or witches—"

"Or pixies?" Johnny interrupted, looking at Orchid.

"Or pixies, or fairies, or werewolves, or anything, the magic won't work and she will die. Do we have a deal?" Daniel said, holding out his hand.

Johnny's eyes were wide as too many emotions for one small boy fought to take precedence. Nodding, he spit in his hand and held it out. Surprised, Daniel spit in his own, and they shook, Johnny's hand feeling tiny in his. Orchid had to get in on it, dropping down to spit on both their hands and dust a bright silver to seal the deal.

Smiling, Daniel leaned in. "You tell your mother that the sickness is in tomatoes. You can tell everyone you want. Don't eat tomatoes. Even ketchup. No tomato soup, no pizza, nothing. Even out of a can. Understand?"

"Okay," he said softly.

Daniel stood, feeling tall beside him. "I have to go to the police and get a lady there who knows how to make the tomatoes safe again so no one gets sick. Can you get home all right?"

Johnny looked at the top of the alley. "I live real close."

"Great, so you be good and tell your mom that Dr. Plank said no tomatoes."

"I will," he said, walking backward to the street, his eyes on Orchid as if he would never see her again. He probably wouldn't.

"Go on," Orchid prompted. "And don't get caught by the big bad wolf."

Grinning, Johnny waved at them. Upon reaching the street, he turned and ran. Daniel listened to the sound of his feet go distant. Tired, he wiped the spit off his hand and rubbed his fingers into his temple. "I sure hope that works."

"Me too," Orchid said as she tucked back into his pocket.

31

Trisk stared at the ceiling, her thoughts on Quen as she pulled her necklace back and forth along the gold chain. Her still-damp hair pressed into her arm behind her head as she lay on the couch of a man who was probably dead. It was nearing midnight, and her box of takeout sat in the trash bin, making the room smell like sweet-and-sour chicken. She'd fallen out of a human's sleep schedule the past couple of days, and after a hot shower thanks to Officer Tex standing guard at the station's facilities, the urge to take a four-hour nap was hard upon her. Hand protectively on her middle, she turned toward the slow scuffing in the hall; Captain Pelhan's footsteps, by the sound of them.

But he continued on, and she winced at the pictures on the file cabinet behind the desk. A nice-looking man in a suit posed with a woman with big hair and a baby. The man and woman were smiling, but the baby stared blankly at something off camera. Sighing, she wondered if any of them were still alive. The baby, probably. Who feeds their toddler tomatoes?

The urge to leave to find Daniel fought with her need to stay and speak to Sa'han Ulbrine. Tired, she sat up and swung her feet to the floor to slip her shoes back on. Her stomach hurt, and she tried to imagine herself with a child and how she was going to keep it a secret. There was so much genetic tweaking going on that elves' genomes were almost public information. Six months after her baby's first prenatal checkup, the elven community would know he or she was heir to the Kalamacks' failing bloodline. Corroborating it was the fact that she'd only been in contact with three elves in the last year, and one of them was Sa'han Ulbrine.

Who is out in the hall talking to Pelhan, she suddenly wondered as she recognized the small man's slow drawl.

Finally, she thought as she stood, brushing at her travel-weary sweater coat before taking it off and leaving it on the couch. Breathless, she tucked the stray strands of hair that escaped her braid behind an ear. She couldn't make herself any more presentable, and still feeling grungy, she opened the office door and peeked out into the hall.

It *was* Ulbrine, looking tired in his trim black suit and tie, a leather briefcase on the floor beside his shiny dress shoes and a dusty overcoat over his arm. The coat was burned about the hem, and her thoughts went to Detroit, wiped off the map. They'd blame the deaths on the plague, no doubt.

Ulbrine's voice was even in conversation, and being unnoticed, she opened her second sight to look at his aura. If he had indeed been a part of the annihilation, there'd be evidence.

Her brow furrowed and she bit her bottom lip. Ulbrine's aura was as ragged as the hem of his coat, the purple haze singed about the edges and thin, held tighter to his body than normal as he tried to heal the damage of channeling too much ley line energy into destruction. She'd seen her classmates with similar auras after finals, but never this thin or . . . fatigued, perhaps.

She must have made a noise because Ulbrine turned. "Trisk," he said, smiling as he and Pelhan shifted to make room for her. "One of the people I wanted to see."

"Sa'han Ulbrine." Trisk came forward, nervously touching her damp hair and thinking herself untidy in the same jeans and casual shirt she'd put on to pack up her life. "I'm so glad to see you." She glanced up at Pelhan and away. It still felt funny using the elven honorific in public, and the worry of the last few days rose up anew. People were dying, but with Ulbrine here, everything would get sorted out and her proposed action would move forward.

Still smiling, Ulbrine touched her shoulder familiarly in greeting. But there was a hesitancy lurking at the fringes of his unspoken thought. It merged with his fond, slightly domineering smile to take her back to being a student and standing on the presentation floor with the shattered protection chandelier strewn at her feet.

Slowly the fear of having done wrong seeped out of the cracks of her resolve. "I heard about Detroit," she said as she pushed the sensation away. "Are you okay?"

His hand dropped from her. "Is there somewhere we can talk?" Ulbrine asked. His smile was gone, and her worry deepened.

"My office." Pelhan's expression was guarded as he watched the play of emotions between her and Ulbrine. "This way," he added, gesturing deeper into the building.

Three abreast with her in the middle, they went down the hall, Ulbrine moving even slower as his stress and the late hour began to show. Most of the few officers still about were dozing at their desks, but those actually working seemed to have a new industry, a show of hope and camaraderie that had crossed the species barrier with an ease she'd never seen before. It was almost as if the lack of humans had reminded them of their shared incongruities, that they were not alone, and that together they were more than the sum of their differences.

"Trisk, I have to thank you," Pelhan said as his gaze rose from his people as well. "Under your counsel, I've been able to bring more of my men back in. We've also had far fewer vamp confrontations once we took your advice to send a ley line witch out with each squad."

"You're very welcome," she said, returning his relieved expression.

"Advice?" Ulbrine said, but Trisk could hear his irritation that she'd voiced her opinion in matters he clearly thought were out of her span of knowledge.

"Our basic assumptions were wrong." Pelhan gestured for them to enter a large office at the end of the hall. There was a secretary desk outside it, but it was unmanned and looked as if it had been for some time. "Without exception, vampires quiet right down at a hint of magic. Their masters have cultivated them to be docile when facing a superior force, but six armed men aren't a threat the way a single witch tapped into a ley line is. That, coupled with uncertainty of what said witch might do, pushed them out of fight mode and into a weird compliant state." Pelhan smiled at her, his gratitude obvious. "They come right in and settle down in the cell with their master. Our biggest problem now is keeping them supplied with the wine they prefer."

"We've always been proud of how Trisk sees a problem and devises a solution," Ulbrine said, but the praise struck Trisk as demeaning somehow. Her name was Dr. Cambri, and the university had never been proud of her for anything. If Ulbrine was publicly acknowledging her, something was wrong, and her foreboding grew as she was escorted into Pelhan's office.

"Let me get that for you," Pelhan said, swooping in past her to take the file box off the room's only visitor chair and putting it on the floor. Trisk gingerly sat. Pelhan's office was a mess, but the clutter looked new. There was a bulky intercom next to a phone on the desk. A typewriter was dead center behind the chair, sitting on a stack of paper and probably taken from his secretary's desk. Three mugs with varying amounts of cold coffee sat in a cluster to the side.

"These are master vampire files," Pelhan said as he leaned out of his office and snagged one of the hall chairs for Ulbrine. "I've been reviewing them when I get an odd hour here and there. You'd be surprised at how structured they are. Very family oriented."

"That's been my experience as well." Ulbrine said as he sat down.

"We're looking into giving a few some power on the street as we've done with the Weres." Pelhan moved the bulk of his clutter to the floor before sitting behind his desk with a heavy sigh. "In the sudden dearth of humans, we think they'll do better policing themselves than us trying to enforce the law. My only question is if it would be better to give the task to a young, rising family or one of the older, more established ones."

"I'd say the older," Trisk said, and Ulbrine's eyes widened, his affront that she had an opinion obvious.

"Why is that?" Ulbrine asked, and she forced herself not to react in kind.

"If you give something to the younger master, the

older will only covet it, and you will have a hidden turf war in three days, dead vampires in four. The undead masters are even more afraid, more volatile than their living children. But if you give them power, they'll follow the rules. That's all the undead have. Rules. The longer-lived undead follow them better than most. That's why they're still undead."

"That makes sense." Pelhan tapped the table in thought.

Ulbrine stifled a frown, clearly not liking where the conversation was going. "Captain," he said pleasantly, "could I trouble you for a coffee? Black. No sugar?"

Clearly reading between the lines, Pelhan looked between him and Trisk, hesitating only briefly before rising. "Of course," he said, just as pleasantly and accommodating. "Trisk. Herbal tea for you?"

"Thank you, I'd appreciate that," she said, her stomach tightening. Ulbrine was getting rid of him, and they all knew it. She'd crossed two thousand plague-torn miles to talk to Ulbrine, and she wasn't sure anymore that she wanted this conversation.

Silent, Pelhan gathered his old coffee mugs and left, closing the door softly behind him.

Trisk's lip curled, her outrage at the unfairness of the world rising thick. "Have you found Kal yet? He's loose somewhere in Chicago."

Ulbrine sighed. "You have no idea of the forces I'm trying to keep in balance."

She uncrossed her legs and set both feet firmly on the floor. "You're going to let him walk, aren't you," she said, making it more of a statement than a question. "Kal modified Daniel's virus to infect my tomato. He's the only one with the skill and motivation, and you're going to let him walk. Unbelievable."

Ulbrine looked up from the floor. "What would you say his motivation was?"

"To destroy my reputation," Trisk said. "Steal my work, maybe. I'm sure the plague was an accident, the idiot not knowing what he was doing."

Ulbrine ran a hand across his stubbled chin, his dexterous fingers rising to push into his temples as if he was getting a headache. He might have one, with that tattered aura of his. "Kal didn't modify your tomato *or* Dr. Plank's virus. We think he created a bridge between the two."

"Semantics—" she said, taking a quick breath to continue when Ulbrine raised a tired hand. "He's responsible. You can't just slap him on the wrist and let him go as if he cheated on a spelling test," she said, pointing at the hallway. "He intentionally bridged the two species without doing the research to find out what might happen, that with a carrier, the virus could pool itself until the toxin levels were high enough to kill. He's a *hack*!"

"Trisk," Ulbrine cajoled, but she stood, her body demanding she do something.

"You're too late to cover this up," she said, fingers tapping her arm in frustration. "They're already figuring it out, and once the general populace realizes eating a tomato can kill you, it won't be long before they put two and two together and get escaped virus."

"Which is why the enclave decided that Dr. Plank will be responsible," Ulbrine said.

Trisk felt her face go slack. "Daniel?" she said as her arms fell from about her middle, but the man didn't even have the decency to look embarrassed. "You can't blame Daniel. It was Kal."

"The virus originated in a human lab," Ulbrine said,

his voice coaxing but his eyes hard. "Even with that TV broadcast about your tomato, very few people, elves included, will know you're an elf. Promoting that the problem is with the virus, not the tomato, won't be hard."

"But that's not what happened," she said, the feeling of betrayal hardening in her.

"What happened is what we say happened," Ulbrine said tightly. "We cannot allow the elves to be the source of the plague." He took a breath, his mood shifting. "We're already on a knife's edge, and if the rest of Inderland knew we were behind the plague—definitively knew—they would hound us into extinction."

She could not believe this. Not trusting her legs to hold her, she sat down.

"Yes, Kal made an error," Ulbrine said, his voice softer as he probably took her abrupt move to sit as compliance. "If it's any consolation, he will not be allowed in a lab ever again."

Her eyes flicked up to Ulbrine's. "You fired him. That's it? Told him to go to his room and spend his parents' money? He's killing an entire species. One we need. One we *all* need. And you want to blame it on humans and walk away?"

Ulbrine's jaw clenched. "You will go along with this, Trisk, or you will be banned from working in a lab and someone else will develop your universal donor virus."

Trisk's lips parted. She couldn't breathe as everything fell into place. "Give me a lab, Ulbrine," she said, no longer able to grace him with the elven honorific he deserved. "I am more than willing to do my job, but I'm *not* going to let a sniveling, copycat, no-talent hack get the credit simply because he has a Y chromosome and all you men feel more comfortable with a blond god saving you than a dark elf from a small family of no note."

"Trisk, it's not like that," Ulbrine said.

"My name is *Doctor* Cambri," she said tightly. "And it is exactly like that, or I would have been awarded a place at NASA three years ago and next year's children would be free of every last genetic defect the demon curse has afflicted us with. Look me in the eye and tell me I'm lying, Ulbrine."

But he couldn't, and they would never understand why she didn't meekly let someone else get the credit for her work. By their reasoning, the world would be saved either way, and she was a petty, spoiled brat for not stepping aside to let another take the credit for it when so many of their people suffered. She should be proud to make that sacrifice, satisfied to be the modest assistant. *Bullshit. Assistant, my ass.*

Neither of them spoke. There was no feeling of vindication in Trisk, only a bitter betrayal that the society she once respected and tried to fit into would reject her over saving themselves.

"I just helped facilitate the deaths of a million people, Trisk," Ulbrine said as he looked at his hands. "Some Inderlanders heeded the church bells and got out, but the old, the young, and the uninformed all died with Detroit's vampire and human populations." His eyes were haunted. "I willingly helped end their lives to preserve the secret of all the Inderland races. I admire you and your work, but have no doubt that I'll do what needs to be done to protect our species."

Her mouth went dry, and she tried to swallow, failing. *Did he just threaten to kill me if I don't go along with his plan to frame Daniel for the death of the world?*

"If you want to be a part of your research, I'll do

everything in my power to see that it happens," he said, and she stiffened, seeing the trap he had made for her, baiting it with her pride and desire. "But in return, we require that you publicly state and uphold that Kal had no part in the mishap. Furthermore, you'll agree that it was a developer error that caused the accidental linkage between your tomato and the human-created virus."

Stiff, she stared at him. *Developer error?* They were throwing Daniel under the bus.

"Be smart about this, Trisk," Ulbrine said as she struggled with her outrage. "I can't give you anything more than that. It is, after all, your tomato that's killing humans."

"You son of a bitch," she whispered, and he grimaced, knowing he deserved it. If she said no, they'd privately blame her for everything. Even without a child, she'd never work in a lab again. She'd never work anywhere again. Her father would be ridiculed. Kal would get credit for her research, and she would be, as he predicted, shelving research materials for old elven men.

Furious, she stared at her hands, clasped in her lap. "Can I think about it?" she said, having no intention of remaining in this room after he left, no intention of staying in Chicago. She would run, go somewhere the council didn't have sway, and then . . . then she would reveal the truth. *DC. I've got to get to the capital. The dewar will help me even if the enclave won't. That's why we have two ruling bodies to begin with.*

"Of course." Ulbrine rose, taking his briefcase with him. "You're a smart woman, Trisk. Don't take too long to decide. People are dying."

Her jaw trembled, and she didn't trust herself to look up. People were dying? How dare he put that onus on her. But the threat was well taken. He wouldn't broadcast the truth about the tomato carrying the virus until she agreed to put the blame on Daniel.

They both jumped at a soft knock on the door, and she forced her expression to a bland nothing when Pelhan poked his head in, three mugs carefully managed in his long fingers. "Tea and coffee," he said, ignoring the tension in the room as he came in and handed the tea to her. "And for you, sir," he added as he gave Ulbrine his mug.

"Thank you, Captain." Ulbrine immediately set it down on the desk untasted. "I need to make a call. Is there a phone with a direct line out that I can use?"

I am not going to let them blame this on Daniel, Trisk thought.

Pelhan glanced at Trisk, who remained stoically placid. "Sure," he said. "Trisk, will you be okay here for a moment? I've got a room for you across the street at the hotel, but I want you to have an escort over there."

"Thank you, Captain, that would be wonderful," she said, thinking it would be easier slipping out of a hotel than a police station.

Pelhan gestured for Ulbrine, and the two headed for the door. "I'm sorry, Trisk." Ulbrine hesitated at the threshold as Pelhan waited in the hall. "Three years ago, this wasn't what I envisioned happening."

Her hands rested stiffly in her lap. "You're not blameless in this . . . *Sa'han.*"

She hit the honorific mockingly hard and he frowned, one hand still on the door as he evaluated her mood. "I'll wait for your answer," he said, and she glared, silent.

The door shut behind Ulbrine with an obvious click. Immediately Trisk stood, angry and frustrated. Daniel could be dead for all she knew. She'd waited too long, tarried behind walls while people languished.

Leaving her tea beside Ulbrine's coffee, she tried the door to find it was unlocked. Turning the knob silently, she opened it and looked out into the hall. Pelhan and Ulbrine were still there, lingering at a crossroads and discussing some small point. She froze as Pelhan saw her. But the witch diverted Ulbrine's attention, ushering him down the hallway and presumably to a phone.

Trisk pulled back into the office, heart pounding. Her eyes closed as she listened at the crack in the door for their conversation to fade. A knot of anger eased; there were people who believed in her. Finally the hallway became quiet and Trisk slipped out into it. She headed for the front lobby, wondering if she should shirk people or pretend she had every right to be wandering around.

"Hi, Trisk," Officer Randy said as she cautiously peeked into the open office floor before passing it. "Can I get you something?"

Pretend I have every right to be wandering around, she decided upon seeing his helpful smile. "Tea, but I'll get it myself. Do you want any?" she said, and Randy shook his head, looking back down at his paperwork. "Hey, maybe you could tell me," she added. "Do you know if they keep records of what person goes to what holding facility?"

"They sure do." Randy stood and went to the next desk over. No one was at it, but it was covered with stacks of paper. "Gordon is supposed to be filing them, but he went downstairs to catch a few Z's. Who are you looking for? The guy you were caught with?"

"Yes—" she said, her voice cutting off at a sudden shout coming from the break room.

"What now?" Randy said darkly, then added, "I'll be right back," as he wove between the desks to the back.

Before he'd even left the room, she was in the stacks of paper, shuffling down and looking for yesterday's acquisitions. "Dr. Daniel Plank," she said in satisfaction when she found him, noting he'd gone to the Chicago Stadium. It was a few miles away. She'd need transportation.

"Get off me!" Daniel's voice filtered mutedly into the large common office. "You have no right to do this. Where's Trisk? I won't let you do this!"

Or I could just go down the hall, she thought dryly, her impetus to run faltering at a familiar clatter of wings. "Orchid!" she exclaimed, then her expression tightened. If Orchid was here, Kal wouldn't be far behind.

"Hide me!" the tiny woman said, and Trisk started, shocked when Orchid tucked in between Trisk's damp hair and her neck. "Daniel's here to rescue you. You have to help him. Saladan and Kal are here!"

Trisk hesitated, then bolted in the direction Randy had gone. "And I should trust you because?" she said as she ran.

"Because Kal's a slug turd," Orchid said bitterly. "Who do you think helped Daniel escape out of that human pen? Me. I did. Go faster! I can't fight Saladan. He throws magic around like Halloween candy. They're going to kill him, Trisk!" Trisk ran faster, tapping a line as she went. "They want to hang the plague around his neck and let him sink, and they'd rather he be dead when they do it so he can't complain."

"Not if I can help it," Trisk said, almost sliding past the open door to the break room. Daniel was on the floor, Randy holding him down with a knee on his back. Kal and Saladan stood over them, the older man looking as if he'd eaten something sour.

"I'm not letting you blame her for this, you blood-sucking hypocrites!" Daniel shouted.

"Then agree to take responsibility," Saladan said as he leaned over the downed man.

"You son of a bitch," she whispered, not sure which angered her more, Saladan's domineering attitude or Kal's satisfied smile as they used her to blackmail Daniel.

Her hands tingled with the force of the line running through her, hot and demanding to be loosed. Kal looked up, a flicker of fear in his eyes. "Trisk," Daniel whispered when he saw her. Pox scarred his neck and face, and something in her shifted sideways with a painful realization. He'd come to find her, risked everything—and he was going to die.

But then Saladan pulled on the same ley line she was, and she dropped, four years of demon studies demanding it.

"Hey!" Orchid shrilled in protest, darting to the overhead light. Trisk rolled, instinct and an utter lack of trust saving her as Saladan's evil-looking ball of purple-tinted energy hit the floor where she'd been, spreading out in a sparkling hiss that smelled of cut chives.

"What the hell?" Randy said, knee still on Daniel's back, and Trisk stared at Kal, betrayal thick in her. Her eyes narrowed, and that fast, her world changed.

He had callously hurt someone she cared about, and that she would not forgive.

"Look out!" Kal shouted, lurching behind the tables when Trisk rolled to her feet, a glowing ball of energy already tingling her palms.

"*Detrudo!*" she exclaimed, then shoved it at Saladan, fully expecting him to deflect it.

"*Rhombus!*" Saladan countered, but his circle wouldn't form because Randy and Daniel were lying too surely across the proposed barrier, their auras interfering. Her curse sped across the distance. Dark eyes wide, Saladan ducked and deflected it.

The charm ricocheted to hit Randy full in the chest. The officer fell back with a pained moan, collapsing into convulsions. Trisk was already moving, her hands glowing with loosed power as Daniel rolled away, free from the imprisoning weight.

Now Saladan's circle formed, and Trisk skidded to a halt to keep from running into it. She'd wanted to slip past his forming circle, but having failed didn't mean she was done.

Shaking, they stared at each other, stray imbalances of force skating like lightning across the molecule-thin barrier humming between them. "You dare to attack me? You little elf whelp?" Saladan said, his face red with anger.

"I'm not taking the blame for this, and neither will Daniel," she said, her knees threatening to buckle. "Kalamack will."

"Not likely." Saladan frowned in disdain. "Even your enclave will look the other way."

She scowled, knowing it to be true. "Perhaps, but I'm not the one hiding in a circle." Her smile became wickedly satisfied, and Saladan's look of confidence turned to affront, then alarm when she placed her palms against his circle, and . . . like a demon, pushed. *Daniel has the plague*, a tiny part of her thought, her heartache swelling. *They must have forced it on him.*

Saladan's eye twitched as he strengthened his hold on the line. Trisk clenched her teeth at the sudden flash of pain arcing through her as Saladan drew more energy into maintaining his circle. She redoubled her force, a cry of frustration rising with the pain, stabbing knives striking her palms, diving to her core, and turning into glass shards with every heartbeat.

"Trisk, Stop!" Daniel shouted, edging forward with Orchid behind him.

Sweat broke out on her, but there was nothing but the small space between her hands as she forced her will against Saladan's . . . until a tiny crack of doubt formed within his certainty. He was good, but she was an elf—and he'd hurt someone she cared about.

Screaming in defiance, she poured her will into it, widening the crack until, with a snap, she broke his circle.

She fell back into Daniel's waiting arms, panting as she scrambled to stand on her own. Furious, she never took her eyes from Saladan. The tall man stared at her in sudden doubt. "You're going to fry for killing Daniel," she said again, her voice raw with heartache.

"Trisk, I'm okay," Daniel said, tugging at her arm. "Orchid pixed me. It's just dust!"

Her jaw dropped, and she blinked at his wide-eyed earnestness, only now seeing the blisters' different texture. "You're okay?" she warbled as Orchid nodded, and he smiled at her.

"Not for long," Saladan said as he reached out and grabbed her wrist. "A no-account upstart isn't going to stand between me and what I want."

Her anger rushed back, and Trisk tucked down and into Saladan, flinging him over her back to slam into the break room floor. Groaning, the man reached for his back, unable to get up. "Me either," she said, breathing hard but satisfied. Lip curling in disgust, she twitched her fingers into a binding spell, watching Saladan go still as it soaked past his aura and took hold.

Daniel inched up beside her, looking down at Saladan. "I didn't know you could do that." He grinned, giving her shoulder a little squeeze as if to test her muscle. "Real ninja-like."

She gave him a grateful smile, so happy to see him alive and well it almost hurt. "You're okay. I thought they'd made you eat a tomato," she said, and then her expression fell.

"Where's Kal?"

32

"**G**one." Orchid dropped from the light fixture to land on Daniel's shoulder. "Kal saw he was losing and left."

Rubbing his chafed wrists, Daniel grimaced at the tables slid out of place, the spilled coffee, and Saladan and Randy still on the floor. "We need to leave."

"Not without Kal," Trisk said, and Orchid gave a bark of pixy laughter.

"I'm not going anywhere with that slug snot," Orchid said, wings moving to make a bright silver dust cascade down Daniel's front. "No way, no how."

"We need him," Trisk said as she picked up Kal's hat and handed it to Daniel.

"For what?" Daniel held the hat as if not knowing why she'd given it to him. "You going to use him as bait for the Were gangs outside?"

Jaw set, she brushed off the hat and put it on his head. Immediately Orchid hid herself under it. "Kal's going to testify that you started the plague," Trisk said. "He can't do that if he's with us. We have to find him before Ulbrine does."

Orchid made a raspberry sound from under the hat. "Fine," she said sourly.

"Thanks, Orchid," Trisk said. "Can you do a sweep of the building without getting caught?"

"Duh." Orchid peeked out from beneath the hat, then jerked back under when a sudden commotion in the hall turned into four officers pushing into the break room.

"It's okay. We're all okay," Trisk said when one of them ran out yelling for Captain Pelhan and the other three went to Randy. "Has anyone seen Kal?" But they weren't listening.

"We had it in impound" came Pelhan's irate voice from the hall. "You're telling me that kid not only got out of his cuffs, but boosted his own van? From impound?"

"We ran out of room so we had to put it on the street," someone said.

"And why the hell am I smelling cinnamon and wine?" the captain exclaimed as they pushed into the break room. Seeing Trisk, he stopped short and reddened, embarrassed for the mild swear word. "Sorry, Doctor," he said, and then his expression steeled when he noticed Daniel beside her, his neck and face marked with blisters.

"He's been pixed," Trisk said, breathless. "He's fine, I promise. Did you see Kal?"

"Thank God," Pelhan said. "You must be Dr. Plank. How did you get pixed?"

"He said I could," Orchid said from under his hat, and both Pelhan and the officer with him started. "I gave him blisters so he could hitch a ride out of the arena on a morgue truck."

Pelhan's eyebrows rose. "Your hat is speaking, Dr. Plank," he said, and Daniel smirked as Orchid peeked out. The tiny woman looked decidedly embarrassed, brushing her dress smooth before taking to the air. "Well, I'll be damned," Pelhan said, clearly charmed as he put his hands on his knees and peered at her. "I haven't seen a pixy since I was twelve and they cut down the park to put in a 7-Eleven."

Orchid's dust turned a dismal green. Any pixies there were long gone. "Are you sure?"

Pelhan nodded. "I'm sorry."

Trisk pushed between them impatiently. "Kal. Did you see him?" she asked, and Pelhan shook his head, sliding out of the way as his officers hustled a groggy Randy out and to the infirmary. Saladan was next, slung between two men, and Trisk's need to leave grew when his hand pushed fitfully at the officers carrying him. The binding spell wouldn't hold him much longer. She'd downed one hell of a witch. She hadn't known she'd had it in her. *Quen would be proud*, she thought, even as she worried about him.

"Where do you think you're going?" Pelhan said, eyeing the dust slipping out from under Daniel's hat.

Daniel took a breath, his expression cross, and Trisk silenced him with a soft touch on his arm. "I'm sorry, Pelhan," she said evenly, ready to fight her way out if needed. "I can't let them do this. They want to blame Daniel for everything."

"And if I don't agree to take it, they'll blame her," Daniel said.

"You misunderstand." Pelhan glanced at the open hall. "You can't stay here. Ulbrine is still on the phone, and I'd rather you be gone by the time he's done. I don't like his plans to make science the enclave's scapegoat."

Relief buoyed her up. "How did you know they were blackmailing us?"

Pelhan's expression became sheepish, his hand on

the small of her back as he ushered them into the hall. "I put a bug in my office last year when someone kept using my phone to make long-distance calls." He held up his hand, showing her a wooden ring that was probably an amulet. "I can hear everything that happens in there."

"You can do that?" Daniel whispered, and Pelhan's eyes flicked to him. Looking uncomfortable, the captain hid his hand behind his back.

"Dr. Cambri . . ." Captain Pelhan said, his voice pained and clearly worried as they continually broke the silence in front of a human.

"I'll deal with it," she said, and Pelhan's hand on her back pressed tighter as he hustled them forward.

"You had better," he said softly as he leaned closer. But then he pulled away, and she breathed easier. "Daniel, I'm sorry for putting you where I did, but I've gotten word that no one new is coming down with the plague at the Chicago Stadium. Thank you for that. In this town, a rumor is as good as a public service announcement."

Daniel met the captain's grin with his own. "Once I convinced them I wasn't a nutcase, the rest was easy." His smile faded.

"I wish I could take you to the TV station," Pelhan said as he snagged a blue police department jacket from a desk they were passing, then another. "But even if it was working, I don't dare. I have very little wiggle room with the enclave here. I can blame Saladan and Kal for you slipping me, but if you're caught again, that will be the end of the rumor, and I want it to keep spreading."

Trisk took one of the jackets and gratefully shrugged into it. "That's why we need Kal. We can't let him make an official statement."

"Way ahead of you." Pelhan scuffed to a halt at the back door, reaching in a pocket to bring out a metal ring. "God, this is weird," he said as he pulled the pin from it and a faint glow swelled and then vanished to a little dot that seemed to hang in the air, just off center of the open space. "Daniel, if you ever breathe a word . . ."

"I know." Daniel stared at it in fascination even as he put on the second jacket. "I say anything, and I'm dead." He looked up, expression placid. "The threat has lost its meaning, but I'm not very eager to tell anyone now."

"Don't worry about Daniel" came Orchid's voice from under his hat. "I'm his watchdog. I'll make sure he dies if he ever makes a peep about us," the pixy said.

Pelhan cocked his head, his amused expression vanishing when Orchid looked out and touched her hip where a sharp spike of metal hung. "I feel safer knowing that," he said, and she beamed. Daniel rolled his eyes, clearly unaware that the pixy's threat was real and utterly enforceable.

"So . . . what is it?" Trisk said, and Pelhan's attention shifted to the ring of metal in his hand

"A tracker. My aunt makes them. We use them with missing persons. Ulbrine had me sensitize it to Kal." Pelhan shifted it slightly as it lay on Trisk's palm, and the bright dot moved. "He's in the streets. I'd say . . . walking." Pelhan pulled back, his gaze going to the closed door and the night visible beyond the thick glass. "Try not to get caught by the Weres," he added. "There's a lot of action on the street, even accounting for the unrest."

"Thank you," she said. She knew she had to go, but was suddenly reluctant to leave.

Pelhan shifted from foot to foot, clearly uncomfortable. "I wish I could do more. I'd give you a pass for the Weres, but . . ."

"But then there'd be a paper trail to you," Daniel said as he peeked out the window at the dark street and the three-story parking structure empty and silent behind it. "Don't worry about it. We can slip a pack of Weres." He hesitated. "It looks clear. Ready, Trisk?"

She nodded, and on impulse, she stood on tiptoe and gave Pelhan a chaste kiss on his stubbly, two-days-from-a-razor cheek. "Thank you. I'm glad you found us."

"Me too. Your advice on how to handle the vamps really helped." His smile faded and he looked at Daniel. "Sorry about leaving you with the refugees, Doctor. But it did get the word out about how to slow this. You made a difference here, too. Thank you."

Daniel flushed, making his pixy rash stand out. "You're welcome."

Nodding, Captain Pelhan ushered them to the door. "Can you by chance shoot?"

Daniel let go of the door, and it swung shut. "Ah, you mean a gun?" he said, eyes wide.

Pelhan made a pained face. "I guess that means no," he said, his hand falling from his hip and the pistol holstered there.

"I can," Trisk said, and Pelhan jerked, surprised. "I minored in security," she added.

"Dark elf. Right," the man said, the snap of his holster obvious as he handed the heavy weapon to her. "I want no magic in my streets. Understand? I'd rather you shoot someone." He hesitated. "In the foot."

Her face warmed as she recalled what she'd done in the break room. My God, it was as if she were a child. No restraint at all. That it had felt good was a guilty secret. "I'm sorry about the break room," she said. "But there were no humans to see it, except for Daniel."

"That's what they thought in Detroit, too," he said

looming over her in threat. "Promise me, or I'll lock you up. Right now."

She frowned up at him. "That's a dumb thing to say after giving me your gun."

Pelhan's brow furrowed right back at her, and finally Trisk heaved a quiet sigh, remembering how his office smelled like a redwood forest, the finding charm he'd made in only a few minutes, and the fact that he was in charge of the only functioning police station she'd seen this side of the Mississippi. "No obvious magic," she said, and he nodded, satisfied. Unhappy at needing a gun at all, she felt the heft of it, checking the safety before stuffing it into her jacket pocket. It was an odd realization to walk away with: to kill with a handgun was preferred to gently holding with magic. Something was wrong with that.

"Cambri!" Ulbrine shouted from somewhere in the building, and Trisk jumped.

"Scoot." Pelhan opened the door. "I'm glad to have met you, Dr. Cambri. It's good to know all elves aren't tricky, conniving bastards."

Scoot? she thought as Daniel all but pushed her out into the night. She turned to thank him again, but Pelhan was already gone, his back visible through the glass as he strode away, his returning shout muffled.

"This way," Daniel said, pulling her into the more certain dark. "I don't want to chance stealing a car too close to the station, but maybe we can find one on the streets."

"I don't know how to steal a car," she said, and he turned to her, his disbelief hard to see in the dim glow from the light at the corner.

"I thought you minored in security."

Her lips pressed. "I was sick the day they covered

hot-wiring cars. Here, you take it," she said as she pushed the finding charm into his hand. "I can't shoot and navigate at the same time."

"Me?" Daniel almost squeaked, shifting the cool metal circle from hand to hand as if it were hot. "I can't do mag—" His voice cut off and he stopped dead in the middle of the empty street, staring down at the ring in his hands. "Wow, it works."

"Congratulations, you're alive," Orchid piped up from under his hat.

Trisk smiled as she tugged him back into motion. "Anyone with an aura can work ley line magic once it's invoked," she said as he stumbled up onto the curb behind her. She wasn't sure what she'd do after finding Kal, but shooting him was now an option. "Which way?"

Daniel moved forward, stopped, turned, then turned back the other way, never taking his eyes off the ring in his hand. "That way," he said, only now looking up.

Kal was either in the building ahead of them or somewhere behind it. Betting it was the latter, Trisk drew Daniel into the alley. The darkness was deeper here, and their pace slowed as they made their way through the dampness. Trisk could smell river over the fading stink of cars and gas. There was almost no sound, and the sky was cloudy, showing very little of the expected light pollution. No wonder the Weres were looking for an excuse to be out roaming in the night. No buses, no cars, no cabs: it was as if the world were empty.

"Daniel," she whispered as they neared the end of the alley, the brighter darkness beckoning them. "Maybe it wouldn't be so bad if humans knew we existed."

He frowned, gaze fixed on the charm. "Yeah, okay," he said distantly.

"I mean, look at you," she said. "You're probably the first human in two thousand years doing a charm. You've met witches and Weres. You're handling it. Maybe we misjudged you."

Daniel halted at the top of the alley, clearly reluctant to step out even if the charm was glowing a bright red now, indicating they were close. "A person is okay," he said, peering into the darkness and the open street. "But when you put a bunch of us together, something is switched on, something ugly." He glanced at her apologetically. "All of us, humans and nonhumans alike, are genetically primed to attack what's different from the collective."

"But what if the collective is all of us?" she persisted.

"I smell Kal," Orchid suddenly said, and Daniel reached for his hat, keeping it on his head as Orchid vaulted out from under it. "Is that him?" she said, hovering between them and staring at nothing Trisk could see. "It is!" she exclaimed, darting off.

"Son of a beaver biscuit . . ." Daniel swore. "I wish she'd stop doing that."

"Orchid!" Trisk hissed, but it was too late. At the end of the street under a flickering light, a shadow hunched at a car straightened, then ducked. Kal's muffled swearing rose, and the dark silhouette flailed at the bright, hot dot of angry pixy.

"Hey!" Daniel shouted when Kal swung a tire iron, and Kal spun, freezing for a moment before taking off at a run. Daniel was close behind, the sound of the sneakers he'd found somewhere odd in the still air. Trisk hesitated for half a second, then pounded after him.

"'Hey'?" she said between her breaths as she caught up. "You said 'Hey'? We could have snuck up on him."

Kal darted into a side street, and skidding, they followed. "He was trying to hit Orchid," Daniel said, and then louder, "Kalamack!"

They'd almost reached him, and with a shout of anger and frustration, Daniel launched himself at Kal's fleeing feet. His outstretched hand caught his ankle, and he hung on as Kal hit the ground, his breath coming out in a whoosh. The tire iron clanged, spinning away as the two men fell to the pavement, rolling.

Tense, Trisk slid to a stop. *No magic. I promised no magic.*

"Why don't you just eat a tomato and die?" Kal snarled, and Trisk's eyes widened when she felt him tap a line. He was going to use magic. In the open streets.

"Kal, stop!" she shrieked, tapping a line as well but knowing that to use it would make things worse. "Kal! They destroyed Detroit," she shouted, and the thump of a fist on flesh sounded ugly to her ears. "For God's sake, don't!"

I have a gun, she remembered, and she pointed it at the two men tussling in the street. "Stop, Kal. Or I'll shoot your head off! I'll do it!"

In a sudden motion, Kal shoved Daniel off him and rolled to stand. He still had a hold on the ley line, and it made the tips of his fine hair float. He stared at Trisk, his hatred and jealousy of her again firmly in place. It had been three years since she'd seen that expression, but it looked right on him the way his flattery and attention the last few weeks had not.

Daniel got to his feet, slapping the street dirt off Kal's hat before putting it back on his head in case Orchid should return. Never taking his eyes off Kal, he scooped up the tire iron, hefting it in evaluation. "I should drop you in the nearest holding center and let them rip you apart."

A smirk twitched the corners of Kal's lips as he looked at the blisters and continued to make the wrong assumption, then he ducked at the sudden clatter of pixy wings. "You are a thumb-sucking slug turd, Kalamack," the pixy woman said as she hovered out of his reach, hands on her hips and a bright silver dust falling from her. "I'd sooner kiss a wasp than look at you. You're lower than a troll's bahoogies, fouler than a fairy's dung heap, as trustworthy as last year's yogurt—and you smell worse. If you move, I'll jam something into your eye."

"You're coming with us," Trisk demanded, arms shaking as she gripped the gun. "Now."

Kal scoffed, his attention shifting between her and Orchid. "Like you'd shoot me," he said, and turning on a heel, he walked away.

Trisk's focus narrowed, her grip on the gun tightening as Orchid's dust turned a furious red. Beside her, Daniel gathered himself to jump him again. *You keep making the same dumb mistakes*, she thought as she shifted her aim low and to the left. Exhaling, she pulled the trigger.

The recoil jolted her more than the sound, and she held her breath, not wanting to smell the spent gunpowder. Kal jerked to a stop, his hands suddenly away from his body as he spun. Daniel looked almost as surprised, the tire iron dangling loosely in his grip as Orchid's dust shifted to a smug yellow. "Move. Now," Trisk demanded. "That way."

"Ah, Trisk?" Daniel said, his gaze going behind them to the end of the street, and Trisk's grip on the pistol tightened. *Shit.* In the distance but coming closer was the sound of a truck running at full throttle. The Weres had heard them.

"Are you insane?" Kal shouted as he ducked Orchid's swoop at him. "You *shot* at me!"

"And I'll hit you next time," Trisk said. "Start walking." She motioned with the muzzle of the pistol back to the car he'd been trying to break into. "Orchid, can you get in there and unlock the car for us?"

"You bet," the pixy said, but Trisk stiffened at the sound of the chortling truck getting closer, the shifting gears loud in the still night. A feeling of being trapped trickled through Trisk. *What the hell good is a gun when I have an entire arsenal of magic I can't use?*

With a sudden yelp, Orchid dove for Daniel's hat, her sparkles quickly vanishing. "Let him go," Daniel said, one hand holding the hat down, the other gripping that tire iron. "We can't afford to get caught, and he can."

"No!" Trisk's hands tightened on the pistol, fully aware that they were obvious under the streetlamp. "We may as well be tried and convicted if he gets to Ulbrine."

Kal smirked, content to do nothing, sure everything would swing his way in a moment. The vehicle jostled around the corner, the headlights shining on them. Trisk felt a wash of despair as she saw the farm truck with its open bed. She could run, but Kal would turn her into more of a fugitive than she already was. She stood frozen by indecision as Daniel pulled at her sleeve, trying to get her to move. "I can't. I can't!" she shouted, then jumped when the truck blew its horn.

No one moved when it came to a squeaky-braked halt as if waiting for them to get out of the way. A shadowy head poked out the front window. "Dr. Plank! Is that you?" a woman's voice called.

33

Daniel spun, his face white in the stark light of the headlamps.

"What the hell?" Kal said, turning to look at the truck as well.

With a smooth motion, Daniel swung the tire iron at the back of Kal's head as if he were throwing a softball.

"Daniel!" Trisk cried out. Shooting Kal in the foot was one thing. Hitting the back of his head with a tire iron might actually kill him, and as much as she hated the man, seeing Kal dead wasn't on her list of things to do at the end of the world.

But it hit with a soft thud, and Kal collapsed. Eyes wide, Trisk fell to kneel beside him, checking to see that his eyes dilated in the headlamps. His aura was strong and his pulse steady.

"Is he okay?" Daniel asked, and she looked up, seeing the anger still in him. She stood, embarrassed now for her outburst, and when she nodded, Daniel let the tire iron fall with a clang. "Good. I'll hit him again when he wakes up," he joked, but Trisk thought there might be a hint of truth to it.

A truck door slammed, and Trisk rose, facing it. The pistol was still in her hand, but whoever was in the vehicle had called Daniel by name, and she hid it behind her.

"Dr. Plank?" a man said hesitantly, and Trisk could see a woman in the truck move across the long bench seat to slip behind the wheel. A little boy was with her, keeping the woman preoccupied as he tried to reach the open window.

"Do you know these people?" Trisk said, and Daniel's expression smoothed out.

"I know the boy," he said, and Trisk put the gun in her pocket.

The man shifted from foot to foot in front of the truck. "You want to bring him?" he asked, and when Daniel nodded, he grabbed Kal's feet. Daniel took his arms, and they tossed the elf unceremoniously into the back, where he slid until he hit the cab.

"Is that her?" the little boy said, finally having crawled his way over the woman, his mother, presumably. "Is that the lady scientist who is . . . going to kill . . . all the tomatoes?" he said between his mother's attempts to pull him back.

"Ma'am?" the man said, holding out a hand to help Trisk into the truck bed. His eyes were pinched. "We don't have a lot of time."

Faint over the night came the sound of wolves, and she shivered. *What on earth did Daniel do in the day we were apart?* she wondered as she fitted her smooth hand into the man's work-calloused one and made the step up into the truck bed.

"Benson, get in!" the woman cried out as an attention-getting bark sounded.

"Drive, woman!" the man demanded, and Daniel lurched in beside Trisk. She held her breath as the man ran awkwardly to the passenger side and dove in. The

Weres were rounding the corner, shouting as the truck sputtered into motion. It bumped onto the curb, making Trisk gasp and reach for the walls of the bed until they found the road and picked up speed.

Pulse fast, Trisk tried to corral the strands of her wildly whipping hair as the Weres howled in frustration, not giving up. But then a man on foot suddenly appeared at the corner, throwing a brick at the Weres before darting into flight. The Weres went after him instead. The truck leaned as they took a corner . . . and then they were gone.

Not believing what had happened, Trisk looked at Daniel beside her, then Kal, still out cold at her feet. Daniel's eyes were wide, one hand on his hat to keep it from blowing off. Orchid must still be under it. Seeing her questioning look, he shrugged. Kal began to move, and panicking, she grabbed his arm, subtly spelling him into a more sure unconsciousness. There was no glow, no telltale sign of magic, and she sighed in relief when Kal went still again.

The wind kept putting her hair into her face, but she didn't dare let go of the cold wood walls of the bed again. The window at the back of the cab slid open, and the little boy's voice grew louder, then was quickly hushed. "Is he okay?" the man said, his face at the open window. "Does he need a doctor?"

Daniel's expression tightened into a grimace. "He'll be fine until he wakes up and I hit him again," he said, then added, "He's fine. Don't take this the wrong way, but who are you?"

The man grinned, twisting even more to stick his work-grimed hand through the window. "Benson," he said as he and Daniel shook. "And this is my wife, May," he said, and the woman driving called out a cheery "Hello!" "And my son, Johnny, who you already met."

Daniel smiled as the little boy pushed his way to the window and kneeled on the seat. "Is that her?" he said excitedly. "Is that the lady scientist who is going to kill the tomatoes?"

"It sure is," Daniel said, and Johnny bounced back to tell his mother.

Benson scooted closer to the open window. "Johnny said you helped him get away from the collection gangs. That you were going to the police station to get a woman who knew how to stop the plague?"

There was hope in his eyes under his disbelief, and Trisk held her hair from her face and leaned closer. "It's in the tomatoes," she said, the relief at telling someone tremendous.

Benson's smile widened as he glanced at Johnny and back. "That's what he said. We came to help." His eyes went to Daniel, then Kal. "Looks like we were just in time."

Trisk's throat tightened as they jostled through the empty streets, the sound of the engine echoing off the building faces. She could sense the new strength in them that her words had started. They had a way to fight. Someday this would end. They could endure it until then.

"My name is Trisk," she said. "Thank you for stopping."

"Benson," he repeated. "It's a pleasure, ma'am." His smile widened, easy to see even in the dark. "It's the least I could do for you saving my May and Johnny."

"It's not me you should thank," she said, her attention shifting to the night at the bark of what she hoped was a dog but was probably a Were. "Can this truck go any faster?"

But Benson only smiled as May took a left down a dimly lit street, clearly headed for the outskirts of town. "We'll be okay. We've got people running rabbit for us, getting caught by the collection gangs so you can get out of Chicago clean."

"They're getting caught on purpose?" Daniel said, aghast, and Benson nodded.

"We can get word into the containment camps that way. No one else needs to die."

Trisk's face warmed in embarrassment. Her own people could stop this if they weren't such cowards. Brow furrowed, she scrunched down as the truck came out into a straightaway and picked up speed. Benson disappeared from the window for a moment, stuffing a blanket through when he came back. "I'm sorry we can't give you more," he said as Trisk shook it out and gestured for Daniel to join her so they could share its warmth. Kal could stay cold on the floor of the truck bed for all she cared.

"It's wonderful," she said as Daniel awkwardly moved closer, smelling like sweat and soap. "Thank you so much."

"The interstates are patrolled," Benson was saying, "but we can do a slow drive past the train station. You can get out that way."

"And go where?" Daniel asked, but Trisk already knew, and she tugged the blanket in place, covering Daniel's shoes. He'd lost his loafers somewhere, and the sneakers with hand-drawn peace symbols looked odd at the hem of his worn and dirty dress slacks.

"DC," she said. "From there, we can get the word out to everyone."

Benson nodded, tucking back inside the cab and closing the window to keep Johnny from trying to climb through it. Trisk settled beside Daniel, appreciating his warmth and hoping Orchid was okay under his hat. "How are you doing?" she asked softly, and his head dropped. "That must have been awful at the containment center. Daniel—"

"I don't want to talk about it," he interrupted, then started, his attention jumping to her when she took his cold hand.

"Thank you for coming to get me," she said, giving his fingers a little squeeze. "When I saw you with those blisters . . . I almost died. I thought Kal had shoved a tomato down your throat or something."

He smiled, a hand rising to touch them. "Orchid says they'll be gone tomorrow. They itch like crazy. Passive pixy deterrent."

"I didn't know she could do that." The engine rumbled soothingly through her, and she slouched, trying to get below the wind. "Why are they helping us?" she whispered, glancing into the cab as she fingered the thick wool blanket. Humans might lack magic, but they made up for it in guile and cooperation. "Everyone is risking their lives for us."

Daniel shrugged, still not daring to take his hand off his hat. His expression was hard to see in the dark, and Trisk frowned when May turned off the truck's lights and even the glow from the dash was lost. "Because I told them we could stop it," he said. Twisting, he looked at her. "Was I wrong?"

She shook her head, biting her lip as she hoped their confidence wasn't misplaced. Then she hesitated, eyebrows rising as she heard the roar of another engine and what sounded like music echoing between the buildings. "Can you hear that?"

"What?" Daniel asked, eyes squinting as he listened.

"Music," Orchid piped up from under his hat. "At least, I think it's music."

"And a car," Daniel said, looking through the cab to the night-dark streets they were racing through.

Trisk sat up as the drums and wailing guitar turned into something recognizable. *"Trouble Every Day"*? she thought, having heard the odd music from Mothers of Invention coming from Angie's radio at lunch just last week.

Angie . . . she thought, a lump suddenly appearing in her throat. She'd probably been the first to die. Maybe she'd get her name in the history books for it.

"That's really close," Daniel said, and Trisk looked up at the sound of a stressed engine. Fear slid through her when the howls of men and wolves joined it. The music was getting louder. Gears were grinding, and someone was shouting.

"Look out!" Daniel shouted, and May shrieked, her arm flashing out to pin Johnny to the seat between her and Benson as she hit the brakes. They squealed a warning, and the van suddenly barreling through the intersection toward them swerved.

This might hurt, Trisk thought, unable to look away as the van majestically slammed into the truck's front fender. The truck rocked to a halt, and from the cab, May screamed. Trisk's shoulder thumped into the wall of the truck bed, but the heavy farm vehicle hardly noticed. Daniel's hand was tight on his hat, his face white as the truck's engine stalled.

Brakes smoking, the van careened to the right as the driver overcompensated, stalling out as well as it hit the mailbox on the corner. The music coming from the van snapped off, replaced with the sound of feminine swearing.

Wide-eyed, Trisk looked at Daniel, his hand still holding that hat on his head. The night seemed both warmer and a lot quieter now that they weren't moving. Johnny was crying inside the cab, but he was probably just scared. "Are you okay?" she asked Daniel, then called into the cab, "Anyone hurt?"

"We're okay, ma'am," Benson said, holding Johnny tight.

May was trying to get the truck started, but something didn't sound right.

Daniel looked dazed as he took his hand down. "I'm okay," he whispered. "Orchid?"

There was no answer, and panicked, he took his hat off. "Orchid!"

But they both looked up at a familiar wing clatter, and relief filled Trisk as she saw that the pixy had flown to safety. "She's okay," Trisk whispered, her attention going to the van. The swearing had stopped. A fan belt screamed and metal groaned as the van, painted with a psychedelic wizard fighting a dragon, backed off the curb and jostled onto the road.

Their truck, though, wouldn't start, and there were Weres in the street.

Howls rang from nearby, the calls sounding odd in the city streets. In a sudden insight, Trisk realized the van didn't hold roving Weres looking for them, but fleeing people. *And they have an Ohio plate*, she thought, seeing the Cincinnati radio bumper sticker beside it.

"Stay here," Daniel said as he levered himself over the side of the truck, his sneakers almost silent as he jogged to the van, whistling and waving for the driver's attention.

"Daniel?" she shouted, her high voice echoing off the buildings, and he turned, gesturing for her to stay.

"They might be hurt!" he called back, slowing as he halted at the open window.

Trisk looked into the truck's cab. May was gathering their things, and the Weres were getting closer. "Why won't it start?" she asked through the open window, and May looked at her apologetically.

"I think I flooded it," she said, handing Benson a grocery bag and taking a tear-streaked Johnny in return.

Trisk watched, not knowing what to do as the small family got out. Kal lay unconscious at her feet. *We're getting out?* she thought, at a loss.

The sound of the van's side door opening rolled through the night, and Trisk's lips parted when a teen-ager got out, his orange pants and red dreadlocks unforgettable. "You have got to be kidding me. It's the bass player," she whispered as he and Daniel jogged back to the truck.

"Let's go, Trisk," Daniel said as they got closer. "I got us a ride. They can get us out of the city."

But she couldn't move as the kid lowered the tailgate and dragged Kal to it. "No way!" he said as he saw her. "The lady scientist? Oh, man. You should have heard the fuzz swearing about you. He's going to toast your candy ass when he finds out you split."

That shook her out of her funk, and sitting down, she scooted to the tailgate. "Yeah? I'm not the one who broke out of jail, stole my van out of impound, and lied to my mom about where I was going."

The kid's mouth dropped open, and then he grinned at her. "Right," he said as he grabbed Kal's feet. Daniel took his shoulders, and together they half ran to the van, Daniel clearly struggling with the added weight.

"Come on, Trisk!" Daniel called as they tossed Kal in.

"Let's haul ass!" a high-pitched voice shouted from

behind the wheel. "I'm not spending Halloween in jail!" the unseen woman added, revving the engine to make the van shimmy.

Borrowed blanket tight about her shoulders, Trisk started after them, hesitating as she realized Benson and May were still standing by their truck as if waiting for the bus.

"There's lots of room," Trisk called, and Benson waved her on.

"Go," he said, voice raised in urgency. "They'll stop chasing you if they get us."

They're going to get caught so we don't? Trisk slid to a halt in the middle of the intersection, heart pounding. She could hear the Weres. They were only a street off. "There's room," she insisted.

"We'll be fine, ma'am," May said, apparently eager to be caught. "It's up to us to save as many people as we can here. We're grateful you told us what to do. Go do what you can in DC. Go!"

"Trisk!" Daniel shouted. Kal was a dark shadow in the van. Daniel waited, one hand outstretched, the other holding his hat to his head. Orchid must be back with him. "They'll be fine!" he exclaimed, and her eyes widened as she saw the flitting shadows at the end of the street.

She ran.

"Hurry up!" the kid demanded, and Daniel lurched through the wide-open door, turning to extend a hand to her. The van was already moving, and breathless, Trisk dove for it, feeling Daniel's grip take her shoulder and haul her the rest of the way in.

"Got her!" the kid exclaimed, and Trisk rolled across the van, coming to rest against a cold wall. The door slammed shut as the van accelerated with the scent of burning rubber. Trisk gasped when they lurched onto another curb, and then back onto the street with a spine-tingling thump before picking up speed.

Eyes wide, she looked up from the shag rug floor of the open van. There were no seats except the two up front, just an empty space filled with black-enameled boxes. Kal was slumped against them, and as they careened through the streets, Daniel began to laugh.

"You find this funny?" Trisk said dryly, then reached for the wall when the van leaned precariously as they took a corner. The brakes squealed in protest . . . and then the van righted itself and they raced down a straightaway.

"Everyone okay?" the driver asked, her childishly high but beautifully resonant voice flowing out along with "House of the Rising Sun" from the radio. It sounded eminently right blaring from the huge speakers as they ran from Weres in the moonless night. The girl's window was down, and her long black hair whipped in the wind as she took a quick glance at them.

"I don't know," Trisk said, wondering if she'd hit her head at some point and didn't remember it. How could she have just left Benson and May like that? And with a little kid, too.

The girl gave her a grin before turning her attention back to the road. With a sudden shock, Trisk realized the driver was sitting on a phone book. Even so, Trisk took in her curves and adjusted her age to be about nineteen. She was just really small. *A Were, maybe?* she wondered, breathing deep for any telltale smell of wolfsbane as she looked from her to the tall boy. They didn't look anything alike, the tiny woman's pantsuit in dark shades of brown and black, and the tall boy in orange-and-yellow bell-bottoms that went with his hair and little else.

Uneasy, Trisk cleared her throat. Kal rolled back and forth as the van wove through the empty streets. Exhaling loudly, Daniel slumped against the wall, his knees bent and his feet spread wide for balance. His hat was leaking silver dust. Seeing her questioning look, Daniel shrugged. "Ah, I'm Trisk, and that's Daniel," Trisk finally said.

"Hey," Daniel said, giving them a little wave.

The gangly adolescent whooped when the van took a bump hard, his smile never dimming. "I'm Takata," he said, pointing to a sticker on one of the boxes stacked up against one side. "And that's Ripley. She's my drummer." He glanced at the driver. "Take it easy, Rip. I think we lost them. You're going to bust my ride."

"I'm not your drummer," the woman said. "You're my bass."

Trisk's eyebrows rose as she realized what the odd-shaped bumps taking up most of the van were. *Pelhan said he was in a band*, she thought, worried when Ripley picked up speed as they headed out of the city.

"We're going to Cincinnati," the kid said as he brushed the dirt from his orange slacks. "If my mom finds out I ditched work to play a gig this Halloween, it won't be the plague that kills me. Then they cancel it. Dude."

Trisk put a hand to her middle, not feeling well from all the sudden shifts and bumps. "It's in the tomatoes," she said. "Just don't eat them."

"That's what I heard!" Takata's gaze touched on Daniel's blisters before turning to the woman. "You owe me a Coke, Ripley. It's the tomatoes."

She flipped him off, but Takata didn't seem to care as he leaned close, whispering, "Your friend is all right. He doesn't have the plague. He's been pixed."

Trisk's lips parted, and from Daniel's hat, Orchid shouted, "You've seen a pixy? Where!"

"No way!" Takata shook Ripley's shoulder when Orchid pushed the hat up, peering out at them as Daniel tried to hold it down. Bright silver pixy dust spilled from under his hand, looking like an aura as the wind ripped it away and it pooled at the back of the van.

"It's a pixy!" Takata exclaimed, and then his face went still, eyes wide as he glanced from Trisk to Daniel, clearly knowing he was a human. "Ahh . . ." he said, looking almost terrified.

"Where!" Orchid demanded, but the kid was tongue-tied.

"It's okay," Trisk said, putting a hand on Takata's shoulder. "I'm taking care of it."

"Like hell you are," Orchid said, and Daniel yelped when she poked at him to stop trying to get her to hide. "If anyone has to kill Daniel, it will be me. Besides, he's not going to say anything," the pixy added. "He's cool with all of us. You know where there are pixies?"

Still unsure, the kid rubbed the back of his neck in what looked like remembered pain. "We had a family of them in the woods behind our house when I was growing up. They might still be there." He chuckled. "I told my mom it was poison ivy."

The dust spilling from under Daniel's hat spun through a kaleidoscope of color, and the tiny woman stared at all of them, clearly torn. "You should go with them," Daniel said softly, clearly knowing the problem, and Orchid's dust turned a blue so dark it was almost unseen. "We'll get to DC okay."

"Not until I know no one is going to kill you to keep the silence," she said, tucking back under the hat, her expression becoming pensive.

Mood undimmed, Takata tapped a rhythm on his knee. "Man, I gotta write a song about this. 'Little death, looking for love.'" He turned to the woman. "Ripley. 'Tiny little death, held captive by silence,'" he sang, shocking Trisk with his beautiful voice. "'Pining for love, made strong by violence.'"

"No," she said, shaking her head. "Just no."

Takata spun back to face them, seemingly undaunted.

"Sorry about running into you," Daniel said, his hand still holding his hat in place. "We have to get to DC to tell the dewar how to stop the plague. Can you drop us at the train station? The Weres are patrolling the roads."

Takata's exuberance didn't so much dim as utterly vanish under a wash of intense concentration. "They stopped all outgoing trains this afternoon," he said, turning to Ripley and telling her not to have a cow and that he knew all the back ways into Cincinnati. "Everything," he added when he turned back to them.

"Great." Trisk slumped into the boxed drum set to feel the road rumble all the way up her spine. "How are we going to get to DC? We can't drive there dodging cops all the way."

"Cincy is still running trains out," Takata said, his pride at his hometown obvious. "They never stop, not for plague, or war, or worker strike. Ripley and I will get you there, and you can hop a boxcar to DC. You can be on the East Coast by tomorrow night, slick as Crisco."

Eyebrows high in consideration, Trisk looked at Daniel, seeing by his shrug that he was good with it. "We'll do that," she said, and Takata bobbed his head, flicking his dreadlocks back as he turned to the front, his long fingers tapping out a complex rhythm that was hard to follow.

I can do this for five hours, Trisk thought as she settled back and closed her eyes. And maybe she could catch a few winks in the meantime. They'd be in Cincinnati by dawn, maybe sooner the way Ripley drove. There'd be a train leaving for the East Coast soon after that—and then everything would be fine.

34

The engine hummed through Trisk while she sat, wide awake and listening to the radio as they raced through the predawn. "Bang Bang," Cher's new single, was on, and Trisk felt the bumps the gun made in the pocket of her Chicago Police jacket as she thought about Kal. It wasn't advisable to keep someone under a sleep charm this long, especially when they'd been knocked unconscious to begin with, but he'd cause problems the moment he was awake, and she couldn't tell her future child that she'd shot his or her father dead—even if it had seemed like a good idea at the time.

Her attention fell on Daniel, across the van from her. His features were soft in sleep, huddled in the jacket that Pelhan had given him. Seeing him next to Kal, it was obvious that he wasn't an elf, his blond hair, slight build, and studious demeanor aside. The glasses gave him away, and his chin wasn't angular enough. His blisters were gone, though, and she smiled at his slight snore. Takata was up front doing the same thing.

Sunrise was a few hours off yet, but she stretched, giving up on sleep. Orchid was sitting on the rearview mirror, and her dust coating the shrunken head dangling from it in a silver glow was decidedly eerie. Nodding her greeting to the pixy, Trisk stepped over Kal to kneel between the front seats and look out at the fading stars. She'd been on her natural sleep cycle for days now, meaning she was most alert at dusk and dawn. She kind of liked it.

"Bang, bang. My baby shot me down."

"Morning," Ripley said, her voice rising and falling to make the two syllables into a song.

"Morning." Trisk coughed to get the cobwebs out. "You want me to drive? It's nearly sunup."

"We're almost there," the woman said with a yawn. "Orchid's been keeping me awake."

The pixy shifted her wings to invisibility. "Two hours, seventeen minutes," she said, then added when Trisk's eyebrows rose in question, "Until sunup. Pixies have great sun sense."

Trisk's gaze went to Takata as the kid mumbled something that rhymed in his sleep. "Thanks for taking us to Cincinnati," she said, and Ripley's gaze lifted from the teenager, going from an expression of fond protection to one more dangerous.

"Do you think you can really stop this?" the Were asked, her concern obvious.

"We've got a good chance." Trisk's knees on the cold van began to ache. "People are starting to figure it out, and that will help. It's the little towns and the really big cities that are in the most danger. Too small of a population, and they can't keep it together and make the right connections to save anyone. The really big cities are just as bad, imploding because of too many people and not enough resources or control. The middle ground has the best chance to survive, cities with a diverse enough population that can figure it out and have a big enough support structure to keep services going, but small enough to keep control. And that might be a problem."

Ripley looked at her, then back to the road. She was driving without headlights, but she probably had better night vision than even Orchid. Besides, there was little chance of losing the road. They were coming in just south of Cincinnati, and the chiseled walls of the foothills rose high to either side. "How?" the woman asked.

Trisk looked back at Daniel with a feeling of guilt. "Humans aren't stupid because they haven't figured out we live beside them," she whispered. "We're just good at blending in. But when everyone around you starts dying, you find out why those who survived made it."

Ripley's small hands gripped the wheel tighter. "You think the silence is cracking?"

Feeling as if it was, Trisk shrugged.

Orchid stood and stretched, her tiny form silhouetted against the last of the stars. "I wouldn't mind coming out. I might be able to find a husband, then. Take out an ad in the paper. Single female pixy looking for like-minded buck to start a family." She snorted as she opened a little bag made of a gum wrapper and used her chopsticks to eat what looked like chocolate frosting. "I've only got a few years left to have kids," she said around a lick. "I really want kids. Lots of them. Maybe twenty."

Trisk's hand went to her middle. She didn't know what to say. Either way, she was never going to work in a lab again. *This is so backward and unfair.*

"Smell that?" Orchid said as she spun to the front window.

"Chili and chocolate?" Ripley said with a smile. "We're almost there."

"No." Orchid's wings hummed to invisibility. "Vampire."

The word hung for two heartbeats as Ripley followed the road around a wide turn, gasping and stomping on the brakes when she saw two cars blocking their way, the cars' headlights bathing each other in a bright glow the curve had hidden.

"Holy pixy piss!" Orchid shrilled, and Trisk grabbed the back of the seats as the van squealed to a stop. Takata slid to the floor, his long arms and legs in a tangle.

"Are we there?" the kid said from the footwell, his eyes wide and suddenly very awake.

"Hold on!" Her arm going across the passenger seat, Ripley turned to look behind them as she jerked the van into reverse.

But it was too late, and two more black cars slid into place, trapping them.

"Goddamn son of a bitch!" the petite woman swore, her high voice making it sound almost beautiful. "I am not going to jail!" she added, hitting the dash hard.

Takata slumped in his seat, long legs cramped. "My mom is going to kill me."

Trisk shifted to make room for Daniel as he came up beside her, rubbing his stubble and yawning. "A roadblock? Swell." Sighing, he tucked his shirt into his pants. "Good morning."

"Is it?" Trisk said, wincing as Ripley slammed the van into park and swore some more.

"God, Ripley. Take it easy," Takata said. "What are they going to do? We live here."

The small woman crossed her arms over her chest and fumed. "I'm not a minor, *Donald*."

Donald? Trisk thought, deciding Takata must be his stage name. "Turn your lights on," she whispered, wanting a better look at the two men standing expectantly before the waiting cars.

Mood sour, Ripley did so, and the two men flinched in the one-headlight glare. The other light was still in Chicago with the van's fender.

Her hand on the gun in her jacket pocket, Trisk looked at the two vampires, quiet and oddly passive in the middle of the road. The taller one was clean-shaven, wearing a trim suit, white shirt, and black tie, his dress shoes scuffing on the smooth pavement as he checked his watch and squinted. The other was in jeans and a tunic, a beaded belt holding it tight around his narrow, almost gaunt waist. His long hair was unbound, and he was barefoot despite the morning chill. As differently as they were dressed, they both had a sublimely confident air about them.

Trisk slumped. *Vampires. Why is it always vampires?* Unhappy, she looked at Kal, then Daniel, but when her gaze fell upon Takata, she took her hand off the gun. He was just a kid. If she used a gun, they'd use a gun. "Open the door," she whispered.

"What?" Orchid shrilled, giving voice to everyone's surprise.

"We can't get past the cliffs," Trisk said in resignation. "Let's find out what they want. Bluff it out, maybe, but we can't fight that. Open the door."

Shoulders tense, Daniel stepped over Kal and opened the wide sliding door. Cool night air slipped in, refreshing and clean and sounding of crickets. Lips pressed tight, Trisk shook the cartridges out of the handgun, checked it again, then threw the unloaded weapon out the door to skitter on the black pavement.

"Dudette, you think that's smart?" Takata asked.

"What are you doing?" Daniel questioned as she dropped the bullets in the van's console.

"Trying to minimize an ugly situation. You see any

humans?" she said, pointing. "If we use a gun, they'll use a gun, and we'll lose. With magic, we've got a chance. If the gun is out there, no one in here is going to make the mistake of using it."

"What if they use a gun against your magic?" Ripley asked, and Trisk frowned.

"They won't," she promised, hoping she wasn't mistaken. "They'll think we're helpless. Trust me on this. Inderlanders are so used to hiding our skills that we don't see them as a threat anymore." Which was a shame. But it would only work once. Vampires weren't stupid.

Watching the two men out the front window, Trisk shouted, "That's the only weapon we have!" Then she hesitated. "Wait a minute!" She turned to Ripley. "Right?" she asked pointedly.

Her expression sour, Ripley reached under the seat, then cranked the window down to throw out a gun, followed by a long, wicked-looking knife in a leather sheath.

Hearing them clatter on the pavement made Trisk feel better. "We don't want any trouble!" she shouted, watching the man in the suit direct two of his men to collect the weapons and fall back. "We just want to come into Cincinnati. No one is sick."

An odd, not unpleasant scent was drifting in the open door along with the sound of crickets. Vampire incense. She'd smelled it on Rick before, but never this strong. There had to be eight vampires surrounding them now, and she reached for a ley line. A sparkling warmth filled her, making her feel better. Behind them in the distance, a light winked on the road and was gone.

The two vampires waited patiently in the glare of

the headlights. The hippie had a bandage on his wrist. There was another on his neck. The young man in the suit looked fine, but he moved with a slight limp. *Living vamps*, she thought. *Maybe they don't know who we are.*

"Am I addressing Dr. Felecia Cambri?" the suited vampire called out.

And maybe someday we'll fly to the moon and back. Trisk grimaced, feeling responsible for everyone in the van, Kal included. Orchid made a surprised chirp, and Daniel and Takata exchanged worried looks. "Who wants to know?" she yelled, and the vampire's smile widened.

"Manners, manners," he said. "You're correct, and I do apologize. I'm Piscary, in charge of the city at the moment until we can get things sorted out. Beside me is Sam. He is assisting me tonight. Could we talk about what happened in Sacramento?"

Trisk thought about it for three heartbeats, then reached for the doorframe.

"Whoa, hold on," Daniel said, pulling her back. "You're not going out there."

She slumped, her attention shifting between his severe expression to Orchid hovering dead center of the van, hands on her hips as she spilled a bright gold dust. Ripley was grim-faced behind the wheel, and Takata, though wide-eyed, was clearly recklessly ready for anything. Kal, of course, just lay there. "Thank you for getting me here," she said. "This is my ride."

But as Ripley and Orchid objected, Daniel lurched to get out of the van ahead of her. "Daniel," she protested, but his jaw was set and she could tell he wasn't getting back in. Orchid, too, zipped out, flying over her head, easily evading her to alight on his shoulder.

"This is my fault, too," Daniel said as he zipped up the jacket he'd gotten from Captain Pelhan, and Trisk slumped. "Coming?" he asked.

"Bad idea. Bad idea," she muttered, then louder, "Ripley, keep Takata in the van." She slipped out, feeling the hard pavement all the way to her skull. "You shouldn't be here," she added as she and Daniel began walking forward.

"When is conversation not a good idea?" Daniel said, convincing Trisk he had no clue.

Behind them, the van's door creaked open, and Trisk spun, a sigh of exasperation slipping from her when Takata began to get out. But it was Piscary who called out, "Donald, get back in the van. I told your mother I'd have you home in time for breakfast."

"Dude! How do you know my name?" the teenager said, then yelped when Ripley reached across the wide bench seat and yanked him back in, telling him to sit or she'd rip off his balls and feed them to the troll under Twin Lakes Bridge.

The van door slammed shut again, and Trisk stopped right before the two vampires. "Promise you'll let them go," she said, feeling responsible. "Do that, and we'll come quietly."

Piscary smiled, his lips tight to hide his teeth. "I intend to," he said, his smooth speech making him sound older than he looked. "We're one man short, though," he said, eyes on the top of the surrounding cliffs as a rock slid and fell. "Is Dr. Kalamack still unconscious?"

How does he know that? she thought as she nodded, both glad and uneasy that Kal was being included in this.

"It's probably easier to keep him that way for now," Piscary said, his eyebrows high as he motioned to the watching men and one came forward. Sam joined him, the light from the headlights flashing on them as they went to the van, chatting with Ripley for a moment before levering themselves in and bundling Kal into the blanket she'd gotten from May.

"You're a vampire," Daniel blurted, reddening when Piscary turned his surprised gaze on him. Still carrying Kal, the hippie vampire gasped, his eyes widening in shock.

"And you're a problem, Dr. Plank," Piscary said, fingers steepled. He was wearing a mood ring, blacker than the night, and Trisk thought it an odd accessory for someone so refined.

"Not usually," Daniel said. "I mean, I'm not usually a problem. I'm always Dr. Plank."

Trisk shifted uneasily. "He can hold the silence. He won't break it. I promise."

"Sir," the hippie vampire protested, and Piscary shook his head.

"Look at him." Piscary gestured at Daniel. "He has a pixy on his shoulder. It is too late. He knows what we are." Trisk blanched as Piscary turned his hard gaze to her. "I see no need to silence Dr. Plank—at the moment," he added as he tugged his suit's sleeves down, smiling to show Trisk his slightly enlarged canines.

"You're not touching him. At this moment, or any other," she said, even as she wondered at the care they took in carrying Kal, supporting his head and making sure he didn't hit anything as they gently lowered him to the earth beside one of the black cars. The driver unlocked the trunk, and her lips parted. "Hang on. You can't put him in the trunk."

Unperturbed, Piscary gestured for them to follow. "There's not enough room in the car. I promise you he'll be comfortable. We need to go. Piscary would like to talk to you."

And you're putting yourself in the third person why? she wondered.

Daniel's frown deepened. "I thought you said you were Piscary," he finally said.

The vampire's eyes followed Orchid as she watched them put Kal in the trunk, the small pixy giggling wildly. "I am, and I'm not," he said as he glanced at the eastern sky just now showing a hint of light. "Shall we?"

Suddenly Trisk wasn't keen on getting in the car, even if Kal was already in the trunk. It had become obvious that Piscary was a true undead, not the young living vampire standing before them. A master vampire in charge of the city's sundry vampire families would be both old enough and skilled enough to possess one of his children so he could see through their eyes, speak through their mouth.

"It's me or the enclave," Piscary said, the threat obvious. "They will be here shortly."

"Why should I trust you?" she asked, Daniel and Orchid again beside her.

Piscary began to look impatient. "I told them you were on a train. They'll discover soon enough that no trains are departing from Chicago. You have my word I won't deliver you to the enclave without an opportunity to publicly air your grievance. I don't like what I'm hearing, and I'm hopeful you can bring some enlightenment." He smiled, but it was devoid of feeling.

Unsure, she glanced behind her at Takata and Ripley watching from inside the van. Daniel looked scared but willing. Orchid stood on his shoulder, and seeing Trisk's question, she clattered her wings. Ripley would ram them if she asked, and with her driving skills and

Orchid's sword, they might evade the vampires for
an hour or two. Recapture was inevitable. Two hours
might be enough to get the word out. It might not. *I
don't want to endanger them.*

"Dr. Cambri," Piscary prompted, "your elven enclave
is not happy. That should be reason enough for you to
trust me for a time."

For a time. Which meant what happened after that
was up for debate. Willingly walking into a master vampire's home was not prudent, but if anyone might be
able to force the enclave to listen, it would be another
high-ranking Inderlander. And so Piscary beamed when
she nodded, her shoulders hunched as she paced to the
car where they'd stashed Kal. "You going to open the
door for me?" she asked the driver, and he jumped to
do so. *This is such a bad idea*, she thought as she waved
good-bye to Ripley and Takata and got in.

The car was luxurious, the soft seats and warm air
coming from the vent soothing in the predawn chill.
Daniel got in after her, but before she could slide to the
other side, the other door opened and Piscary levered
himself in. Uncomfortable, she sat in the middle of the
long bench seat, caught between Daniel and a master
vampire seeing through one of his children's eyes.

"Thank you," Piscary said as he settled himself. "I'll
see you shortly," he added as the driver and Sam got in
the front and the vehicle began to shift back and forth
to get back on the road properly. "Let Leo know if you
need anything. The shops are open, and it's likely that
we'll have some time before the witch's coven of moral
and ethical standards clears their spokesperson. There's
a Were representative to be found as well."

Coven of moral and ethical standards? Trisk thought,
wondering why the witches were getting involved,

but Piscary had promised she could air her grievances. "Thank you," she said, but Piscary had slumped.

Gasping, his head snapped up, almost as fast as it had fallen. Eyes wide, he took a deep breath, his hands on his knees almost white-knuckled.

Daniel leaned to look around Trisk. "Are you okay?"

"Fine, thanks," the man beside her said, his voice higher, almost apologetic. "Sometimes he forgets to breathe enough for me is all." Eyes pinched in worry, he leaned forward to see them both. "I'm Leo. Do you need to pick anything up on the way?"

Daniel stared; the change was obvious. Leo was upfront where Piscary had been calculating, attentive where Piscary had been detached. "A-ah," Daniel stammered, but Orchid, still on his shoulder, hummed her wings, filling the back of the car with her sparkling dust.

"Slugs in beer!" she swore, hovering inches in front of the man now trying not to sneeze. "I've never seen that before. You're Piscary's scion, aren't you?"

Leo nodded, looking exhausted, as well as proud, and scared. "For the last few days," he said, wiping sweat off the back of his neck. "His usual scion is unwell." Leo's eyes flicked to Trisk, then back to his hands. His mood ring had shifted to a fiery red, and he made a fist to hide it. "The faintest taint of sickness, and they won't touch us. It's becoming a problem."

From the front, Sam said, "Those of us not ill are taking on an undue burden," he said, holding up his bandaged wrist in explanation. "It's hard keeping up."

"We'll manage," Leo said, a hard determination stiffening his shoulders. "We won't allow our masters to make Cincinnati into another Detroit."

Clearly confused, Daniel leaned close, whispering, "Scion?"

"An undead vampire's aide who does his or her day-light work," she said, adding, "I'll explain it to you later." She turned to Leo, seeing him trying to recover. "You'll be okay," she said, and he looked up, his fear quickly hidden. "Your family will be fine."

Wan, Leo nodded, clearly not convinced.

All the vehicles had worked themselves back onto the road, and Trisk felt a new ribbon of unease wind around her heart when Takata and Ripley were escorted onto the expressway heading into Cincinnati. She watched the van go distant, a black car before them, one behind.

But then she looked out the front window, her lips parting in amazement as the car rolled into Newport, just across the river from Cincinnati. There were cars on the road and people on the sidewalks despite the predawn hour, and yes, the shops were open unusually early. She wondered if the plague had somehow skipped them, but then Orchid's wings drooped when a bus with MORGUE spray-painted on it rolled past, stopping when someone waving a red dishcloth came out of an apartment building.

"Are they all Inderlanders?" Trisk asked, and Leo followed her attention to the people pausing to pay their respects to the anonymous shroud-wrapped body. Yet the city was functioning, and she couldn't help but compare it to the locked-down fear that held Chicago.

"I'd say most are," Leo said as they bumped over a railroad trestle. "Simply because of the hour. This isn't Cincinnati's first plague. We know what to do, especially the old ones." His smile faded. "They started a new cemetery up by the museum. Spring Grove is already full with cholera victims from the 1800s."

"Old ones?" Daniel questioned, and Orchid flew

back from the rearview mirror where she'd been charming Sam and the driver with her pert smile.

"Don't worry, Daniel. I'll stick with you," she said as she landed on his shoulder. "It's a fact that even old vampires leave you alone when there's a pixy on your shoulder. Right, Leo?"

Leo looked at her, and Orchid touched the tiny blade on her hip. "Sure," he said, his attention going to the elaborate Victorian house the car was pulling up to. It looked as if every light was on. A small marina lay to one side, and a restaurant on the other. A huge stone-foundation barn that had probably once held carriages was set behind it under even larger trees. Sleek cars and old vehicles were parked before it under security lights, with no regard to age or style. It was here that they stopped.

Immediately the driver and Sam got out, the trunk popping up so they could get Kal. Leo put a hand on Daniel's knee, stopping him from opening the door. The dome light made odd shadows on his face. "Have you met with the undead before?" he asked.

Daniel stared at him. "I don't think so."

"Just one," Trisk said. "And he blew up my truck with us in it."

Daniel's expression went empty as he began to put it all together.

Leo took his hand back. "Some advice. Piscary appreciates manners above all. He will forgive untidiness, but not disrespect. You," he said, looking at Daniel. "Don't eat anything in front of him, even if he offers. You can drink if he hands it to you, but otherwise, no. It's probably a good idea if you don't even talk." Leo's brow furrowed as he turned to Trisk. "Are you sure you want to bring him down? I can keep him entertained upstairs."

"I'll be fine," Daniel almost growled.

Orchid snickered. "He can handle it," she said, then punched Daniel's ear in a show of fondness. "I won't let him eat you, Daniel. Promise."

I feel so much better now, Trisk thought as the back doors opened and they all got out.

The predawn morning was warm despite their being right on the river, and when Leo headed for the barn instead of the house, she balked. "Ah, I don't think so," she said, and Sam, currently carrying Kal over his shoulder, snickered.

"It's this way," Leo insisted. "There's an entrance downstairs from the old whorehouse, but I'd rather bring you in through the business door. You're his guests."

A smile, real this time, came over his face, but it still didn't feel safe as she followed Leo into the cool depths of the barn. The echoes were almost nonexistent, and she could tell there hadn't been a horse in here for more than a hundred years. Now it housed old cars under tarps and furniture in the rafters, everything lit with new, modern lights. There was even a corner holding an efficiency kitchen and a plastic-top table where drivers could relax, complete with a couch and a color TV. A man watched them pass before him, the *thump-thump . . . whap* of the Super Ball he was throwing against the wall getting on her nerves.

"We're putting in an elevator next week, or at least, we were," Leo said as he opened a pair of double doors. They looked like mahogany, dark from age and incredibly thick. There were burn marks on the outside. "Shipping has slowed dramatically. Sorry about the stairs."

"No problem," Daniel said, and Orchid's dust glowed as they spiraled down two stories. Wondering if she'd ever walk back up, Trisk clasped her arms about herself.

Leo used a key, then whispered a password to open the metal fire door at the base of the stairs. Lips pressed into a bland smile, he passed ahead of them to hold the door. Sam went first with Kal, and then she and Daniel followed, Orchid still on the man's shoulder as promised. *Not a password, a charm*, she thought at the tingle of magic prickling through her aura when she crossed the threshold and stopped, gaping.

Trisk wasn't sure what she had expected, but the height of the ceiling surprised her, even if the walls were the original stone. The room felt airy, too, as if the evenly spaced banks of closed curtains might have a view of the river instead of bare wall should she twitch them aside. It was tastefully decorated with wood floors that threw back the glow of the numerous lights.

Being about the size of the barn upstairs, the large space was like one big living room, with modern-looking couches and chairs clustered in several areas. One centered around a color TV, currently muted and showing the news. Another had a large album collection with two turntables. A third sported a wet bar. The artwork on the walls was flamboyant and colorful, very much not her taste. There wasn't even a hint of musty dampness, surprising her. It was warm, and she unzipped her jacket.

"Wow, that's a smell you don't forget soon," Orchid said, and Daniel breathed deep, shrugging. The musky scent was pleasant, like incense.

"All I can smell is pasta," Daniel said as he took his police jacket off. "This is amazing."

"Do you like it?" a man at the bar said, and Trisk started, not having seen him. "It began as a hole under the stables, a place to hide escaping slaves. They were free once they were on the other side of the river and in Ohio."

The man set his glass down and came forward. It wasn't a suit he had on so much as an elegant housecoat, something an Englishman of the eighteenth century might wear before retiring to bed. His face was clean-shaven, and there wasn't a hint of hair on his head to give away his age. There was a youthful tightness to his features, but his eyes were old, the pupils so wide that his brown eyes looked black. Even with the slippers he wore, he looked more in charge than if he had been wearing this year's suit with a briefcase in his hand. *Egyptian?* Trisk wondered as he stopped before them, a pleasant, closed-lipped smile on his face. "It's a pleasure to meet you both," he said, and Daniel gasped when the man's lips parted to show very long, sharp canines.

"Knock it off!" Orchid said, smacking his ear. "You're embarrassing me."

"My God," Daniel whispered, a bright red as he ignored Piscary's proffered hand.

"No, but close." Piscary turned to Trisk. "Dr. Cambri?" he added, taking her hand.

Her pulse quickened; a predator who killed without a thought was kissing the top of her fingers. "Piscary," she said, having to try twice before her voice worked.

"And Dr. Plank," he said, trying again now that Daniel had recovered. Trisk breathed easier when he looked away. Daniel cautiously extended his hand, his breath coming out in an odd, stressed almost-giggle, causing Orchid to dust an embarrassed red. But honestly, the man was doing remarkably well for not even having known vampires existed three days ago.

Has it only been three days?

"And that must be Dr. Trent Kalamack," the master vampire said when Sam unceremoniously dumped the unconscious man on one of the couches. "Sam," Piscary admonished, and the man propped him up to look as if he had simply fallen asleep watching TV. Leo had gone behind the bar, and Trisk was ten times thirstier when he poured what looked like lemonade into three tall glasses.

"Thank you, Leo. Could you stay?" Piscary said, and the soft-spoken man went to sit in a far chair facing an unlit fireplace as Sam left. The door clicked shut, and Trisk stifled a shudder.

"Do you need anything?" Piscary said, playing the gracious host as he led them to the bar and handed them each a condensation-wet glass. "Are you warm enough? We're under a time constraint, of course, but I believe we can grant you time to relax, perhaps eat."

Trisk cautiously reached for her glass, her sip turning into an appreciative gulp at the tangy, sweet lemonade. Realizing Piscary was smiling at them as if they were wayward children he'd taken in, she set the glass down. Orchid was perched on the rim of Daniel's glass, grumbling as she ladled a portion of his lemonade out into the cup she carried tied to her waist.

"A dark-haired elf," Piscary said, and Trisk jerked, stiffening when he reached to run a long-fingered hand through her travel-dusty hair.

"Hands off!" Orchid shrilled, but Trisk had stepped out of his reach.

"My apologies," Piscary said, actually giving her a little bow. "I spend so much of my time with my children that I forget the outside world has personal space. I've never seen a dark elf. I can't help but wonder if your blood is as dusky as your hair."

She didn't know what to say, but she set her glass on the bar. "If this is a choice between being your blood slave or being blamed for the plague, I'll take the plague," she said, and Piscary laughed. It sounded natural enough, but it ended fast.

"No," the man said, turning his attention to Daniel. "Dr. Plank," he said, and Daniel almost choked on his drink. "I find myself in the odd position of needing to thank you."

"For what?" he asked suspiciously, but it only made Piscary more delighted.

"For not being afraid," he said, moving toward the nearest cluster of chairs and gesturing for them to sit. "I wasn't expecting that. It makes it easier to talk to you."

Daniel sat down, holding the glass in his hands between his knees. "I'm too tired to be afraid," he said, and Piscary laughed again. It was putting Trisk on edge.

"Don't get me wrong, sir," she said as she gingerly sat on the edge of a chair, "but why are we here?"

Piscary settled deep into the cushions, a careless hand waving in the air. "To die, of course."

Daniel tensed, Orchid whispering furiously in his ear to keep him from standing again. Trisk didn't look away from Piscary's eyes as they dilated in response to Daniel's sudden fear, but she'd give the master credit where it was due: that was the extent of his reaction. Trisk glanced at Leo, hunched in his distant chair, staring at the empty fireplace. Perhaps the master had just fed. It would make resisting temptation easier.

"Trisk." Daniel rose in alarm, and Trisk took his hand, trying to pull him back down.

"Sit, you lunker!" Orchid hissed, pinching his ear. "He's not going to kill us."

"That's correct," Piscary said, inclining his head solicitously. "But I'm sure someone will try. I want to talk to you, and perhaps change the outcome if the truth is to my liking."

Trisk slowly exhaled, not knowing she'd been holding it. Daniel, too, sat down.

"Just so," Piscary said, then relaxed into a taut las-
situde. "I want to know what passed before it's clouded
by elven lies. My range of easy movement is limited,
so I plotted to bring everyone to me." Smiling again,
he inclined his head to indicate Trisk. "You're quite the
draw, Dr. Cambri. Sweet honey to the stingless bees
that surround you."

Trisk frowned, the lemonade not sitting well, but
Piscary's next words were forestalled when a narrow
door set to the side opened and Sam came back in, his
pace fast and smooth. Eyeing them, he whispered in
Piscary's ear. Trisk knew it was about them when Pis-
cary's attention touched on them as he rose. "Already?"
Piscary glanced at his watch. "It's not even sunup yet."
Then he turned with a closed-lipped smile. "I apologize.
I thought we'd have more time."

"They're here now?" Trisk all but squeaked.

Daniel was white-faced. "You said you'd let her talk
first."

But Piscary had taken off his housecoat to reveal a
white linen suit underneath it. Leo stood from his distant position, coming close to take the coat. "And I will,"
Piscary said as he scuffed off his slippers and donned
the slip-ons that Leo gave him. "Cormel can keep you
company as I speak with them first." He touched Leo's
shoulder. "Fetch Rynn."

Housecoat in hand, Leo slipped out the small door
Sam had come in through.

"Rynn?" Trisk said, not knowing if that was another
vampire, or maybe his dog. "Piscary, why are we here?"
she asked again, and he turned to her, still adjusting his
suit.

"To prevent what happened in Detroit," he said as he ran a hand over his bare skull.

"They destroyed Detroit," Daniel whispered, and Orchid dusted a pale pink.

Piscary's smile took on an anticipatory gleam. "Which is why I lured not just the elven enclave to me, but the witches' coven of moral and ethical standards. The Weres haven't had a ruling body since they lost the focus, but by an incredible stroke of luck, I obtained the ear of the only Were who might speak for all, having followed Dr. Plank's virus from its onset."

"Colonel Wolfe?" Daniel guessed.

Piscary beamed as if he thought Daniel incredibly clever. "The same." He turned his gaze to Orchid, and the tiny woman's wings faltered. "We even have a pixy to weigh in. The rest can decide collectively what to do." He turned to go, pausing to add, "If the majority of us agree on my proposed course of action, that is."

"And what is that?" Orchid asked, and Piscary stopped at the small door.

"Agree to break the silence," he said, and Trisk felt a wash of both fear and desire that made Piscary's eyes flash black. "I want us to reveal ourselves to save humanity," he added carefully. "And in the process, save ourselves. And, incidentally, your life, Dr. Plank."

"Oh, is that all?" Daniel said breathlessly, but Piscary was gone.

35

The small door shut behind Piscary with the sound of a lock sliding into place. Trisk was sure the other doors set in the corners and behind the bar would be locked as well, and she didn't insult their host by trying them. Instead, she sat at the bar and drank her lemonade down to the ice. *What have I done to Daniel?*

"Lemonade." Oblivious to the danger, Daniel went behind the bar to find the pitcher and refill her glass. Shaking his head, he began to laugh weakly. "I am standing in a vampire's *lair*, and he serves me lemonade."

Trisk set her glass down and he filled it tinkling to the rim. "I've heard citrus helps vampires maintain control of their bloodlust. Covers the 'I'm scared' pheromones."

Daniel looked at Orchid, and the pixy nodded, even as she poked a hole in a sugar packet and delicately fingered the sweet grains right off her sword tip.

Something stronger would have been welcome, but Trisk didn't dare, even if liquor was tastefully displayed behind the bar in neat rows, the expensive labels under spotlights. Ulbrine was somewhere close. She could almost smell him.

Daniel's laugh turned into a sigh as he leaned into the counter toward her. "I'm a scientist, Trisk. Vampires, witches, werewolves, elves?" He winced as Orchid's dust turned a happy silver. "Pixies," he added. "You're all real. And you're ruling the world."

"Not really, but after this?" She winced. Something was going to break, and break hard.

But Daniel seemed comfortable behind the bar, even if his hair was untidy and his conservative vest and slacks were dirty from riding cross-country in a boxcar, followed by sleeping on the floor of a band's van. Though not as suave or continental as Kal, he had an air of adaptable confidence, even with the stubble on his cheeks. *I still don't know what happened to his dress shoes*, she thought as she slipped out of her coat and set it carefully on the stool beside her.

They all looked up at the faint click of a distant door, and a man in brown slacks, a button-down shirt, and a homey-looking brown sweater-vest came in. He was clean-shaven, average height, perhaps a little thick from being behind a desk too much. But his brown eyes quickly took them in as he paced eagerly forward with a contagious enthusiasm.

Orchid rose up, brushing the sugar from her as if embarrassed to have been eating it. "Hey, hi," she said, her dust a faint pink. "You must be Rynn Cormel."

"Senator Cormel, actually, but call me Rynn," he said, a slight Bronx accent making him seem even more easy-going. "Piscary asked me to keep you company and answer any questions while he's attending his other guests."

Trisk's first worry vanished as she decided he was a living vampire, not a dead one. "Ulbrine," she said, and Cormel nodded. He looked exactly like a politician, young, idealistic, and clever with words.

"Among others," Cormel said, reaching across the bar to Daniel to shake his hand. "Dr. Plank," he said before taking Trisk's, the rings on his fingers glinting. "Dr. Cambri."

Cormel turned to Kal, asleep on the couch, and Orchid piped up. "Dr. Dumb-Ass," she said, and the living vampire chuckled to show his small but pointy canines.

"That's Kalamack?" Quick on his feet, Cormel went to stand over him. Trisk's eyes narrowed when the vampire's eyes closed and he breathed deep, as if scenting Kal. He might be. Elves were uncommon enough that he might not have ever met one before. "I thought he'd be taller."

Orchid flew to hover beside Cormel, and the man's eyes flashed open at the clatter of her wings. "I thought he'd be smarter," she said, her high voice holding a world of disdain.

Cormel smiled, hand dipping into a pocket to bring out a silver wire. "You should wake him up. It's either now or before the council."

Trisk clamped down on a flash of fear, not liking that Cormel noticed it. "He's only going to lie. Try to get away. In that order," she said.

"Truths will be outed." Cormel crouched to fasten the silver around Kal's wrist. "He can't do magic now. Or at least not ley line."

Orchid snorted, a burst of dust coming from her. "He couldn't do that much magic before," she said, and Daniel, content behind the bar, muttered about it being more than he could do.

"What is that?" Trisk asked suspiciously as Cormel stood, and she touched her wrist to indicate the metallic band around Kal's. "Charmed silver?" she guessed. "Where did you get it?"

Cormel grinned, looking very unvampiric. "Vampires use witch magic all the time. How else do you think Piscary could look so good? He's over five hundred years old."

"No way." Daniel looked up from wiping a stray spill of lemonade off the bar.

Cormel ambled back to the bar and took the glass Daniel had poured for him. "It's true, but I agree, highly unusual. Piscary himself is . . . unusual. Most undead live only forty years after their first death. It's only those who are clever enough to convince new living vampires that they love them and to willingly give them the blood they need who last longer. That's why Piscary is concerned enough about the decreasing human population to take action when instinct says to keep still, stay in the shadows." He took a sip of the lemonade, eyes lingering on the ice. "I tell him not to worry, that balance will find itself, but he has no soul, so he cannot believe it on faith."

"You don't just take it? Blood, I mean?" Daniel asked, and Orchid gasped, clearly embarrassed by his question. Cormel, though, didn't seem to mind.

"Not for a long time," he said. "It gets you noticed and there's no need. There're enough living vampires to meet demands." His eyes went to the bar. "Or there were. The undead won't take blood from the ill or young." Cormel looked behind him at the couches and chairs around the long oval coffee table. "Are you going to wake him or let Ulbrine do it?"

"Go on, wake up the lunker," Orchid encouraged. "I want to see his face when he finds himself in a vampire's basement."

Agreeing, Trisk broke the sleep charm with a whispered word of Latin.

Kal snorted awake, his hand immediately going to his face to judge how long he'd been asleep by the thick bristles. Unlike Daniel, he'd gone two days without seeing a razor, and his infant beard made him look surprisingly . . . dashing. Daniel cleared his throat, and Kal's gaze jerked from the high ceiling, stone walls, and thick carpet to the bar where they stood. Trisk's eyes narrowed at his sudden flash of hatred directed at her. Smug, she raised her glass and took a noisy slurp, knowing he had to be parched.

"Where am I?" he rasped, a hand going to his throat as he coughed.

Orchid zipped to him, coming to a short stop that sent a gray dust spilling over him from momentum. "Cincinnati," she said tightly. "Can't you smell the chocolate in the chili?"

Trisk's smile became even more self-satisfied when Kal tugged at the thin band around his wrist, frowning when he realized he couldn't do magic. "Nice," he said, then went still, evaluating Rynn Cormel as the man crossed the room and set a full glass in front of him.

"I'm Rynn Cormel," he said as Kal reached for the lemonade and downed it, his Adam's apple bobbing. "You're in Piscary's living room. Sa'han Ulbrine is in the next room over." Cormel took a step back, his disgust showing in the curve of his lips. "You may want to brush your hair. You'll be giving your account soon. Such as it is."

Kal came up for air, gasping for breath. "They won't believe Trisk over me," he said as he set the glass down. Cormel pointedly moved it to a coaster. "A pixy and a . . ."

"A what?" Trisk said, warming, but it was obvious. A dark elf. Second-class citizen.

"Yeah?" Orchid darted in, wings clattering in outrage when Cormel reached out, caught her foot, and pulled her to safety. "Well, you're troll turds, Kalamack. Troll turds on a stick!"

But the truth of it was, he was right, and Trisk found little comfort in Orchid's outburst.

"It was her tomato, his virus," Kal said as Cormel sat across from him, one leg atop the other knee. "You really think I'd upset the balance intentionally? She's framing me for her ineptitude."

Trisk's grip on her glass tightened, and Daniel took it out of her hand.

"I take it back," Orchid said. "He's a troll turd with maggots in it. No, he's the maggot eating the troll turd."

Cormel halfway hid a smile. "I don't care who started the plague," he said. "Actually, I would shake his or her hand if they were in this room. It's lowered the numbers of humans such that Weres, witches, and even vampires can come out of the closet and not be targeted unduly. Especially if we work together to help our weaker kin." He smiled impishly. "It's my idea, you see. But it will take Piscary to sell it."

Daniel nodded slowly, but Trisk thought it was because coming out would save his life more than anything else.

Kal inched forward to the edge of the couch, clearly wanting to stand and stretch his legs. "You think we should come out?" he said, settling back into the couch when Cormel all but growled at him. "After we decimated their numbers?"

"No, I think *you* should hide," Cormel said lightly. "Hide as the rest of us come out and fix what you broke. The elves *should* take the brunt of humanity's hatred for their mistake. It will enable the rest of us to come out of the shadows and flourish. The enemy of my enemy, yes?"

Kal's eyebrows rose, his doubt obvious. Satisfied, Cormel remained standing before Kal when a set of double doors at the other end of the room opened and the sound of casual conversation slipped in. "Dr. Plank, it might be better if you didn't say anything unless asked a direct question," Cormel said, and the usually outspoken man nodded in agreement.

Trisk couldn't see into the hall, but she slid from her stool when Piscary came in. Kal remained seated until Sa'han Ulbrine followed, tight on his heels, the shorter man darting his gaze about until he found them at the bar, and then Kal on the couch. Kal's shoulders rose in an embarrassed shrug when Ulbrine grimaced at him.

A tall man in an outdated suit from the forties came in after them, looking like an older, drastically more frumpy version of Daniel. He walked with Leo, Piscary's scion, who pushed a bandage-swathed man in a wheelchair. The scholarly man touched Leo's shoulder familiarly in passing as Leo took the injured man to a distant corner and settled him at the outskirts.

Behind them was Colonel Wolfe, with a haughty-looking older woman in a trendy business dress on his arm. The military officer nodded to Daniel, then dismissed him, making Daniel turn red and fume. Trisk knew they'd met only once, and briefly at that, before the government had taken control of his virus and shut him out.

The petite woman beside Colonel Wolfe looked nothing like him, and yet somehow . . . they were a matched pair. Both were in their late forties, both clearly accustomed to giving orders that were taken without question. He had little ribbons and chevrons, and she had high heels and a diamond-covered watch.

"Thank you, Rynn," Piscary said, moving with an eerie, unusual quickness until Cormel cleared his throat and Piscary jerked into a slower pace. "Allow me to make the introductions. This is Professor Thole from Cincy's university."

The tall man who'd come in with Leo adjusted his glasses and lifted a hand as he headed for the bar. "Good morning, everyone," he said, his resonant voice loud, as if addressing an auditorium of restless students.

"He teaches advanced physics of two varieties," Piscary said, sidling between the couches and chairs to give Kal a visual once-over. "Thole does my spell fittings for me, but it's his connections to the witches' coven of moral and ethical standards that bring him here today."

Trisk's eye twitched as Daniel slid down to make room for the taller man behind the bar. The rising scent of redwood said he was a practicing witch of note. Unable to resist, Trisk unfocused her second sight to check his aura, not surprised to find it streaked with black. He played with the dark stuff, and she looked away when he noticed her interest. Relief rose that her aura was clean—her smut for the forget curse now on Kal. Guilt was quick behind it.

Kal took a step toward the bar, only to be shoved back onto the couch by Rynn Cormel.

"And I think everyone knows Colonel Wolfe," Piscary said as Cormel moved to stand right behind Kal to make sure he didn't get up again. "As I understand it, he's been catching holy hell about his new tactical virus that Dr. Kalamack signed off on as being safe."

Kal opened his mouth, shutting it when Cormel cleared his throat.

"That's one way to put it," Wolfe said, going to the bar to take the glass Professor Thole was filling.

"And last but not at all least, the resplendent Mrs. Ray," Piscary said, graciously inviting her to sit. "One of Cincy's own successful businesswomen."

Beaming, the woman gracefully sat in the chair at the head of the low table. "Let's be honest, Piscary. I'm Cincy's *only* successful businesswoman," she said as she coyly played with her pearls, the white orbs seeming to flow like bubbles around the tattoo of a koi on her neck. "But that's going to change. My daughter will soon give the men in the boardroom something to chase." Her head tilted as she accepted the glass that Colonel Wolfe handed her. "Thank you," she said as he settled in to stand behind her, not in protection as much as . . . unity.

"You're Weres," Daniel whispered, then flushed as everyone in the room looked at him, shocked that he'd named them, calling out the truth of their heritage. It was probably the first time they'd heard it spoken aloud so brazenly.

"And you are . . . a human," Mrs. Ray said, a lifetime of hiding making her reluctant to say the words aloud. Expression cross, she turned to Piscary. "You brought us together to witness a minor breaking of the silence? Piscary, we all have full plates right now."

Daniel leaned across the bar to Trisk. "I thought Weres were rough. You know, like bikers and hippies," he whispered, and Trisk cringed.

Mrs. Ray made a delicate snort. "And we have excellent hearing," she said, then added, "The higher your pack status, the more refined you tend to be."

Red-faced at having been overheard, Daniel pulled

himself straighter. "Then you both must be alphas," he said, and Mrs. Ray beamed, clearly liking him.

Wolfe strode forward with a military precision. "I'll do it," he said shortly.

"No!" Trisk slid from the stool, her hand outstretched.

Orchid was suddenly in the air, a dangerous red dust spilling from her. "You go through me, puppy," she said, and the Were stopped short, the threat well taken. Daniel had backed to the shelves of bottles, his face ashen as he stared at the military man's hands, clenched into fists. *What was he going to do? Choke Daniel to death?* Trisk thought. Professor Thole eyed them both, two full shot glasses in hand.

"You are *all* my guests," Piscary said, voice low but demanding. "Wolfe, Dr. Plank is exempt for the moment. If he's to die for having witnessed a breaking of the silence, I claim him as a blood slave. God knows I'm going to need them if this plague continues."

Daniel edged closer. "He's kidding, right?" he asked, and Trisk gave him a sick smile.

Wolfe frowned when Orchid landed on Daniel's shoulder like a tiny lioness protecting her territory. "Why am I here if it is not to maintain the silence?" the colonel asked, sullenly sitting on the end of the couch beside Mrs. Ray when she patted the cushion in invitation.

Piscary sat as well, leaving Rynn Cormel to loom over Kal and Ulbrine on the opposite couch. Professor Thole remained behind the bar with Daniel, arms crossed as he leaned back against the shelves. "I want Inderland to know the truth of where this plague began," Piscary said, and all eyes went to Ulbrine. "Seeing as it landed on my doorstep, I asked you in."

Ulbrine's expression became a study in controlled

anger. "You shouldn't have run, Trisk," he said coldly. "Only the guilty run."

"I wasn't running away," she said, voice even. "I was running toward something."

Kal sat deep in the cushions, his arms defiantly over his chest. "Am I being detained?"

"I prefer to think of you as my guest," Piscary said. "But you will remain until I hear the truth."

Ulbrine pushed himself to the edge of the couch. "I told you what happened," he said irately. "Dr. Kalamack was to check that Dr. Cambri's work made Dr. Plank's tactical virus safe for Inderlanders. Before Kal could tell me his disastrous findings, the virus escaped and spontaneously attached to the tomato she was working on."

"And that's why he signed off on it the day before it went rogue?" Trisk said. "Why he cleared the PTV going to live trials? There was no connection point between Daniel's virus and the T4 Angel until *he* made it," she said, looking at Kal. *Damn it, is that a smirk?*

"Clearly she gave Dr. Plank's virus the same attachment points as her tomato," Ulbrine continued, ignoring her. "Cutting corners and resulting in the plague we're now forced to deal with. It was an error, but an innocent one."

"Bull pucky!" Trisk exploded. "Kal intentionally made a bridge between our two products. I could tell you how if he hadn't destroyed my lab and all the evidence."

Ulbrine spread his hands to the assembled Inderland representatives. "Clearly she shouldn't have been allowed to work without supervision. But she's a good researcher and I'm sure she'll work to see an end to the plague. I apologize for her lack of experience. It was my fault. I put her in that position."

You little bastard, she thought, seething as Daniel reached across the bar and she pushed his calming hand from her.

Professor Thole was sourly eyeing Trisk over his glasses. "You allowed a tactical virus to attach to your tomato? That is a stupid error."

Furious, Trisk took a breath to tell them all to go to hell, her words catching when Rynn put a finger to his lips. Slowly she exhaled, no less angry but trusting his half-hidden smile.

"Trisk is telling the truth," Orchid said, and Kal's eyes shot murderously to the pixy. "I was there when Kal made the bridge between the virus and tomato."

Ulbrine stiffened in the sudden silence. Orchid's wings turned pink as she blushed at everyone's eyes on her. "I don't fly in your garden anymore, Kalamack," she said, bobbing up and down to make her dress waft. "You told me you wanted to prove her work was dangerous and yours was safe. If you cared about what was safe, you wouldn't have promised Saladan you'd give him manufacture and distribution of Trisk's other work."

"He did *what!*" Trisk exclaimed.

"You did it to hurt her, Kal," Orchid said, her dust so bright it was hard to look at. "To help yourself, not help your people."

"You're going to take the word of a pixy over mine?" Ulbrine said, but he was sweating, and Piscary casually reached out, catching Orchid's foot as she flew murderously at Ulbrine. Fuming, she backwashed in her own dust, shrilling at Piscary to let her go.

Ulbrine stood, his expression drawn. "Release Dr. Cambri into my custody. I'll see about beginning to mend this," he said, but the Weres had their heads together, whispering, and Professor Thole's lips were pursed in thought as he stood behind the bar with Daniel.

"I have a doubt," Piscary said, voice mocking and low.

"The proof was destroyed in the fire. A fire *she* set," Ulbrine said, and Kal stood, only to be shoved back down by Rynn Cormel.

"This is outrageous!" Ulbrine said, fuming when Piscary's brown eyes flashed black. "I demand you release Dr. Kalamack and Dr. Cambri to me."

"Demand?" Piscary said, so still on the couch that he didn't look real anymore.

Ulbrine's eyes narrowed, and Trisk stiffened as she felt the enclave member tap a line.

"Perhaps you're right," Piscary said, and Daniel exhaled at the visible easing of tension in not only Ulbrine, but the Weres and Cormel. From behind the bar, Professor Thole fingered a worn ley line charm. "I was dearly hoping to avoid this," Piscary continued, "but as you say, the evidence of who tampered with the connection points between the species was destroyed in a fire. I have no problem with the testimony of a pixy, but others will."

"Thank you, Piscary," Orchid said primly, flying back to sit on Daniel's shoulder.

"Then you release them to me?" Ulbrine asked, his smile faltering when Piscary's attention went to the far corner of the room.

"Rick?" the master vampire called, and Trisk's eyes shot to the bandaged man in the wheelchair. Her jaw went slack as she remembered what Niles had said when he tried to burn them alive in her truck. *My God, Rick was burned into his second life?* Undead vampires did not feel love, but they did feel pain.

Ulbrine sat down fast, his expression empty as Leo wheeled the bandaged man forward.

"Rick?" Daniel said, and the figure shifted a wrapped hand up in acknowledgment. "The news said you were dead!"

"I am," Rick rasped, and Trisk blanched when a weird, wispy burbling rose up. He was laughing. "I am," he continued, the awful noise gurgling to nothing. "Kal burned me alive when I realized he'd tampered with the Angel tomato and Dr. Plank's PTV. He hid within his circle when fire dripped from the ceiling like liquid sun. He watched me burn, and did nothing."

Trisk shuddered when the white-wrapped figure turned to Kal, the hunger and hatred behind the bandages easy to see. The black orbs rimmed by red didn't even look like his eyes anymore. "You think your journey here was painful?" Rick rasped, his beautiful voice gone. "Perhaps someday I will thank you for moving me to my second life. But not today."

Professor Thole's fingers began to drum on the bar. Ulbrine began to distance himself from Kal, and seeing it, Piscary frowned. "I'm sorry, Rick. Thank you," Piscary said as he gestured for Leo to take him out.

Rick's eerie, rasping laughter hissed over them all, and Daniel turned to Piscary, his face white. "Is he going to be okay?"

Piscary seemed surprised by the question. "It remains to be seen. His insurance will be sufficient to set him up safely from the sun, but he has no scion to see to his other needs. If he does not find one soon, the blood he takes from my family will no longer support him. He can't hope to win his own scion while burned. It was an ill-timed death. Niles is most upset."

Orchid's wings clattered as she rose up and down,

landing herself on the sugar packets. "See?" she said as she helped herself, apparently feeling as if she deserved it now. "I told you! But does anyone listen to a pixy? No-o-o-o. We're apparently too small to have a brain."

Ulbrine stood, his expression haunted as he watched Rick slowly rolling away. "I knew nothing of this," he said, and Professor Thole scoffed. "Kal, I'm disappointed."

With an ugly snarl, Kal leaped at Ulbrine. Rynn Cormel was faster, yanking Kal back into the cushions and pinning him there with a ring-bedecked hand as Ulbrine backed up, appalled. "You hypocritical bastard," Kal seethed, but Trisk was having a hard time finding any joy in it. Ulbrine had been using them both, betraying Kal now to try to save his own skin.

Ulbrine edged farther away, and the Weres gave the elven dignitary a disgusted look. "This is the first I've heard of this atrocity," Ulbrine insisted, but clearly no one was buying it. "You have my apologies."

A high laugh chortled out as the door closed behind Rick. Kal pushed Cormel's hand off, hatred in his eyes as he stared at first Ulbrine and then Trisk. Even as relief filled Trisk, it left a tiny spot of worry that began to grow. This wasn't over yet.

"So," Ulbrine said, his voice holding a forced joviality, "if you'll allow us. Dr. Cambri, Dr. Kalamack, and I need to get to a lab and figure out how to stop the plague."

"Burn the Angel tomato fields," Trisk said, having no intention of going anywhere with him. "Destroy all products made from it. This year's. Last year's. Everything. When there's no more carrier, the virus will die. In the interim, don't eat them. That's it. I made sure

Dr. Plank's virus couldn't kill an Inderlander, even with a massive overdose."

Piscary's hands were steepled, his attention fixed on Ulbrine as the man scrambled to find a way to come out of this without smelling like dung.

Professor Thole shook his head. "Are you saying the plague began because of an elven power play?" he said, both hands flat on the bar as he leaned over it. "Half the human race dead or dying, us on the verge of being exposed, all because of an elf's greed? Please tell me you wouldn't allow an entire species to vanish to hide the blame of one man?" He looked at Ulbrine. "Or is it two?"

Still on the stool, Trisk put her back to the bar, feeling confident with Daniel behind her. "In Kal's defense, I truly believe his only intention was to discredit my work so he could claim my other research. I don't believe he wanted to start a plague. It was an accident due to his impatience and using species he was unfamiliar with. If he's guilty of anything, other than Rick's murder, it's pride."

Kal turned his anger from Ulbrine to her, and she wondered if she'd gone too far. The only thing worse than starting a plague on purpose was being stupid enough to start it by accident. And Kal would rather be thought of as ruthless than ignorant. Professor Thole, though, was nodding. Trisk could almost hear his thoughts: *Foolish, prideful elves. It wasn't on purpose. It was an accident.*

"This is beyond reason, Ulbrine," Colonel Wolfe said. "I call for your abdication from the enclave."

Ulbrine's eye twitched. Behind her, Professor Thole sucked in his breath as if slapped. Trisk's knees buckled as someone—probably Ulbrine—yanked on the nearest ley line, taking in a huge amount of energy.

"Down!" she shouted, shoving Daniel, who fell whooping to the floor behind the bar. Orchid flew away, inking a black dust. Daniel rose up, shocked to find himself safe with Professor Thole behind his circle. Pulling hard on the line, Trisk took a breath to invoke her own protection circle. She was Ulbrine's largest thorn. It was her his magic would come for.

Then Ulbrine was on her, shoving her into her still-forming barrier, breaking it.

"Get off!" she cried as they hit the floor together, then gasped as she slammed into the inside of his larger circle. She slumped, Ulbrine half on her. His eyes shone with hate, and his hands went around her throat. She was trapped in here with him, a master of elven magic.

"You fool," he rasped, and she screamed as pain arced into her, becoming her entire world. "You will all die here, and everything will go on as before."

"Aaaaaaaaagh," she gasped, clawing at the hands around her neck, the gold of her necklace feeling like ice against her fingertips. She couldn't say a spell, couldn't even think one, the pain was so bad. He was an expert of what she dabbled in, and she could do nothing. "Gallllllaak," she tried again, eyes bulging. Black sparkles gathered at the edges of her sight, threatening to swamp her. Pain and a lack of air were going to kill her. Behind Ulbrine, she could see Rynn Cormel hammering on the barrier, but nothing would come through. It was strong enough to hold a demon.

Demon . . . It might be too late. The sun could be up. With a desperate need, she stopped trying to fight, patting passively at his hand as if wanting to speak. And like the proud fool he was, he eased up, letting a slip of air into her. "What?" he said as she sucked in the air gratefully in huge gasps.

Eyes watering, she looked up at Ulbrine's self-satisfied smirk, wishing she could tell Daniel to go hide somewhere. It was going to get really ugly in here really fast. "Algaliarept," she rasped, and Ulbrine's eyes widened. "I summon you."

36

Ulbrine's hands sprang away from her neck. Horrified, his gaze went to the barrier over his head and back to reassure himself it was still there and that a demon wasn't materializing in it with them. "Y-you . . ." he stammered, clearly knowing she had summoned a demon without a protection circle. "What have you done?"

Eyes watering, she sucked in air. His aura-tainted barrier hummed so strongly, it was almost an ache in her skull. "Probably killed us all," she rasped, hand on her throat. The sun would be up soon. All she had to do was survive until Algaliarept was pulled back across the lines—unless the sun was already up and it was too late.

But with an almost inaudible pop, a dark blot materialized in the center of the room.

Trisk sat up, her skull and back tingling where they'd touched the inside of Ulbrine's barrier. Above her, Rynn Cormel straightened. The barstool in his hand slowly touched the floor, no longer hammering on Ulbrine's circle. Orchid hovered above him, and Trisk followed the pixy's attention to the haze sending out tendrils of smoke as if searching for the limits of its prison.

"Mother pus bucket," a gray voice echoed into the silent room. "I am . . . loosed?"

"Stop!" Professor Thole jerked Daniel close, as if he might break the circle they were in.

"Hey!" Daniel shouted, his word of affront seeming to ripple through the haze of nothing in the center of the room, pushing it into something that almost had a shape.

"I am loosed!" a voice boomed, and as the Weres backed into a corner, the black swirled, grew, and became . . . a demon. "Felecia Eloytrisk Cambri!" The grotesque form had goat-slitted red eyes. They were the only thing she recognized. "Have you called me to bargain?"

Orchid's dust turned a frightened black, and the pixy darted to hide in the ornately carved hearth surrounding the fireplace. "My God," Trisk whispered. Algaliarept's form had no skin, the striated red muscles bulking up and relaxing as he watched the Weres scramble for cover. She'd never seen him in this guise, but it was obvious it was Algaliarept.

"You should be so lucky," Algaliarept said, but his attention shifted when Piscary rose, Rynn Cormel ghosting to stand at the old vampire's side. Flat, blocky teeth grinned with ill intent as Algaliarept breathed deeply, nothing but a homespun loincloth between him and the rest of the world as his flayed body leaked blood to pool on the floor.

"No one summons me free of a circle and survives to see another sunrise this side of the ley lines," Algaliarept said, and Trisk's nose wrinkled at the reek of burnt amber.

"Hold, ancient worm!" Piscary all but hissed. "You may be immortal, but even a god dies without his head."

"I have no issue with you, vampire. Let me take my prey and go," Algaliarept said, a haze coating him for a brief instant. It soaked in to leave elegantly embroidered linen and a dusky skin, taut with a wiry strength. His head expanded, a muzzle and pointy ears forming. With a shaking shudder, the Egyptian god Anubis stood in Piscary's living room. The jackal-headed monstrosity licked his long muzzle, a throaty laugh bubbling up and over sharp teeth.

Piscary growled, the elegant man vanishing under a thousand years of instinct. Hunched, his hands made into claws, he advanced with an unreal grace. Hate scented the air with vampire incense. Behind him, the Weres began creeping to the door.

Algaliarept followed Kal's attention to them. His long face split into a tongue-lolling wolf grin. "*Lentus*," he said, his voice thunderously low, brushing the edges of the audible range, like an elephant's inaudible rumble.

"Move!" Colonel Wolfe shouted, forming a living front as Mrs. Ray bolted.

"Look out!" Trisk shouted, and the woman turned, her eyes wide in panic as she slid to the floor, her heels hitting the door as a black ball of loosed energy hissed over them. It slammed into the old oak panel, and a black goo spread, creeping out as if alive.

Colonel Wolfe exclaimed in disgust, the sound evolving into a high-pitched howl as he brushed at his front. A drop of black had hit him, and it had begun to burn.

The demon's laugh seemed to push upon the very air, darkening it in bands of ripples spreading from him in waves. Licking the spittle from his lips, Algaliarept turned to the undead vampire and performed an elegant bow of invitation.

With a silent fury, Piscary leaped at him, a long hand snagging a floor lamp even as he was in the air. It swung in a fast arc, smacking into Algaliarept's raised palm when the demon put his entire hand over Piscary's face. Still laughing, he shoved the vampire across the room.

Cormel was half a second behind, the cord from the lamp in his hand. As Algaliarept watched Piscary skid across the floor and slam into the wall, Cormel spun the cord around the demon's thick neck, wedging it above the elaborate collar of gold and stones.

Snarling, Piscary launched himself at the jackal-headed god, bowling him over with his sheer will. They hit the floor, crashing into the coffee table and shattering it. Standing above them, Cormel tightened the cord, trying to strangle the demon.

Trisk stood. Ulbrine's circle hummed over her head. Choking the demon wouldn't work. Algaliarept need only vaporize and reappear.

"What were you thinking?" Ulbrine said. "You killed them, all of them. God knows why. Help me hold my circle until the sun rises."

She stared at him, lips parted. "Why do you think I summoned him?"

Ulbrine froze, fear widening his eyes. "You summoned him to make a trade? With me?" he said, and she recoiled, amazed he could think her so foul. Her intention had been to create a distraction to get his hands off her neck. Surely a member of the enclave, a professor at the university, and an undead master could together dispatch a demon. But seeing the horror and sudden fear on Ulbrine's face, she knew she'd made a mistake.

"A trade?" Algaliarept said, and Cormel called out a warning as the demon was suddenly not under him anymore, having dissolved into a gray fog that solidified behind the vampire.

"We can work something out!" Ulbrine shouted in fear, still believing her intent had been to give him to the demon. But his attention jerked behind her, and he ducked when Rynn Cormel crashed into the bar beside them.

Now you want to work something out? she thought bitterly. *Coward.*

"Stay in your circle!" Professor Thole exclaimed as Cormel put a hand to his head and fell down, unconscious. Beyond them, Piscary wrestled with the Egyptian god, Algaliarept's jaws snapping inches from the incensed vampire's face as they rolled into tables and artwork.

"Fight!" Orchid shrilled, darting in and out, her tiny sword scoring on the jackal-headed god and making Algaliarept snap at her like a dog. "All of you! Alone you will be picked off. Attack together, or we all die! Has peace made you so tame that you've forgotten how to battle?"

Grunting, Algaliarept shoved Piscary from him and swatted at Orchid. The vampire howled as he flew across the room. Arms splayed, he hit a chandelier before falling to the floor. Piscary levered himself up, dazed as he slipped back down to one knee, struggling to focus.

"You summoned me for a trade?" Algaliarept said. "Mar-r-r-rvelous!" The demon dissolved into a mist that re-formed as his usual crushed green velvet frock and blue-tinted glasses. He eagerly paced forward, peering at Ulbrine cowering behind Trisk. "A member of the enclave?" he rumbled, tugging his white gloves tighter. "I amend my earlier words. I misjudged the depth of your determination, Felecia Eloytrisk Cambri."

Trisk's own fear swelled. She wanted to survive, yes, but she didn't want to be known as a demon practitioner to have done it. She'd be a pariah among her people. There was a beating at the door as Piscary's children tried to get in, and then more screams when that black goo slipped through the cracks and began to burn whoever it touched.

"Well?" Algaliarept asked Trisk, and she blanched. "I must hear the words, little bird."

"I didn't summon you to take him. I . . ."

Algaliarept's thin lips curved into a smile as he looked at the imprint of Ulbrine's fingers on her neck. "Are you sure?"

Why isn't the sun up yet? Behind him, Orchid darted to Professor Thole and Daniel for a whispered conversation, her dust pooling on the surface of Thole's circle.

"Shove him into his circle and give the worthless sod to me," Algaliarept said, not looking as he flicked a sparkly ribbon of black at Piscary. It wound around the vampire, tripping him to the floor, where he writhed and cursed in what sounded like Hebrew. "I promise you'll be . . . safe." Algaliarept grinned, tapping on the circle between them to make dimples of stress ripple out. Ulbrine's hand tightened on her arm. "Or don't you trust me?" The demon's eyebrows were high as he looked at them over his glasses, a curious quirk to his expression. Checking his watch, Algaliarept tugged the lace at his sleeves out. "I'll even make sure your name gets on your research."

"In return for Ulbrine?" she said, and Ulbrine's grip on her arm tingled from the force of the ley line he was channeling. "It hardly sounds fair. You wanted my soul before."

Algaliarept snickered as he turned to look behind

him at Kal and the Weres. "Black suits you, my dear. Suits you so very well. Giving me the worm beside you will make you halfway again to being mine, soul included. Think of it as me letting the fruit mature on the vine. And in the meantime, I can pay my rent."

"Dr. Cambri," Professor Thole whispered in horror, and Trisk's face warmed even as she denied the jolt of knowing he might think she could do such a thing. To do such evil was a power in itself.

"So . . . do we have a deal?" Algaliarept gave Piscary a sideways glance to make sure the vampire was unmoving before turning back to her, his goat-slitted red eyes eager. Orchid was with Piscary, whispering in the old vampire's ear. "Tick-tock." Algaliarept brushed the lace at his throat. His gaze landed on his gloved hand and the dull gold ring on it. "The sun waits for neither vampire nor demon."

"Don't you dare," Ulbrine said, sweating.

"Why not?" she snapped, and Algaliarept smiled. "You tried to choke me to death so no one could stop you from blaming Daniel for the plague Kal started. How is giving you to a demon less horrific than you two killing a quarter of the world's population?"

Ulbrine brought his darting gaze back from Kal. "They're just humans!" he said, truly mystified.

"What the hell?" Daniel said indignantly, red spots of anger showing on his pale face.

Algaliarept winked at Trisk's outrage, then spun, the clatter of pixy wings giving him warning. Piscary and Rynn Cormel attacked together, their savage rage tempered with a plan.

"Now, Thole!" Piscary shouted, and the professor stepped from his circle, a globe of green-tinted power in his hand.

"Abrie!" the high-magic user shouted, and Algaliarept bellowed, flinging Cormel at the witch. But the spell was away, and it hit Algaliarept square in the chest. The demon rocked back, laughing gleefully, head shaking to make his hair fly out as he absorbed what would probably kill anyone else.

"You, little witch, have potential. I will put in a library with your sale," Algaliarept said even as he swung a thick fist at Rynn Cormel, now on his feet and lunging across the bar. The living vampire saw it coming, dropping to the floor so it skimmed harmlessly overhead as Orchid shrilled a battle call from the ceiling. Cormel flipped to his feet, but Algaliarept was gone, having vaulted over the bar for Professor Thole.

"Back!" Thole shoved Daniel behind him and out of the way. *"Rhombus!"* the witch shouted, and Algaliarept bellowed in frustrated anger as Thole's circle sprang up anew, this time with Algaliarept inside it.

"No!" Algaliarept shouted in frustration, a red mist sweeping the floor for any crack, any conduit out. The circle had been drawn in haste, but it had been drawn by a master, and as Algaliarept gave up and coalesced down to a sullen, angry demon, Thole collapsed to lean against the bar, his hand trembling.

"Save me from fools," the witch said as his eyes found Trisk's.

Algaliarept wasn't fighting the barrier, but she'd never seen him so angry. "You shouldn't have tried to kill me . . . Sa'han," she said bitterly, then shoved Ulbrine into his circle.

The barrier dropped and Ulbrine moved away from her, unknown thoughts circling behind his furrowed brow. Trisk's nose wrinkled. The room reeked of burnt amber, and pixy dust hazed the lights. Daniel rose up from behind the bar, fumbling backward until he found his way out. White-faced, he took Trisk's arm, pulling her farther away from Algaliarept, who was fuming in a silent rage. "Thanks, Orchid," he whispered, and the tired pixy dropped down onto his shoulder.

"You all just needed someone to take charge," she said, her dust a pale orange.

"Banish him," Professor Thole said wearily, his lips twisted into a wry grimace. "Unless you intend to give all of us to him."

"That's not why I summoned him," Trisk said. Turning to Algaliarept, she took a shaky breath. The demon's silence held more threat than his gleeful raging. "Demon," she said, not wanting to say his name aloud again, "I banish you to the ever-after."

"Indeed," Algaliarept said dryly. "I will be back for you, Felecia Eloytrisk Cambri."

With an inrushing pop of air, he vanished. Trisk shuddered at his last words, but as she looked at the shaken, relieved faces around her, it seemed only she heard them. Even the Weres coming out from behind the couch seemed oblivious. "It was never my intent to give Ulbrine to him," she said as she stumbled to the nearest chair and collapsed into it. Her gut hurt, and her neck still felt the grip of fingers around it. "I'm not a practitioner."

"You are a foul guest," Piscary intoned, and she looked up, eyes widening as the master vampire rose from beside a dazed Rynn Cormel.

"You always let your guests kill one another?" she said, then gasped, adrenaline a pulse of fear as Piscary launched himself at her. "Hey!" she managed, and then he was on her, pinning her to the chair.

"You are a foul guest," he repeated, his canines inches

from her cheek. He held her shoulder down, his fingers twined in her hair to pull her head back and expose her neck. She held her breath, terrified. His eyes were dead black, and an odd tingling coursed through her, desire and fear all mixed up into one heated emotion that threatened to overwhelm her.

"I . . ." she managed before her thoughts turned to blind terror when his weight pressed deeper. The Weres were shouting, and Daniel, too. Orchid's dust was sifting over them, the sparkles seeming to prick like fire. "Please," she managed, thinking fast. "He's a gift."

"Gift?" Piscary snarled. "You gift me with filth? Filth you brought into my home?"

"Piscary!" Cormel exclaimed. "Not now. Not like this!"

"She brought abomination," Piscary said, and Trisk got a clean breath of air when he looked away. "She opened the door, invited him in."

I did not survive one nut job to die at the hands of another, she thought. "He's a gift! A gift!" she tried again, becoming breathless when Piscary's eyes found hers again. "You heard his name," she said, sure she was on the right path when Piscary's grip eased. "You can summon him. Contain him with witch magic." It took everything she had, but she looked away from Piscary to Professor Thole. "Yes?" she said, and it seemed as if Piscary's weight on her grew less. "There's an earth-magic circle that he can invoke himself to contain a demon."

Professor Thole nodded, his gaze troubled.

"He's a gift," she echoed once more as the hunger in Piscary was replaced by thought. "You have a demon. He will grovel before you, and you can give him information for favors or information in turn. You'll be the first vampire to have one. Ever."

For three heartbeats she met his black eyes, waiting. Almost imperceptibly, his pupils shrank, and she couldn't help her gasp when he was suddenly not there. "A gift," Piscary said, and she sat up in the chair, shaking at how close it had been. "Write his name down lest I forget."

Nodding, she stood, no longer comfortable in the chair. Her knees wobbly, she cast about for Daniel. He always had a notebook and pen on him. Seeing him by the bar beside Professor Thole, she walked over, hand protectively on her middle. *Will I ever see the sun again?*

"A gift?" Daniel said as he handed her his palm-size spiral notebook.

Orchid hovered close, and Trisk let her stay, knowing the pixy wouldn't know how to read. It took three tries for the pen to work, and Trisk stared at her shaky handwriting. It didn't even look like hers. Resigned, she ripped the page free and folded it over to hide the print.

"Give it to me," Rynn Cormel said, and Trisk pulled the paper closer. The man arched his eyebrows. "You smell like a melty chocolate chip cookie right now. He put you back on the counter untasted once. He won't do so again. Stay here. I'll give it to him."

Trisk glanced at Piscary, reading the truth in those words by the stiff way he was holding himself apart from everyone. "Thank you," she said as she gave Cormel the note. "Tell him I apologize for the way I introduced him to the demon, but at least now he knows what he's dealing with and will be careful enough to survive."

Rynn Cormel tapped the paper against his other palm, glancing between her and Daniel, Orchid now back on the man's shoulder. "I can't decide if you're serious, or if you're trying to kill him." Head high, Cormel headed for Piscary, stopping to talk to the Weres on the couch to give the undead vampire more time to find his self-control.

Daniel exhaled, taking her elbow as he helped Trisk onto the high barstool. "Are you okay?" he asked, and she stifled a bitter laugh.

"Peachy," she said, feeling her throat. It was raw and sore, and she thought it might be time to make a new life plan, one that didn't include demons, or crazy peers, or even crazier superiors. Ulbrine could still try to blame her for everything.

Eyes narrowed, she looked over the room, not seeing him. "Where's Ulbrine?"

"Ah . . ." Daniel hesitated as he looked over the room as well. "Kal is gone, too."

"How did they get out?" Thole said, looking up from a narrow glass full of something amber colored. Trisk assumed it wasn't iced tea.

"There," Daniel said, pointing to one of the narrow side doors, just now swinging closed. It was then that the large oak doors covered in black goo splintered apart and a handful of distressed vampires spilled in, all fire and spit. Piscary turned his back on them and shook, not because he didn't care, although he didn't, but because he couldn't handle the emotional outflow. Clearly knowing it, Rynn Cormel hastened to cut them off, bundling them back into the hall. Trisk was amazed they did as they were told, like children. *But that's what they are, in essence.*

The hallway grew quiet, and Cormel returned, looking as if he didn't know what to do. He wasn't Piscary's scion, but he had enough clout that the lesser members of Piscary's house would listen. "Perhaps you should have given Ulbrine to the demon," Rynn Cormel muttered, and Piscary turned. Seeing the master vampire's questioning look, he added, "Someone has to be blamed for the silence being broken. If he's in the ever-after, he can't refute it."

Colonel Wolfe stood, tugging his uniform down. "The silence isn't broken," he said, his gaze going to Daniel. "Not beyond repair."

Orchid clattered her wings, not rising up from Daniel's shoulder. "No one is touching Daniel," she said, and Wolfe's eyes narrowed.

Rynn Cormel rose from having helped Piscary into a chair. The slip of paper with Algaliarept's name on it was in his hand, and Piscary tucked it in his suit coat pocket.

"Killing Daniel won't stop the silence from breaking," Cormel said, his smile soothing. "Humans will survive the plague in numbers too high to ignore, too low to not protect. As Dr. Cambri has observed, they're realizing immunity runs in family lines. They will find out why soon enough. That we are not human."

Professor Thole was shaking his head. "I don't want to come out," he said, taking a gulp from his glass. "We tried that once. It didn't work. They all but destroyed us."

Mrs. Ray came to the bar as well, nervously tucking her hair back in place. "Just as many humans were killed as you witches."

Professor Thole scowled as he reached for a bottle to top his glass off with. "When your family is burned at the stake, we'll talk."

Rynn Cormel took the bottle out of Professor Thole's hand and returned it to the shelf. "We should come out now, before we are forced out," he persuaded in his thick Bronx accent. "It's a singularly unique opportunity to gain humans' trust as we help them, earn a debt of gratitude that will rub out their fears, both imagined and real." He turned to Piscary. The vampire was still sitting across from Trisk, his frown puzzling, as it had been his idea to break the silence in the first place.

"Some humans may choose immortality to escape the plague," Cormel added, and Piscary's frown deepened. "A welcome relief for us seeing to the needs of the undead."

Mrs. Ray waggled her finger as she perched on the barstool. "No, no, no," the petite woman said as if she hadn't been cowering behind the couch just minutes previous. "I see your intent, Piscary, and you won't be allowed to increase your numbers. Adding human-based ghouls to your population is a short-term solution that will create a larger problem in the future. If humanity's numbers are dropping, you will be expected to take a loss as well."

Piscary grimaced, and Trisk felt a new danger rise. The population balance between witches, Weres, and vampires had been fairly stable for thousands of years, but every time it wobbled, there was a war until it equalized again.

"I agree with Mrs. Ray," Wolfe said, staring mournfully at his empty shot glass before pushing it to the center of the bar. "Piscary, I understand your predicament, and if there was something we could do, we would. No one wants your people to suffer, but the health of your old ones won't be given priority over the well-being of the rest of Inderland."

Gaze distant, Piscary shook his head. "There will be no population bubble. Only those born as vampires make the leap to the undead with no help. The subclass of human ghouls created to get us through this crisis will die when their masters fail to elevate them. Even so, I worry that this is only a slow decline, the beginning of a new era of madness."

Professor Thole was rummaging for more alcohol. "There are too many maybes," he said, affronted when Rynn Cormel took the new bottle out of his hand and put it back on the shelf. "If we come out, the laws preventing human takes will become human laws, and we all know how humans love their litigation."

Piscary idly motioned that Thole could have the bottle, and Cormel smacked it back into the professor's hand. "What do you suggest?" Piscary asked. "We're between a rock and a cliff."

"I have an idea," Trisk said, and Wolfe started.

"The elf speaks," he said dryly, the crack of the bottle's seal loud as it broke.

"And you should listen," Orchid said, making Rynn Cormel hide a smile.

Seeing Piscary gesture for her to continue, Trisk tugged her tired T-shirt straight. "Seems to me all you need is a drug that increases metabolism and blood production so one living vampire, a scion, could supply their newly undead master with enough blood so they don't have to go into a new, possibly dangerous blood pool."

"A drug?" Piscary shocked Trisk with his intent gaze. "You can do this?"

"Me? No," she said, and he frowned. "But Kal can," Trisk added, not liking that the dweeb stood to make a fortune from this. "One of the compounds he used in his graduate thesis increased blood production to the point where it was a detriment. I'd be willing to bet he could work from that, making a product that would allow one or two living vampires to safely supply a master with enough blood."

"That works for me," Mrs. Ray said, eyeing Professor Thole right back when he stared at her in betrayal. "I say we come out," she said as she proffered her shot glass and he filled it. "As long as the elves provide a metabolism booster to the vampires."

"You're serious?" Professor Thole said flatly.

"Why not?" She sipped her drink with an appreciative *mmmm*. "Are you telling me the media campaign you've been waging the last twenty years was for nothing? All that positive PR you've been pumping into Hollywood was so you could remain hidden? Cormel is right. It's time. They aren't ignorant savages anymore." She looked at Daniel, her smile bright. "And neither are we. They need help, and as Dr. Plank exhibits, they're willing to accept it and us."

Professor Thole shook his head, and on Daniel's shoulder, Orchid clattered her wings, frustrated. "I've been out there," Daniel said, his voice almost bland after the rich tones of the Weres and vampires. "They're hurting, and they won't care if help comes in the form of a witch spell or a neighbor who can turn into a wolf on the way to get you some groceries."

Unconvinced, Professor Thole capped the bottle and put it away. "You're only trying to save your skin," he muttered.

"Are you blind?" Orchid shrilled, startling Daniel as she rose up on a column of bright silver sparkles. Even Piscary turned to look. "Listen to me, you lunkers. Breaking the silence is likely the only chance for my people to survive. I've been everywhere the last three weeks, and I have yet to find a mate. It's because we have to hide. It's killing us one species at a time. The only people flourishing since the industrial revolution are those who can pretend to *be* human. That's not living. It's not even surviving anymore. It's our world, too."

Colonel Wolfe made a low growl of discontent. "Do you realize how difficult it would be to get a consensus from all the various Inderlanders? In time to be useful?"

"Do you know how hard it will be to remain hidden?" Trisk countered. "Because it's coming out whether you like it or not. Thanks to the plague, our combined numbers are now greater than theirs. They're shaken, looking for a way out of the madness. Unless you *want* to destroy Cincinnati, New York, Boston, the entire world? How many Detroits do you think Inderlanders will put up with before they rebel against their own leaders?"

But clearly both Professor Thole and Wolfe refused to budge, and Trisk's hope faltered. If she couldn't convince them, there'd be no hope of convincing any others. They had to come out of this room united.

"I think we can all agree that elves have made a shitfest out of this," Cormel said, and Trisk frowned. "The question is, can we turn the dire prospect of the faltering human species into a boon? Can we find the courage to be the monster and save them?" Hands spread wide, he smiled with a professional warmth that said all would be well. Much of it was his vampire charisma, but Trisk didn't care since it wasn't being used against her. "The question is simple," he said, hands falling. "Do we break the silence to save humanity, or let their numbers drop even more due to secondary diseases and throw them and us into a new dark age?"

Eyes averted, Professor Thole set his empty glass in the sink as Colonel Wolfe sat down, a grim expression on his face.

"Oh, for God's sake," Orchid said, startling Trisk as

she flew from her. "Don't be so scared of the wasp in the room. Not everyone has to come out. If a family wants to remain in hiding, they can, continuing to masquerade as human. God knows you've gotten good at it."

The silence grew, and Trisk fidgeted as Piscary looked at each one in turn, his eyes narrowing when they landed on Professor Thole.

"Fine," the witch finally said, and emotion zinged through Trisk. "I'll inform the coven of moral and ethical standards what has passed here along with whose fault this really is. They can decide. I still think it's a mistake."

Beaming, Trisk gave Daniel's hand a tight squeeze. They'd done it. Or at least half of it.

Mrs. Ray slipped from the stool, her pace confident as she went to collect her purse, inclining her head in good-bye to Piscary and drawing Wolfe to his feet. "Wonderful. Wolfe will get a consensus from his superiors. If the military Weres agree—and I know they will if Wolfe puts his mind to it—the business community will follow. As for myself, I'm eager to stretch into a run without having to go to Montana or the Canadian woods to do it."

Rynn Cormel looked to Piscary. The master vamp dismissed him with a finger twitch, and the living vampire hesitated only briefly, an unknown thought flitting behind his eyes before he hid it with an expansive smile. "I admire your logic, Miss Orchid," Cormel said as he came forward to leave Piscary in his chair. "Would you accompany me to DC? I have to bring this to the Columbia vamps for approval and immediate action. They can make a decision for the entire vampire state, and you'll have one more garden to look for a husband in."

Orchid glanced at Daniel, clearly loath to leave him,

as she'd taken on the responsibility for his continued safety. But when he nodded, the tiny woman rose up on green and gold dust. "You bet, short-fang," she said cheerfully, circling the man in a maddening circle until he made a grab for her and she darted out of reach with a little giggle.

"What about the elves?" Professor Thole asked as he came out from behind the bar. "I doubt they'll approve."

Piscary stirred, breaking his eerie stillness. "As it is their fault, I suggest we all agree to uphold that they're dead at the hands of the virus they created." The master vampire looked at Trisk, and she shrugged. They'd been in hiding for two thousand years. It was a small thing.

Professor Thole shook the master vampire's hand. "I hope this works," Thole said as their hands parted. "I know you face a difficult choice."

A flat smile crossed Piscary's face. "Thank you. Could you stop in next week?"

He'd need a powerful charm to contain Algaliarept, and the tall witch nodded, uneasy as he glanced at Trisk. "I will. Until then, be well, old friend."

Piscary dismissed him with a wave, and Professor Thole left, taking the Weres, Rynn Cormel, and Orchid with him. "I can't believe you want this," Wolfe said loudly as they picked their way past the broken door and into the hall, and Mrs. Ray laughed.

"My dear Wolfe," she said, her arm possessively on his, "if vampires are reliant upon a drug for their well-being, that will be as sure of a population check as we have ever had."

Piscary grimaced, the old vampire knowing it as well. And yet he was still for it. A drug would allow them to set aside the mantle of predator, a must if vamps were to make the jump from the shadows to polite society.

Feeling as if they needed to go as well, Trisk took Daniel's elbow and drew him to his feet. "We should find a radio station," she said, eager to be gone and back under an open sky. The sooner they could start telling people how to avoid getting sick, the better.

Daniel glanced back at Piscary, the old vampire preoccupied by his own thoughts. "So much for my career. You know anyone hiring?"

She sighed, too tired to even chuckle. Too tired, and too depressed. The need to publicly announce that it was her tomatoes causing the plague was both an itch and a fear. It would cast a shadow on not just her future, but her past. It wasn't her fault, but she'd never work in a lab again. "Sorry about the mess," she said as she stepped carefully through the chunks of door, her mind already on how to find a way out of here. Perhaps Leo could drive them.

"Where are you going?" Piscary said, and she and Daniel froze, the hallway feet away.

"Ah, to find a radio station," Trisk said, exchanging a worried glance with Daniel. Piscary's pupils had widened to a thick black, and she stifled a twitch when he stood in a smooth motion, buttoning his coat and running a hand over his clean-shaven skull.

"You misunderstand," he said as he ghosted forward. "We do not come out, and no mention of the T4 Angel plague will be announced, until we find Dr. Kalamack and he agrees to provide us with a drug that allows one scion to supply a master with enough blood for a chance at immortality." He looked at her pointedly. "I hope you have a firm will, Dr. Cambri. I fear Kalamack will be most reticent and need much encouragement. If he doesn't agree, I won't allow anyone to break the silence. In any way whatsoever."

Trisk's lips parted. She'd been so anxious to get the word out that she'd forgotten Daniel was still in danger. Her hope died, then rose again as she saw Piscary standing ready. "You'll help us find him?" she asked, and Piscary's black eyes glinted with the hunger of a hunter.

"Absolutely," Piscary said, taking a huge breath of air. "Le-e-e-o-o-o!"

37

It was Halloween, though no one trick-or-treated. Trisk and Daniel had been looking for Kal all day to no avail, joined by Piscary after the sun had set. Trisk sensed a quiet restlessness in the master vampire, now sitting in the front seat of the large luxury sedan. A tiny Asian woman was driving, all in black silk and smelling of cherry blossoms. Leo and Daniel were with Trisk in the back. Another car full of Piscary's men was behind them, and she couldn't shake the feeling that she'd fallen in with a mob boss as they cruised through not only Cincinnati, but also the small city of Newport across the river, where Piscary actually lived.

After several hours, the tension in the car had become palpable, and she clenched her jaw as Leo cracked his knuckles, starting with his pinkie and working his way down until he reached the end and started over. Daniel seemed oblivious, slouched into the car door as he yawned.

"Keeping you awake?" Leo said, flushing in embarrassment when Piscary frowned in disapproval.

"Sorry." Daniel stretched where he sat, only to immediately slump back against the door to stare out at the dark city. "Long day."

Which was true. On Trisk's advice, they'd gone to the airport, using the finding charm they'd gotten in Chicago to see if Kal was trying to flee with the refugees. There'd been no ping of magic on their slow drive-by.

From there they had crossed the river to cover every inch of Cincinnati in a half-mile grid pattern. Their afternoon had been spent at the outskirts, physically checking in at the vampire-manned roadblocks. Sunset had them back to Newport to get Piscary. The need to produce results had become unbearable, and Trisk was starting to think Ulbrine and Kal had vanished into the ever-after.

"Dr. Cambri, is there any indication from your charm?" Piscary asked, his eyes on one of his watches. He wore two of them, in case one failed. Getting belowground before sunrise wasn't simply prudent, but the difference between life and death. Or undeath, perhaps.

Her gaze dropped to the tiny disk in her hand. If not for the tickle of energy running through it, she'd say it was just a hunk of metal. "No."

"You think it's even working?" Daniel asked, his voice as tired.

"No," Trisk said again, nervous when Piscary's eyes dilated at her sudden surge of fear. Exhaling, she calmed herself, not liking the uneasy glance Leo and the Asian woman shared through the rearview mirror.

"Be easy, Dr. Cambri," Piscary said, clearly having noticed her angst. "There is more than witch magic to find the missing." He looked at his watch again. "Ellen, Fordges probably has something by now," he said, and without a word, the woman took the next right, wheeling the car off the sporadically lit main street and into a more certain dark.

"Fordges?" Daniel asked, but Trisk thought it was more to wake up than out of true interest.

"My informant." With a confident grace, Piscary flipped open the glove box and took out an envelope. He turned in his seat, handing it to Leo as the car smoothly parked at a nondescript corner store. The nearby streetlight had been broken, and only the light spilling out the windows lit the cracked, weed-choked parking strip in the depressed area.

Immediately Leo got out, his smile wide and showing sharp but small canines. "Be right back," he said as the chill night slipped in with the scent of garbage and chili. The door shut, and he sauntered into the store.

Trisk watched as he stood at the register and talked to a bearded man, a Were by the look of it, who gestured wildly, then clung to Leo when the vampire began to leave. Her pulse quickened when Leo glanced at the car, then turned back to the rough-looking man to listen.

Good or bad? she wondered, settling back into the plush leather. There was a plethora of ley lines in the area, most of them on the Ohio side of things. It would be a nice place to work—even with the large vampire community. At least the stores would be open all night. She didn't mind that the streets were darker here than across the river in Cincinnati—darker and somehow more dangerous, though the buildings were lower and wider spaced.

She'd been seeing darting shadows at the edges of the light all night, as if people were out tasting the wind to see what was changing. Piscary had said nothing would be announced until Kal agreed to manufacture the metabolism booster, but clearly the city knew that those in power were considering breaking the silence.

"Here he comes," Daniel said, but her hope faltered as she took in Leo's hunched shoulders. "We'll find him," Daniel whispered, seeing it as well.

"We've been at it all day. Every hour we wait, more people die," she said, and he gave her hand a squeeze.

"No one eats tomatoes for breakfast," Daniel said, and then his eyes widened in alarm.

She turned to look, her intake of breath pulling Piscary's attention as well. A shadow of a man had detached itself from the building and was striding after Leo. Her lips parted to call out a warning, but Leo had sensed him and spun.

"Ellen," Piscary said shortly, and the woman reached for her door.

More car doors were opening as the vehicle behind them emptied and the lot began to fill with wary vampires. Yelling at them that he was hers, Ellen jogged forward. The shadow stopped, a hand raised in placation.

Trisk felt her expression go blank. "Quen," she whispered, recognizing his silhouette. "That's Quen!" she shouted, fumbling for her door. "Don't hurt him. Quen!"

"Dr. Cambri, get back in the car!" Piscary demanded, but she was out and pushing her way past the tall vampires between her and the storefront.

"Get out of my way!" Trisk shoved the last man aside. Her eyes widened. "Stop!" she shouted as the Asian woman did a martial arts move and Quen hit the ground, his hand on his stomach as he tried to breathe. Running forward, Trisk tapped a line, loath to actually use it in the street. "I said stop!" she cried out. "What is wrong with you people! He's my friend!"

Quen looked up. Guilt flashed over him, and then his eyes dropped. The woman's domineering posture shifted as she looked past Trisk to Piscary, now out of the car. He must have told her to back off, because her hand drawn back to strike slowly extended to help Quen up. He took it, rising to his full height, then stumbled back when Trisk crashed into him.

"Whoa. Trisk," Quen said, and she gave him a hug, arms wrapped awkwardly around him as the scent of honey and shortbread puffed up between them. "Hey . . ."

She let go enough to look up at him, sorrow crossing her face as she saw the healing pox scars past the thick stubble. The rash was gone, but it would forever mark him. "I—I thought . . ." she stammered. "How did you find us? You ran away like an old cat to die!"

He smiled down at her, his short-cropped hair catching the light coming out of the store window. "I never left you," he said, his fingers touching her hair, running down its length to straighten the necklace he'd given her. She'd never taken it off, finding strength in it.

"What do you mean, you never left?" she asked, letting go of him when she realized the watching vampires were chuckling at them. But then she thought about it. The distraction with the Weres in Chicago, the flash of distant light and the falling rock at the ambush, and now this. "That was you? Why?"

Quen took her arms and bodily shifted her back a step. "Because I'm a fool," he said, reluctantly letting go of her as he looked past her at Daniel, who had boldly pushed through the ring of vampires as if they were just everyday people. "Human blood is not a shame, but an honor," he added, and Daniel seemed to lose some of his frustration. "I'm sorry. I shouldn't have left."

"If not for you, we never would have gotten away. Just don't do it again," she said, simply glad he was back. Still holding his arm protectively, she turned to

Piscary. The elegant, somewhat small man looked out of place in front of the tired, dilapidated store.

"Sir," Quen said respectfully, and Piscary stepped forward, eyeing Quen's healing pox scars.

"Leo said someone followed him from the road-block." A pale hand lifted, almost touching him. "You were so beautiful. Like a warrior poet of old."

Quen's eyes narrowed in warning, but it wasn't until the Asian woman visibly stiffened that Piscary's hand dropped. "He still is," Trisk said, and the vampires behind them chuckled.

Clearly more put off than afraid, Quen watched Piscary's men begin to break up. "I saw Kal," he said, and hope spilled back into her. "Ulbrine was with him." He turned to Trisk. "When he left Piscary's in such a hurry, I knew you were safe. Trisk, I shouldn't have left you. Sick or not."

"It's okay." The fervent pressure he gripped her with was worrying. "Where are they?"

Quen's gaze lifted to the night. "Hiding with those seeking comfort. The basilica."

Leo whistled, arms moving to point at two of the better-dressed vampires, then the night.

"We're within a half mile," Piscary said as his entire posse except Ellen vanished on swift feet, their orders either silent or already known. "Why is your charm not working?"

Head down, Trisk thumped the ring of metal against her palm as if it were a malfunctioning radio. "I don't know. Perhaps Ulbrine is blocking it." Quen's hand on her elbow, they started back to the car, a new hope quickening their steps.

"Hold," Piscary said suddenly, his feet scraping to a halt. "I have people there now."

An unsettled feeling of wrong tripped down her spine as she pocketed the useless charm. Piscary's eyes were unfocused. Ellen stood by, the jealous slant to her eyes both a warning and promise, protecting her master while he was vulnerable. His breathing was faster, and it was obvious he was seeing through someone else's eyes. Leo's, perhaps.

Piscary's focus sharpened, then his gaze went pupil black, chilling her when his smile tightened with anticipation. "This way," he said, breaking into an easy jog into the dark.

Ellen was at his elbow, and after a moment's hesitation, Trisk followed. Quen's hand slipped from her, and he ran beside her.

"We're going to run?" Daniel said, his jog reluctant and slow. "What about the car?"

Quen leaned close, whispering, "Cars are noisy, and we hunt."

Pulse fast, Trisk watched her footing, glad that they were running perpendicular to the direction Piscary's men had gone. "And this is a good thing?" she muttered breathlessly.

Quen's teeth shined white as he smiled. "Be ready. They're flushing them to us." Never slowing, Piscary looked at him, surprise in his dust-eddied eyes, and Quen shrugged. "It's what I would have done," Quen said in explanation, and Piscary turned back to the night, satisfied.

Daniel's panting grew loud, and worry furrowed Trisk's brow. It was more than him spending his days in a lab. He wasn't as strong simply because he was human, and when surrounded by those who weren't, it showed.

"Hold!" Piscary whispered as they came out on a

dark intersection. A smoldering bonfire sat at the center, the blinking streetlight above it making more of a statement than the circle that someone—probably witches—had etched before the flames. The muffled shout and clatter of rapidly retreating footsteps gave evidence that they'd scared someone off. Piscary slowly moved out into the firelight's reach with the powerful grace and command of a lion taking over a kill.

Ellen was tight to his elbow, head swiveling as she scanned the cut the night made above the two-story buildings facing the street. Brick and mortar, metal and stone—not even a tree to relieve the downtown shops. An appliance store spilled light onto the street, the display TVs still on as a late-night comedy show played to no one.

Staggering, Daniel lurched to the storefront stoop, collapsing on it to put his head down between his upraised knees. "Are you okay?" Quen asked Trisk, and she nodded. "Hey, your smut is gone," he added as he took her arm, and guilt flashed through her. "You didn't call him again, did you?" he whispered intently.

"I'll tell you about that later," she said, pulling out from his grip.

"Ellie?" Piscary said softly, and the woman's attention jerked down from the empty second-floor windows. "Minimize the noise," he said, and immediately the woman jogged down the street. She gave a hissing whistle, and what were probably living vampires came out from behind closed doors and alleys. They clustered around her in the shadows, then fanned out.

The bonfire made orange shadows on the storefronts, and Piscary backed into the dark to vanish. Trisk grasped Quen's hand, dragging him with her to leave the intersection at least looking as if it were abandoned.

A thrill was spilling through her, embarrassing somehow. Not all of it was because they were going to find Kal. They were hunting. It was that simple.

"Daniel!" Quen all but hissed, and the man looked up, lips parting as he realized he was alone. "Get out of the light!"

But it was too late, and Trisk waved him to stay at the sound of shoes on the pavement. "No, don't move!" she whispered loudly, and Daniel sank back down, pressing into the door. Tension coursed through her, and her skin tingled from the line Quen had pulled into him.

"There," Quen murmured as Ulbrine and Kal ran down the street.

"I'm telling you, we're being driven," Ulbrine said, clearly struggling.

"You're blocking the tracker, aren't you?" Kal slowed at the edges of the bonfire's light, clearly not wanting to pass into it.

"Of course." Ulbrine jerked to a halt, grabbing Kal's arm as Piscary stepped from the darkness. The vampire's smile widened. There was no one behind Piscary. He didn't need anyone backing him. His entourage was to comfort those in it, not him. He wasn't just the city's master vampire, he was the city's apex predator. More, he was enjoying his night out, free of the restraints that a watching human might otherwise impose. What looked like a memory lit his expression.

"Ulbrine," Piscary said, his voice smooth with promised threat and anticipation. "You left my meeting prematurely. There's something important you need to bring to the enclave's attention." His eyes slid to Kal. "And I have a small task for you, Dr. Kalamack. Dr. Cambri told me you know of a metabolism booster. Is that true? Be careful; your life depends upon it."

Kal jerked his arm free of Ulbrine, the remembered betrayal of the enclave member haunting his eyes. "I do," Kal said, and Piscary beamed. The expression seemed practiced on the master vampire, but was effective nevertheless.

"Grand!" Motions fast, Piscary made a gesture, sending Leo for the car, presumably. "There will be no more ruckus tonight. You'll stay in Cincinnati and make your metabolism booster for all of the vampire society. Something clean and without undesirable side effects."

"I will not," Kal said clearly, and Piscary jerked to a stop, his eyebrows high.

"I force no man to do anything," Piscary said, and Trisk surreptitiously tapped the nearest ley line, laying a thought among it so light that even Quen beside her couldn't feel it. "But if your answer remains unchanged, you alone will take the entirety of blame for the plague."

Kal drew himself up. "I hold a chartered name that can be traced back to our beginnings. You can't force me to do anything."

Piscary's eyes went to Ulbrine, who was standing deathly still with no expression. "The enclave will do anything to hide that the Angel tomato plague was the elves' fault," Piscary said. "Sacrifice you without thought. He did so once already. If it's allowed to become public knowledge that the elves caused the unbalance, the world would band together and finish what the demons started." Piscary's smile shifted from one of practiced, fond persuasion to one of pure dominance. This one was real, and Trisk shuddered, glad it wasn't directed at her.

"Tell me I lie," Piscary said to Ulbrine, and the man's jaw clenched. "One elf, even from as high a house as yours, is a small sacrifice to save your species."

Kal's confidence faltered as he turned to Ulbrine and the man looked away. Slowly Kal's expression went blank. His finger twitched. It was one of his tells, and Trisk took a huge breath.

"Look out!" she exclaimed, dropping back even as Quen jerked her behind him. Tossed, she spun to the pavement, hitting Daniel to send them both sprawling. Quen stood before them, and she winced, feeling it when his circle sprang up around all three of them, undrawn but firm.

"*Detrudo!*" Kal shouted, and cries rang out as everyone outside Quen's circle was bowled over by an expanding bubble of air. Leo rolled almost into the bonfire. With a whoosh, the flames sprang high only to nearly go out when the wood scattered.

"Catch him!" she shouted from the ground, but Kal had pulled Ulbrine to his feet, dragging him to the large circle the witches had etched in the pavement before the bonfire.

"Stay back!" Kal shouted as a huge bubble rose up around them. It was too large for any but perhaps a coven of witches to hold comfortably, but Kal held it alone, impressing Trisk. "I will *not* be betrayed a second time," he muttered as he pushed Ulbrine out of the way and used a half-charred stick to etch an even smaller circle within his larger one.

A circle within a circle? Trisk thought, fear a cold spike when she figured it out.

Piscary found his feet, his hands on his hips as he stared at Kal as if he were a spoiled child throwing a tantrum. "This is getting tiresome. Ellen, how did he get the charmed silver off?" he asked, and she shrugged.

"What are you doing, Kalamack?" Ulbrine said as he

stood, eyeing the circle that kept the vampires at bay. "There is nowhere to go."

"You'd give me up? Twice?" Angry, Kal tossed the stick aside. "I'm no one's scapegoat. You set me to this task, and I *will not* be punished for it." Biting his lip, he spat blood into the small circle and invoked it. "Algaliarept, I summon you."

Trisk felt ill, clutching at Quen when power swarmed up out of the earth. Edging backward, Ulbrine went pale. "No," he whispered as understanding filled him. "You can't!"

"What is he doing?" Daniel asked, and Quen's eyes narrowed.

"Committing suicide," Quen said, his expression shifting to one of guilt. "Trisk. I'm sorry."

Trisk shook her head. It wasn't suicide, but it was close. They were in the open. Anyone could see. If Kal didn't make the booster, they wouldn't come out of the closet, and if that didn't happen, Cincinnati would be destroyed as Detroit had been. "Kal!" she exclaimed, pulling strands of her hair from her face. "What are you doing!"

But it was too late, and with no fanfare, Algaliarept appeared within the smaller circle.

"I will not be dragged about," the demon intoned, his goat-slitted red eyes finding Trisk over his blue-tinted glasses. "You spread my name like butter across bread. You will live a thousand years in pain for this."

"I summoned you, demon. Not her," Kal said boldly, and Algaliarept shifted, his surprise genuine as he saw Kal with Ulbrine, the older elf nervously backing up. "You forgot something in your haste to leave this morning."

Algaliarept's smile widened.

"Quen, help me circle them!" Trisk rasped, and she

patted her jeans for her absent chalk. Taking a stick of charred wood, they traced a new line around Kal's barrier. With a sigh of relief, Trisk watched a new circle spring up to create a double-walled circle. Three circles glowed in the night. Now, even if Algaliarept should get past Kal's barrier, the demon would not escape.

"I'm listening." Algaliarept poked a gloved finger at Kal's inner circle, testing.

Trisk let the burnt stick fall, walking backward to Daniel as all her plans began to dissolve. She never should have summoned Algaliarept, and certainly not where an entire room of Inderlanders could hear. Her grandmother might have been smart, but *she* was an idiot.

"You want him?" Kal looked at a horrified Ulbrine. "I'll give him to you, but I will walk away from this clean. Not a hint now or ever that I or my family was involved in the plague. Blame it on a ladybug. I don't care, but not me."

"Difficult, but not impossible," Algaliarept said, eyeing Piscary.

"And I want her research on the universal donor virus," Kal added. "If I am to do this, I want everything."

"What!" Incensed, Trisk took a step toward the bubble. "You can't do that." She looked from a stiff-faced Kal to a grinning demon. "You promised my name would go on my research!" she exclaimed, shrugging off Daniel's calming hand.

"I'm a member of the enclave," Ulbrine said, eyes haunted. "You can't give me to him."

Kal's lip twitched. "You made a mistake, Ulbrine," he said, an odd, dangerous, lost light in his eye. "My family can trace our name to the elven warlords that fought in the ever-after. Yours only goes back to the slave pens. I have no problem sacrificing a bishop to save a king."

"You are no king, Kalamack," Ulbrine whispered, but he was afraid, and Algaliarept began to laugh.

"Done and done," the demon said, holding his gloved hand out. "Give him to me, and it will be as you say."

Trisk stepped closer until Algaliarept's image became wavy from the triple bubble. "You promised my name on my research."

"Let it go, Trisk," Daniel said, and she rounded on him.

"You think this is about my pride?" she said bitterly. "If Kal walks away from this, we are dead. I can't make Piscary's metabolism booster, and if that doesn't happen, we don't come out of the closet, and then we all die for breaking the silence, you included! *That's* how he gets his name on my research. We're all dead!"

"He wouldn't . . ." Daniel looked behind him to Piscary, going white as he realized the vampire would.

Algaliarept actually bowed, short and stilted because of the narrowness of his prison. "My dear mistress, I have already fulfilled my end of your bargain."

"You have not!" she exclaimed, and Algaliarept's lips twitched in a flash of ire.

"I have. Did I not suggest you roll with him? Did you not take my advice? You are pregnant, and is not the father of the child bound by elven law to marry and support you?"

She went still. Quen sighed. She heard it clearly in the night air. She couldn't look away from Algaliarept, even when Piscary began to laugh. Daniel's shoes scraped, and she flashed warm, blushing as Algaliarept began to pull his glove off, one finger at a time.

"Is he not required by law to sta-a-a-ay with you," the demon drawled, clearly enjoying this. "See that you and your child are well treated, fed, and have all the best a little elf can give an elfling?"

"You're pregnant?" Kal blurted, and she flushed deeper at his horror.

"You *slept* with her," Ulbrine muttered, and she clenched her jaw.

"Trisk?" Quen said, and she jumped when his hand landed gently on her shoulder.

She nodded, furious that she was going to have to sacrifice her own happiness to get what she thought she wanted. She'd be alive, though, and Daniel, and what was left of the world. "I will stay in Cincinnati," she said in a low voice. Kal's lips twisted in annoyance, and she lifted her head defiantly, knowing that custom and law would demand Kal remain with her. "I will stay!" she exclaimed. "And you, Kal, will stay with me."

"That child might not even be mine," Kal said, and Algaliarept smirked.

"It is," the demon said, and Trisk glared at Kal, hating him. "It's a boy." Algaliarept cocked his head, breathing deep. "A healthy boy. Or he will be, with a little tinkering. Blond with brown eyes, but Kal, you can change that with your bride's research so the little tyke won't offend your mother." He eyed Kal over his glasses. "I'd say yes. Your code is so tattered that you'll never manage a child without the hybrid vigor of a dark elf."

Trisk burned, hating them all now.

"Do you still wish to trade, Trenton Lee Kalamack? Or will you simply marry the bitch and create a drug that a fifth of the world will want?" Algaliarept leered at him. "Need. Pay for."

Kal turned to her, seemingly shaken that the demon knew his full name, and she shrugged.

"Well?" Piscary prompted.

Kal looked at Ulbrine, his disgust obvious. "I will marry Dr. Felecia Cambri," he said, voice low and without inflection. "I will make what the vampires need, but I will set the price."

Ulbrine sighed, a pleased, relieved smile blossoming over him. Trisk hated the glint in his eye. He knew he'd won again, and it disgusted her that he'd played them all.

"But I'm giving Ulbrine to Algaliarept anyway," Kal said, shoving the unaware man at the demon. Bellowing in anger, Ulbrine hit the circle holding Algaliarept, then stumbled when Kal dissolved it, too. Algaliarept beamed down at Ulbrine. White-faced, Ulbrine looked up, realizing there was nothing between him and the demon, nothing at all.

"No . . ." Trisk whispered as Ulbrine shrieked. He backpedaled, too late as Algaliarept reached an arm out and jerked him forward.

"Fool," Algaliarept said as he stepped over the drawn line, clearly intending to take Kal as well.

"Hold!" Kal said, self-preservation making him back up a step. He hit the inside of his circle. It fell, but the one Trisk and Quen had drawn held firm. Red spotted his cheeks as he faced Algaliarept, but he pulled himself forward, alone with nothing but his words to keep himself free. "Take me, and you will have sundered our bargain. You promised my name on her research, and for that, I need to be alive and in reality to marry her."

Algaliarept said nothing. Then he snickered, the low chuckle rising to a belly laugh and finally a full-blown howl of amusement. Ulbrine began shrieking as the two of them dissolved, vanishing until even the demon's laugh died.

With a thought, Trisk sundered her hold on the outer

circle. The name on her research would be Kalamack, but since she would be married to the bitter sod, it would still adhere to the earlier bargain she'd made with Algaliarept. *Son of a bitch, I hate being a foregone conclusion.*

Daniel sighed, sitting down right there on the pavement. "I'm starting to miss my lab," he said as he took off his shoe and shook out a pebble. "That's better," he said as he put it back on. "I've had that in my shoe since Chicago."

Kal edged out of the defunct circle, chin high as he took in the surrounding vampires. His eyes landed on Trisk, then dropped to her flat middle. She was shaking, and she felt more alone than she ever had when Quen's hand slipped from her, and, head down, he rocked away to make room at her side for Kal.

"I can't believe you did that," she accused Kal as he stopped four feet away from her. "You gave a person to a demon. In front of witnesses. Are you crazy?"

Kal gave Piscary a respectful nod, then turned to Trisk. Slowly his expression shifted to one of odd vulnerability. "He betrayed me twice," he said, voice flat. "Will you do the same?"

She took a breath to protest, then exhaled, knowing that on this, all things would turn. She looked at him, seeing past the stained tie, limp hair, and fatigue that hung on him like a badly cut suit, recognizing the courage it had taken to stand before a demon with no protection other than the trust in a pact made between unequals. She saw the strength in him as he refused to be anything other than a peer to Piscary. She remembered the hard promise in his eyes, and knew he would do anything to protect what was important to him. And suddenly, she wanted to be on the right side of the line—even if she never liked him. "No, I won't betray you," she said.

He considered her for a moment in the last glow of the bonfire. "I can live with that," he said suddenly, and she jumped, startled. "I need three days to get my grandmother's ring."

Oh God. She was going to marry him. "Fine," she said, hoping she was matching his cool, calm tone. "It will take that long to convince my father I'm not insane."

A smile flickered at the edges of his mouth, softening his eyes as he looked at her middle again—and then it was gone.

She was never leaving Cincinnati again. She would make it her garden.

Suddenly her throat closed, and she turned away before Kal could see her face twist up as she forced herself not to cry. Quen had his back to her. Daniel . . . Daniel just looked lost, left alone as the vampires around them began to disperse.

"Piscary? I need access to a lab in the meantime," Kal was saying, and she wiped the hint of tears away. "A good one. That's short-term. I will also need several low-interest loans to cover payroll and the initial setup for manufacturing. Can I count on you?"

"I'm sure we can come to an agreement," Piscary said, and somehow, she found the courage to look at the master vampire. His expression was wary, but it gave her strength. It had all ended with a whiff of brimstone and burnt amber, a fading laugh, and a scream—Algaliarept taking Ulbrine in exchange for . . . nothing.

Arms wrapped around her middle, she stood in the intersection and looked up at a night without stars. She would marry Kal, but it would be a flavorless arrangement. Perhaps it was what she deserved, and seeing

Quen five feet away with Daniel and Leo discussing the logistics of how to get to the nearest radio station, she realized how badly she had served herself in her quest for recognition. *I won't betray you.*

Daniel clapped his hands once, beaming as he left the two men and headed to her. "Trisk. Leo is going to take us to the radio station. We can get the word out tonight."

Feeling ill, Trisk looked to her left at Kal. Never ceasing his conversation with Piscary, Kal looked pointedly down at his right side as if waiting for her to join him. "You go ahead," she said, and Daniel's lips parted.

"But . . ."

Eyes smarting, she gave him a hug. It was allowed, especially when he started, clearly feeling the good-bye in it. "Go," she repeated as she rocked back. "I have to stay here."

Daniel looked over her shoulder to Kal, a reluctant nervousness in the pinch of his eye as he realized everything had shifted. "Okay," he said as he kissed her forehead and the lump in her throat hardened. "Bye, Trisk. I'll stop in and see your lab when you get settled."

Leo groaned impatiently by the open car door. "Now, you little snack."

"I'd like that," she said, knowing she'd have to be circumspect about her friends from here on out, even if friendship was as deep as it went. "I'll give you the full tour," she said, her voice rising to a squeak.

Daniel drew back, his hand leaving hers reluctantly. In the distance, the basilica's bells began to toll, cheerful peals of sound that rolled out over the river valley in an unexpected wave. Everyone turned to look into the night as the noise was picked up by first one, then another church, until they were all ringing.

"What is it?" she asked, following Piscary's attention to the color TVs on display in the store window. "My God, they're going to extirpate Cincinnati?" she said in sudden fear, but Piscary had a hand up in a gentle admonishment.

"Perfect timing," Piscary said, pointing at the appliance store and the TVs still on behind the window.

Trisk's brow furrowed, then evened out as she saw Rynn Cormel on TV. Orchid was on his shoulder, and the man's confident voice rolled out, his smile saying everything would be fine.

"You are not alone," the senator said, Orchid's dust spilling down his front as her wings fanned. "We have always been here. Today we came forward to save our society, and tomorrow we will work openly together to build it anew. Witch, vampire, Were, and human."

Trisk started when Kal came up beside her, standing too close but well within his rights. "It's my decision that we will not come out," Kal said softly, his eyes on the glowing TV. "I wish to remain on the rolls as human." His eyes flicked to hers and held. "Understand? No magic from here on out."

Her eyebrows rose. "What I do in the privacy of my garden is my business."

His lip twitched. "You don't have a garden."

She eyed him up and down. "Get me one. Wall it off. I want pixies."

Behind them, Quen chuckled, muffling it when Kal looked at him.

Bothered, Trisk turned to Piscary, now done directing his people to spread the word door by door if need be. "You said you wouldn't allow anyone to come out if we didn't have Kal to make the metabolism booster," she accused, and the master vampire smiled, making him look soft and pleasant. It was a lie, but it was a comforting one.

"I knew you'd accomplish it," he said as he gestured at the cars now rolling up. "And many people enjoy eating ketchup on their eggs, do they not? Every life we save puts us closer to a new balance that much sooner." Nodding confidently, he breathed deep of the night. "It is done. Excuse me." Piscary walked away. "Leo!" he called, and the young living vampire held the door for him. Apparently he wanted to go to the radio station, too.

Together the remaining three turned to the car Piscary had left for them. "So, where do you want to live?" Kal said. "There are no virgin woods here."

Trisk could feel the heat from his shoulder near hers, but not touching. "I like the field, but if you want a woods, by all means, plant one."

Quen jogged ahead to open the back door. The gesture would have grated on her but for his smile. "Sa'han?" he said almost mockingly, and Kal got in first, the rims of his ears a bright red.

"Behave yourself," she whispered to Quen as she gracefully folded herself into the supple leather seats to find Kal brooding, his brow furrowed in thought.

Giving her a wink, Quen shut the door with a firm thump. His motion to cross in front of the car held a curious excitement, and once he settled behind the wheel, they slowly drove away.